BY RORY POWER

Wilder Girls
Burn Our Bodies Down

THE WIND-UP GARDEN SERIES

In a Garden Burning Gold
In an Orchard Grown from Ash

IN AN
ORCHARD
GROWN
FROM
ASH

IN AN ORCHARD GROWN FROM ASH

BOOK TWO OF THE WIND-UP GARDEN SERIES

RORY POWER

NEW YORK

Published in the United States by Del Rey, an imprint of Random House, a division of Penguin Random House LLC, New York. Published in the United Kingdom by Titan Books, a division of Titan Publishing Group Ltd., London.

Del Rey and the Circle colophon are registered trademarks of Penguin Random House LLC.

Hardback ISBN 978-0-593-35500-8
Ebook ISBN 978-0-593-35501-5
Export ISBN 978-0-593-72272-5

Printed in Canada on acid-free paper

randomhousebooks.com

2 4 6 8 9 7 5 3 1

First U.S. Edition

Για την Γιαγιά

AUTHOR'S NOTE

The fictional setting of *In an Orchard Grown from Ash* is inspired by various parts of the world but is not intended as a true representation of any one country, culture, or language at any point in history.

For a list of applicable content warnings, please visit the author's personal website at itsrorypower.com.

DRAMATIS PERSONAE

*denotes deceased

THYZAKOS

*Aya Ksiga, or Irini Argyros, a saint thought to have lived in the Ksigora before becoming consort of Vasilis Argyros and mother of Alexandros, Rhea, Nitsos, and Chrysanthi

*Vasilis Argyros, the Stratagiozi of Thyzakos and father of Alexandros, Rhea, Nitsos, and Chrysanthi

Alexandros Argyros, the second to Vasilis Argyros and Rhea's twin brother

Rhea Argyros, or Aya Thyspira, a newly made saint, and Alexandros's twin sister

Nitsos Argyros, son of Vasilis Argyros

Chrysanthi Argyros, daughter of Vasilis Argyros

Yannis Laskaris, the Thyzak steward of the Ksigora

Evanthia Laskaris, consort of Yannis and mother of Michali

Michali Laskaris, son and heir of the Ksigoran steward and consort of Rhea

Kallistos Speros, son and heir of the Rhokeri steward

Giorgios Speros, the Thyzak steward of Rhokera

Dimos and Nikos Vlahos, suitors at Rhea's winter choosing

Athanasios Kanakaris, a leader of the Sxoriza

Andrija Tomic, a high-ranking member of the Sxoriza and an Amolovak refugee

Piros Zografi, a high-ranking member of the Sxoriza and an Amolovak refugee

Lefka, a horse

TREFAZIO

Tarro Domina, the Stratagiozi (called Stratagorra in Trefza) of Trefazio

Falka Domina, the second to Tarro Domina

*Luco Domina, the first Stratagiozi (called Stratagorra in Trefza)

Ettore Domina, a relative of Tarro Domina

MERKHER

Zita Devetsi, the Stratagiozi (called Ordukamat in Merkheri) of Merkher

Stavra Devetsi, the second to Zita Devetsi

CHUZHA

Nastia Rudenko, the Stratagiozi (called Toravosma in Chuzhak) of Chuzha

AMOLOVA

Ammar Basha, the Stratagiozi (called Korabret in Amolovak) of Amolova

IN AN
ORCHARD
GROWN
FROM
ASH

ALEXANDROS

The guards were discussing his overcoat. They had been since Legerma, where Lexos had been passed into their care, and they were not being quiet about it.

It was, according to them, quite ugly and in need of mending, along with a good wash so that it might stop stinking up the carriage. One of the guards had even tugged on the hem a few minutes ago, as if expecting a seam to give and the whole thing to come apart in his hand.

Lexos had said nothing then, as he did now, sighing and settling more deeply into the corner of the carriage before shutting his eyes. He knew he looked quite Thyzak in his dour black coat and that its sleeves did nothing to hide the beautiful silver bracelets that had been bent around his wrists—ornamental chains to mark his status as a captive of Tarro Domina. But he was warm, and he could tell, from their occasional shivers, that the guards were not. They were dressed for a standard spring; the weather they found themselves in these days was anything but standard. Snow was still falling, even as the season began to tip toward its end. It melted quickly, to be sure, but it left the ground unsteady and the air heavy with mist that took too long to burn off.

It was a shame. Trefazio was meant to be beautiful this time of year. Rhea had told him once that it was her favorite place to make a marriage, although it had been some time since she had married anyone outside of Thyzakos, since their father's efforts had turned toward securing the support of his own stewards.

It didn't do, lately, to think of his sister, but he couldn't help it. Every night on his trip across the countryside he fell asleep remembering the look on her face that day at Stratathoma, in the silence after he'd finished reciting the prayer meant to end her life. Her shock, that he had tried. His, that it hadn't worked. Wherever Rhea was now— and he was very sure that she was still alive, sure to his bones—it was with the matagios on her tongue, a little black spot marking her as their father's eldest child and successor. Had she made any peace with it, he wondered. She had never wanted that power. Especially not at the end.

But power or no, she was free. He hoped she was pleased with that, because he could not be pleased for her, not when he was stuck in this carriage on the latest leg of his tour of the countryside. Every few days they would stop, and Lexos would find himself in some city or town he'd never heard of before and be given hardly a minute to catch his breath before being paraded down the street: the Argyros prince, federation traitor, and fugitive, captured once more. He'd asked one of the guards if this was a popular Trefzan hobby—if there were other parades on the off days, perhaps for anyone who had worn a non-Domina shade of green—but apparently this was a custom Falka had invented just for him. Lexos couldn't decide if that was flattering or not.

At least Tarro had gone back to Vuomorra. The first few cities had been the worst, when Lexos and his guards had been accompanied by Tarro and Falka both, the two of them riding at the head of their dubious little procession, waving to the people and basking in the wrath Lexos could not keep from clouding his expression, much as he tried to seem unaffected.

He'd gotten better at that part. The guards had to work harder to get a rise out of him and even sometimes switched from Trefza to poorly accented Thyzaki, as if the problem was simply that Lexos couldn't understand them. Never mind that he spoke Trefza very well, and never mind that of everything that had gone catastrophically wrong in his life over the past season, being dressed unfashionably was the most palatable.

The least was that after years of serving his father and of keeping the Argyros family safe and well, the four siblings were scattered. Chrysanthi was probably following her older sister, or charming her way into some secluded rich household in the countryside if she knew what was good for her, and Nitsos . . . well. Lexos couldn't begin to imagine what his younger brother might be busy with. Nitsos had stepped into the garden as a man in control, and meanwhile Lexos had still been picturing him as a child sulking at the dinner table. What else had Lexos missed? Who else had Nitsos taken for his own?

"Wake up, Argyros," one of the guards barked from across the carriage, and Lexos jolted upright as an elbow connected with his ribs. Somehow the guards all managed to make Trefza sound harsh, a true feat. "We're almost there."

"There" meant Vuomorra, a return at last to the capital. Three months ago, Lexos had been quite prepared to vomit over the side of the ship at the sight of Vuomorra's port on the horizon. Now he bent low to get a good view out the carriage window, and when the green dome of the palace came into view, a wave of gratitude threatened to overwhelm him. At last, out of this gilded Domina carriage, and off the rattling Domina roads, and into a comfortable Domina bed.

Which he would then object to, on principle. Just as soon as he got a good night's rest.

The city seemed busier than when he'd been here last, as though more people might have trickled in from the countryside when their fields did not thaw and their crops did not grow. Lexos watched carefully as the carriage eased down the main thoroughfare, searching for signs in each face that he passed. What was Rhea doing out there? What had she done, letting winter linger through spring? Her consort had been dead when she'd arrived home at Stratathoma. Everything had been set up to continue on as normal.

"Are we going to the palace?" he asked the guard opposite him.

Tarro would be there, along with his second, Falka, the very woman who had stripped the mark from his left hand. He needed to see them both to, if possible, get a sense of what maneuvers they'd begun since their last real meeting.

The guard laughed. "Not the way you're thinking."

Lexos was about to ask what he meant when the carriage cornered sharply and turned from the broad street cutting through the center of Vuomorra onto a smaller, cobbled alleyway. Still neatly kept, as all things in Vuomorra were, but he could tell that they were headed away from the main set of entrances open to the public, through which Lexos had entered when he'd come to Vuomorra last.

"Why not?" he asked. "Aren't I due for another parade?"

This, apparently, did not warrant an answer, and the ride continued in silence, with only amused glances and barely muffled laughter exchanged between the guards. Lexos began to brace himself. Whatever waited for him at the Domina palace might be something even his recent experience in humiliation had not prepared him for.

Finally, the carriage came to a halt. Lexos and his quartet of guards sat there in the stilled cabin for a moment, enjoying the quiet that the clatter of the carriage wheels had obliterated for so many weeks. Then, the most senior of the guards clapped his leather-gloved hands together and said, "Let's get him inside, shall we?"

Lexos barely had time to take in the small courtyard where the carriage had stopped before he was bundled through a door cut into the stone wall. From there, he was escorted down a low, dimly lit corridor, the guards leading him on ahead even as smaller branches of the hallway split off and disappeared into the dark. Oh dear, Lexos thought, somewhat hysterically. Was he being taken to a tiny, damp cell, where he'd be left to rot? That hadn't seemed like Tarro's intent, but the man had lived a long life, and would live a longer one still—it was entirely possible he'd just forgotten he had Lexos in his custody at all.

But he needn't have worried, because the corridor soon opened and emptied into the sort of room Lexos had spent time in when he'd previously been Tarro's honored guest. This one was a portrait gallery, the floors a polished wood that had been laid in an angular pattern and the walls so thoroughly hung with portraits of Dominas past and, in Tarro's case, notably present, that Lexos could barely see the stone behind them. At the far end, a pair of double doors stood shut, each side manned by two armed guards, and in the middle of it all, sitting perfectly still on a single plain chair, was Falka Domina.

She looked well. Falka always looked well. This time, though, she looked well when Lexos knew he very much did not, and he resolved to take it as a personal insult.

"Alexandros," she said at last. One of her heavily jeweled hands twitched as she seemed, impossibly, to sit up even straighter. "Welcome back."

Lexos said nothing, only narrowed his eyes. He'd been transferred often enough without ever encountering a Domina, let alone the family's second-in-command. So what sort of play was this, then?

"I hope you've enjoyed your tour of Trefazio." Falka rose slowly. Her long, wide trousers rustled gently as she crossed the room toward him, her heavy dark braid draped over her shoulder. "The countryside has so much to offer."

"I've been cramped in a carriage for more than a fortnight," Lexos said. "I wouldn't know."

Falka laughed, and immediately he felt his cheeks go warm with embarrassment. A whole season with only Domina guards for company had done quite a lot to blunt the blade he'd spent all those years under Baba sharpening. He would need to watch his words more closely now that he was back.

"Well, don't worry," Falka went on. "That's why you're here. I've got something else in mind for you."

She was close now, close enough that Lexos was reminded of the last time they'd stood like this—the two of them in one of the gardens surrounding this very palace, Falka already halfway to framing him for an attempt on her father's life. He'd been a fool then. Very likely, he still was, but there was nothing left for it to cost him anymore.

"Why don't you just bundle me off to my next holding cell?" he asked. "It's been a long day. I'd like to rest."

"Because," Falka said, gesturing to one of the guards at the opposite end of the room, "you've got a bit more travel still to go, I'm afraid."

The guard reached behind him and began to haul open one of the large double doors. Sunlight spilled in from the corridor beyond, and Lexos caught a glimpse of a white colonnade and a garden. Was he staying here? He was ready to forgive Falka for all manner of things if she let him stay in Vuomorra, where he would have half a chance at getting his next move in order.

"Your escorts will take you to the boat," she said and hooked one finger around the silver bracelet on his right wrist, tugging him forward. "They'll see you on."

He let her guide him for a few steps before slowing. "To where?"

"You'll see." Falka smiled. "But it's a wonderful place. Lots to do. Plenty to keep you busy. I might even pay you a visit sometime."

"Wait," Lexos began, but she was already turning away, and the guards at his back had taken her place, closing ranks around him to keep him from following her. He could only watch as she continued down the colonnade, where someone stepped out to meet her at the far end. Someone with a tumble of blond hair and an unassuming posture that Lexos could recognize even from here.

Nitsos Argyros. Lexos's younger brother, here in Vuomorra.

Of all the ways he had ever imagined encountering another one of the Argyrosi, this particular scenario had never come up. So he had nothing to say at all as Falka greeted Nitsos, or as Nitsos looked down the hall toward him and held up one hand in a surprisingly warm wave.

"Right," said the guard to Lexos's left. "Let's get him moving."

What was Nitsos doing here? He'd barely left Stratathoma during their father's reign—Lexos could remember those conversations, the longing on Nitsos's face as Lexos described his latest trip to Agiokon, or to see a steward in eastern Thyzakos. And yet he'd made it here after the attack on their home without so much as a mark on him. Lexos had never bothered before to wonder whether Nitsos might have helped welcome the Dominas to Stratathoma; now it was impossible not to.

Before he could consider it further, the guards began to move, their armor at Lexos's back forcing him forward. He stumbled as they guided him sharply to the left, around the edge of the garden and toward another colonnade that led deeper into the palace, and despite his best efforts, he lost sight of Falka and his brother, hedges rising between them.

For just a moment he let himself hope that Nitsos might help, might bargain for his freedom, but that hope crumbled under the memory of Nitsos that day in the garden at Stratathoma. It stung, still: how quickly Nitsos had dismissed the idea of creating a creature in his image. Because Lexos would always do exactly as Baba asked; Lexos was not worth controlling; Lexos was nothing to be afraid of.

He set his shoulders, clenched his jaw. That was a family quarrel, and it was beneath him to keep dwelling on it. Whatever Nitsos was doing here in Vuomorra was bigger, which meant Lexos now had to add another player to the game he kept in his head—bright painted triangles on a round board, called Soldier's Teeth to a winner and Saint's Grave to a loser. Lexos had had quite enough of playing Saint's Grave these days.

He and his escorts moved quickly through the palace. Elsewhere in the building, he knew, regular citizens were visiting, enjoying the art and the gardens, but the guards kept him to private passageways, their walls dark and paneled, and it wasn't long before they emerged onto a small lawn. It was bordered with high stone walls, one of which was cut through by an archway. Under it flowed a narrow canal that ran like a channel down the middle of the lawn and ended almost at Lexos's feet in a set of gentle marble steps. There, waiting on the water, was the boat Falka had mentioned—a little thing, built for three or four people, and manned by an oarsman who was already at his post.

"This is it?" Lexos said in Thyzaki. Let the guards be confused, or even afraid. There was nobody here worth communicating with anyway. *"Mala."*

It made him nervous to see, as he was led toward the boat, that the pillows lining the seats were in Domina green, the family's crest stitched in with gold thread. Where was he going, if this was how he was getting there? To Tarro? Why would Tarro be away from Vuomorra?

He was left without answers as he took his seat on the boat. Two guards climbed in with him, one taking up a second pair of oars, and slowly, as the oarsman counted out the strokes, the boat began to move, drifting toward the arch in the wall and the continuing canal beyond.

Lexos craned his neck to get a last look at the palace before it disappeared. There was the pale green dome, rising above the stone and the greenery. There were the branches of a nearby cherry tree, reaching over the wall to drop their petals into the canal—it was still spring, after all. And there, perched on the lowest one, was a white bird that watched his boat pass with sharp, interested eyes.

There was no guarantee, of course, that it was one of Nitsos's creations. But Lexos lifted his hand and made a rude gesture all the same.

Enough with Vuomorra. He would find his freedom elsewhere.

CHAPTER TWO

RHEA

There was nothing Rhea despised quite like these meetings. It wasn't that they were particularly long, or even all that difficult to stay attentive during. It was more that the other people attending them so clearly wished she was elsewhere.

This time, she and the Sxoriza's leadership—half a dozen of the rebel group's oldest and most powerful members—were gathered in one of the few remaining undamaged tents, standing around an uneven pile of crates, atop which were spread an assortment of maps. Rhea was focusing very intently on the nearest one, trying to ignore everyone else's matching grim expressions.

They hadn't always been like this. When she'd met some of them back in Ksigori before midwinter, they had been polite, albeit distant. But she'd understood that attitude then; they knew that her presence meant Michali's death as her consort. And now she'd fixed it, brought him back, and still they looked at her as if she'd cut his throat herself.

Luckily the people outside didn't seem to feel the same way. They loved her, loved her in a pure and uncomplicated way that Rhea had yet to grow accustomed to, and it was on the strength of both their good opinion and Michali's devotion that she was here in this tent at all, listening as a woman who looked very much like Michali's mother finished reporting on the status of Sxoriza camps across the Ksigora.

"Stefanos is moving his people out of the mountains," the woman was saying. "And he recommends a rerouting of supplies away from the eastern roads."

"Avoiding bandits?" one of the men opposite Rhea asked, and the woman's expression darkened.

"Trefzan soldiers under a Domina banner," she said. "They're riding north from Rhokera."

Rhea managed not to flinch as the woman's gaze landed on her. Dominas in Thyzakos: That was Rhea's fault, as far as this council was concerned. Never mind that she'd had nothing to do with Falka Domina's betrayal of the Sxoriza—not even Rhea's sainthood could wash off the stain that being a Stratagiozi's daughter had left on her.

Since the sacking of Stratathoma, the Dominas had taken the whole of Thyzakos under their control, leaving Stratathoma empty and establishing Rhokera as a powerful Domina outpost. According to the reports that Rhea was allowed to see, most of the country continued on as it always had—an indictment of Baba's actual power if Rhea had ever heard one—but Domina banners flew in cities all along the southeastern coast, and everybody seemed to accept that it wouldn't be long before they made a real attempt to bring the Ksigora to heel. If the Sxoriza knew what was good for them, they would be gone by the time that happened.

Some of them already were, to be sure. The smaller camps had been sent west weeks ago, toward Agiokon, where Thyzakos bordered both Merkher and Trefazio, and the larger were meant to follow in stages. Why it made sense to avoid the Dominas in the Ksigora by moving closer to their country of origin, Rhea had yet to comprehend, but every time she'd asked about it, she had been assured by Sxoriza leadership that it was a wise decision.

"Is it Tarro that's in Rhokera?" she asked now. "Or one of his children?" Perhaps if Tarro was keeping residence in Rhokera, the Sxoriza meant to move on Trefazio while he was away.

But if that was the case, nobody in the tent with her gave any indication. "We haven't heard," the woman said, which was so blatantly a lie that Rhea almost rolled her eyes. "Why do you ask?"

She lifted one shoulder, hoping she didn't look as exasperated as she felt. "Just curious."

For a moment she imagined what this meeting would have been like with Michali at her side—Michali as he had been, a sense of command draped around his shoulders like a cloak. They would have listened to her then. They would have answered all of her questions, hung on her every word. But he had not come with her, not for many weeks now, despite every invitation she extended. Instead he begged off, claiming to be too busy or too tired, and spent these hours waiting back at the tent they shared, leaving Rhea to muddle through alone.

Nobody, Rhea thought, was very happy about that, least of all the leadership.

"Well," the other woman said, "I think that's all we have today."

"Are you sure?" Rhea looked from person to person, searching for some kind of warmth. "Nothing else I need to be made aware of?"

"No," a woman replied. "Not at this juncture."

It was a dismissal, and one Rhea was quite tempted to heed, but she lingered at the makeshift table even as the others began to step away, heads bent low as they spoke quietly amongst themselves.

"I don't mean to be a nuisance," Rhea said, a bit louder than she intended, "but has there been any word of my brother?"

Most of the leadership gave no sign that they had heard her, instead continuing their conversations. One, though, an older man who spoke Thyzaki with an accent Rhea still could not place, looked over his shoulder at her.

"Alexandros Argyros," he said, "remains in the custody of the Dominas, in Trefazio."

"No, I meant . . ." She cleared her throat. "The other. Nitsos."

It had been a point of contention in this little council when she'd asked for scouts to be sent after her youngest brother. She'd been unable to explain exactly why; the truth about her initial involvement with Michali and the Sxoriza, and the power of that little hummingbird Nitsos had built, was something she kept to herself. Instead, she'd done her best to blame him, however vaguely, for summoning the Dominas and ultimately for the collapse of the Sxoriza's plans. The advisors had agreed that two scouts might be sent to find word of Nitsos, but no more, not when most of their resources were needed for the next phase of their plans. A phase which, Rhea was constantly reminded, she did not need to be let in on just yet.

"Thus far," the older man said impassively, "I'm afraid we have no new information to impart."

Right. They never did. For all they knew, Nitsos was still back in that garden, watching the sea for more ships.

"Thank you," she said. "I'll see myself out, then."

She left the leadership to tidy up the maps and exited the tent, sparing a moment to nod to the nearby Sxoriza guard who kept watch. Another would be in the trees, ready to follow her back to camp. There was always someone like that around her now, someone at her command, but it all meant nothing, didn't it? As much as the people in the camps loved her, and as much as they counted on her as someone to worship, as a sign of the old days returning, she had no real power— not to guide the Sxoriza as she'd hoped to and not to protect herself from those threads she'd left loose.

One of those, whether she wanted to admit it or not, was the man currently waiting for her back at her tent in camp, the man toward whom she walked now, hoping her ambivalence wasn't too obvious.

He was still himself, really. She would argue that with anyone, although of course nobody dared. He was still challenging and thoughtful, and he still believed in her with that same expectation in his eyes. His hair fell in the same curls, and he still draped his coat over the foot of his bedroll, rather than get another blanket.

And she still loved him. That felt important to remember.

But there was no denying the way her steps slowed as she approached the edge of the camp and caught sight of his tent—hers, too, if anyone asked. Chrysanthi's was right next to it, and her sister was probably there, ready to sulk and complain to Piros (or to nobody, as she had never really required an audience). Rhea was tempted to join her there. She knew, though, any sisterly visit was simply putting off what Rhea needed to do next. She might as well get on with it.

It was always a strange experience to walk through camp. Nobody seemed to know what to do. Some people gathered behind her, walking with bowed heads. Others hurried to line up in front of her so that they might offer their hands as she passed. In her early days with the Sxoriza, she had stopped to bless each one. There simply wasn't time for that anymore.

The guard that had kept their distance during her meetings was close now, cutting through the crowd to walk at her elbow. They were young, but hardly a new arrival. In fact, Rhea thought she could remember blessing them on that very first day in the snow. That seemed a long time ago now.

Michali was waiting when she arrived at their tent. Not smiling, but then that had never been his way, even before. His eyes were dark and solemn as he watched her pass, his chin proud above the high collar of his black coat, and for a moment none of it had happened—she had never pulled him from his grave, never heard the new contours of his voice. It was midwinter; he was waiting for her; one day she would go home again.

She let her gaze drop from his as she ducked into their tent, leaving her guard behind. Michali would join her momentarily, but she got a breath of respite before she had to look him in the eye.

It had been so easy between them when she'd first pulled him out of the earth. He'd hardly let go of her for that whole first week, his steps so closely following hers that they left only one set of tracks in the snow. And though his voice had come back to him slowly, it hadn't mattered. She had kissed him, kept him close, and the first thing he had said had been her name.

But the more he returned to the role he'd filled before his death, the more uncomfortable he became. For meeting after meeting with the Sxoriza elders he'd lingered at the edge of the tent, brow furrowed as he listened without offering any opinion. Finally, at one particular gathering in a ramshackle lean-to tucked into a ravine farther north, Rhea had lost her patience and asked him directly just what he thought

they should do next. Instead of answering—instead of being the leader
he was meant to be—Michali had only stared back at her with a wild
confusion.

Afterward, lying together in the dark, they had not spoken; the embarrassment wrapped around Michali had said enough. And no matter how many times she'd led Michali back to the threshold of that tent
since, he always turned away. She didn't think anyone could blame her
for not trying anymore.

Rhea shut her eyes tightly for a moment, and then sat down heavily
on a nearby pile of cushions. None of this was supposed to happen this
way. She'd never been meant to be doing this alone. Maybe it would
have been better if she and Lexos had switched places. Him here in the
mountains, plotting and advancing, and her a Domina's prize, trotted
out for ceremony and shame—that, at least, she knew how to do.

"May I?"

She turned to see Michali hesitating halfway through the tent flaps,
one hand reaching up to brush the snow from his hair. "Of course,"
she said. "It's your tent."

"Our tent," he said and stepped all the way in.

That was a bit pointed, Rhea thought, but she resolved to let it pass.
She could hardly blame him for being a bit upset; she'd been happy to
share a bedroll with him at first, and he'd no doubt noticed the change.

Rhea slid sideways and patted the empty space beside her on the
cushions, raising an eyebrow in invitation. He did not deserve her fear
or her anger. He had not meant to die.

"What have you been busy with today?" she said.

Michali approached slowly. "Piros and I rode ahead a ways." He sat
down next to her. Rhea shivered. There was a cold to him now, even
through his coat and furs. "And then Chrysanthi needed tending to."
He reached across her lap to take her hand. "She hates to eat alone.
Although if she were here, I think she would say that eating with me is
no different."

Rhea smiled and pressed her shoulder to his. It was like home, to
hear of Chrysanthi's complaining and to see Michali's annoyance
creasing the corner of his mouth.

"Thank you," she said. "I know it isn't your preference—"

"Yes, I would rather be with you," Michali interrupted. "But you asked me to look after your sister."

He said it so simply, Rhea thought. As though all she ever need do with him was ask. Why could she never give him that same devotion in return? Why was it she slept in Chrysanthi's bed most nights instead of here, with her consort? Tonight she would lie alongside him and match her breathing to his. If he wanted her company, he would have it. She owed him that.

But there was something a bit uncomfortable to get out of the way first. It was already dark outside, and Rhea could tell that it was time. The hour for the dead, come just as it had for her father every night.

Michali must have seen the dread in her expression because he rose from his seat next to her to kneel at her feet, gently grasping one of her hands. "Now?" he asked quietly.

She nodded. "Almost."

"You know I wish I could bear this for you."

"I know." She took hold of his coat in her free hand, the roughness of the wool rooting her to the earth. "You shouldn't worry, though. It doesn't hurt. It's only a bit odd, that's all."

"Still," Michali said, but Rhea was no longer listening. The names had begun to pile up in drifts like snow at the back of her head.

She'd always wondered if her father was lying when he'd said he never picked the names of those about to die, and that they just arrived in his mind as if torn from a dream. But she'd carried the matagios now for a dozen weeks, and every night they came, tapping against her brow like drops of rain borne on the wind. Strangers, always. Names from across Thyzakos and farther still.

She never spoke them. Her father had been quite happy to wield his power, and hand down death before dinner, as though it whetted his appetite. That had been his way; it did not have to be hers. So every night the names came to Rhea, and she waited for them to dissipate like mist, but they never did. They never would until she spoke them aloud.

The longer she refused to, Rhea was alarmed to admit, the more it hurt. Tonight was no exception. Only Michali had ever seen her like this, hunched over with her forehead pressed to the heels of her palms. It was like a headache, she had told him once, if only a headache were not in fact a headache but rather a sword fresh from the fire jammed from temple to temple.

"You know," Michali said quietly, "nobody would fault you for doing as your father did. It seems to be your duty."

"It's one I didn't ask for," she snapped, even though she knew that changed nothing. But really, it was Lexos who had wanted this. Lexos who had been, as far as they'd known, the firstborn. Lexos who had killed their father and—she flinched at the memory—tried to kill her.

She sighed, shut her eyes briefly, and willed her head to clear. Instead, she heard only the distant whisper of, *"Nikolaos Papageorgiou."*

"Excuse me," she said and got to her feet, tugging her hand free from his. "I need a bit of fresh air."

Michali let her go—he did not really have much choice—and she slipped out the back of the tent, away from the rest of camp. It was bracingly cold without the braziers, and only a bit of light reached this far back, barely enough to outline the narrow path into the trees that Rhea had cut through the snow a few days prior. Still, her steps were steady; she had come this way more often than anybody knew. Anything to get a moment to herself.

The names were beginning to subside, thankfully. There were not as many as she had dreaded there might be—death, she supposed, had a number of other methods available to it outside of the natural order—but each one was painfully vivid. Rhea had wondered, at first, if she would ever forget them. And of course she had, but that was beside the point.

She stopped just as the trail began its incline toward the flat of the nearby clifftop. In daylight she might have continued, but too often she'd nearly tripped and fallen while carrying that cursed humming-bird, and as strong as the temptation always was to chuck it off said clifftop and turn away before it hit the riverbed, Rhea was not yet ready to begin playing with that particular fire.

It was not always with her, the bird, but it was tonight, wrapped carefully and tied at her waist in a blue fabric pouch. It was dangerous to carry it, she knew, but it often seemed more of a risk to leave it out of her sight. She did not know quite what Nitsos had meant by his little speech that day in the garden, or what would happen to her, specifically, if the bird was damaged, but it was certainly nothing good. Perhaps even more alarming, though, had been Nitsos's insinuation that he no longer needed the hummingbird to take hold of her heart and mind. Whether that was a bluff or a real threat, Rhea meant to handle her brother before she could find out.

She yanked her skirts up out of the snow and sidestepped into a clearing just off the trail. Here she could see the stars dotting the sky above and her own breath forming in the black. The names were almost over. She could tell—it was just before the last that her nose always began to bleed.

Not too much, nothing she couldn't wipe away on her sleeve and pretend had never existed in the first place. Enough, though, that if Michali or Chrysanthi saw, they would certainly have something to say about it.

She turned the cuff of her sleeve inside out and wiped at her nose before examining the fresh stain. It did worry her, if she was honest. All of it did. The snow that kept falling, and the way Michali's eyes never left hers. She'd known what price she was offering up when she'd raised him. The seasons would pass only with the death of one consort and the claiming of another—or with the death of her entire family, and no performance of the proper rituals to pass their power on—and still she had never wavered, never hesitated in calling Michali home. But nothing had prepared her for the despair in Piros's face when yet another cart broke, its wheels frozen through one too many times. Food caches along the mountain trail remained empty; people arrived from the villages below with nothing in their packs.

And all the while, Michali looked at her with his too-dark eyes.

They did not always look different, and sometimes she could convince herself that she'd imagined it, that black glimmer in their depths. But when it appeared, it was unmistakable, though what it was she couldn't say. If it reminded her of anything, it was the power her mother had been said to have as a saint: the blackness behind the stars. That same darkness seemed to beat in the matagios on her tongue, to carry between her and Michali like a shared breath. Something waiting, something familiar.

Mama, Rhea thought, as a trickle of blood ran down the back of her throat. Maybe it was Mama, back from the dead like Michali.

She scrubbed at her eyes, pressed her hands to the snow covering the path, and let the melt of it carry the blood from her fingertips. That was wishful thinking; Mama was gone, and there was nobody to help her with the mantle she'd chosen to take up. Time, now, to go back and see if she could weather the night next to Michali.

It was as she turned to head back to camp that something in the sky caught her attention. An odd collection of stars directly overhead, arranged in a way she had never seen before. She stopped and tipped her head back. She had never spent too much time watching Lexos exercise this gift, but she had seen its effect, and there were two constellations that were not supposed to be where they were.

One looked something like a wave, if she squinted. An ocean, perhaps. And the other—well, the other was a little bird, wing raised in flight.

A hummingbird, Rhea thought bitterly. That had to be Lexos, didn't it? Her twin brother, sending her some kind of message from wherever he was, attempting some version of writing her name in the stars.

Well, whatever the rest of the message was, she had no care to hear it. He'd made his choice when he'd sent her to the north alone, in service of his own plans, and he'd done it again that day in the garden. Besides, he was no longer the brother she was most interested in hearing from. No, that honor belonged to Nitsos. Nitsos, who she had promised to kill one day. She'd meant it then; she still did.

She spun on her heel and tramped back to the camp, one hand clamped around the pouch at her belt. He was out there somewhere, with plans of his own. He had to be found.

CHAPTER THREE

ALEXANDROS

The trip along the canal was shorter than Lexos had expected. When Falka had mentioned his new prison, he'd imagined some dingy cell at the bottom of a remote fortress, days away by ship, but the little canal boat seemed only equipped to carry him a day's travel from Vuomorra at the most. The channel was perfectly straight save for where it occasionally opened into circular ponds so that a boat might turn around if necessary. The passage was bordered on both sides by stone walls, and overhead was covered by glass panels, with small openings cut into them here and there to let in fresh air and rain. Lexos spent most of the journey with his head tilted back, marveling at how the glass stretched from wall to wall with almost no visible support. Perhaps this was the work of some ancient smith under the banner of Luco Domina himself, the first of the Stratagiozi.

But no, Vuomorra was all Tarro's work, wasn't it? Before him, the Dominas had ruled from cities all across the continent. Even Thyzakos had been part of Trefazio under Luco. What a world that would be, Lexos thought wryly as the boat drifted farther down the canal. He might have been Tarro's favorite son. Or he very well might have still found himself in chains, or worse, as was so often the fate of Tarro's children.

It was passing sunset, the glass panels above washed to orange and gold, but around him the Trefzan guards gave no indication that they were about to stop for the evening. In fact, Lexos was not sure where they would make camp, as there were no banks to this little river.

He cleared his throat. "Excuse me?" he said in Trefza. "Does anyone have any water?"

One of the guards looked his way and, after a long moment, fished for something on the boat floor before tossing Lexos his discarded helmet. "The canal is clean."

"Yes," Lexos said, eyeing the helmet distastefully, "but I am not sure you are."

"Leave it be," said the guard closest to the bow of the boat. "We're nearly there anyway."

"Really?"

Nobody answered, so Lexos leaned forward and craned his neck, trying to get a better look. The canal did seem to corner up ahead, which it had not done so far. But this was still very close to Vuomorra. If he could make it out of here, he would not have far to go to reach Nitsos and Falka, for whatever purpose he cared to indulge. Either this suited Falka just fine, or she had failed to consider the risks, and Falka was much too clever for that.

The oarsman dragged his oars in the water, slowing the glide of the boat toward the bend in the canal. It began to tilt to one side as the guards shifted over and reached out, palms raised in case the boat should come too close to the wall. Lexos held very still. He had never been particularly fond of water travel, and this was doing very little to change his mind.

This corner led to another, and then another, but finally the canal straightened again, and as the guards sat back down, their light armor clanking gently, Lexos could see what awaited him.

Hanging across the canal was a golden sluice gate, molded intricately in spirals and leaves. It was currently lowered, but the guard at the bow reached for the pulley mechanism set into the wall and tugged on the gold-capped lever. Smoothly, without even the slightest groan, the gate began to rise.

Beyond it, the canal widened, rigid lines giving way to a wash of blue and green. Lexos blinked. It was a pond that lay ahead of them, or something like it—still water closed in by the same high stone walls and vented glass dome overhead, but stretching broadly in every direction. Floating on its surface were a number of lily pads, as wide across as Lexos was tall, and between them grew strange green stalks that towered over the water, some almost as tall as a house. Lexos tipped his head back to get a look. Whatever these were, they seemed like flowers growing from the water, their petals casting a dappled shade below.

"What is this place?" he asked, and though he hadn't had much hope of getting an answer, the guard nearest to him nodded toward the far side of the pond, unease written plainly across his face.

"Summer palace for the family," he said, which made Lexos scoff. What was there to be afraid of with a summer palace? "They're being kinder to you than I'd have been."

Lexos followed his gaze ahead of the boat to where a bank of neat grass ran like a ribbon across the far shore. On it, and set a bit back from the water, was a large building, the mass of which seemed to continue out of sight. The portion he could see was washed in warm terracotta, its faded walls showing the wear that none of the Domina buildings in Vuomorra ever did.

When, he wondered, had Tarro been here last?

The boat continued on its path across the pond, skirting the lily pads with the aid of the guards. Lexos kept his eyes trained on the fading sky. It was difficult to tell how low the sun had sunk since his departure from Vuomorra and harder still to discern its true direction from beneath the canopy. None of his travels in Trefazio had ever taken him much outside the capital city, but he remembered mention of Tarro's preference for the rock beaches that dotted the southern coast. Perhaps Lexos had found himself there, although the air carried no hint of the salt tang Lexos knew so well from Stratathoma.

They were nearer now, almost to the far shore of the pond. Only one lily pad remained for the boat to maneuver around, and it was as the guard at the front gripped the upturned edge of it, his gauntlet clanking noisily, that Lexos realized—these were not plants. Not natural, and not truly green. They were copper, built by the hands of man and set to drift in Tarro's summer garden.

Lexos leaned over the edge of the boat to get a better view. Yes, now that he looked closely, he could see the supports under the water, holding the false lily pads in place. And he could see, too, spots where the verdigris had not turned the copper all the way green. The flowers overhead had to be artificial, too, then. All of this was. And it looked, unfortunately, very familiar.

There was no guarantee, Lexos told himself as they slipped past the lily pad and toward the little stone dock ahead. Surely there were many craftsmen in Trefazio capable of something like this. But he had seen Nitsos in Vuomorra and spent long enough living amongst Nitsos's designs to recognize them elsewhere. How long had Nitsos been making inroads with the Dominas? How many favors did Tarro owe him? Even one was too many, and more than Lexos could ever hope for.

The boat bumped gently against the dock. He waited as the guards disembarked, eventually hauling him to his feet and all but carrying him ashore and up onto the lawn. They were speaking among themselves, presumably discussing what to do with him next, but Lexos hardly paid them any attention. He was more concerned with the house up ahead.

And it was a house, not a palace as the guard had said, and not anything like the Domina citadel in Vuomorra. It had seemed quite large from the canal entrance. Now that he was closer, Lexos thought perhaps the whole of it could have fit inside Stratathoma many times over.

It could not have seemed more different, though. Stratathoma was done in thick stone, its warren of passages marked by the many hands of many Stratagiozi. This house seemed plainly built, without the ancient hollows and tricks that lived at home.

"Here," a guard said, drawing Lexos's attention. He was holding out his hand, and in it he held a large brass key. "You'll need this."

"I'm sorry?"

"For the door."

Lexos took the key, looking to the house again. Ah—there, set just where the stone walls that bordered the pond butted up against the house, a lonely little door was waiting for him.

"You're not going to see me inside?" he asked.

The guard nearest let out a bark of laughter as he began climbing back into the boat. "This is as far as we go," he said. "Look out in there, Argyros."

"Look out? It's an old house. I think I'll be all right."

The guards left him there then, turning the boat slowly toward the golden sluice gate across the water. Lexos watched from the lawn as the boat slipped into the canal. This was it? No chains and no guards left to keep watch. Just an old house and another of Nitsos's gardens. How little, he thought bitterly, things seemed to change.

But it was getting dark, and he was hungry. So he turned away from the water and made for the door. It was probably a stray shadow that had those guards on edge.

Despite the rust clinging to it, the lock opened easily, and the hinges didn't complain as Lexos pulled the door open. Immediately, he caught the smell of a kitchen's dried herbs and milled flour. For a moment it reminded him so much of home that he half expected to see Chrysanthi inside. If only she were here. Anything to spare him from having to eat his own cooking.

He left the door open behind him and stepped inside, the last of the sunlight drifting in over his shoulders. The kitchen was dominated by a great plank table, the softened edges notched here and there by the stray cut of a knife. Along the side was a rack of vegetables, grains, and dried meats, somewhat depleted. At the far end of the room, difficult to make out in the shadows, a hulking brick oven lay quiet.

All told, it was only enough to last him a week, if he was careful. And who knew if he would ever be brought more? But, he reassured himself, he hardly planned on being here very long.

An archway opened into more darkness opposite the table, and so Lexos crouched by one of the hutches cluttered with spices to find a candle and a match. Once he'd got a flame sputtering, he began to venture farther into the house.

First was a dining room, its gilded chairs covered in a fine layer of dust. Beyond that, a double-height entrance hall, with a simple wooden staircase running up one side to the second-floor mezzanine. There were portraits here, hung in odd groupings across the plastered walls. Dominas, certainly. Lexos didn't bother giving them a second look and continued on, ignoring the second floor for the moment.

He was hoping to find a study, perhaps, or even better, a coterie of servants ready and waiting to aid him. What he found was a sitting room, equipped with two couches that seemed to be competing to be the ugliest thing in view.

Maybe, he thought, they were what the guard had been referring to.

Lexos peeled off his traveling coat and tossed it onto the rug that covered the slate floor before he collapsed onto the least offensive of the couches. Overhead, he could see the ripple of the pond reflected onto the ceiling, the light magnified by the room's lopsided crystal chandelier.

They had not let him bring much with him from Stratathoma that day they'd taken him, and everything he had been able to scrounge up had been confiscated the minute he arrived in Vuomorra anyway, distributed amongst the lesser Dominas as signs of Tarro's favor. So there was nothing to do now—no luggage to unpack, no books to pile up by his bed to make it feel more like his. This was a prison, not a guesthouse. He was here to pay for his crimes against the Dominas. Him, and not his siblings, who he'd tried to protect.

He shut his eyes tightly. None of that mattered now. What mattered was that the Dominas could've sent him anywhere. A cell beneath Vuomorra, or the gallows in the city square. And yet he was here, alone and, for the moment, safe, despite the warnings of the guards. He was here because somebody meant him to be. Whether that was Falka, or Tarro, or even Nitsos, he wasn't sure, but whoever it was, he wouldn't make the mistake of thinking they were an ally. This time he would look after himself.

CHAPTER FOUR

NITSOS

One more dinner with the Dominas, Nitsos told himself, and then he'd be on his way.

It really would be a shame to leave. Everything about Vuomorra had gone as he'd wanted it to. After Stratathoma, he'd waited for Lexos to be brought here before making his own arrival some weeks later, once he could be sure that his last name alone wouldn't get him tossed into Lexos's prison cell. Yes, he'd been courting favor with the Dominas for years, sending information for their spies and designs for their metalsmiths, but favor fell apart so easily, didn't it? Better than anyone, Nitsos knew that sometimes, a bit of patience went further than anything else.

And, as predictably as one of Nitsos's own creations, Tarro had welcomed him with open arms, given him a room to sleep in and materials to tinker with, and—whether he'd known it or not—an introduction to all manner of influential people. Half the Stratagiozi Council had been in and out of Tarro's halls. Nitsos had made inroads with all of them—one in particular.

"Argyros," someone said. Nitsos looked up. A few yards ahead, her pale blouse and trousers stark against the gathering dusk, Falka was waiting where the hedge-lined gravel path they'd been walking opened onto a broad pitch of grass. Some of her siblings were already there, the younger set playing some insipid game with a ball, the older well into their glasses of wine, as they always were at this hour. "Are you coming?"

He cleared his throat, said, "Oh, yes," and hurried after her, toward a table where he could sit and wait for the dinner bell to be rung. Perhaps Falka would circle the lawn, chatting with her siblings and reinforcing the pact she'd made with them to keep them from taking her place as Tarro's second. Or perhaps she'd join him, which he wouldn't object to at all.

He liked Falka, and oddly enough she appeared to like him. As different as they were, Nitsos could recognize in her the same urge he often felt: to pry the world open and rearrange what he found inside. How reassuring to sit with her in the blue of the evening and know exactly what she might be thinking about. He'd had to work so hard to understand Lexos and Rhea, had needed all one hundred of the years they'd spent alongside one another.

Chrysanthi, of course, had been different—he could imagine her now, preening at the thought—but he'd been aware, even as she helped him in his garden, how much she'd resented the bond she shared with him. That, he understood very well. He'd never asked to love his siblings, and yet he thought of them still: of their portraits along the corridor at Stratathoma, and of his workshop in the attic, the table there littered with glass lenses, all waiting to be tinted Argyros blue.

Nitsos sidestepped a gaggle of children, their Domina green clothes stained with grass and dirt, and found himself a seat at one of the little tables set up around the edges of the lawn. Only moments later, a servant brought him a glass of water topped with a wedge of lemon. It was probably, Nitsos thought as he took a sip, Domina water with Domina lemon—everything in Vuomorra that could possibly carry the family's name seemed to have it tacked on. Baba had not been like that. Neither, it seemed, was Nitsos's new benefactor.

He hadn't been sure, at first, who might best serve his interests, but it had come down to a decision between the wealth and ancient influence of Zita Devetsi and the pure might of Ammar Basha. Ammar would have made great use of his creatures, both in and out of battle, and Nitsos had been sorely tempted to answer that particular summons, but Ammar was of the same sort Baba had been. The power he wielded would never sit properly in Nitsos's hands. Zita, though—she'd held Merkher almost as long as it had existed. She had helped build the federation, and it was in her service he might find just the right way to make it fall again. Then, when there was quiet at last, he could set about designing something better.

Nitsos had finished with his first water and started another before Falka broke from her rounds and dropped into the chair next to him, her head tipped back as she let out a sigh.

"Something to drink?" Nitsos offered.

"Yes, thank you."

She reached for his glass. He moved it away. "I didn't mean mine."

They fell silent for a moment, the air filled instead with the sound of conversation and, in the distance, the wails of whichever young Domina had just been knocked down during the game on the lawn. Was this a good time, Nitsos wondered, to tell Falka he would be leaving? Or would it be better to not tell her at all and simply slip out of the city before the sun was fully up tomorrow?

"He'll be fine," Falka said suddenly, speaking now in Thyzaki instead of their customary Trefza. Nitsos looked sidelong at her, one eyebrow raised, and she added, "Your brother."

Ah. Nitsos had found himself surprisingly glad to see Lexos; he did not think Lexos had felt the same, which annoyed him. What grudge could Lexos really justify holding? Everything that had happened at Stratathoma had been Lexos's fault. At least Rhea had a real reason to dislike him.

"Lexos is always fine," Nitsos said. "It's his great talent."

Falka scoffed, and Nitsos supposed he could understand why. She hadn't seen Lexos keep his spot as their father's second through decades of failure and missed opportunities. Even Lexos himself didn't seem to realize how long their family had teetered on the edge of ruin.

They could have survived—flourished—ruled for centuries just as the Dominas had, if only anyone had let him do anything at all.

Suddenly, the Domina chatter around them was too much. Nitsos stood sharply, jostling the table and nearly knocking over his glass.

"Nitsos?" Falka said. "Is everything all right?"

He really did like Falka. But she'd got what she wanted, and he was still where he'd always been. Surrounded by power, with none of it actually his.

No, it was well past time to leave Vuomorra.

"Excuse me," he said. "I'm feeling rather ill."

Falka did not call after him, but he felt the weight of her gaze on his shoulders long after he'd started up the path to the palace.

Back in his room, Nitsos knelt next to his already packed bag and began to reorganize it, as he had done every night since accepting Zita's offer. Her instructions had been vague, but from what he knew about Vashnasta, he wouldn't be allowed to bring in much. And even then, whatever he was allowed would be picked through by the guards at the Navirotsk.

A flare of excitement burst in his chest as he thought of where he'd be heading before the sun was up. He'd dreamed of the Navirotsk for nearly eighty years now, since Lexos had first mentioned it offhandedly and sent Nitsos digging through every bit of Baba's correspondence he could get his hands on, looking for more information. The largest library on the continent, older than the saints themselves—he could think of absolutely nothing more worth his time, even if he did have to spend some of it looking for whatever Zita was after.

He sat back on his heels, staring down at the contents of his bag. This was it; he had everything he needed. Spare shirts, a dagger, thick socks for the deeper cold up north, and tucked on top of the rest, carefully wrapped in a blanket, a collection of gears and worked metal. Though the pieces had yet to be assembled, Nitsos could see the finished creation so clearly in his mind's eye. The gossamer wings, the gold body, and, of course, that flash of Argyros blue.

A smile started at the corner of Nitsos's mouth. Old habits were hard to break.

CHAPTER FIVE

CHRYSANTHI

There was quite a lot to be said for not being stuck behind the same stone walls every day. Since leaving Stratathoma, Chrysanthi had tried spices she'd never heard of before and seen mountains taller than she'd thought possible, and though all of it was very exciting, her favorite novelty was, without question, this: riding out into the Ksigoran woods in the early morning, her paints tucked in a bag at her side, as she searched for new subjects to capture and new colors to match.

This particular morning had already gifted her with a brown she'd spotted in the knot of a birch tree, so pale and cool it was almost lilac, and a strange shade of silver that seemed, in the diffused light, to rise off the snow like a layer of fog. One of her most successful outings, really. The only thing that might have improved it would have been Rhea's company, but that was in short supply these days, which meant Chrysanthi was alone. Well. Almost alone. Riding silently behind her, just as he always did, was Andrija Tomic, his hulking figure keeping her sheltered from some of the wind that came down from the peaks.

He'd been assigned to her by Piros, meant to keep her from getting into trouble, and when they'd first met, Chrysanthi had been greatly optimistic—surely nobody's company would be as dull as Michali's, who often seemed just as dead as he was alive—but Andrija had proven himself to be a man of few words. Or, more accurately, a man of one word, and that was "No," offered to Chrysanthi in a northern accent when she asked if she could ride on ahead without him, or if she could stay out beyond camp borders past sundown.

At least he looked at her, though. Michali was always too focused on Rhea to pay her that kind of attention, but Andrija seemed to take notice when she pointed out a particular bird or set of tracks in the snow that she found interesting, and that made his presence much easier to bear. Besides, she couldn't pretend she wasn't used to it. Silence and solitude had been so much of her life at Stratathoma. Whenever Rhea was gone, and Lexos lost to some dispute between stewards, Chrysanthi had spent her time wandering the grounds, pausing here and there to touch up spots where the stone perimeter wall looked in need of a bit of moss, and keeping an eye out for Nitsos.

She clutched tightly at the reins, urging her horse forward as a pang of guilt sliced through her. She was not meant to think of him anymore—not fondly anyway. Rhea had explained everything about that day in the garden, from Mama's past and Lexos's murder of Baba to the true purpose of the hummingbird Chrysanthi had seen so often flitting about in Nitsos's clockwork garden. And though Chrysanthi believed her sister with all her heart, she found it difficult to leave Nitsos behind entirely. It was second nature to worry about him, to wonder how he was managing without her to look after him. Wherever he was now, she hoped it was with people who would help him keep his blond curls trimmed; he'd always hated it when they got in his eyes while he worked.

Behind her, a horse whinnied gently. She turned, half expecting to see Nitsos approaching, but of course it was Andrija. He'd bent low in the saddle to whisper something soothing in his horse's ear. Chrysanthi held back a smile; maybe he spoke to his horse in single syllables, too.

"Everything all right?" she asked. Andrija nodded, not looking up. "Then shall we continue on?" They were close to the river here, she thought, and she was eager to spend some time with her paints on its banks—its color was proving deliciously difficult to replicate.

Andrija straightened slowly, appearing to think before saying, "No," which was not unexpected.

They stayed quiet for the rest of the ride back to camp, which was not unexpected, either. Sxoriza scouts had broken the trail before the rest of the camp followed, and so it grew wider the nearer they got to the site, enough for Andrija's horse to draw up alongside Chrysanthi's and then slip past. Andrija probably hoped that Piros, who would be waiting up ahead for her return, wouldn't realize he let Chrysanthi proceed first into the wilderness, unguarded.

Piros stood right at the edge of the campsite as they rounded a copse of pine trees, his beard dotted with snow, a heavy cloak draped over his broad shoulders. He had been responsible, on their ride across Thyzakos, for keeping Chrysanthi fed and out of trouble, and though he had since been replaced, he was still the one sent to fetch her whenever she was needed; apparently the rest of Rhea's runners did not like to be talked at quite so loudly.

"Piros!" she called as they approached. "What can I do for you today?"

"Oh, thank goodness," he said, visibly relaxing. "I've been waiting here for ten minutes."

He was always in a hurry, Piros, always late to something or in search of someone who was late to something else. Chrysanthi liked to dawdle whenever he was in charge of taking her somewhere, just to see how red she could get his face to turn.

"So sorry to delay," she said as she pulled her horse up short and began to dismount. "I saw a ruby-throated warbler that just had to be admired."

Still seated on his own horse, Andrija made a small noise that might have been laughter, but a quick glance at his face showed no expression.

"A ruby-throated . . ." Piros started before trailing off wearily. "Yes. Of course."

"What was it you needed?"

"Your sister," Piros said, gesturing over his shoulder toward camp. "She's asking for you."

Chrysanthi raised her eyebrows. "Me this time? Not Michali?"

Something shifted in Piros's face—a twitch of the eyelid, perhaps—and he shook his head. That was interesting. Another little moment for Chrysanthi to file away next to every time Piros all but refused to look Michali in the eye. This was unusual not just because Piros had, apparently, been one of Michali's most trusted advisors prior to his return, but also because in general Piros was one of the most affable people Chrysanthi had ever met. Upon their arrival at the first of the camps some months ago, he had even given her his spare coat and a pair of his trousers to help her keep warm, which had been very kind, if only they had fit at all.

"All right," she said. "Let's go, shall we?"

She turned to gather her horse's reins and tie him at the nearby post so that someone else might collect him, but Andrija was already there, one gloved hand hooked around her horse's bridle.

"Go," he said. So she did.

The tent wasn't far, but to get there, they had to cut through the center of camp, which always turned into something of an event. People were constantly lingering nearby wherever Michali could be found—his novelty as proof of Rhea's power had yet to wear off—and newer camp followers gathered, too, in little clusters to get a look at Chrysanthi herself. That, she understood. She was quite something to see.

Rhea attracted that sort of attention, too, although it was much more reverent, which seemed to weigh on her. But that was only one of the things that worried Chrysanthi about her sister's current situation.

"How is she?" Chrysanthi asked Piros as they continued through the camp. The paths had been laid with wooden planks meant to keep the mud and slush from seeping too deeply into people's boots. They were not working.

"Busy," Piros said. "She missed her breakfast again this morning." He paused. "I'm not sure I was meant to tell you that."

Chrysanthi was glad he had. Rhea was all too happy, lately, to let meals pass her by, and Chrysanthi absolutely would not stand for it. Her sister needed to eat, and yes, Rhea could call herself a saint and pretend that it gave her some inhuman holiness, but Chrysanthi was fairly sure that saints were allowed to enjoy a stuffed pepper just as much as the next person.

They skirted a row of canvas shelters, keeping close to the trees that lined the camp's clearing. There were crocuses growing at the roots, spring flowers in spring bloom just as they ought to be. But their colors were muted, an odd green-brown running up from the center where a vivid yellow should have been. Chrysanthi felt her palms begin to itch and thought about taking out her paints. She could fix this spot before they left. But then, what good would it really do? Her gift wasn't nearly as effective now that she'd been removed from Stratathoma.

She put all that out of her mind as they approached the tent that the leadership used for their meetings.

"Wait here," Piros told her. "I'll see if she's ready."

"Oh, that's all right," Chrysanthi said and pushed one tent flap open. "I can make my own way."

She heard Piros stuttering behind her but continued in, ducking slightly to keep the canvas from mussing her hair. Inside, Rhea was standing at a shoddily built table, poring over a stack of maps. Her dark hair was loose around her shoulders, caught here and there on the metal studs that covered the bodice of her gown.

Sometimes Chrysanthi tried to understand what worshippers in camp felt when they looked at Rhea. She'd seen the way their eyes went wide, the way their cheeks flushed and their hands began to shake; was that love? Or was it something stranger? Whatever the case, she could not imagine that any of them held Rhea as dearly as Chrysanthi herself did.

"I told Piros I wasn't ready yet," Rhea said.

Chrysanthi rolled her eyes. "I didn't want to wait outside. It's cold out, if you weren't aware." She loved Rhea very much, but that didn't mean she couldn't also think she was a bit annoying.

"Well, fine." Rhea beckoned Chrysanthi closer. "You're here, so come and see this, will you?"

Chrysanthi did not move. It was her first good look at Rhea in a few days—they were often separate during daylight, spending only the dark hours together under their heavy blankets—and it was alarming. Rhea's skin had gone terribly pale, her veins standing out in purple ribbons beneath, and the line of her jaw seemed too sharp. She looked very little like the sister Chrysanthi had known for a century, had spent countless hours with at the dinner table while their brothers fought for a sliver of their father's attention.

"Rhea," she said. "Are you well?"

"Very." Rhea was in the middle of rolling back one map to lay bare another. "Really, come over here."

"Because you look ill."

"That's very kind."

"I mean, beautiful, of course. You take after me. But I think we should get you something to eat, perhaps. I can send Piros for some cabbage rolls, if you would like. Or Michali could fetch—"

"There is no need for that." Rhea looked up from the table. All good humor had left her face. "I'm fine. And every person in this camp wishes they had more to eat than they do, so forgive me if I don't take food out of their mouths just to put it in mine."

If there was one thing Chrysanthi did not like, it was to be scolded. Yes, she had lived so long at Stratathoma, and yes, there was quite a lot she didn't know, but she was, shockingly, not as stupid as Rhea seemed to think she was. In fact, of all her siblings, Chrysanthi thought she might be the only person who understood the value in letting the opportunity for an argument pass her by.

"Very well," she said and approached the table, coming around to stand next to Rhea to get a look at the map. "What's this, then?"

Rhea tapped a small symbol in the bottom corner. It was not labeled—nothing was—but Chrysanthi could reasonably infer that this was their current campsite's location.

"Oh, excellent," she said. "Are you planning where we go next? Might I make some suggestions? I'd prefer somewhere without snow, although given your recent misadventures, I'm not sure that's an option."

She'd meant it as a friendly jab, the kind they'd always exchanged as sisters, but Rhea bristled and straightened next to her.

"I'm doing my best, you know," she said. "I'm trying to protect you, and me, and the people who follow me, and it's quite a lot to keep in order, so—"

"Rhea. Rhea, I was only joking. I promise." Chrysanthi leaned in close, putting on her very best sisterly smile—this one usually got her what she wanted, from almost everyone. "You used to joke about this sort of thing, too," she said. "You used to be fun."

Rhea's frown deepened. "Find something else to joke about. You are far better off than most of the other people in this camp, *kora*."

"That doesn't mean I have to be happy," Chrysanthi said. She could hear herself turning shrill, which was mortifying, but there wasn't much she could do to hold herself back. "Do you understand what this has been like for me?"

Rhea opened her mouth to answer, her eyes darting to the map before flicking back to Chrysanthi's as she hesitated. That was a grim little face she was wearing, which was saying something, given everything they'd undergone in the last three months.

"What is it, then?" Chrysanthi said. "Go on."

"Well," said Rhea, looking down at the map again, "I'm afraid I need to ask you a favor."

CHAPTER SIX

RHEA

She'd been dreading this. For days she'd been trying to find a way around the option she was left with now, but there was nobody else she trusted well enough. And nobody else with Chrysanthi's particular charm, a quality that was nearly a Stratagiozi gift of its own in its ability to be both incredibly persuasive and incredibly irritating.

"It's not a task you will like very much, I'm afraid," she began. "But this will be a chance to see something new." She moved to the table and pointed to the map. But Chrysanthi did not follow her gesture and instead was looking at her with an expression Rhea recognized from the deer that Nitsos used to build to roam the grounds at Stratathoma. "*Koukla?* Are you all right?"

"You're sending me out?" Chrysanthi said at last. Rhea could see her working to look calm, much as she'd seen her working to look like any other Sxoriza member, in her threadbare clothes and lank, grimy hair, although even months of travel couldn't dim the Stratagiozi shine in her. It was a costume she'd put on, really, and Rhea knew from experience how ill that fit over time.

"I hoped this would be welcome news to you," Rhea said. "I know you have not always found the camps quite to your liking."

"And you have decided that I will fare better alone on the trail in the wilderness?"

"Not alone," Rhea started, because of course she wasn't planning to feed her little sister to the wolves, both literal and figurative, but Chrysanthi barreled on.

"You and Lexos, you know. You both think that you can treat the rest of us like we are all children."

That was too far. "I am nothing," she said sharply, "like Alexandros."

Chrysanthi scoffed, unafraid. "No? He sent you to the Ksigora, and now you send me to . . ." Her anger dissipated somewhat as she glanced down at the map with a furrowed brow. "Where? For what?"

An opening, Rhea thought, and she leaned over the table again, drawing the map of the continent closer as she pressed her shoulder to Chrysanthi's. It was marked with the few pieces of intelligence she'd been able to gather thus far as to Nitsos's whereabouts—that is, a little X across Stratathoma, another smack in the middle of the Vitmar, and another on the edge of Trefazio, near the Vuomorra harbor. This was the sum total of it: everything her scouts had been able to cobble together since she'd left Stratathoma. It made her flush with embarrassment if she thought about it too long. How this must look compared to the work Lexos and Nitsos used to do.

"I need to find him, Chrysanthi," she said. "I need to find Nitsos."

There was a slight pause, and she could see her sister trying to hold back the words that inevitably did come out of her mouth: "What for, though?"

What Rhea really wanted Nitsos for was to break the link that still lived between her and that little hummingbird. And then, once he'd done that, to kill him, and bleed him out the way he'd had done to Michali. But Chrysanthi had spent more time with Nitsos than anyone else, and though she was doing her best to be quite furious with him, Rhea knew that her sister still dreamed of a family dinner, the siblings pulled back together from across the continent and Baba's seat left empty. Nothing Rhea could say would change that; Chrysanthi would have to learn the truth of her brothers for herself.

"I think he knows something," she said. "Something important, about Lexos and what happened with Tarro."

Vague, and ultimately meaningless, but technically correct. And much more appealing to Chrysanthi than the actual truth.

Still, her sister seemed unconvinced. "You can't reach him yourself?"

"I could," she answered, "or I could send someone like Piros. Like your guard. But Nitsos won't come back with those people. You know that."

"And that's what you want? For Nitsos to come back to us?"

"Yes."

"Alive?"

Rhea let out a long breath. If she said yes, Chrysanthi would recognize it for the lie it was. "I want to speak to him," she said instead. "Everything happened so quickly at Stratathoma. We didn't have a chance to talk properly. And I'm afraid we might not ever get it if I send a stranger to go and fetch him. But if I send you?" She gritted her teeth, forcing out the rest. "If I send someone he knows, someone who loves him? That's how I see a way forward."

Chrysanthi's face fell, a blush suddenly bright on her cheeks; Rhea winced. Most of the time, she admired how easily her sister loved people and how deeply. Using it now as a way to prod Chrysanthi into action felt like something Baba might have done, but she could think of no other way to set things in motion.

"*Elado,*" she said and nodded to the map again. Perhaps if Chrysanthi focused on the task at hand, she might stop looking like Rhea had just blamed her for stealing the last kymitha even as its crumbs were still caught in Rhea's own hair. "Can I?"

Chrysanthi gave her one last lingering stare before turning her attention to the map. "Fine. These are where he's been seen?"

"Vuomorra, most recently," Rhea said, tapping the mark by the city. "But it's this I'm most interested in." She dragged her finger up to the north, to the *X* in the Vitmar. "He wasn't sighted, but one of my scouts saw something that might have been one of his creatures." A familiar white bird, in fact, but that wouldn't mean much to Chrysanthi. "I expect he'll be there shortly, if he isn't already."

" 'There' being?"

"Vashnasta," Rhea said. "At the Navirotsk." She paused, waiting for Chrysanthi to react, to be upset, but she only stood there, her jaw set in that mulish way she'd done since they were children. "Are you familiar with the Navirotsk?"

"Should I be?"

"I— Yes, you should." She'd known Chrysanthi lived a sheltered life, but really, the Navirotsk was as famous as the monastery at Agiokon. "It's an archive. A library of sorts."

"Sounds boring." Chrysanthi's mouth twitched, a smile flickering to life. "Of course that's where Nitsos is."

"No," Rhea corrected, "not boring. In fact, you'll need to be paying quite close attention. It's a difficult area at the moment, and if you're not careful—"

"I haven't said I'll go yet." Chrysanthi met her eyes, and for a moment she looked so like Baba that Rhea nearly flinched. But then Chrysanthi lifted one shoulder in a lazy shrug and moved around the table to look at the map from a different angle. "Keep talking."

Rhea took a deep breath and let it out slowly. "Ammar and Nastia have kindly refrained from open war over Vashnasta, but it's bristling with troops, according to every report. Entrance to the city and the Navirotsk are both tightly controlled, particularly on the Chuzhak side. So you'll go through Amolova."

Chrysanthi appeared, at least, to be considering this. "How?" she asked finally. "The mountains are barely passable farther north."

"Ah. Here." Rhea pulled a second map over the first, this one a much more detailed sketch of Thyzakos's northern border. One portion of it was crosshatched in red and marked with a number of winding dotted lines. "This is a section of the border between Thyzakos and Amolova. It's a notch in the mountains and the only safe passage."

"Then won't it be full of Amolovak soldiers?" Chrysanthi asked. "They'll take me in as soon as they see me."

She was, unfortunately, mostly correct. Like the other Stratagiozis, Ammar had sided with Tarro, and though their quarrel was primarily with Lexos, Rhea was fairly certain that they would happily add another Argyros captive to their collection.

"So," she said, "you'll need to get through."

"Oh, would you like me to assassinate them all with one of my paintbrushes?"

"I do hope you come up with something else, but at least you have a fallback." Rhea stepped back from the table, the studs on her gown scraping her palms as she pressed them to her stomach. "It's important, *koukla*. I wouldn't ask if it weren't."

Chrysanthi had not looked up from the map. "And you're sure there's nobody else?"

Rhea choked back a laugh, but it burbled up again anyway. "Very sure."

"Then I suppose," Chrysanthi said, sighing, "that I will do what I can to find our wayward brother."

Rhea could have fainted with relief. "Thank you," she said. "Truly. And you won't be alone. I'll send someone with you. Anyone you like." She would miss Piros's help, but Chrysanthi would want him with her.

Chrysanthi tilted her head, eyes fixed for a moment on the tent flap over Rhea's shoulder. "I think I have just the person."

"Oh?"

Her smile was full of mischief, and Rhea was reminded, suddenly, of standing at the foot of the stairs in Stratathoma's atrium, an assortment of suitors waiting ahead of her, Chrysanthi's hand clutched in hers.

"Andrija Tomic," her younger sister said. "He can come with me."

That was a new name. Rhea hardly knew everybody in the camps— she saw far too many faces every day to keep them all straight—but surely somebody who could inspire that particular smile of Chrysanthi's would have stood out. "You trust him?" she asked. "I'll need to ask Piros what he thinks, and—"

Chrysanthi waved a hand. "Piros will agree."

She was always so sure. That, out of everything, was what Rhea felt most jealous of. Not Chrysanthi's idle time at home, or the ease with which Baba had loved her, but the way she never hesitated, not once she'd made up her mind.

"Well," Rhea said softly, ignoring the slight sting of tears at the corner of her eye. "If he'll keep you safe, then all right."

"He will," Chrysanthi said and leaned in to kiss Rhea's cheek. "He'll hate it."

She left then, whistling a cheery tune that Rhea recognized from their earliest days at Stratathoma. It seemed pointed, somehow, but whatever its meaning, she could not remember (or had, perhaps, chosen to forget). All she could think of now was that here it was again—a break between her and her siblings. Another goodbye, and Chrysanthi sent out alone. She could not have imagined it a year ago, and now it seemed the only thing left to do.

Resolutely, she bent again over the table. That was done. She would need to meet this Andrija before Chrysanthi's eventual departure; Chrysanthi had never placed much value on drawing minimal attention, and both she and her traveling companion would need to leave camp and pass through Amolova without calling any to themselves. But Rhea could leave most of it with Piros, who always knew how to keep things quiet. And she could turn instead to the heart of the matter: luring Nitsos home.

She pushed the maps aside until she found a blank bit of parchment and something to write with. Chrysanthi had the best shot of bringing Nitsos back, but her presence alone would not be enough. Rhea would have to offer him something. Something he wanted and could get only from her. She bit down on the inside of her cheek, the pain dull and distant, and began to write.

> Kouklos,
>
> I hope you are well. I know we parted last in anger, and I understand if you are hesitant, but I would like for us to meet and discuss the situation we find ourselves in. I think there must be some solution to all this, but I have no hope of discovering it alone.

I recognize that you have little reason to trust I am being sincere, so let me offer this as well: Should you agree to meet with me, I would be willing to perform the same rite for you that I have used once already. I have my beloved back. I may give you someone back as well.

She would not write down the name. Partly in case Chrysanthi failed and the message fell into different hands, and partly because she could not bear to see it spelled out. It was difficult enough to make the offer already, to imagine her father climbing from his grave the way Michali had climbed from his. But that was the only thing Nitsos had ever really wanted, and badly enough to force him into some kind of mistake—another chance at being his father's favorite. She could give him that.

If it was what she had to do to get her knife in between his ribs, then there was no other choice.

CHAPTER SEVEN

CHRYSANTHI

Chrysanthi had expected that she might have a week or so to prepare herself for this journey Rhea was sending her on, but as it happened, she had closer to a day and a half, and she meant to hold a grudge about it for the rest of her natural life. They were in Chrysanthi's tent, the two of them, Rhea sorting through everything Chrysanthi had packed for the trip and reclaiming the items of clothing that had initially been stolen from Rhea's own closet. With every piece that her sister took back, Chrysanthi added on another year to the length of her grudge. At this point she would have to live quite a long time; luckily, as a Stratagiozi's daughter, that was what she'd been born for.

"This is too much," Rhea said quietly, sitting back on her heels. The saddlebags in which Chrysanthi had packed her things were scattered around her, and a well-made black gown had spilled out of the nearest one and into her lap. "It's a ride through the mountains, *koukla*, not a party. And besides, I need this for myself."

"I know it's not a party," Chrysanthi said. "But it is a ride through the mountains toward something that is very much not mountains."

She had never been out into the world alone before, and she rather thought it was good, in a situation like this, to be prepared for anything. "If you're going to send me into the wilds to meet a tragic end, you might as well give me something nice to die in."

Rhea rolled her eyes and folded the gown back up. "Fine. This you may keep."

"Your kindness astounds me."

"But the rest . . . You have only the one horse, Chrysanthi. Better not to break its back, don't you think?"

Chrysanthi didn't bother answering. They were both nervous; she could hear it in every word that came out of Rhea's mouth and could certainly feel it in her own body, a tight sort of humming that kept her checking over her shoulder to see if anyone was there.

"Are you bringing anything practical, at least?" Rhea asked after a moment. "Anything you can defend yourself with?"

"Yes. I'm bringing Andrija."

"I'm serious." Rhea took Chrysanthi's left hand, the saddlebags forgotten, and turned it palm up. "It's dangerous. For anyone, yes, but especially for someone with this kind of mark."

Chrysanthi couldn't help swallowing hard, her mouth gone dry. The followers here in camp treated Rhea's marks and power so reverently. Frankly, she had forgotten that out in the wider world there would be people who hated them in equal measure.

"We'll be careful," she said, as much to herself as to Rhea. "Get to Vashnasta, find Nitsos, and come back again—it's simple. And I can write to you the whole time."

"I'm not sure that you should," Rhea replied. "We can't risk anyone intercepting your letters."

"Even with the hummingbird?"

Rhea's expression darkened. "He'd recognize it," she said, and Chrysanthi knew she meant Nitsos. Unfortunately, she was right. Chrysanthi had a chance at getting him home, but the more warning he had of her coming, the smaller it got.

"All right," she said, her voice trembling slightly. "I'm sure everything will be fine."

She must not have sounded as convincing as she'd meant to, because Rhea squeezed her hand and said, "Vashnasta, then. I'll send the hummingbird to meet you there. Even if the camp moves, it will know how to find me."

"Really? I can write to you then?"

"You can."

"Thank you." Chrysanthi felt herself loosen as her worry faded. She flicked her hair over her shoulder, waving Rhea away. "But I probably won't have time to. I imagine I'll be back before you've even started to miss me."

"Too late." Rhea kissed Chrysanthi's temple. Her lips were cold and dry. "I already do."

Chrysanthi watched as her sister resumed packing. She really would be fine on the road, wouldn't she? That was what Piros had insisted, and while Andrija himself had said nothing of the sort, he hadn't seemed skeptical, either, when offered the job. He'd simply stood there in Rhea's tent and listened, and when Piros was finished, had looked over at Chrysanthi and nodded once. She supposed she would get a better measure of his confidence in her when they left in a few hours. Until then, she would try to relish this last bit of quiet with her sister and remind herself that it could have been worse—Rhea could have sent Michali along with her.

When the time did come, and the sky was well past dark, Chrysanthi followed Rhea out of the back of the tent and into the trees. She was not sure exactly why they needed to leave unseen—something about the Sxoriza leadership was all she'd been able to gather from Rhea's mutterings—but if it meant that nobody saw her dressed as she was now, in a pair of ill-fitting trousers with her yellow hair wrapped under a ratty scarf, she was more than willing to go along with it.

"This way," Rhea said from up ahead. They were taking a path that Chrysanthi had never seen before, one that led east from camp. Chrysanthi narrowed her eyes, trying to make out the shape of the mountains between the trees. They seemed higher in this direction, sharper and more dangerous. Would Rhea mind very much if she immediately turned around once she and Andrija were on their way?

And speaking of Andrija, where was he? Had he somehow wea-seled his way out of this obligation?

He had not. He was there, up ahead in a small clearing, waiting next to a pair of horses. Rhea stopped in the tree line, still hidden, and lifted her hands to her mouth. Chrysanthi watched with amusement as Rhea made a sound that seemed meant to be a birdcall of sorts.

"What is that for?" she asked.

Rhea shot her a look and gestured for her to be quiet.

"It's all right," came Andrija's voice through the dark. The sisters both jumped; Chrysanthi didn't think she'd ever heard him say more than two words in a row before. "I'm alone."

That was good enough for Chrysanthi. She stepped forward, push-ing the pine branches aside to make room. Behind her Rhea let out a small noise, and Chrysanthi felt a tug on the back of her coat, but she ignored it and emerged into the clearing. Rhea followed a moment after, struggling to look dignified as she nearly tripped on a root hidden under the snow.

"Right," Chrysanthi said. "Which horse was more expensive? I think that one will be mine."

Rhea smiled, and there was something so familiar about it—Rhea in the doorway of the kitchen at Stratathoma watching her work, Rhea across from her at the dinner table reassuring her as Baba went on about something she didn't understand—that for a moment Chrysan-thi's heart stopped cold in her chest and only started again when her sister's expression melted into something more resigned.

She looked so sad. She looked . . . old. What did she know that the rest of them did not?

Well, lots of things, but Chrysanthi did not much like considering any situation in which she was not the expert, so she looked back to Andrija, who had dropped the reins on one horse and was leading the other toward her. It was gray, with gentle brown eyes and a sweet face, and its saddlebags were loaded with some of her things, another bun-dle tied across its haunches.

Chrysanthi was not afraid of horses, necessarily. She'd ridden them through the mountains here without much issue. It was just that the ones she'd encountered for most of her life had been Nitsos's creatures, mechanical and predictable and certainly not the sort to toss you off their backs if they were startled. This horse, like the others out here beyond Stratathoma's walls, warranted a bit of caution on first meeting.

Gingerly, she approached, Andrija easing back to make room for her by the horse's shoulder.

"What's its name?" she asked.

"This is Lefka. Give her her head on the trail, all right? She knows what to do." Rhea's voice was gentle as she reached out to rub the horse's nose. "She's looked after me for a while. I thought she might look after you, too."

Chrysanthi glanced sidelong at her sister. Was this supposed to be meaningful? It was a horse.

"We should get moving," Andrija said from just behind her, "if we want to be away by morning."

"Of course," Rhea said, her eyes glassy in the silver light. "I know."

Suddenly, she was moving, and Chrysanthi found herself tugged forward into her sister's arms. The embrace was so tight that she could barely breathe, but she returned it, pressing her face into Rhea's hair.

"Come back, all right?" Rhea whispered roughly. "I mean it."

Chrysanthi let a great shiver rack her body and then wrested herself away, swiping under her eyes at the lone tear that had dared fall. "Don't tell me what to do," she said, and Rhea laughed.

They had parted before. Over and over, in fact. There was no need for all this carrying on.

She turned back to Lefka, and while the mare was not too tall, still Chrysanthi accepted Andrija's offered hand as she climbed into the saddle. From up here, she could make out his features—his furrowed brow and the twist of his mouth as he concentrated on tightening her stirrups. Was he nervous, she wondered. Did he know what sort of danger they might be walking into?

"Is she ready?" Rhea asked. She had drawn her cloak around her and looked every inch the saint these people thought she was.

Andrija nodded. He tugged on her saddle one last time before stepping back. "We'll be off."

"You take care of her," Rhea said. There was a menace to it that Chrysanthi had started hearing more and more often. "Your life and hers—they're the same. Do you hear me?"

This, Chrysanthi thought, was a bit alarming, as Andrija's life seemed to consist entirely of wearing black and frowning at things, but Andrija did not look bothered. He only nodded again and went to the other horse, mounting it quickly.

Rhea came closer and grabbed Lefka's bridle, beckoning for Chrysanthi to duck down. "You have the letter?"

Tucked under her shirt, bound to her chest with a length of linen. "I do."

"Good. Find him, pass it on, and get him home."

"I know," she said, half exasperated. "You've only told me about a hundred times."

Rhea's mouth quirked up slightly, but Chrysanthi could see the sister in her disappearing, perhaps forever without Chrysanthi there to remind her of who she'd been.

"Off with you, then," she said, waving Chrysanthi away as she stepped back. "And don't dawdle. You have a job to do. You can see the sights some other time."

"There go all my plans."

It was a tradition of sorts for them to carry on this way before parting, but this time Rhea did not answer. She was instead staring up at the starred sky wearing a look of annoyance so pure that for a moment Chrysanthi thought Lexos had to be nearby, as he was the only person she'd ever seen make Rhea look like that.

"What?" she asked. "What is it?"

Rhea remained quiet for another breath, and then said, "Oh, for goodness' sake," and clicked her tongue.

Baffled, Chrysanthi followed Rhea's gaze up toward the sky. Perhaps one of Nitsos's creatures was hovering there, watching them. Or was it approaching sunrise already? Surely not. All she could see was the black of the sky and the usual collection of constellations. Usual except for one, directly overhead, which seemed to take the shape of a hummingbird.

"It's just ridiculous at this point," Rhea said, and she hardly glanced at Chrysanthi again before turning around and stomping her way back across the snow toward the trees and the camp beyond. "Be safe," she tossed over her shoulder.

Moments later, she was gone. Soon the woods were quiet once more, and it was only Chrysanthi and Andrija, and the heavy breath of their horses.

"Well," Chrysanthi said, nudging Lefka around. "Shall we?"

CHAPTER EIGHT

RHEA

Would he never learn? Would he never understand that if he did not get what he wanted on the first try, he did not in fact need to keep trying?

Rhea stormed through the trees back toward camp, Chrysanthi and Andrija long since out of sight. Of course Lexos had no way of knowing that she was in a particularly foul mood this evening, having had to say goodbye to her youngest and favorite (and only) sister, but still, Rhea was quite happy to blame him for his horrible timing. She was afraid for Chrysanthi and for what would happen when Nitsos read the contents of that letter; she did not need to deal with Lexos on top of that. Whatever he wanted to tell her—whatever that humming-bird in the sky was meant to say—it could wait.

She didn't have long now until morning, and she needed to sleep, to carry on as if nothing had happened. Chrysanthi's departure, when the council and the rest of camp learned of it, would be news to her just as it was to everyone else. And she would pass it off as a family matter. A long-held grudge finally come to the surface between the two of them.

Camp was quiet as she arrived back. A few sentries were posted nearer to the northern edge, and she knew another would come this way in a moment, but Piros had been posted to guard her tent for the evening as she'd requested, and there he was, holding the flap open and looking deliberately the other way.

"Piros," she whispered, still hidden by the trees. "Is it safe?"

He did not move. "Oh, no," he said. "My tent. It's stuck." She rolled her eyes but hurried across the slight gap between the forest and the tent and slipped inside. Immediately, the flap dropped shut behind her, and she heard Piros sigh and say, "Good. My tent. It's fixed."

It was hers that she'd ducked into, the one she shared with Michali, when she wasn't sleeping alongside Chrysanthi next door. But it was empty. Wherever Michali had gone, he'd left the bedroll made up neatly, a lantern burning by its side and a fire-warmed rock tucked between the blankets to keep out the chill.

She swallowed back the lump in her throat. Did he do this every evening? Even when she didn't show up? She would make use of it tonight, at least.

She was halfway into her nightclothes when the tent flap opened again and a figure ducked through. Michali, cloaked in black, brushing snow from his hair.

"Ah," he said. "Piros told me you were back."

She finished pulling a woolen nightgown over her head and stepped out of her crumpled gown beneath. "Were you out looking for me?"

"I prefer to know where you are." He was unlacing his own boots, and once finished, he came toward her across the layered rugs and knelt to gather up her dress. For a moment Rhea was back in that first Sxoriza camp she'd ever visited, blood on her hands as she blessed him. "What were you doing outside so late?"

"A walk," she said. "You know I like time to think."

Michali made a small, wry sound. She'd claimed that excuse quite often recently, and while she'd hoped he hadn't noticed just how much time she seemed to need to herself, apparently he had.

"Well," he said, "I'm glad you're back. Are you hungry? Thirsty? I can call in some fresh water, or bread, or—"

"I'm fine." He was looking up at her, his face so earnest, eyes so dark. He was still here. Chrysanthi was gone, and Lexos . . . Lexos was gone, too. Yes, Michali was changed, but so was she. And he was here, always, no matter what. She laid her hand on the side of his neck and felt his heart beat slowly against her palm. "Just tired."

They settled down to sleep, Michali at Rhea's back. He was cold to the touch as he pressed his body to hers, his left hand hesitating over her hip before settling on her stomach. Rhea stared straight ahead at the last of the lantern light and did not pull away. When she dreamed, it was of that hummingbird in the sky moving its wings and beating away, over the horizon.

She was still in Michali's arms come morning and had to move slowly to extricate herself without waking him. He needed rest, she thought. More sleep, to ease the circles that never seemed to fade beneath his eyes. Hopefully he could still find it even without her near, because as much as she wanted to hide in her tent for the day—for as long as possible—and wait until Chrysanthi came home with some news, she had to carry on. There was still quite a bit more to be done.

Piros was waiting outside the tent, looking tired enough to rival Michali on his worst day. He said nothing as he escorted her, still in her nightgown, to Chrysanthi's tent next door, where the bulk of her belongings were kept. It was only when she had dressed herself for the morning and come back out that he cleared his throat, scuffing one boot against one of the tent pegs.

"What is it?" she asked. "Not—"

"No, nothing with your sister." He kept his voice low, but he needn't have, as it was too early for most of the camp to be out and about. "It's the leadership, I'm afraid."

Rhea only just managed to keep from rolling her eyes. It always was. What a miserable little collection of people. "What about them?"

Piros's gaze flicked sidelong, toward where the meeting tent sat on the other side of camp. "They're gathering this morning. Now."

"Without me?" She didn't wait for an answer. Skirts gathered in one hand, she took off toward the tent, slush spraying underfoot. Piros stumbled after her. "Why didn't you hurry me along?"

"You weren't dressed!" he answered, a note of hysteria to his voice that Rhea would've found amusing on another day. "I couldn't very well send you in there in a nightgown."

"You could've at least told me not to dawdle. I spent a good five minutes choosing this dress."

"I'll remember that for next time."

They were both a little winded by the time they'd made it around the rocks and through the pines to where the tent sat at a remove. Rhea had to stop a few yards back to make sure she didn't look a fright before approaching the pair of guards who stood at the tent's entrance. They were both young and new enough at their posts that they didn't even attempt to stop her from brushing past them and into whatever meeting was going on inside.

And it *was* a meeting. Piros had been right. The council was gathered in their usual setup around their usual table, in the midst of a conversation that skidded to a halt as soon as they laid eyes on her. This was ridiculous. She'd always known she wasn't necessary to their proceedings, but they'd at least done her the courtesy of inviting her. She was a symbol of the future. She was a saint, for goodness' sake. To leave her out of this was near sacrilege.

"Oh," she said as airily as she could manage. "Are you busy? I didn't think anyone would be in here."

She watched as they exchanged glances. There was always one person who seemed to be dealt the task of speaking with her while the others got to stand back and whisper to one another about more important matters. This time, her designated conversation partner appeared to be the youngest member of the council, a man she could faintly remember being friendly with Michali during the midwinter festival on the lake in Ksigori. He seemed nice enough. It was just that he looked like he would rather pluck out his own eyeballs than be the one speaking to her now.

"I'm sorry," he began. "That is, we . . . we do apologize."

Was that it? "Whatever for?" she asked. She hoped he was prepared to do a sight better than that.

The young man shifted from foot to foot. Idly, Rhea wondered if she should bother learning any of their names. "We've gathered."

"I can see that."

Suddenly, the man was nudged aside, and another stepped forward. He was visibly aging, but still stood straighter than almost anyone else. This one, Rhea did know—Athanasios, who Piros had identified as being the longest-serving (and perhaps most respected) member of the Sxoriza.

"My young friend here is using a dull knife where a sharp one would be better." He reached out to the table and tapped a sheet of parchment that Rhea recognized as a map of Thyzakos. "We have been discussing our plans. Wondering whether our time up in the mountains might be over. And when looking at the targets available to us, your judgment is not one that we trust."

Rhea's mouth dropped open. For a moment she heard a ringing in one ear. "Excuse me?"

"Come," Athanasios said. "Look. Rhokera. Patrassa. Myritsa. These are your cities, no?"

They had been once. They were not anymore. Although, based on the stern look in Athanasios's eyes, that distinction wouldn't matter to him.

"That should only mean I can be of more use, not less," she said. What reason had she ever given these people not to trust her? She had given up everything, everything she'd ever known, and thrown her lot in with them. She was the reason any of them were still here in the first place. "And while we're having this discussion, I should make clear that I don't take kindly to being treated like this."

"Like what?" came a sarcastic challenge from the back of the group, but Athanasios ignored it, continuing to consider her. Rhea felt her skin begin to prickle. She managed to ignore it most of the time, but so close to this man, who was himself so near the end of his life, she was reminded how horrible it was—age. Perhaps she should feel sorry for this man and the others, too. They didn't know what it was to be free of that sort of thing.

And then Athanasios said, "I was being kind when I said they were

your cities. What I meant was that these are your past entanglements."
And any thoughts of feeling sorry for him disappeared quite quickly.

"I'm not sure I heard you," she said. "My entanglements?"

"The Vlahos brothers in the west country. The Speros boy in Rho-kera." He paused, as if to give her a chance to argue with him. But there was no argument to be made against the utter preposterousness of all this. "You have a history with these families that nobody else does. And we do not know you well here. We cannot be sure that your interests and motives will align as closely with ours as they should."

They'd been waiting for it, hadn't they? For any excuse to get to the heart of the matter. Past entanglements—it was a farce. But they would pretend it wasn't, as long as it let them call her untrustworthy.

Rhea gave over to the sneer tugging at her lips. There was no point trying to appease them anymore. "The idea that any of those people is worth my time is laughable." She looked down at the map and at Rho-kera, where Kallistos Speros, her particularly odious suitor from her final choosing, no doubt still lived. "That said, let me know which city you end up picking. You're right. I suppose I do have my history to consider."

It felt wonderful to leave the council behind, somewhat speechless, as she strode back outside. It felt better still to hear Piros apologize on their behalf once they'd returned to Chrysanthi's tent and to hear him say, over and over, how valuable she was. How wrong the council was.

Unfortunately, though, none of it lasted very long, and soon Rhea was sitting with her head in her hands doing her level best not to cry.

Why had she bothered going back to the Sxoriza after Stratathoma at all? She could have vanished into the countryside, lived on horse-back with none of the guards and provisions and camp followers, and she was fairly sure that she'd have had just as good a chance at finding Nitsos that way as she did now. This was not power. This was not hope.

But what could she do? She had already sent Chrysanthi out into the wilds. She had put her only ally into play. And now she was alone, positioned at the head of an organization she had no real control over. She needed help, someone here at her side she could trust to be honest with her. Piros was all well and good, but he was not enough.

"Hello?" someone said from outside the tent. "Rhea?" Michali, then. Nobody else left in camp called her that. "May I come in?"

He was the ally she'd been meant to have. Maybe there was still a way.

"Yes," she said, tidying her skirts, "of course."

Michali was still half dressed—Rhea realized she had not been at that sham of a meeting very long—and his eyes were soft, hair mussed. She barely had time to smile at him before he pulled off his coat and draped it around her shoulders, leaving him only in his nightshirt and a pair of unlaced boots.

"Thank you," she murmured as he knelt at her feet.

"What is it?" He lifted a hand to her cheek. Cold, he was always so cold. "You seem upset."

"I am." This was the test of it, she supposed. He had faltered when asked to make real decisions, but if she could confide in him now and get back some kind of actual advice, that was all she would need. A partner, just like he'd promised to be. "I was in with the leadership," she said, taking one of his hands in both of hers. "They met without me this morning. I only found out because of Piros."

"Without you?" Michali frowned, but it seemed to be more bafflement than displeasure. He squeezed her hand. "I'm sure it was just a coincidence. I can't imagine anyone genuinely trying to keep you from something like that."

"But they did," she said. "And it was important, too. Do you remember the other suitors at your choosing?"

"I suppose." He shrugged, one corner of his mouth ticking up. "Having regrets?" It startled a laugh out of her. Michali's eyes crinkled with delight, and he tipped forward, his chest pressing against her knees. "You had your chance to be without me," he went on. "I'm afraid you've squandered it."

She shook her head fondly. "We all make mistakes."

"Indeed." As quickly as it had come, the warmth in his expression faded, and she wondered if he was thinking of the same thing she was: the last meeting he'd attended, and the way they'd been too embarrassed even to argue afterward. It had not been respect for her office that kept him from speaking his mind that day. She was sure of that. It had been something more like surprise that she would even ask him to.

"Michali," she started, but he held up one hand.

"I know you're upset," he said, his retreat obvious. "But it was nothing, I promise. That council would not leave you out if they could help it."

That was a lie and they both knew it. Rhea had seen almost every member—except Athanasios, which felt notable—approach Michali when they thought he was alone, to seek his advice or maybe coax him into attending a council meeting without her. But she had never brought it up, and she wouldn't now. It wasn't his fault; it would only start an argument.

"Of course," she said. "I'm sure you're right."

As they ate breakfast, Rhea found herself watching Michali. She'd been so glad to bring him back, so eager to be loved the way he'd loved her before midwinter. Wasn't she still? Couldn't she be happy with that?

Maybe, she thought, but there were things that needed handling first, and Michali wouldn't be any help with that at all.

That night, Rhea snuck away from Michali and into the woods to listen to the names of the dead. The clearing was waiting for her, her bootprints the only ones marking the snow. She sank onto a fallen tree trunk and propped her elbows on her knees. She spent altogether too much time in clearings after dark. Maybe that was where she was going wrong.

So: no Chrysanthi, and now no Michali, too. Who else could she turn to? There had to be something she could do to change her position here, or some string she could pull that would make the council see just how important she was to their success. Something that would make them follow her to Nitsos's doorstep and help her take his life. But as she tilted her head back to the sky and thought, and thought, nothing came. There was nobody left to help her.

Above her, the hummingbird constellation shone again amongst the stars, its outline clearer than the night before. Not so, it reminded her. You have one other option.

Rhea eyed it for a minute and then at last relented. "Fine," she said. "Yes, all right. Fine."

Some time later, her own hummingbird flitted out of Rhea's tent. She watched it from the threshold, biting down on the inside of her cheek, until finally it disappeared into the trees.

Needs must, she told herself, and went back inside.

CHAPTER NINE

ALEXANDROS

Two days in Tarro's abandoned summer palace, and all Lexos had to say was that he was sick of pasta, thank you very much.

His first investigation of the kitchen had revealed a number of ingredients available to him, but his second had revealed that almost none of them were something he knew how to prepare, and so both mornings in his spacious new prison, he had stood over the stove watching a pot of water refuse to come to boil, before pouring in a pile of dried pasta and eventually slurping it down with a wince as it turned to mush at the back of his throat.

He was not, he thought, meant to live alone.

The rest of his time he'd spent exploring the house as best he could. He'd found a sunroom of sorts off the sitting room, its roof made of a warped glass, and had spent the first night there trying to find a hint at Falka's plans in the way she'd stitched the stars. He'd also found a bedroom in the back corner of the building, and that was where he'd spent the second night, tucked in under dusty linens as the house settled around him. It was old, quite obviously, but not in the way that Stratathoma was. Stratathoma had felt impregnable and solid as the earth beneath it. This house wore its age like decoration—even the knife marks on the kitchen table looked artful.

There were other things, too, that reminded him he was not on Argyros land anymore. Extra locks built into every door, and scuffs here and there on the floorboards, left over from some struggle between Domina children that was one of so many they could not all be remembered. How many seconds had died here, Lexos wondered. Was he simply expected to waste away until he joined them?

On this, his third morning, he was resolved to at least try to do something other than make a meal that tasted like dirt and lie on his back in the sitting room feeling sorry for himself. He'd come here intent on leaving immediately, in whatever manner he could manage, and while the house's lower floor and lawn provided no opportunity, there was still a large portion of the house he hadn't explored yet.

With a groan, he sat up in bed and clambered to his feet. His boots were discarded in the corner, along with his coat and the other layers of clothing he'd been traveling in, each filthier than the last. From here, he could see through the bedroom doorway to the hall, to where a pair of double doors stood open, connecting the back side of the house to the atrium with its grand staircase.

Why he hadn't gone up yet, Lexos didn't know. Perhaps it was the respect for Tarro and his family's stature that he still couldn't quite shake, despite being a Domina captive. Or perhaps it was that it looked dark up there, and he did not know where to find a lantern.

"Enough," he muttered and ambled out of the room, across the hallway, and into the atrium.

It was late in the morning, verging on noon. The light that came in through the large front windows was pure and buttery, its warmth comforting as he stopped at the foot of the stairs. They were carved out of a dark wood and widened as they ran up to the second-floor mezzanine, from which a hallway ran off in each direction.

Slowly, he began to climb. Unlike some of the rooms he'd been in previously, these stairs did not creak with each step, and he could hear only his own breathing as he neared the top. The mezzanine was deep enough to accommodate a small sitting area off to one side: a pair of armchairs positioned around a little table and just under one in a series of windows that let in sharp shafts of sun.

They looked comfortable, the chairs. They looked used. Because this was a *house*. That was the oddest thing and something Lexos found himself returning to. A very secure house, certainly, and not somewhere he wanted to be, which was something you often found with prisons, but it was comfortable. It was spacious. It was . . . a kindness.

That did not make sense at all.

He turned left, the corridor waiting ahead. A number of doors were dotted along the wall, all of them shut. Carefully, Lexos approached the first and tried the handle. Locked, as nothing had been downstairs. When he bent to look through the keyhole, the room inside appeared to be simply another bedroom like the one he'd slept in, this time decorated in a more palatable color. A shame he couldn't get inside; he'd have much rather slept there.

The next door was also locked—a closet, it looked like—but the third, this one on the other side of the corridor, wasn't, and so Lexos pushed it open, and sidled through into the room.

It was a study, paneled dark wood walls and large matching desk somewhat incongruous against the daylight that poured in through the large windows that overlooked the water. Lexos left his post in the doorway and approached the desk. Like the rest of the house, it had clearly seen a bit of use, from the corners where the varnish had chipped off to the large, scrolling letter *D* someone had carved into the side.

If Tarro had lived here once, perhaps he had left something behind.

Lexos took a seat in the tall chair, its scrolled arms digging into his elbows, and surveyed the desk in front of him. The desktop was clear, save for a large, polished stone that served as a paperweight for a stack of sketches, each one a different version of the view from the window, done in charcoal pencil. Tarro's work, possibly, but Lexos had never thought of him as much of an artist. Maybe some other fool had been unlucky enough to find themselves kept here once.

The left-hand drawers, when he tried them, opened smoothly, only to reveal themselves as empty inside. The right-hand drawers were the same, except for the topmost one, which held a few sheets of blank parchment neatly stacked, beside which sat a gold ring.

It was so small that it would have been snug on his little finger. And it was in perfect condition, too, despite the disrepair that could be spotted throughout the rest of the house. Although, really, that was hardly a surprise. Most everything the Dominas owned was of the finest quality.

Lexos walked it over to the window so he could get a better look. It was plain gold, entirely ordinary at first glance, but now that he'd got hold of it, there was something strange about the weight and shape. The band of the ring was perfectly round, instead of flattened to fit closely against one's finger. And it felt insubstantial—far too light to be solid gold.

He bent over it, eyes narrowed. Could it possibly have been hollowed out? He'd never seen anything like that before—trust Tarro Domina to have something unique and leave it forgotten in a drawer. But there would have to be a mark somewhere on the ring, a place where it had been joined. Sure enough, after a long moment of scrutiny, Lexos found a nearly invisible line running across the ring where someone had fused the two ends of the band together. Which meant, maybe, that there was something protected inside. A message, perhaps, rolled up tightly and slotted in. Or a map showing a secret way out of this place. Or something even better.

He was absolutely going to have to break this beautiful ring.

It wasn't difficult, as it turned out. The joining, while it looked perfect, gave way after only a bit of forceful leverage against the desk, leaving the two ends pried apart widely enough that Lexos could see the darkness of their hollowed-out centers. He'd been right; there was space inside and probably a message waiting for him. Surely it had been designed for just this purpose. Maybe Falka had left it for him, or at this point, he would even take Nitsos.

Eagerly, he shook the broken ring into his palm.

A bit of hair fell out.

He recoiled immediately, yanking his hand back. The ring hit the floor with a clang and skittered under the desk, while the spray of hair drifted down to rest by the foot of the chair. Lexos could feel his heartbeat in his throat, could feel his cheeks going hot.

So, not a message to him, then.

The strands were dark and had been formed into a very slender braid tied off on both ends with a bit of twine. Some were broken here and there—Lexos's treatment of the ring couldn't have helped—but the care with which the braid had been assembled and then slid into the ring was evident.

Whose was this? And who had preserved it in this ring, only to leave it here, in a house nobody would enter for many years?

He could only assume the ring was a memento of some sort for one Domina remembering another, but then, he supposed he had no proof of that. Many of Tarro's children were dark-haired, but just as many were not, and regardless, Tarro had never seemed the sentimental sort. Lexos couldn't even imagine him discarding such a ring here, let alone ever carrying it with him.

With a sigh, he shuffled around to the front of the desk and felt underneath it until he'd grabbed the ring. As quickly as possible, he slid the lock of hair back inside and dropped the ring into the drawer where he'd found it. Whatever it was, he wanted nothing more to do with it.

He left the study then and headed back down the corridor toward the stairs. Perhaps he'd go outside for a moment, or even for a swim— one of those giant metal lily pads had looked like it might also serve as a dock for that sort of thing. And while it was not quite the most productive use of his time, there was a part of Lexos that had already given up the idea of ever escaping this house. If this was what it meant to forgo power, it wasn't quite so bad.

First, though, he stopped in the kitchen, his mouth dry from the dust he'd stirred at the desk upstairs. Water was delivered to this house through a set of pipes that Lexos recognized as being part of Vuomorra's network; he'd seen them in the palace on his last visit, providing a number of rooms with running water, although his bedroom had not been fancy enough to be one of them. A reminder, again, that this house could not be far from the city at all. And yet he felt alone—

beautifully alone—as though the rest of the world had crumbled and left only this place standing.

He went to the sink to fill the kettle, meaning to set it to boil for a cup of kaf. But the kettle was not there, which was odd, as he was quite sure he'd left it next to the sink the night before. He frowned and began to check the rest of the room: the shelves by the door, and the cupboards under the counter, then the table in the middle of the room, where he finally saw it, perched on a little stone square to keep it from marking the tabletop.

And next to it sat a fresh cup of kaf, steam rising off the top.

Oh, Lexos thought faintly. It seemed he was not alone, after all.

The most unnerving thing about it, really, was that Lexos had spent two days here already and all the while there had apparently been another person roaming about, staying out of sight for reasons Lexos could only imagine were less than honorable. The second most unnerving thing was that Lexos did not, at present, have a weapon on him.

Without taking his eyes off the door that led to the rest of the house, he felt behind him for one of the heavy iron skillets that hung from hooks all along the wall. It would do in a pinch, if he needed to stave somebody's head in. But then, this mug left here, hot and fresh—was it meant for him? A gift? A peace offering?

A peace offering filled with poison?

Lexos shut his eyes briefly, giving himself a little shake. Only two and a half days alone and already he was coming unraveled. It was a cup of kaf. If whoever his companion was wanted him dead, they could have very easily accomplished that while he'd been asleep and utterly defenseless.

He left the skillet behind then and took the mug with him into the next room, its ceramic warming his hands. There was a little bite to the air that meant the first sip of hot kaf was very pleasant indeed and delightfully strong compared to the muddy water Lexos had been able to coax out of the pot.

He had half expected to find his new housemate waiting in the other room, but it was just as empty as it had always been. There were no additional footprints in the dust that coated the corners of the room, and the chairs at the dining table were just as Lexos had left them. Everything was. He looked down at his mug and took another sip. Please, let him not have made this himself.

It was as he paused at the foot of the grand stairs that he heard it—a splash. It was coming from outside, where the pond was dotted with those giant metal lily pads that Nitsos, he was sure, had designed.

Mug still clutched in his hand, he made for the large double doors opposite the staircase and pulled the nearest one open, allowing the sunlight to flood through. For a moment he couldn't see, but as his eyes began to adjust, the pond and its greenery took shape. Giant metal lily pads floated on the water's surface, so wide from edge to edge that Lexos could have stretched out on one quite comfortably. Rising high above them, tall mechanical stems led to sculpted flowers, their petals always in bloom, the canopy of them some fifty feet overhead where they almost brushed against the enclosure's glass dome. Lexos had been to the continent's most massive cities—he'd stood at the foot of the great rock spire in Agiokon—and yet nothing had made him feel quite so small. Like one of Nitsos's miniatures, he thought, a clockwork beetle taken from its home in the grass and placed on a game board to be moved about at will. So what did that make his apparent companion?

There, across the shimmer of the water, stood a man. He was poised at the edge of one of the lily pads, his head lifted to catch the light, his chest bare. As Lexos watched, he stretched, arms swinging, and dove into the water.

Lexos felt his mouth go dry and took a sip of kaf.

When the other man surfaced, his closely shorn dark hair was bristling with water, and it scattered into the air as he climbed a small ladder attached to the lily pad and shook himself dry. His trousers had been rolled up to just under his knees and were belted high around his waist with a length of fabric that now, as he took a moment to examine it from even this distance, Lexos thought might have been torn from one of the curtains in the sitting room.

Who was this, then? A guard left behind to keep watch? Or another prisoner, so deeply forgotten that nobody had bothered to tell Lexos he was here?

Just then the man finished scrubbing at his hair with what must have been his shirt and turned toward the shore, stopping short when he met eyes with Lexos. For a moment they only looked at each other, and though Lexos was too far away to be sure, he could have sworn the man's broad smile faltered.

It was without much thought that Lexos lifted his mug of kaf into the air and said in Trefza, "Sorry. Was this yours?"

The other man's laughter was sudden and brash, a kind of unbridled sound that Lexos himself had no experience making.

"No apology necessary," the man shouted back to him. "I saw your meagre attempt yesterday morning and thought you could use the help."

Lexos wasn't quite sure what to make of that. The informality of it all, along with the fact that he was still alive himself, suggested that he had little to fear from this man, but still, it gave no hint as to why there was anybody else here at all. The stranger's Trefza was perfect; that didn't mean much, though. Lexos's own was very good, and only people so elevated in Trefazio as the Dominas ever really noticed that he was not a native speaker. This man could be anyone. A member of a rival Trefzan family, or a captive from some excursion beyond Tarro's borders, or someone else besides.

"Why don't you come in?" Lexos called. He needed a better look and a proper introduction. And also some lunch. "You can teach me where the good spices are."

"So you can burn those, too?" the man replied. "All right. I'll only be a moment."

Lexos watched as he wrung his shirt out and laid it flat on the lily pad to dry before diving back into the pond, disappearing into the blue gleam for a long stretch before surfacing almost halfway to shore. He swam well, elbows sharp and strokes long. Lexos thought he might have even managed to swim the currents at the beach at Stratathoma.

Finally, having reached the shallows, he stood, the water lapping at his knees as he approached. Now Lexos could see the strong line of his brow, the rich tan of his skin—it seemed this man spent a good deal of his time out in the sun—and the delicate shape of his skull, bared as it was by the close cut of his hair. He was taller than Lexos, but not by much, and by the time he was standing on the grass, bare torso dotted still with water, Lexos had been overcome with a strange sort of familiarity. Why, he was not sure. Was this one of Tarro's old seconds, perhaps? Someone he'd met in Vuomorra and not given another look before being run out of town?

"Alexandros," he said, holding out a hand to shake. "I think this is your house?"

The man considered his hand for a moment, and then clasped it suddenly with both of his, skin startlingly warm despite the coolness of the water. "Ettore," he said. "What's mine is yours."

It had been quite some time since Lexos had met somebody like this: no Domina guards over his shoulders and no shackles holding him tight—not even the silver bracelets Lexos had been so kindly given to mark his status, which he'd pried off with a kitchen utensil on his first afternoon here. He could see Ettore's eyes flick to the stripes they'd left around his too-thin wrists where the skin was cleaner, paler. Embarrassed, suddenly, he withdrew his hand.

"Shall we?" he said. "I imagine you must be hungry after all that exertion."

"I'm always hungry." Ettore clapped him hard on the back and then turned, leading the way back into the house.

Lexos hesitated on the threshold. Was that it? Surely Ettore had questions for him, just as he had many of his own. Or if not questions, a knife to be held to his throat, or a favor to be asked, or a penance to be exacted (well, beyond the fact of his imprisonment). It didn't seem possible to him that something should go so simply.

"Are you coming?" Ettore called from inside.

He seemed affable. He seemed like good enough company. And he was here, tucked away out of Tarro's sight. There had to be a reason.

"Yes," Lexos answered. "I'm right behind you."

Ettore led him inside without a backward look. Lexos expected him to direct the two of them toward the dining room, or perhaps the kitchen, where he'd found the cup of kaf, but Ettore waved a hand in the direction of the sitting room and said, "I'd rather be comfortable, wouldn't you?"

Lexos had been in several situations over the years that had thrown him off balance and forced him to find some path forward that he had not planned to take. This, he told himself as they entered the sitting room, was no different, although he had to admit that he felt quite keenly the absence of a mark on his palm and the power that came with it.

Ettore sat first, sprawling on his back across one of the couches. Rather than try to squeeze himself in by Ettore's feet, Lexos subjected himself to one of the chairs opposite, grimacing when his elbow knocked painfully against the wooden arm.

"Your house is lovely," he said. "Thank you very much for having me."

It had seemed the polite thing to say—ignore the circumstances by which they both found themselves here, Lexos had told himself, and acknowledge the other man's seniority, such as it was—but it only made Ettore raise one eyebrow.

"It's full of dust and the mattresses are as old as I am," he replied. "It used to be much nicer." He frowned as he glanced around the room, taking in the cracked paint and sagging curtains. "I suppose you'll just have to take my word for it."

Lexos found himself smiling and leaned back in his chair, crossing one leg over the other. "Have you been here long?"

"Oh, ages. Alone for most of it, too. What did you do to get thrown in with me?"

"My father," Lexos said. "He and Tarro were not friends." That was true enough. It would do for the moment.

"Is that so?" Ettore met his gaze with a sharpness that did not match the airiness of his voice. It reminded Lexos of some great bird of prey, wheeling high overhead in the moments before it dove. "Your father sounds like someone I might enjoy. You could say I'm not a family favorite, either."

"You're a Domina, then?"

"Despite my best efforts." He sank lower on the couch so that his body was nearly horizontal. "Let's see. That accent of yours is Thyzak, no doubt. A Katsaros, perhaps? No? Vlahakis?"

Lexos did not recognize either of those names. Whoever they were, they were not steward families, at least. "No," he said and then paused. Was there any worth to lying about it? Ettore had suggested that he and Tarro were not close—that he and the Dominas at large were at odds. And someone who had been kept hidden away for so long might not know anything of his father's fall, of the problems that had arisen in Thyzakos under his rule. "Argyros," he finished. "Alexandros Argyros."

He expected something in Ettore's expression to change. But the other man just looked at him blankly and said, "I'm not familiar."

Lexos felt himself flush. "They say you can recognize us by our eyes."

Immediately, that seemed like the most ridiculous sentence that had ever escaped his mouth. But Ettore paid it no attention and instead jumped to his feet, one hand scrubbing over his scalp as his mouth stretched into an uncomfortably wide smile.

"Well, it's good to meet you, Alexandros Argyros," he said. "And I'm very glad you're in here with me."

"Are you?"

"Yes." He leaned in, and his voice dropped to a whisper. "You see, with you, I can finally get out."

CHAPTER TEN

CHRYSANTHI

They had been on the road for a day and a half and already Chrysanthi was wondering just what bodily harm she could threaten Andrija with to make him speak more often. She'd been hopeful after he set a new personal record the night of their departure—Multiple sentences! All in the same breath!—but since leaving the camp behind, Andrija had once again fallen quiet, leaving only the hush of the woods between them. Now, sitting across from him over a tragically small campfire, Chrysanthi was reaching the end of her patience.

She understood the value of silence. Really, she did. Especially out here, in what Rhea had been so insistent was dangerous country. But she had spent so long alone, with only her brothers for company, that it felt incomprehensible to her to pass up any opportunity for conversation. Perhaps Andrija would learn that from her. He would teach her to gut fish or skin deer or start a fire with nothing more than a bit of wood and the memory of a match, or something like that, and she would teach him how to laugh when she made a particularly good joke. An equal trade in skills if ever there was one.

She adjusted her position on the ground—the blankets Andrija had allowed her to layer underneath her were doing very little to keep out the cold—and leaned in toward the meagre fire. "Are we close yet?" That seemed a guaranteed way to get her a response.

Andrija glanced up from where he was very methodically turning a very small dead animal, mangled beyond recognition, over the flames. "To what?"

Ah. She had not thought quite that far ahead. "The border. A bath. A meal other than whatever that is. Take your pick."

He considered her for a moment. "Somewhat. The river, yes, but it's too cold for that. And no."

Chrysanthi was briefly too surprised to respond. Luckily she overcame it very quickly. "What can you tell me, then, about the border crossing? From what I've heard, it will be very difficult for us to pass."

Andrija nodded. He had returned his attention to their dinner and had left off turning the spit to stoke the fire.

"Why didn't we head west, then? Surely it would be easier to pass through Merkher and then north to Vashnasta. It doesn't seem that we're saving much time coming north first."

"We aren't."

She waited for more and, when it did not come, said, "So why?"

Andrija sighed. Annoyance! She was delighted. It was the first indication that he could be made to respond in any way beyond his control.

"There are large stretches of Amolova left unsettled," he said. "We stand a better chance there of passing by undetected."

"Undetected and also quite uncomfortable."

"I would imagine being dead to be a bit more so."

She grinned, cheeks aching in the cold. "And that's a guarantee in Merkher?"

Andrija lifted the dead animal off the fire and pressed it to the snow beside him. It steamed viciously for a moment before he lifted it again. Against her will, Chrysanthi felt her mouth water.

"The Amolovak Stratagiozi has always stood against your family," he said finally. "The Merkheri is a recent convert. I believe if you must face one or the other, choose the enemy you know."

Chrysanthi hid a smile. His Thyzaki was very good, but his accent had changed briefly, shaped itself more softly around "Amolovak." Not Chuzhak, then, but Amolovak himself. Andrija was returning home.

"So you know Amolova," she said. "What about Merkher? Have you been there?"

"For a time." He shifted, the snow underneath him creaking lightly, and cleared his throat. "Have you?"

She blinked. "I . . . no. No, I haven't."

Nitsos had always wanted so badly to go, to leave Stratathoma behind the way Rhea and Lexos were allowed to. She had never dreamed even once of seeing Merkher. Should she have?

"Here," Andrija said suddenly. She looked up from the fire to see him holding out half of the spit, with what was meant to be her dinner still hanging off it. "It's squirrel."

She had never dreamed of trying squirrel, either.

They spent the night there at their little camp, asleep under a low shelter of pine boughs Andrija managed to construct. When Chrysanthi woke, there was fresh snow caught in her eyelashes and dusted over the top of her blankets. Perhaps Andrija was right that Merkher was the more dangerous option, but a few more nights like this and she thought she might just die anyway.

Still, she put on her very best smile as soon as she rose from her bedding, and asked Andrija if he'd always kept his hair that long while he packed up the camp, and commented on the color of his horse while waiting for him to help her onto Lefka. Somebody had to do something to pass the time.

Though it was difficult riding, Rhea had been right; Lefka was very capable, following Andrija's horse with ease. Chrysanthi only had to correct her a few times, otherwise keeping her grip on the reins so loose it hardly counted. As it was, when Andrija held up a hand near midday to bring them both to a halt, she was not yet in need of rest and quite ready to continue.

"I'm fine," she called to him. "I don't even need to stretch my legs. You know, I think I'm adapting rather well to the wilds. To think, all this talent could have gone undiscovered if—"

"Respectfully," Andrija snarled, twisting in his saddle, "be quiet."

Chrysanthi froze, her mouth still open.

As she watched, Andrija leaned toward her and whispered something in a language Chrysanthi did not recognize. Lefka, however, seemed to understand. She lurched forward in response, carrying Chrysanthi up until she had drawn even with Andrija. He had straightened and was peering closely into the woods ahead of them, right hand resting on one of the knives he kept strapped at his hip.

"What is it?" she whispered. Lefka, perhaps picking up on her nerves, stamped impatiently, settling only when Andrija reached across the gap between their horses and knotted his fingers in her mane.

"Voices up ahead. Amolovak border patrol, probably."

That, as far as Chrysanthi understood it, was bad news. "Can we go around them?"

Andrija's stirrup knocked against Chrysanthi's as he urged his horse backward, Lefka moving with him. "What's to say there won't be another?" He looked quite grim, which was saying something. "There wasn't supposed to be anyone this far out from the crossing."

"What do you mean?"

"I mean a patrol like that is no doubt looking for travelers like us. And if we're caught, there's no lie we could tell that they'd believe." Andrija shook his head. "We're better off just taking the main trail up."

The main trail—that sounded promising in terms of comfort, which was always Chrysanthi's priority. But when they reached it, it was little more than a beaten track up the mountain, much like the other paths except in this case wide enough to accommodate two horses. The height of luxury.

They stopped and dismounted a few yards back from the trail itself, still somewhat hidden in the trees. The original plan had been risky enough, as far as she understood it, but now they would have to spend another full day on the main road. It would make them targets for the handful of bandits that kept outposts near the border and put them in the path of more guards than they'd prepared for. Thankfully, she had just the thing.

While Andrija rearranged their saddlebags, hiding their more valuable belongings under a layer of ratty tarp that he seemed to have brought for expressly this purpose, Chrysanthi took out her paints. Rhea had packed them very carefully in a lovely wooden box that she'd had made for Chrysanthi soon after their arrival at the camps. As Chrysanthi lifted the lid now, she caught a whiff of salt and sweetness. Rhea had tucked a sprig of therolia in with the paints.

"What do they do?" Andrija asked. He had finished with the saddlebags and was watching her now, a twitch in his hands that looked suspiciously like nervousness. It occurred to her that in all likelihood he had never heard of her or her gift before she arrived in the camps. Not like Baba and the particular power of the Thyzak matagios, or like Rhea, whose Thyspira was famous across the continent.

"They decorate," Chrysanthi said brightly. It was her favorite way to describe everything she could make her paints do. And it very conveniently left out how much of their functionality had been destroyed now that she was no longer at Stratathoma.

"Decorate how?"

"Everything can always stand to be a little prettier." She frowned up at him, and the words slipped out before she could keep them back: "Although in this case, we might have reached our limit."

Andrija raised one eyebrow. In a bid to look anywhere but directly at him, she plucked the therolia from the box and held it to her nose. It smelled like home, like a Stratathoma spring. This time of year, bundles of this herb and many like it would be hanging in the kitchen and more still growing fresh out on the grounds. She might spend an afternoon picking some to bake into a pita for whenever Baba and her brothers were finished for the day.

How easy would it be to return there now? To give up on all of this, and just go home?

No, she could not go without Rhea. Not even without her wretched brothers. She ground the therolia between her fingers and pressed it against her neck. Maybe the scent would linger, or maybe it wouldn't.

"I can't do as much as I would like," she said, waving Andrija over. "I shouldn't waste them. I don't have the right materials with me to make more. But I can keep us from being too recognizable."

"Yourself, you mean. Don't waste them on me."

"No? Isn't there anybody who might recognize you?" He was Amolovak, wasn't he? Well traveled as he might be, he must have spent some time here in his home country.

He shook his head. "I looked quite different when I was here last."

"Do you mean to tell me you haven't been the size of a mountain since birth?" Andrija did not laugh, and though she knew it was pushing her luck, Chrysanthi couldn't resist. "What about your family? Where are they?"

He remained silent, his eyes stern. Her own family could always be baited into action, into argument. Speaking to Andrija, though, felt very much like leaning against the thick walls at Stratathoma.

That was fine. She would wring more out of him eventually. Nobody could ever resist her for long.

The darkest of her current array of paints was a shade somewhere between brown and black. A little of it would go far toward disguising her hair. Chrysanthi scooped a bit out with her fingers and slathered it between her palms before scraping them across her scalp. She could tell from the way Andrija's mouth opened ever so slightly that it was having the desired effect. It would wear off within a day or two, this far removed from home, but that would be enough to get them through the border crossing and muddy the waters for anyone trying to find her.

She finished things off by smearing the excess paint across her open eyes—that would alter their Argyros blue—and then blinked a few times to clear her sight. Andrija's face came back into focus; he looked horrified.

"What?"

"Nothing," he said and glanced away and back again before adding, "You touched your eyeball."

Chrysanthi allowed herself an amused smile. "I did."

"Unnatural," he grumbled. "You Stratagiozi. Are you finished, then?"

She was, and so he waited on horseback while she tidied up the paints and tied her now brown hair back at the base of her neck. When she was settled on Lefka again, they rode out onto the main trail and resumed their trek north.

If it was possible, Andrija seemed even more silent than before. Chrysanthi could feel the tension coming off him and could see it, too, in the rigid hold of his shoulders as he guided the horses forward. Was he more nervous than he needed to be? Or was she misunderstanding the danger of their situation?

She spared a thought for how startled she had been that morning the Domina ships arrived at Stratathoma and decided there was no need to answer either of her questions.

Soon the trail began to widen farther. By the time they made camp for the night, it was even cleared of snow in spots, enough so that little markers were visible here and there—an arrow chiseled into a low boulder, or a series of notches cut out of a thick root that ran across the path. Chrysanthi did not understand them, and she wanted to ask Andrija about them, but there was no opportunity; as soon as he'd dismounted, he set about building them a shelter with what materials he could find and chastised her with a single look when she asked when he planned to build the fire.

Chrysanthi spent the night warmed only by the knowledge that Andrija was probably as uncomfortable as she was.

It was, he told her the next morning, only a few more hours to the crossing. They would likely encounter an increased guard presence on their way; she was to keep as quiet as possible and let him do the talking, which made her snort derisively. But she did her best to follow his instructions, and it did get easier—by the time the third patrol of men passed them going the opposite way, dressed in uniforms of black and blue, Chrysanthi barely looked up. Still, it was strange to see livery that was not her father's. These were soldiers of Amolova, Ammar Basha's men, and in his service they were made enemies of the Argyrosi. Chrysanthi suppressed a shiver and urged Lefka forward, closer to Andrija's familiar presence.

Not long after, the trail began to climb sharply, and the ground on either side grew steeper. Banks of trees turned quickly into tall rock faces, and overhead the sky was suddenly visible, its midday blue unblotted with clouds. If Chrysanthi was remembering the map Rhea had shown her correctly, this was the southernmost point of the ridge—if they did not cross through this pass, they might have easier going for a few more days skirting its edges, but soon they would come up against cliffs like these, only each one some hundreds of feet taller. Attempting to cross in either direction was asking for death.

Still, she thought darkly as Lefka sidled too close to the rock wall and gave Chrysanthi's leg a scrape, it might be worth it.

"Easy," Andrija said a few minutes later. "We walk from here."

It was so cold that Chrysanthi could see steam rising off Lefka's haunches as she dismounted. When her boots hit the ground, it crunched, frozen solid even without a layer of snow. She shifted uncomfortably, all too aware that if they did not travel quickly and make it through the crossing without issue, they would be forced to sleep out here; she couldn't imagine it getting much colder than it was, but certainly, it would after dark.

"It's absurd," she muttered. "Somebody has to speak to Rhea about this. Isn't it supposed to be spring?" Andrija made no response, but she caught the alarmed look he sent her. "What? I said speak to Rhea, not kill Michali. Although really, it's not as if he hasn't died before. I'm sure he's used to it by—"

Andrija cleared his throat. "Yes, all right."

After a few more turns in the path, the pitch leveled out, and the gorge around them broadened. Here and there Chrysanthi spotted felled trees, and up ahead an empty hitching post, at which a donkey was tied while its master repacked the bags it carried. Judging by the tracks in the snow, it had come from the border.

They kept on. As the trees thinned out around them and the cliffs leaned back away from the trail, the guard outpost came into view. She could see a pair of men, dressed in that black-and-blue livery, keeping watch on a balcony that ran around the halfway point of the double-height timber hall. Another trio were standing on the road in front of a wooden gate that stretched from the hall to the opposing cliff face. As Rhea had said: Sneaking through would have been very difficult indeed.

"Remember," Andrija said, "I'll do the talking."

Chrysanthi stumbled to a halt. "What, we're going now?"

He frowned. "Why wouldn't we?"

"I'm just . . ." She cast about for a good reason to delay. Lefka leaned in and nudged her shoulder with her nose. "I'm nervous," she admitted.

"All right." He waited for a moment, adjusted his belt with one chapped hand, and then said, quite dryly, "Are you still nervous?"

"Oh, honestly."

They kept on and were soon close enough to the hall that Chrysanthi could see firelight coming through its warped glass windows. The air smelled of woodsmoke, a stream of it rising from somewhere on the roof, and if Chrysanthi breathed in very deeply, she could catch the scent of something cooking, too.

The guards watched them approach without response until they had drawn even with the hall. Finally one held up his hand. "Stop there," he called. Andrija halted so quickly that Chrysanthi stumbled into his back. "Step aside from the horses."

Inspection. Right. They were prepared for this, Chrysanthi reminded herself. There was nothing to be afraid of.

One of the guards remained by the gate. The other two crossed the hardpacked trail, buckles on their heavy blue coats glinting in a sudden slash of winter sun. She eyed their weapons as she stepped away from Lefka. Well armed, all of them. If anything did go wrong, the small, plain knife she'd hidden in her boot would be of very little help.

She glanced to her right—if Andrija wasn't nervous, she would try not to be, either—but there was only Lefka. The horses were between them, obscuring her view, and she was alone now as one of the guards stepped up to her, his face startlingly young under the brim of his fur hat.

"Hello," she said in Thyzaki, immediately anxious when he didn't respond in kind. Had she given the game up already? Should she have attempted some Amolovak? And maybe her accent was the wrong kind.

"Where have you come from?" he asked gruffly, looking her up and down in a way that made her want to back up. Thankfully, though, he'd used Thyzaki, too. Right, of course—he must meet people from all over. He wouldn't find it that unusual.

"Ksigori," she said. She and Andrija had agreed that it was the only story that made any sense. Anywhere farther west and the sensible path north for a traveler would be through the center of the continent.

"And where are you headed?"

"Not sure yet," she said, hoping she looked properly disaffected. "Bosmara, probably." She nodded toward where Andrija was undergoing his own questioning. "He'll decide."

The guard appeared to consider this for a moment before nodding and waving her aside. She hurried out of his way, heart hammering in her chest. Almost done, and then she'd be away from here and if not safe, then at least safe from this particular danger.

He rummaged quickly through her saddlebags, barely pausing to take a second look at any of her clothes or provisions. They had anticipated that Andrija would get a more thorough examination, especially since he was armed, and that was why Chrysanthi's paint box was still in with her things, instead of hidden in his. As they'd hoped, the guard didn't even open it all the way before shoving it back into the bag.

She was not all that sure what he was looking for, in fact. Other weapons, maybe, or contraband—whatever that was—but she wondered if perhaps Ammar cared more about being seen to guard the border than about actually keeping anything in or out.

She could hear the other guard speaking from a few yards away, although he was speaking Amolovak, which meant Andrija must have been as well. Her own Amolovak was all but nonexistent. She would have to get Andrija to teach her as much as possible before they arrived in Vashnasta.

"Fine," her guard said suddenly, and she returned her attention to him. He had stepped away from Lefka and nodded now to where her saddlebags were still in some disarray. "You can pack back up now."

She hurried to do as he said, hoping he'd leave her to it, but he stayed to watch. She could feel the weight of his gaze; he was so much younger than she, and by so many more years than he would ever know, yet he'd still learned the cool, evaluating stare that had never come easily to her, not even after so many years of seeing it in her father's eyes. Uneasy, she pressed on, tucking her body closely against Lefka as she worked one of the buckles into place.

"Wait," the guard said. She stopped, Andrija's name hovering at the back of her throat. "Let me see your hand."

"My hand?"

She looked down at where her right hand was poised over one of the straps. Perhaps he thought she'd slipped something into the saddlebag. She held it out, visibly shaking despite her best efforts.

But he shook his head. "No. Your left."

It dawned on her so slowly. Not as she extended her left hand, and not as he grabbed hold of her bare wrist and twisted it violently up to the sky, but only as he pressed her palm flat, and tapped the three black lines that ran just under the first knuckle of her little finger. Her Stratagiozi's mark, given to her by her father so many years ago that she often forgot it existed.

"What's this?" the guard said. Chrysanthi's heart dropped into her stomach. "I think we've got someone here who shouldn't be."

There was no time to react. Or if there had been, she had not been quick enough to use it, and before she could do anything, the guard had yanked her forward, her back slamming into his chest as his arm locked around her neck. Moments later his free hand covered her mouth, muffling her cry.

"*Korabretski*," the guard shouted. It was Amolovak, but Chrysanthi knew what he'd called her. A Stratagiozi's child.

She kicked violently, struggling to get free, but the guard didn't even seem to notice. The breath burst out of her as he dragged her away from the horses, her boots trailing in the dirt. Another yell from him, and soon Andrija and the other guard came into view.

Andrija looked furious; the guard, astonished, but already his sword was out and held toward Andrija, whose empty hands were outstretched.

"It's a mistake," he was saying, now in Thyzaki. "It's a mistake, that's all."

"You're lying," the guard holding her spat, and Chrysanthi flinched. Her shoulder twinged as he shoved her to her knees. She twisted away, trying to get free, and when that didn't work, clawed at his hands where they were gripping her. It was no use—his gloves were too thick, and his hold was too strong.

How could she have been so foolish? How could she have forgotten to cover her mark? She'd disguised everything else, and this—this small thing—had ruined everything.

Andrija took a small step forward, and his guard yelled something she couldn't understand. "Don't," she told him, but that only earned her a kick from her guard, sending her sprawling forward.

She had to think quickly; there was a way out of this, a way that didn't end with her speared on the tip of this man's sword. But her mind was fuzzy with pain, and how strange, to feel something like this—aching in her muscles and tears fresh in her eyes. In all her years she had never expected it might happen to her.

"Please," she said, shielding her head with her hands. "I'm sorry we lied." She waited a moment, in case another blow was coming, but there was only quiet. "Whatever it is you want, I can give you. Money, or . . . I don't know. I just know I can help you. Please."

All she could see was the gray of the road and the awful brown of her hair. She shut her eyes tightly, imagining the flash of a blade as it swung toward her, or the face of the guard bending low to look into hers.

Suddenly, a hand grabbed the back of her coat, and she was hauled upright so quickly she could barely get her feet underneath her.

"Inside," the guard said in her ear.

She was only too happy to obey.

Andrija was quickly divested of his own sword and escorted after her. She avoided his eyes as they trudged toward the hall, her cheeks burning. She didn't need to see his face to know he'd be angry with her, embarrassed by her incompetence. This was all her fault.

Inside, the hall was plain but warmer than anywhere Chrysanthi had been since Stratathoma. She edged closer to the hearth that dominated one end of the room and moved to hold her hands out toward the fire before thinking better of it, before realizing that seeing her mark again might further anger the guards.

"Over there," Chrysanthi's guard said, pushing her toward a bench on the opposite wall. She went and sat dutifully. Andrija was not sat next to her; instead, they made him kneel a few yards away and bound his hands with a length of rope. When they left hers free, Chrysanthi was too ashamed to be grateful. She tucked them inside her coat, brushing the outline of Rhea's letter once to be sure it was still there, tucked against her breastbone.

As she watched, the guard nearest to her removed his fur hat before testing the weight of Andrija's confiscated sword. He inspected the hilt for a moment before putting it aside onto the nearby mess table.

"So," he said. "Which one?"

Chrysanthi blinked. "Which one what?"

He let out a huff of annoyance, and Chrysanthi wished not for the first time that she knew any other language than her own. The guard reached for her and again grabbed her arm, pointing to the mark on her palm. "Which one?"

"He means which family," Andrija said. His voice was tight, his teeth gritted. "Which country."

Chrysanthi hesitated. She could lie, but there didn't seem to be enough to gain to make it worth the trouble it would cause later. Out of the corner of her eye, she saw Andrija shaking his head slightly, but she couldn't tell if he meant for her not to lie or not to tell the truth.

"From Thyzakos," she said finally.

The guard's eyes narrowed. In this light, the glow of the fire cast along his cheek, he did not look so young anymore. "Argyros?" She nodded fervently. "Where are you going?"

She knew the lie she was supposed to tell this time. Nobody was meant to know the errand she was on. But the story stuck in her throat, fear clutching her tightly.

"Bosmara," Andrija cut in before Chrysanthi could speak.

"I asked her."

"No, he's right. It's . . ." She swallowed hard, pressed her hands to her stomach to settle herself. "Bosmara, like he said."

For a moment nobody spoke. The fire crackled; Chrysanthi could hear her own breathing, ragged and quick. And then the guard was moving, Andrija's sword drawn from its scabbard and held now to its owner's throat.

"No lies," the guard said. "Where are you going?"

She couldn't. Andrija knew that, too. He would not expect her to give up the answer. But she couldn't let them hurt him, not the least because it would put her in even greater danger.

These guards had been told to look for her kind. They knew what a mark looked like—not everybody did, as she had learned quickly in the camps. Ammar must have prepared them, and for something more than just standard border control: to protect something in Amolova from the other Stratagiozi, perhaps? Whatever it was, it meant that these guards knew something she did not, and Chrysanthi had lots of experience turning that sort of thing to her advantage.

She sighed and let herself collapse, shoulders sinking, her back slumping against the wall. "I'm sorry," she said. "You're right."

The guards exchanged smiles, but the sword at Andrija's neck did not lower.

"I didn't want to lie," she went on. "Really. And I can help you. That part is true. But, well . . . you do know what this is." She held up her left palm, fingers spread so her mark was clearest, and then dropped it to her lap again. "So I think you probably know where we're going, too."

The other guard leaned forward and whispered something into his counterpart's ear. Chrysanthi strained to hear, but it was too quiet. What was not too quiet was the armed guard's reply: something quick in Amolovak that very clearly included mention of Vashnasta.

Her eyes snapped to Andrija, only to find that he was already staring at her. Whatever these guards were worried about, were protecting, it was there in Vashnasta. Where they were already headed, and where Nitsos was rumored to be.

She knew her brother. Nothing he ever did was by accident—not baiting Baba into a fight over dinner and not this. He was clockwork, running in patterns and gears; if she could just find the right key, she would be able to understand it all.

"Look," she said, pulling the guards' attention back to her. "I know you have a job to do. But I'm afraid you can't keep me here. There are quite a few people who will come looking."

The guard holding the sword frowned. "The Argyrosi are dead. Who is looking for you?"

"Only my father is gone," she said. "The others are waiting for me. Some in Vashnasta, but others not very far from here."

Get free, then get them talking. Surely one of them would spill their secrets eventually.

But Andrija was moving. Slowly, so slowly she thought at first she was imagining it, he lifted his bound hands, inching them closer to the blade of the sword where it hovered at his neck.

She tried not to let her alarm show. Not yet, she wanted to say, not just yet.

But if he was going to make a move, she had to help him. She had to keep the guards looking at her.

"You've been kind to us," she said. "I can tell my family that. I can protect you. But only if you let us both go now. Don't you see how wise that would be?"

She had barely got the words out when Andrija lunged forward and trapped the blade of the sword between his bound wrists. In one quick motion he wrenched it from the guard's grip. The weapon clattered to the floor.

"Hey," the guard yelled, and he reached for the sword, but too late—Andrija had already sliced the rope binding his hands along its gleaming edge, freeing himself. Chrysanthi watched, mouth agape, as he snatched it up and scrabbled to his feet, shoving the guard away from him.

"Go," he called to her.

"What?"

"Hide!"

One of the guards began to circle Andrija, his weapon ready. The other came toward her, but slowly, his hands lifted as though he were gentling a horse. In fact, Chrysanthi thought he seemed almost afraid.

What rumors about Stratagiozi children had come this far east? What did he think she could do?

A roar came from behind him as Andrija raised his sword and brought it down hard. His opponent only just managed to parry. He would win that fight, Chrysanthi was sure, especially if she could keep her guard occupied, but what about the others? Two on the balcony, one still by the gate. They might hear the commotion. They might come to see what was wrong.

She bolted. Left, away from the fight. Her guard shouted, and she felt him tug at her coat, but she shrugged free of it, let it fall behind her as she cornered hard and made for the door. The heavy beam used to bar it was propped against the wall, and she wouldn't be able to lift it, but she could at least try to hold the door, keep the other guards from coming in, and give Andrija a better chance.

But she'd only just reached it when the guard caught her again, his hands tangled in her hair. He yanked her back and her head knocked against his shoulder; for a moment she could see only black.

"Where do you think you're going?" he said in her ear.

It was not instinct. She had to will herself into it—the reach of her hand down into the shaft of her boot, and the curl of her fingers around the handle of the knife. He was shaking her, her neck drawn taut as he pulled her head to one side, and she hurt. She hurt every-where.

"I'm sorry," she told him. "You should have let me go." With a cry, she lifted the knife and plunged it into his ribs.

His grip on her went lax. She squirmed around to face him, her hands slick with his blood as she pushed him away. He was not dead. Instead he was looking at her with strangely alert eyes, and his jaw was working as he tried to say something. She could only stand there with her back pressed to the door as he fell to one knee, and then two.

Over his shoulder, Andrija had the other guard on the ground and his sword was raised. Chrysanthi shut her eyes before it struck. She had seen enough.

When she opened them again, Andrija was coming toward her. He had put his blade away already, the scabbard buckled again at his hip. From the look of his clothes, he had managed to stay clear of the other man's blood, for which Chrysanthi found herself absurdly grateful.

Her guard, however, was still breathing. "I don't know," she said, half to him and half to Andrija. "What . . . what are we supposed to do?"

"Are you hurt?"

"No, but—"

Andrija ducked down to get a look at the wound she'd delivered. "Go get your coat," he said quietly. "There's nothing more for you to do here."

The guard tipped forward, one hand holding him up, before collapsing to the floor. "Please."

"He wants something," Chrysanthi said softly. "He's asking for—Andrija, he wants something."

"They say that, sometimes."

The guard began to cough, blood burbling up between his lips, but it wasn't long before he had stopped and gone very, very still. Out of the corner of her eye, Chrysanthi saw Andrija shake his head.

"That's it?" she said. She stared down at the dead man's face; some of his hair was stuck to the wet, red line of his mouth. "That fast?"

Andrija took hold of her elbow, the press of his palm warm and solid, and stepped in front of her, until the buttons on his jacket were all she could see. "Yes," he said. "Now, we need to go."

They left out the back of the hall, through a guards' entrance that emptied into the trees. The cold was a welcome distraction, but still Chrysanthi let Andrija bundle her back into her coat as they hurried on.

"Lefka," she heard herself say. "What about the horses?"

"They'll come." He lifted his fingers to his lips and whistled, the sound like a hawk's cry. "Keep moving. The rest of those guards will be looking for us. We have to get as far as we can before dark."

They continued through the woods, as far from the trail as they could manage. Chrysanthi kept her eyes forward, even as Andrija checked over their shoulders every few steps. Keep moving—that was all she could do. Keep moving and try not to think about how it had felt to slide that knife into that man's flesh. It was still there, wasn't it? Still stuck in his body. She had forgotten to take it out.

It wasn't long before the horses caught up with them. They were, for the most part, unharmed, but there was a wide slash running through one of Andrija's saddlebags, as though a guard had tried to stop his horse as it passed. Andrija paid it no mind and mounted immediately, wheeling his horse around so that it followed Chrysanthi and Lefka on the trail, between her and anybody coming from the outpost.

"You ride on," he told her.

"What? Where?"

"Just follow the trail. Rest when you can't go any farther. I'll be right behind you."

"I can't go alone," she said. "I can't, I—"

"You can. You have to."

She could not make out his expression. But she took strength from it anyway, from the hit of the sun against his fair hair, the tight grip of his hand around the reins, and the knowledge that if he did let her die, it would be because he was dead, too.

"Be careful," she said. With one last look over her shoulder, she urged Lefka on, into the darkening trees.

CHAPTER ELEVEN

CHRYSANTHI

For hours, she rode alone. Evening came in close and quiet; sweat formed on her brow and froze before melting again as she continued. Sometimes she heard another horse not far behind and turned to see Andrija following her. Sometimes she thought she was the only person for a hundred miles.

Finally, once Lefka had slowed considerably, Chrysanthi steered her toward the side of the trail and dismounted. Her legs ached, and her eyes were so dry she could barely blink. She needed water, and shelter, and rest.

The trees were still thick here, but the walls of the gorge had widened, and she was able to lead Lefka off the trail. Together, they picked their way through the underbrush. She didn't know how to build the kind of lean-tos that Andrija did, but maybe she could find a clearing, or some kind of overhang.

What she found was something much better. After a few minutes of walking, the toe of her boot thudded against something solid, hard enough that she gasped and her eyes watered. Stone, she realized quickly. A piece of rubble, left over from a wall, and there beyond it, the remains of a little house.

It was too dark to see much, but it seemed similar to the ones she and Rhea had passed by in Ksigori. Thick walls, although these were mostly collapsed, and a sturdy stone-tiled roof. Enough of the structure was still intact that it would do quite nicely for the evening. Yes, it would keep her and Andrija hidden, but more important, it meant that she would wake the next morning without a fresh layer of snow covering her. She could hardly wait.

Still, though, she needed Andrija to be able to find her when he caught up, so she dug in her saddlebags for her paint box. She might not know how to make a fire, but a line of sunlight painted on what was left of the door would do the same trick. Andrija would find that hard to miss, if he was still alive.

He proved to be very much so when, an hour or so later, he came tramping through the trees, his horse following slowly behind. He was not even very horribly injured. He simply looked tired, and there was a scratch across his cheek that had not been there when she'd seen him last.

"An arrow?" she asked, hurrying to her feet. "Sit down. I'll clean it for you."

He waved her off, his head bowed almost shyly. "It was a tree branch. I'm fine."

"Are you sure?" He was all right—she could see that with her own eyes. But so much blood had come pouring out of that soldier, just from the point of her knife. It was so easy, it seemed, to die.

Andrija only reassured her again and set about building a fire. Even though he kept it small, it was still enough to warm Chrysanthi all the way to her bones. She huddled near it, waiting for some water to heat up so that she could wash the blood from her hands.

"The other guards," she said after a moment. "Did they catch you?"

Andrija shook his head. "Two came close. I led them off the trail. If we keep moving tomorrow we should be clear."

"But they're alive."

He looked at her from across the fire, head tilted slightly. "Yes," he said. "They are."

"Good." She stared down into the little pot of water, waiting for the first bubble to rise to the top. It would be much too hot. That was all right. She had plenty of time to let it cool again.

"Was that . . ." Andrija cleared his throat, and she braced herself. "Have you ever seen it before?"

She didn't need to ask to know what he meant. "No," she said. She took a deep breath. That was quite enough of that. "So. Vashnasta."

"Right," he replied after a moment. When she glanced up at him, his face had softened slightly—that is, as one rock turning into some other, infinitesimally softer rock—but there was no pity there, which Chrysanthi and her ego both found very gratifying.

"We know why Nitsos would be there," she said, thinking of the Navirotsk, although she couldn't imagine what could really be that enticing about a room full of moldy parchment. "But why has Ammar got his guards talking about it?"

Andrija lifted one shoulder. "He's been fighting over that territory for centuries. I'm sure it's been a topic of conversation amongst his soldiers for just as long."

"I suppose," Chrysanthi said, "but then Vashnasta and the Vitmar are northwest of here. Why would that conflict be important to a handful of guards on Amolova's southern border?"

"Ammar has his reasons."

Chrysanthi raised her eyebrows and said, "You sound very sure of that. Are you familiar with him?"

Andrija watched her for a moment, the quiet between them long enough that Chrysanthi felt a horribly familiar unease begin to climb up her throat. That was too far, wasn't it? She should have known better than to ask, to push her way into these parts of living that were not meant to be hers.

"I am," he said finally.

The plainness of the answer startled Chrysanthi into silence. Where was the deferral she'd learned from her family to expect? Where was the refusal, or worse, equivocation?

Andrija cleared his throat, gaze drifting from hers as he continued. "In Amolova he is . . . hard to avoid."

Ah, there it was. Well, she supposed nobody was entirely immune. And she would allow him a little bit of privacy, considering how easily he'd given up the rest of it in agreeing to travel with her.

That didn't mean she wasn't curious. About so many things, yes, and some of them much more than whatever had happened to Andrija Tomic before he'd met her—didn't most people she met find that it was only then their lives really started?—but it pricked at her, his ease in the world. How had he known what to do back there with the guards? How had he learned to speak languages other than his own so well? And if somebody had taught him all those things, why had nobody thought to teach her?

It's all right, she told herself, thinking of the portraits she'd left behind, the flowers caught in a half-finished dapple of sun. Andrija could keep his expertise in all that. They were useful things, and she despised usefulness.

She would, however, make an exception for Rhea. Her sister was right—nobody else would be able to get Nitsos home both willingly and alive. But what had been a fairly complicated errand to begin with was even more so now that another Stratagiozi was possibly involved. Andrija could think what he liked; Chrysanthi had trouble believing that Nitsos and Ammar Basha were not interested in Vashnasta for the same reasons.

Granted, she still had no real idea what they might be. Rhea had described the Navirotsk as an archive, but that could mean anything. What did archives have in them anyway? Scrolls nobody had read in five hundred years? Statues with the arms broken off? The Navirotsk was so old it predated the mandate for cremation over burial. It might even have actual bones in it.

Suppressing a shudder, Chrysanthi conjured up the image of the hall: the guards in front of her, Andrija on his knees to the right. What had they said exactly? Was there anything she'd missed that might hint at Ammar's interests? Amolovak was different from Modern Thyzaki, and it didn't operate by the same rules, but maybe there were words she could guess at, meanings she could infer, if she could only remember what they'd said.

Too late, she opened her eyes, but the memory had already changed from the guard's face to his fumbling hands and vacant stare as he dropped to the ground. That was her fault. She had taken the life from him. Dinner after dinner with Baba, hearing him recite that prayer, and yes, she had known to some degree what it meant, but it was another thing altogether to see a man die like that. And to know she had done it with her own hands.

It would take a long time, in this cold, for the fire to burn his corpse. His fellow guards would be stoking the blaze for days. Or maybe they wouldn't—what did she know? Maybe they'd begun digging a grave for him, or covered him in the deep snow to wait for the ground to thaw.

She didn't know how anybody bore it, how they laid those markers to remind themselves of what they'd lost. Personally, she would always choose to forget. Her father, in Nitsos's garden. Her mother, in some lost grave on the grounds of their old house. She'd never laid eyes on either one. And as far as she was concerned, she never would.

CHAPTER TWELVE

NITSOS

Getting into Vashnasta had been almost disappointingly easy. A lie here, a name dropped there—he had learned at Vuomorra how easily those won people over—and he'd been wished a pleasant stay and let through the gates and into the city. The Navirotsk, on the other hand, had been quite the trial, and it apparently wasn't over yet.

He had followed his guide down through the passages that led toward the library's bottom floor, and he was waiting now in a large, almost subterranean-looking chamber while his paperwork got looked over by yet another official. The floor here was wet. He found that disconcerting.

Vashnasta was a tall city—that had been his first surprise. Both the spread of the nearby lake and more than a century of siege from both sides had necessitated huge fortress walls around the whole city, which nobody dared build outside of. Instead, the city had grown upward, houses and shops stacked together so precariously that it was not unheard of for them to collapse. But Vashnasta was poised at the crossroads of a number of age-old trade routes. Despite the costs, nobody seemed quite ready to leave.

The Navirotsk, for better and for worse, was at the bottom of its particular stack. It was an ancient thing, older even than the saints that had come before the Stratagiozis. Personally, Nitsos thought that whoever had built it could've done with a bit more respect for concepts like order and sense, but then, he often found that was hard to come by.

"You've been approved," came the voice of his guide, a tall, willowy woman with a shaved head and the expression of someone who would much rather be somewhere else.

Nitsos smiled, ignoring the twinge of protest in his cheeks. "Thank you. I really do appreciate it."

"This way," she said, nodding toward the iron door set into the far wall. "The entrance is just through here."

He followed her to the door and looked aside politely as she used a large ring to open a series of intricate locks that were hidden in the curves and corners of the door's embellishments. Finally, she grabbed hold of the handle and began to pull. The door slid sideways, disappearing into a pocket in the wall.

Nitsos cocked his head. On the other side sat another room. The floor seemed not stone but black, rippling water, its surface set some feet below the level of the hallway. Beyond the door, a lip of rock jutted out, forming a little ledge over the water where it stretched from wall to wall. Overhead, the ceiling was raw rock, and other than a pair of torches mounted on the rock ledge, there was no light.

"I'm sorry," Nitsos said, even though he wasn't. He stepped across the threshold and turned in a slow circle, examining the room. "Where are the books?"

His guide stared at him. "Books?"

"Yes. It's a library, isn't it?" And he had already seen the other halls of this building, shelves from floor to ceiling packed with volume after volume in a dozen different dialects and alphabets, most of which he hadn't known existed. He'd expected more of the same.

"It's an archive," the woman corrected icily. She and her colleagues were apparently referred to as the Navirotskovai, but Nitsos thought it was much easier to simply think of her as a librarian. "Your benefactor has requested that you be given access to all our materials on her chosen subject. This is how you access those materials." She stepped back to the other side of the door, leaving Nitsos alone by the water. "I hope you find what you're looking for."

The door seemed heavy; he was not sure how she managed to get it shut so fast. But she did, and now he was stuck here, with the door at his back and water ahead, the librarian's last words ringing in his ears.

What *was* he looking for? Zita had sent him here, had told him it was a research errand, but she'd also been in direct contact with the Navirotsk about what that research concerned, clearly only prepared to trust Nitsos so far. He couldn't blame her, really, but he did want very much to know what a Stratagiozi could want that might be found here, in a room swallowed up by the lake.

Tentatively, he approached the lip of the ledge. Below waited the water's surface, smooth and not at all inviting. It was too dark to see beneath, to the bottom of this place. Perhaps there was none, and this only continued deep into the earth.

But the librarian had to have led him here for a reason. He could not imagine a scenario in which it benefited her to lie and trap him here. Well, unless she was working for Rhea, but that seemed highly unlikely. His sister was spending her spring as she had her winter, up in the Ksigora with that creature she called a consort. He remembered the threat she'd made in the garden back at Stratathoma—he'd have been a fool to forget it—but it carried with it quite a lot less danger when his scouts told him Rhea had hardly moved more than fifty miles in the last three months.

So if not a misguided attempt at assassination, this was perhaps just what the librarian had said it was: access to the requested materials. Nitsos peeled off his boots and his coat and dropped them on the stone floor. He hoped the water wasn't too cold.

Unfortunately, when he had sat himself on the ledge and dipped his feet in, he found that it very much was. This room—cave, actually, was probably the correct term, judging by the raw stone ceiling—was well underground, and the water here had not seen the sun in years, if ever. Nitsos felt his skin prickle. It wasn't going to get warmer while he sat here. With his eyes shut, he pushed himself off the ledge and dropped into the pool.

It took a few minutes' swimming around the perimeter for his heart to settle and his lungs to relax. As he swam, he examined the rough stone walls for any markings to indicate what might be waiting for him below. But there was nothing. Just the door on the far wall still shut, and the torches flickering as a thread of fresh air burrowed in through some invisible crack in the rock. It made him nervous. Nitsos did not like to be nervous.

He swam to the center of the pool and treaded water there, his head tipped back to keep his face dry as long as possible. He'd learned to swim at the beach at Stratathoma. Rhea and Lexos on the shore, Chrysanthi in the water with him. If she were here now, she would already be below, swimming down toward whatever waited there. She'd never been afraid. At least, not of the right things.

Nitsos took a deep breath and dove. Deeper, deeper, stroking away from the light at the surface. He could barely see a foot in front of him, and already his chest felt like it might burst, but he kept on. There had to be something here.

Finally, the floor of the cave came into view. Whatever this place was, it continued out in two directions, beyond what Nitsos could see. Tunnels, he thought, and probably other caves, all tangled together under Vashnasta. Perhaps the people here had used them once, before the water filled them. It seemed likely, given that a few feet away stood the bottom half of a stone plinth, its shattered top half scattered in bits across the ground.

Nitsos swam closer to it. There was nothing else here—this must be what he'd been granted access to. His head was aching now, and his vision seemed to blur. He could surface and try again, he knew, but he couldn't wait. He had to know.

He ignored the top half of the plinth and kicked down to hover by its base. It had been a simple thing, a cylinder of rock with what looked like decorative carvings etched around its base. Each one was intricately composed, distinct and seemingly unrelated to those around it.

Frankly, Nitsos thought the carvings were a bit ugly. At least the library above hadn't been adorned in a similar style.

He pushed off the plinth, swimming around it in as neat a circle as he could manage. There had to be something else. A written inscription on the base or another ruin nearby. Surely the Navirotskovai hadn't sent him here to drown.

But there was nothing to be found. Not on the plinth, and not in the rest of the cave. An air bubble slipped out of Nitsos's mouth as he returned to the carvings. Perhaps they weren't decorative, after all.

In fact, now that he looked more closely, their shapes seemed deliberate, chosen not for their beauty but for what they might represent. Here and there, lines tucked into each carving formed shapes with bare simplicity: a house, or the sun, or—

Or a person on their knees.

An idea began to form at the back of Nitsos's mind. People had never knelt to the Stratagiozis like that. No, that was how, long ago, people had worshipped their saints.

Was it possible? All of Zita's secrecy—the vague invitation she'd extended, and the lengths she'd gone to in order to keep Nitsos from realizing her exact area of interest—in service of this. Zita Devetsi was looking into the saints. And Nitsos had no idea why.

The inscription would give him some idea, certainly, but he'd need time to translate, and more time than he had breath left. Still, as he traced the shape of each symbol with his index finger, committing them to memory, one's meaning was immediately so clear that Nitsos felt a chill run through him.

A box, long and narrow, and underneath, a series of half-moons, lines extending up to graze the box's bottom edge. People, he thought, carrying a coffin. The symbol repeated every so often, dotted between the others as though the whole line of carvings was itself a procession. A memorial for the dead.

Above, torchlight glimmered on the surface of the water. It was not far. He had the breath for it still. Nitsos pushed off from the plinth and swam.

The saints had been here once. And no, they weren't anymore, but once Nitsos translated that inscription, he would know where to find them.

CHAPTER THIRTEEN

RHEA

It was colder today. The previous afternoon had been rich with sun and warm enough that the snow still lingering in the mountains had begun to melt in earnest. Rhea had stood at the edge of camp and shut her eyes, letting a balmy breeze tug at her hair. Spring, she'd thought, was coming no matter what. But of course today it was back to the same: a bit of snow in the morning, and sunlight so weak she couldn't feel it as she held her hand out over the glittering surface of the Dovikos.

She had come with Michali—or rather, Michali had come with her—to the river early in the morning, for some privacy and some time to think, and the two of them were still on the rocky shore now some hours later. Back at camp, she knew, the council was having a meeting. They were probably discussing the increasing presence of Trefzan soldiers just south of the Ksigora, but she wouldn't know, as it was yet another meeting to which she had not been invited. They had given up pretending that she was anything other than a living portrait for the Sxoriza followers to worship.

Next to her, Michali drew one leg up against his chest, the movement sending some of the smooth, worn pebbles on the shore tumbling into the water. It was near to bursting, the river, after so many extra months of snow. Wherever the council meant to move the camp to, they would need to find new routes through the mountains; scouts reported daily that another of the crossings had been flooded too deeply, or that one of the ancient bridges had been damaged by the current.

This was her fault, for bringing Michali back, and for taking no new consort. She knew that, and yet it felt at the same time very distant, and not like anything she wanted to apologize for. Instead it seemed only right that every day she should wake to the same grim weather—that the world should not continue on just as it always had when everything about her old life had disappeared. And besides, everybody had been so pleased when Michali had returned. The Sxoriza leaders had even told her not to worry about the winter. They'd said it was worth the sacrifice.

Whether they felt that way today, she wasn't sure, but it didn't really matter, did it? If they wanted to end the season, they knew perfectly well how it might be done.

"Do you remember?" Michali asked. "The first time you saw it?"

"The first time I saw what?" she asked, voice rough. It had been some time since either of them had spoken. Still, she'd felt his eyes on her the whole while. He was worried about her; that was what he'd said the previous night as she lay awake, hour after hour. She supposed she understood why.

"The river," he said.

She nodded. They had crossed it on their way to Ksigori. It had borne witness to an attack orchestrated by Michali to convince her to trust him. "A man died that day."

Michali made a small noise, and she turned to look at him. His face had taken on the sort of wistfulness he seemed to favor these days. "That's right," he said. "Do you know— I've forgotten his name."

It would have been appropriate for Rhea to take that moment to remind him of it, but she had forgotten, too.

The water was beautiful: a bright blue that she had seen replicated elsewhere only once, at the base of the cliffs at Stratathoma her very last morning there. It made her want to sink under, to open her eyes there on the riverbed and watch the sunlight glance off the surface.

"It's remarkable, isn't it?" Michali said, interrupting her thoughts. He looped his arm around her waist and she leaned into him, even as she imagined pushing him away. "I remember watching you that day. The first time you saw it. I remember I thought you were meant to be here."

"In the Ksigora? Or with the Sxoriza?"

His answering smile was indulgent, if a bit baffled. "No. No, with me."

He kissed her then—the first time he had in a few days, at least, if not longer—and Rhea shut her eyes so tightly that purple sunbursts appeared behind her lids. This way she could pretend it was as it had been: her first visit to the mountains, black kohl from temple to temple and something honest held between them. It wasn't so different now, was it?

They returned to camp soon after, following a trail so narrow that Michali, who would usually find a way to walk beside her no matter what, was forced to fall into step behind Rhea. She liked it this way. Empty woods ahead of her, so that she could imagine she was alone. She had never been alone much before all this—at Stratathoma she had always sought out her siblings, and away from home she had been Thyspira, at her consort's side until the very end. Now the few moments she did get to herself did not seem enough.

Just at the edge of the tents, Rhea stopped, waving Michali on past her. He did as she told him after kissing her forehead, and when she blinked, for a moment they were somewhere else entirely—her first day in a Sxoriza camp, her blessing given in blood as he knelt at her feet. But it was gone again, and so was Michali, his bootprints heading into the camp the only sign he'd been there at all.

Rhea sighed. Her body still felt alive with the cold and the blue of the Dovikos—awake and full. It would be so disappointing to go back to Piros telling her about yet another decision she'd been locked out of and to Chrysanthi's empty tent. As important as her sister's errand was, Rhea wished sometimes to wake up alongside her again, her nose buried in Chrysanthi's hair. She wouldn't even mind when Chrysanthi kicked her shins to bruising in her sleep. Anything, to feel that belonging for just a moment.

A mechanical whir in the air caught her attention. It was a familiar sound—her hummingbird, returned after some days away. She had tied her message to Lexos to its leg and sent it off, confident it would be able to find him. Now she caught sight of it descending through the trees and held out her index finger to give it somewhere to rest.

It alighted with a little chirp and looked up at her with its head cocked, its Argyros eyes unblinking. There was a piece of parchment tied to its leg. Rhea undid the twine securing it with a shaking hand. What if the bird had failed and was returning with only her own message? Or what if Lexos had not meant for her to find him and was refusing her request to meet?

In fact it was neither of those, and a new message waited for her, written neatly on the parchment.

Two days past the full moon, a mile east of the Drakolemnos bridge. Come alone, if you wouldn't mind.

So, Rhea thought, not Lexos, then. The handwriting was too neat to be his and the language too polite. Someone had intercepted her note. Whoever it was, they couldn't be far removed from Lexos—they had used him to get her attention, with those symbols in the stars, and besides, her hummingbird had proven itself an unerring messenger. That meant this new correspondent was likely a Domina, which certainly complicated things.

She'd heard of her brother's tour across Trefazio, but she'd paid it little mind. What happened to Lexos no longer concerned her, she'd told herself, except now it seemed that it very much did. If she wanted his help finding a strong position here amongst the Sxoriza, she would need to deal with his minders first.

And yes, she knew it would be a risk to go to this meeting. Argyros and Domina were two names that did not mix well these days. But

Rhea was not as her brother had been three months prior; she was not some powerless fool. She was a Stratagiozi with a matagios on her tongue. She was a saint. No matter who met her—no matter how many—there was no power they could hold that would equal hers.

Rhea gathered up the hummingbird and tucked it into her coat before hurrying back to camp. He'd threatened her, Nitsos, that day at Stratathoma as she'd plucked it from the branch of the cherry tree. The hummingbird was in her possession, he'd said, because he didn't need it to direct her anymore. That had scared her once, but more and more she caught herself thinking, Let him. Let him walk her right into the Dovikos until the water closed over her head. For every day that he didn't, she got one closer to finding him again. And when she did, she would bring him to his knees and sever the bond between them, even if she needed Lexos and his mystery Domina to do it.

CHAPTER FOURTEEN

RHEA

er new friend had not specified a time in their note, and so when Rhea snuck out of the Sxoriza camp, it was so early in the morning that the stars were still clear enough for her to see the message written there—the hummingbird again, only this time with what looked like a little hourglass clutched in its talon. Now, it told her. It's time to go.

Yes, I'm aware, thank you, she thought as she steered her stolen horse around a low-hanging branch and ended up with snow down her back. She knew Lexos would not be at this meeting, but on the off chance he was, she would absolutely begin the proceedings by smacking him upside the head.

It made a sort of sense, she supposed, that he'd ended up in Domina hands. As firm as Lexos had been in his support of their father, she'd heard it in the way he spoke of Tarro and seen it in the effort he put into their lessons in Trefza—a longing for a power like the Dominas'. Old, storied, and steady as stone. She couldn't really blame him for it, but if she'd noticed, surely Baba had, too. How, she wondered, had Baba felt about that? And how might he feel about things now?

Would he be proud that she had forged a new seat of power for herself, or would he recognize it as the false throne it was?

Shaking her head slightly, she urged her horse on, ducking low to its neck and focusing her eyes on the trail ahead of them. He was dead—that was all done with. She would never have to be his child again.

After a few hours of riding, the trees on either side of the path began to thin out, and she heard the roar of the river as the water itself came into view, its current stronger than it had been farther upstream. Rhea dismounted from her horse, sparing a moment to think of Lefka, who was hopefully taking good care of Chrysanthi, and started down the path. It was steep, dotted with bared roots and jagged rock, but luckily after the initial descent it leveled out and she was able to walk comfortably, the high collar of her coat protecting her from the spray of the water. At her shoulder, her horse whinnied, and urged her forward.

The bridge appeared in the distance not long after: dark gray stone arcing over the river in a nearly perfect semicircle. Rhea had been skeptical upon first seeing it—it looked like a sketch of a bridge rather than an actual one, too narrow and too steep to hold the scores of people the Sxoriza needed to get across. But they'd passed over easily, and it would support her now.

She climbed the little cobblestone ramp that led onto the bridge itself and began the crossing. The hollow knock of her horse's hooves against the stone followed her with every step. She resisted the urge to shut her eyes against the narrowness of the bridge and the height of its arch, and focused instead on the opposite bank, on the trail that could be seen leading into the trees.

Michali was probably awake now, she thought. He would be asking Piros where she'd got to, and then berating Piros when he did not know. Eventually, she assumed he would get on his own horse and go looking for her. She'd left tracks—there had been no way around it—and so she needed to finish whatever conversation there was to be had with this Domina envoy before anybody caught up with her.

Off the bridge, then, and back onto her horse. The trail was harder to follow the farther she got from the river, and after a few minutes she had to abandon it entirely and rely on the sun, still on its way to noon, to keep her headed east. The trees thickened; the ground rose again, layered with snow. She was beginning to sweat, despite the chill numbing her hands.

"Probably Lexos's idea that I meet them here," she muttered to herself. "Stuck in some Trefzan shackles and he's still making life harder than it has to be."

It was then that she saw the first flower. A single violet, tied to the trunk of a nearby tree with a matching ribbon.

How odd.

There was another flower some yards ahead, this one a pink lily tied up with its own paired ribbon. And if Rhea squinted, she thought she could make out a third spot of vivid color—yellow, this time. She swallowed hard and continued on, following the trail that had been set in front of her, from flower to flower.

"Hello," she said. It felt silly, but she wanted as few surprises as possible. "This is a lovely welcome you've left for me. Thank you for making it so easy to find you."

She rounded a large beech tree and found herself on the edge of a clearing. In the center, a slab of rock came jutting out of the ground. Someone had covered it with a sheet of rough blue fabric and set out a meal on top of it—bread, fruit, and a pitcher of wine, along with a tray of sliced meat. And across the table from her stood that someone: a woman dressed in rich, dark clothes, her black hair knotted at the nape of her neck.

"You're welcome," she said. "And thank you for coming. My name is Falka Domina. I'm very pleased to meet you at last."

Rhea's heart jumped in her chest, and she felt her mouth drop ever so slightly open. She had been expecting a Domina, yes, but not this one. Falka's name had come up before, first discussed by Michali as a Sxoriza agent inside the Domina family and then revealed as a double-crosser when the Dominas invaded Stratathoma using Sxoriza intelligence. Rhea had thought about that betrayal for many days after fleeing her home. It had felt, for some reason, as though it had been meant personally—as though Falka had meant for Rhea herself to suffer. They were both Stratagiozi's children, and if anybody could have understood what it meant to leave that inherited power, to seek your own somewhere else, it would have been Falka.

"I hope the trip wasn't too difficult," Falka went on. "I would've come to meet you, but—"

"You aren't welcome with us," Rhea interrupted, not so surprised that she'd lost her voice entirely. "Not after what you did."

"I know." Falka's pleasant smile turned a bit bemused. "That's what I was about to— It doesn't matter. Won't you sit? It would be a shame to let this food go to waste, and besides, we have lots to talk about."

"Like what?"

"Your brother, perhaps? He's very well, you know. If you were wondering." She tilted her head. "I'm not sure that you were, though."

Rhea couldn't help the snort of laughter that slipped out. She'd wondered so many things about her brothers in the months since parting from them; never had she wondered if they were *well*.

"Is he with you, then?" she asked. "Or have you left him back in Trefazio?"

Falka sat down on the other side of the table. Rhea watched as she poured two glasses of wine and pushed one forward. "He's back west, yes. But he's being looked after, I assure you."

"Do what you like with him."

"Oh, I'm sure you don't mean that," Falka said as she busied herself arranging some of the meat on a piece of roughly sliced bread. "We're lucky to have the siblings we do. We should cherish them." She glanced up now, dark eyes focusing on Rhea's empty hands. "You didn't take the flowers?"

"What? No. I didn't."

"They were for you."

"That's very nice. Listen—"

"You can take them on your way back, I suppose."

"Falka," Rhea said, voice cutting sharply through the silvered air. "What am I here for? Surely you didn't call me here to discuss my brother."

"I did, actually, but that can wait a moment." Falka's expression was still fixed somewhere between indifference and genuine warmth. "To start, I really think you'd be much happier if you sat with me and had something to eat. You must be cold after your ride."

Fine. If that was what it took to get answers out of her, Rhea would do as she asked. There was another small rock deliberately positioned on her side of the table; she sank down onto it, her knees pulled in against her chest. "Well?"

Falka pushed one of the wineglasses toward her. "Your brother is a very generous man, you know."

"Is he?"

"Quite. He was more than happy to share his gift with me." Rhea watched as Falka laid her left-hand palm up—resisted the brief urge to take it, as though it would be rude to not—and there it was, Lexos's old mark copied on Falka's palm. It was, as far as she knew, impossible. But she recognized the flatness of the color, and the way the black line was neither part of Falka's skin nor separate from it. It matched the other patterns on Falka's palm, markers of gifts Rhea did not recognize. This was no trick.

"Share?" she asked faintly. "Or something else?"

Falka smiled. "Yes, 'share' might have been skirting the truth a bit."

Rhea swallowed hard and continued to stare down at Falka's palm. How was this possible? She had never heard of a gift being transferred like this; as far as she knew, it could be achieved only through the death of its wielder. And even then, if the right ritual was not performed in time, a gift would only return to the matagios it had come from.

So either Falka had killed Lexos and performed the ritual, or she had some power, some gift of her own, that nobody had ever encountered before.

"If my brother is dead," she said, proud of how unafraid she sounded, "you might as well just say so."

"Not at all," Falka answered. She leaned in farther, brow furrowed. "Really, Rhea, he's fine. I wish I could offer you some token of proof, but I assumed you wouldn't—" She broke off, lifted one shoulder in a half shrug. "I suppose all I can say is that he hasn't outlived his use. And my father leaves nothing to waste."

That, Rhea could believe. She allowed herself to relax and eyed her wineglass. If Falka was in the habit of taking gifts, what would be easier than to poison Rhea's wine and take the Thyzak matagios for herself? Still, if she had let Lexos live, maybe she had a fondness for the Argyrosi. Or maybe, like Lexos, Rhea had not outlived her use, either.

Nitsos's face flashed into view, blond curls in his eyes as he tended his garden. Rhea blinked hard as her mouth went dry. For once, he was not the brother she needed to consider right now.

"I will take your word as proof enough," she said. "And do what you want with Lexos, although you hardly need my permission."

Falka let out a low laugh. "I appreciate it, but rest assured, Alexandros's only suffering has come in the form of humiliation."

Rhea could only imagine how poorly that had sat with him. Did Lexos have anything left now? Any shred of power? Or had Falka taken it all? It was difficult to imagine any scenario in which she hadn't. Rhea certainly would have, in her position, although she wasn't sure it made Lexos any less dangerous to be without a gift of his own.

"It was you, then," she said. "The hummingbird in the stars."

"It was," Falka said, and she looked pleased. "I heard you have a soft spot for them."

Rhea would have to look into that. It was entirely possible Falka had simply heard Rhea described by one of the rumors that traveled out of the mountains, but it was equally possible that the hummingbird's true function and purpose were not as secret as she intended them to be. Forget caution; she snatched up her wineglass and took a long sip, wishing it were something stronger.

"I suppose that's how we've ended up here," she said. Her voice sounded hoarse; she felt as though she must look ridiculous, with her cheeks flushed and sweat still fresh on her brow next to Falka's unblemished complexion and general air of superiority. "You still haven't told me why, though."

"Isn't it enough to want to share a meal with a new friend?"

"No. It isn't."

Falka laughed quietly—she had been joking, of course, and having misunderstood made Rhea want to bury herself in the snow—before leaning forward, turning her marked hand over, and resting the tips of her fingers on Rhea's wrist. The touch sent a chill running up through Rhea's arm.

"I thought it was strange we'd never met before," Falka said. "You must have traveled quite a bit as Thyspira, and yet I never saw you in my father's house."

Rhea shifted in her seat, drawing herself away from the other woman. "It's been some time since he sent any suitors."

"Imagine." Falka's smile lessened into a small, hidden thing. "What fun we might have had if he'd ever sent me."

It rankled her in a way it hadn't before, to hear it spoken of so lightly—the marriage that had cost Michali and so many others their lives. "My consorts didn't seem to enjoy dying, but to each their own." She rose to her feet abruptly. What was the point of this conversation? She had accepted the invitation thinking it would help her stand against Nitsos when the time came. But it would be madness to put any trust at all in Falka after what had happened at Stratathoma.

If Rhea's disruption had startled Falka, it didn't show on her face. "Do you need to go?" she asked while examining a piece of fruit, ultimately putting it back down. "I thought we had a bit longer, but I'm not sure of your schedule."

"All right. Enough with the food and the flowers."

"I thought they were a nice touch."

"Why am I here? What is it that you actually want?"

Falka stood, every movement smooth and serene. She came around the stone table, and Rhea wondered briefly if she should flee, but then Falka was close, and getting closer. She was just about Rhea's height, and she smelled of oranges, somehow, even though Rhea had never seen one growing anywhere this cold.

"That," Falka said. She tapped Rhea's mouth with her index finger. "That is what I want."

For a moment, Rhea did not understand. She thought—

And then: of course. The Thyzak matagios. She clenched her jaw and lifted her chin, and Falka let her finger drop.

"That stays with me, I'm afraid," Rhea said. "You could have killed me from the minute I arrived. You could have had soldiers hiding in the trees, slipped poison into my wine. If you want it, why not take it?"

"I will one day, if I must," Falka said, as though it was obvious, "but I'd rather do it this way, and I can afford to wait for you to come around." She cleared her throat delicately. "Call it a debt repaid. I was glad to see you made it out of Stratathoma." For a moment, she was silent, a heaviness hanging in the air, and then she smiled. "And anyway, why kill you for your matagios today when tomorrow you might want very much to be rid of it?"

"Why wouldn't I want it?" But Rhea knew some of the answer already. The names that sounded in her head, and the sleep that either never came, or drew her under too quickly and too deep.

Falka watched her, eyes narrowed. "Write to me if you change your mind. You'll find I'm never far." She raised her glass as if making a toast. "If hummingbirds aren't your favorite, what are?"

Rhea shook her head. "Goodbye, Falka."

She turned and began making her way back toward where she had left her horse. Over her shoulder, she heard Falka call, "We can discuss that next time, then."

There would be no next time. Rhea had fought too hard to have any kind of power. Never mind that she hadn't wanted the matagios in the first place; it was hers now, and she would hold on to it no matter what.

CHAPTER FIFTEEN

ALEXANDROS

Ettore told him he didn't need to know the full plan—that was first on the list of things that had Lexos nervous as he lay flat on his stomach on one of the metal lily pads floating in the pond. Second on that list was the smile Ettore had given him as he'd ushered him out the door early that morning.

"Stay hidden until my mark," he'd said, without adding what that mark was. And Lexos's questions had all gone without answers (or at least, without useful answers, which were most people's preferred kind).

A week with Ettore had taught him very little about the other man, but what he had learned left him conflicted. Some days Ettore was as warm and relaxed as he had been on the day of their first meeting, and they would share meals, read together on the upper mezzanine, or spend the afternoon in the water, racing sometimes from one side of the pond to the other. Other days Ettore did not come out of his room, and Lexos was left alone to cook a pathetic little meal that he ended up tipping into the sink just as often as he ate it.

It seemed clear to him that Ettore was not the lesser Domina he made himself out to be. For one thing, he'd had a prison to himself, one much nicer than the cells that Lexos had heard lay below Vuo-morra, and for another, the guards had been on edge escorting Lexos here. Giving him the key to the house, leaving him alone on the shore as they turned back toward the sluice gate: It was as if they'd been afraid of Ettore.

But today Ettore was in a good mood. He had burst into Lexos's bedroom before the sun was fully up and forced him to keep him company in the kitchen while he cooked a large breakfast with the last of their food stores. They were due for a delivery today, he had said. And that was how they were going to get out.

A whistle came from across the water. Lexos lifted his head; there was Ettore on the grassy shore, waving to him.

"Nearly noon," he called. "Are you ready?"

"For what?" Lexos returned, hoping they were close enough now to their goal that Ettore might give up something more, but Ettore gestured as if to say he didn't know, and Lexos dropped his chin back onto his folded hands with a sigh. Ettore reminded him of Baba sometimes. They shared an aloofness, a sense of something else hidden behind the white curve of their ribs that Lexos wanted to get his hands on. And if Baba had taught him anything, it was how to maneuver around this sort of man, how to follow behind until a new path split in the right direction. Ettore could keep secrets as much as he liked; Lexos would win out in the end, just as he had with Baba.

And what a short-lived victory that had been, he thought bitterly. His gift gone, his sister the new Stratagiozi—why had Baba never told him? Why had he switched their order in the first place and called Lexos his firstborn?

There was little time to wonder. The sun had just hit its zenith, throwing Lexos into shadow, and as if on cue the golden sluice gate that kept them penned in began to lift. He shrank back on the lily pad, ducking below the rim of metal around its edge.

"Stay there," Ettore had told him, as his only other piece of instruction. "You will be out of sight. Trust me."

Lexos was not sure yet if he did, and for an instant he had the wild impulse to stand up, to wave to whatever vessel was coming through the gate and give up this whole plan, if it could really be called that. Instead, he gritted his teeth and remained still.

After a minute or two more, he heard the water slapping against the side of the lily pad. A wake from the boat, small enough that it matched with what he remembered of the one that had brought him here. The dock was opposite him on the shore; once the boat reached it, he could be reasonably sure that nobody would see him if he lifted his head.

He was still working up the nerve to, though, when he heard Ettore exclaim something in Trefza, too quick for him to understand. And then, louder: "Yes, he's inside. Upstairs somewhere, I think. And listen, I know we've done this a time or two before, but I still think it's only polite for you to ask me first before you get started with all this."

All what? Lexos carefully lifted his head until he could see over the rim of the lily pad, across the water to where Ettore was standing on the dock, now flanked by two guards. One seemed to be in the process of binding Ettore's hands—not with the silver bracelets that Lexos had worn to mark his status as a prisoner, but with rope and iron chain.

That, Lexos thought, was a little excessive. Not just because neither he nor Ettore had weapons available, but also because the guards outnumbered them at least five to two. Only one, though, was left to stay with Ettore as the others went into the house. He watched, waiting for the door to shut behind the last of them. Surely Ettore's signal, whatever it was, would come soon after. They didn't have long until the guards discovered he was not where he was meant to be.

The guard was speaking to Ettore, too quietly to be understood no matter how Lexos strained to hear. He was considering slipping over the side of the lily pad and trying to move closer when Ettore threw his head back, laughed loudly, and slammed his elbow into the guard's throat.

The guard dropped, stumbled backward with a muffled gurgle. Lexos watched, mouth agape, as he lost his footing and tipped over the side of the dock into the water below.

"All right," Ettore called. "Anytime now, Alexandros!"

Lexos shook himself and wriggled forward, up and over the edge of the lily pad. The water was warm, soft, and smooth as he cut through it, making for the spot where the guard had disappeared under the surface.

What was Ettore thinking? This would just make things worse for them if they got caught, especially if the guard died. Lexos had to hurry. He swam harder, remembering how it had felt to muscle through the waves off the beach at Stratathoma, and then, a few yards out from the dock, he held his breath and dove.

The world turned deep, cool, and green, the shadowed shape of plants swaying below on the pond floor. There was the guard, sinking slowly, his eyes closed as he left a trail of air bubbles behind him. Ettore's hit had knocked him out cold. There wasn't much time. Lexos pushed himself down.

Finally, he drew level with the guard's body and got a good grip on his shirt. The guard's armor was thin, and only partial, but one glance told Lexos it was heavy enough to keep them both below. His chest aching, vision beginning to blur, Lexos undid the buckles holding the armor in place. As he glanced up, he thought he could see the refracted silhouette of someone standing at the edge of the dock. Ettore, he hoped. But he had to surface one way or another.

The armor free and the guard light enough, he began to struggle back up. Bubbles streamed out of his nose as his lungs convulsed once, twice. He spared a look down at the guard's body—his eyes shut, blood clouding in the water as it trickled from his nose. Would they be able to wake him, once they got him onto dry land?

A pair of tied hands broke the surface, reaching down toward him. Without a thought, Lexos grabbed for them, and his shoulder ached as he was hauled upward. Ettore dropped him as soon as his head was above water, and he gasped for breath. His hair was in his eyes, tangled and dripping, but there was the dock, and it felt blessedly warm when he grabbed the edge.

"I've got him," he said, chest heaving. "Here. Pull him out."

"For goodness' sake," Ettore said. "You weren't supposed to bring him back up."

"Maybe if you had told me the plan ahead of time—"

"I have no confidence that would've improved things." Ettore's tied hands clasped the back of Lexos's shirt, and he found himself unceremoniously dragged onto the dock, his torso scraping painfully against the edge. "Undo these, will you?"

Lexos peered down into the water, where the body of the guard was beginning to sink once more. It wouldn't take much time to get him out, but then, he could hear the other guards inside the house, could hear the clanking of their armor, could hear them calling his name. They would be here soon, swords drawn. Whatever was next, he and Ettore had to hurry.

He scrambled to his feet and set about loosing the rope that kept Ettore bound. There was a chain, too, but the tiny padlock keeping it in place wasn't even locked.

"I've never understood what that was for," Ettore said as Lexos undid the chain. "Superstition, I know, but really. Haven't we grown past that?"

Lexos blinked. "Superstition? What do you mean?"

Ettore didn't answer. Instead he made for the boat the guards had arrived in, only a few yards down the dock. Lexos barely had time to drop the chain and take a step after him before he had climbed into the boat, grabbed one of the oars, and shoved off from the dock.

He was leaving. More specifically, he was leaving Lexos behind.

"Wait!" Lexos said. "Ettore, wait!"

The other man did not slow and in fact began paddling harder. Lexos stepped back from the dock edge, mind racing. He'd known they weren't friends, but Lexos would never have abandoned Ettore. It hadn't occurred to him, not once. Unbidden, a bitterness formed at the back of his throat. This man was a Domina. He had let himself forget that. He would not do so again.

With a running start, he dove into the water. Some twenty yards ahead of him, Ettore was still working to get the boat moving, but as Lexos began to stroke toward him, he could tell that Ettore was having trouble. The boat was too big for one man to row by himself; the bow was already beginning to drift.

"You need me," Lexos called, keeping his head above the water as he continued to swim. "You won't get away clean without my help."

Ettore did not look back, but still, Lexos could see him considering it in the hunch of his shoulders. Lexos would just have to make that decision for him.

He took two hard strokes and surged forward, one hand outstretched to catch hold of the boat's stern. He managed to grab one of the decorative carvings on the gunwale, wincing as a splinter bit deep into his palm. Without any help from Ettore—indeed, without Ettore even slowing down in the slightest—he managed to pull himself up over the side and collapsed, his cheek near the heel of one of Ettore's boots.

"I think," he said, "that next time I really will insist on hearing the plan beforehand."

By the time he was upright again, seated on the little bench behind Ettore's, Ettore was reluctantly holding out the other oar, his head turned to one side so that Lexos could see the clench of his jaw and his downcast eyes. It looked almost like embarrassment, Lexos thought as he took the oar and they began to row, making for the sluice gate.

Behind them, the yells of the guards were louder, and when Lexos risked a look back, two of them were standing at the edge of the dock while another tread water and shouted a name he didn't recognize. After a moment, another guard surfaced, shaking his head. He was dead, then, the guard Ettore had hit. If Lexos wasn't careful, it would be him next—he'd been left behind once already.

A familiar resentment began to stir, but he knew better than to give voice to it. It was his job now to keep the peace, to make Ettore see how valuable he was, even if this escape attempt failed.

They were almost at the gate, but what they would do once they were out, Lexos didn't know. Surely someone would see them before they could get all the way to safety, especially if the guards hadn't come alone. "Are there others down the canal?" he asked Ettore.

"I don't know," Ettore said. It was the first thing he'd spoken since trying to leave Lexos on the dock, but he sounded just as he had in the moments before—neither worried nor afraid. "I suppose we'll see."

The bow of the boat slipped under the lifted gate. Both Ettore and Lexos drew their oars close, ducking their heads to keep from clipping the golden scrollwork. As soon as they were past, out from the pond and back into the narrow canal, Ettore dropped his oar and swung a leg over his bench, pivoting to face Lexos.

"Keep us going," he said. He fished for something in his pocket, his eyes fixed on a point over Lexos's shoulder. "I'll make sure they can't go for help for a while yet."

"How?"

Ettore opened his clenched fist. There was the ring Lexos had found in the study at the house. Gold and hollow, with a lock of dark hair inside.

"It's yours?" he heard himself say.

Ettore's eyes flashed as he glanced up. "Keep rowing."

Lexos did, more out of reflex than anything else. Most of his focus was still on the ring and on the practiced way Ettore bent it out of its circle and tipped the thin braid within into his waiting palm.

"Right," Ettore said. "Let's lock the door, shall we?"

He began to unravel the braid. Lexos had assumed it was an ancient thing, left there in the house to rot, and he expected the strands to disintegrate under Ettore's less than gentle handling. Instead the hair flexed and bent as though freshly cut as Ettore looped it into a simple knot and then, his eyes shut, pulled it tight.

The quiet of the canal shattered; a crash came echoing from behind their boat. Lexos looked over his shoulder just in time to see the gate slam shut into the water and then crumple and twist as if someone had taken a hammer to it.

Lexos's mouth opened and closed, his oar stilled. The boat continued to drift ahead on its own momentum, and he distantly heard the scuffle of Ettore returning to his position.

"Excuse me?" Lexos said. "What did you just do?"

"Oh, don't look so surprised." Ettore waved him off. "We Dominas have always had the knack for gold."

He began rowing again, but Lexos could not move. A knack? This was more than that. This was—he didn't know. He and his siblings were gifted, yes, and other Stratagiozis' children were even more so. Lexos had learned the truth of that at the hands of Falka Domina. But there were limits still. There were things they could not do without the power that lived in their tools and in places like Stratathoma. None of it stood up against what Ettore had done.

"I'd start helping if I were you," Ettore growled over his shoulder, and Lexos hurried to join in, fumbling with clammy palms. Ettore's strokes were powerful; he was stronger than he looked, and Lexos was reminded sharply that Ettore had been planning this without him for who knew how long. Lexos was interchangeable: a gear in one of Nitsos's machines. If he had to ignore what he'd just seen to endear himself to Ettore, he would do it. He had certainly done worse before.

But as they continued on, he could not keep from wondering: If Ettore's gifts were unlike those of a Stratagiozi's child, what did that make him? What if he was not a Stratagiozi's child at all?

CHAPTER SIXTEEN

CHRYSANTHI

The Vitmar was farther north than Chrysanthi had ever been and colder than she felt it had any right to be. She and Andrija were huddled close to their fire in the tree line, their shoulders almost touching. Earlier he had handed her a flask from his saddlebags, full of a bracing, clear liquor. It was all but frozen to her hands as she took a sip and shut her eyes, letting it ripple through her.

Thank goodness this would be their last night out in the wilds. Vashnasta was up ahead, perhaps a mile out; they had reached it too late for Andrija's liking and would make their attempt to enter tomorrow. From here, its lights could be seen dotting the sky, flickering gold against the black bulk of the walls.

Chrysanthi did not know much about it. What she did know had created a strange sort of shape in her head, one she couldn't match to the silhouette before them now. Andrija had explained that once the city had been a fortress, woods on one side and a lake on the other. The trees had long since been cut back, and the lake had grown, pulling the original fortress under the earth. Now the city grew upward every year, houses stacked on houses, Vitmar history drowning day by day.

For all the territory's complications, crossing into it had been as easy as taking a few steps off the Amolova border trail, which left Chrysanthi feeling a bit silly for all the preparation she'd insisted she and Andrija do in the stretch of days it had taken for them to arrive there— the rehearsed stories, the lessons in Amolovak and Chuzhak (and in telling the difference, which, while apparently very important, seemed to Chrysanthi not to exist). Ammar was apparently quite happy to let anyone in Amolova cross into the Vitmar, presumably because he considered it part of Amolova—that was, at least, what Rhea had told her.

Nevertheless, she knew it had been good practice for entering Vashnasta. Though the Amolovak checkpoint was said to be more lenient than the one on the Chuzhak side of the city, it would be difficult to pass through without being questioned, and just the thought of another set of Ammar's guards approaching her, swords at their sides, was enough to send a shiver down Chrysanthi's back.

She had tried so hard to forget it, that fear that had gripped her at the Thyzak border, but it was following her still. Close behind every turn on the trail and lying alongside her every night when she closed her eyes and tried to rest—the reflection of the hall's hearth in the guard's eyes as he'd approached and the feel of a knife in her hand. All of it a reminder that there was damage she was capable of dealing out, when it came down to it.

This time would be different. This time she would do everything right.

"Tell me again," she said, leaning toward the fire. "I want to make sure I have it."

Andrija cleared his throat, and she felt his body tighten and relax next to her. "We approach the Amolovak gate, on the eastern side."

Chrysanthi peered into the dark, trying to find the spot in the distant shadow where a gate might be. "Right, and then?"

"I have a set of false papers for both of us. They should be enough to get us through, provided we take care."

"We will," she said. Her hair was freshly darkened with her paints, and the mark on her palm was covered, too. She had scarcely allowed more than a minute to pass without wearing some kind of disguise since leaving Thyzakos.

"At which point we find a safe room in a safe inn. I know a place."

"Let me reiterate my preference that it not be underwater."

"I've noted that."

He sounded as though he might be smiling; Chrysanthi snuck a sidelong glance to check, but his face was thrown into shadow.

"From there," he went on, "I stop riding in front. You tell me where we're going."

That meant the Navirotsk. Rhea had told her Nitsos might be here, but she had not been sure, and even if she was right, Nitsos would have been able to move more freely than Chrysanthi and Andrija. He might very well have come and gone since they left the Sxoriza camp. Regardless, it was the last anybody had seen of Nitsos. Chrysanthi would have to start here to see where he might have gone next.

"You said the Chuzhaks hold the city for the moment?" she asked.

Andrija nodded. He took the flask back from her, knuckles knocking hers, and drank deeply. "Back at camp," he said when he'd finished, "I heard that the Chuzhak Stratagiozi had moved her seat here. To keep her hold strong."

Chrysanthi felt her chest tighten briefly at how he pronounced "Stratagiozi." She could hear the word he wanted to say in Amolovak, and something about the deliberateness with which he spoke each syllable of Thyzaki made the corners of her mouth twitch.

"Nastia," she said. "My sister told me she's called Nastia Rudenko."

"That's right."

"And if she is here?"

Andrija got to his feet. Chrysanthi was about to protest at the rush of cold air when she realized he'd unclasped his cloak, and it was crumpled next to her hip. For her? Or had he forgotten? "Her banner will be flying, for one thing," he said, nodding toward Vashnasta. For a moment he paused, his gaze flicking down to the cloak and then back up to meet hers. "And she might be someone you want to see."

"She might." Tentatively, she picked up the cloak, waiting for him to stop her, but he turned away as soon as her hands touched the fabric, seemingly satisfied. She drew it around herself and hoped it would not be quite this cold inside the city walls. "I'm not sure yet if I'm prepared to give her a reason to see me, though."

"No?" Andrija asked. He had finished inspecting the fire and crossed to where the horses were tied loosely to one of the last of the trees. Lefka did not look bothered by the weather. The warmth of her body under the saddle had been one of Chrysanthi's only comforts. She would miss it dearly once they'd stabled her in the city.

"No," she said. She shut her eyes, trying to bring to mind the maps that had covered the table in the Sxoriza tent, searching for some detail she might have forgotten since then that could help her now. "Not after the welcome we got from Ammar. I think we're better off going unnoticed."

She heard a crunch in the snow. When she opened her eyes, Andrija had left the horses and was facing her across the fire, arms folded. Back by the tree, his horse was munching on something that looked like an apple. She hadn't known they'd brought any.

"All right," Andrija said. "No Nastia, then."

Chrysanthi sighed and sank more deeply into the borrowed cloak. "What are they fighting over anyway? Rhea said it's been centuries of back-and-forth. I can hardly think of anything that might be worth it."

Andrija shrugged. "It depends who you ask."

"I'm asking you."

"Let's see." He held up one hand, ticking off each finger as he went: "The Amolovaks who live here, the Chuzhaks who live here, the farming fields up north, Vashnasta itself, the Navirotsk. There's a reason to suit everyone, even the *poklatsai*."

"The what?"

"It's Chuzhak," he said. "Really it's whatever came before Chuzhak, but it's the word for the old kind. The ones who still follow the saints."

Chrysanthi supposed she ought not to have been so surprised—she'd just left an enclave of that sort behind in Thyzakos—but it was still strange to hear the practice discussed so openly. Baba had talked as though he'd eradicated it altogether, the mere mention of it enough to send him into a rage. Even now she could feel a tension begin to roll down from her shoulders, body bracing as though her father might arrive at any moment.

"What's their reason?" she asked. "The *poklatsai*. Is the Navirotsk one of their churches?"

Andrija shook his head. "There's a rumor," he said, sounding more dismissive than she'd heard before. "An old story. They say the saints were buried somewhere in the Vitmar."

"Buried? As in, their actual bodies?"

"Like I said. An old story."

Chrysanthi tipped her chin up to the sky, letting the cold slip under Andrija's cloak for a moment. Graves for the saints—she had never considered them before, but why shouldn't they exist? Why shouldn't the story be true? The saints had all died at the hand of Luco Domina, long before cremation was common practice; it stood to reason he'd had to put their bodies somewhere.

"Is this the sort of thing everybody knows?" she asked. "Ammar, Nastia, I mean. Would they have heard this story?"

"Certainly." Andrija snorted. "One of them might have even been the one to start telling it."

"You seem very certain there's nothing behind it." Did Andrija not consider himself one of the *poklatsai*, then? He'd come to follow the Sxoriza and Rhea, and while not everybody up in the Sxoriza camps worshipped the saints, enough did that she had considered it a foregone conclusion.

"I think a thousand years is a long time," Andrija said. "How we think of the saints now is likely not at all how people thought of them when they died."

Though she could understand his skepticism, she couldn't share it. She'd seen how hard Baba had worked to stamp out any mention of the saints. And she'd seen, too, how deeply the worship of them could move a person—even her sister. Control over their graves, over whatever was left of their bodies, would be invaluable to someone like Nastia or Ammar. And to someone like Nitsos. Chrysanthi had spent their years at Stratathoma thinking of her family, of the suitors Rhea summoned and dismissed; meanwhile Nitsos had spent them straining to see over Stratathoma's walls. She could imagine him following a story like this one. Power of a different sort than their father's—it seemed as if her siblings were all in search of that now.

How, she thought, was she ever meant to tempt Nitsos home again?

"I think I'll take a walk," she said and got up, brushing the snow off her riding trousers.

Andrija glanced over his shoulder, toward Vashnasta. "Once you're back, I'll go make sure our route for tomorrow is clear."

She bundled his cloak into one hand and held it out to him as she passed, making for the edge of the trees. "Here."

"Keep it."

"It's yours."

"I'm two feet away from the fire. Keep it."

She met his eyes for a moment, waited for him to look away, but he looked evenly back at her.

"Fine," she said. "Yes, all right, fine."

It was a well-made cloak, she thought as she stepped into the darkness. Andrija had barely worn it during their trip—the difficult riding kept them both warm—but still it seemed of a piece with the portrait she had begun painting of him in her head: dark colors, certainly, and strong, purposeful lines, but smooth strokes. None of the sharpness an Argyros portrait would demand.

She had called it a walk, but Chrysanthi stopped as soon as she could no longer make out Andrija's figure by the glimmer of the fire. She needed light, still, to do what she meant to, and she did not like to be too far from help. Checking to make sure she was alone, she reached into her coat and pulled out the letter Rhea had sent her here to deliver.

She hadn't read it. Rhea hadn't specifically told her not to, but the implication of the seal across the flap had been clear. And on first setting out from the Sxoriza camp, she had been happy to leave it be. Or perhaps not happy, but certainly used to it. How comforting, to once again be kept out of the know by one of her family. But Vashnasta was huge and terrifying in the dark, and the road to get here had been so cold. She was tired of the task already, and she'd barely borne any of it at all.

Carefully, she slid her fingernail under the wax seal, already partially loose from wear, and popped it up. Inside, her sister's handwriting was laid out in neat lines, the same little flourishes and stray marks she recognized from notes Rhea would leave on her door back at home. Ignoring a pang in her chest, she tilted the letter toward the glow of the campfire and read.

The beginning was nonsense, all little platitudes and pretty words. They would never lull Nitsos into the kind of complacency they were designed to create, but Chrysanthi recognized them all too well as the sort of pleasantry both she and Rhea fell back on in moments of uncertainty. What mattered was the end: Rhea's offer to perform the rite she'd used on Michali, this time on someone else. On Baba.

Chrysanthi felt something strange pricking at her eyes. Her hands felt as though they weren't all there—was she still holding the letter? Perhaps she'd dropped it.

Baba, brought back. What would that mean for her family? For her? Would she be drawn back to Baba's side, to serve again as the head of his household, managing all those tasks nobody had ever realized existed? Would she be his favorite as before, and worse, would she enjoy it? She had for a long time, had resented her siblings for upsetting their father. And she could feel it in her still: that wish for easiness, for comfort over everything else. It bloomed every night as she lay down to sleep on the hard ground. If Baba came back, she wasn't sure she'd be able to ignore it. She wasn't sure she'd want to.

She could see why Rhea had offered, though. It had been plain to her how deeply Nitsos wanted Baba's respect and, the older they'd gotten, how deeply it had cut him to be reduced to wanting his attention. The promise of another chance would draw Nitsos back anywhere, whether Rhea meant to make good on it or not.

And she didn't. Right? Surely she understood how deeply Baba's return would ruin all of them. It would open a chasm between each sibling that Chrysanthi would never be able to bridge. Lexos and Nitsos back in competition, and Rhea? Rhea utterly undone. She had loved their father so much more than she allowed herself to understand.

Chrysanthi was taking no chances. She bent over the letter once more—she had not, in fact, dropped it—and then crumpled it up, so quickly the letter's edge sliced the bottom of her thumb. She would not carry this to Nitsos. If Rhea wanted to scold her for it when she got back to the Sxoriza, that was fine. But she would find some other way to get him home. Something in Vashnasta would present itself. Something, or someone, and just thinking about the number of people that must have been living and breathing and talking amongst themselves less than a mile away made her stomach turn. The Ksigora had been enough of a shock after a century of isolation at Stratathoma; Vashnasta, from what she had seen of it, would be many times larger. And now, as Andrija had said, it was her turn to ride in front.

The east gate, and a safe inn, and then some time to think, she repeated to herself. Nitsos had been or was still here, and he had to have left some kind of trail behind him, even if it was just a series of poor impressions on other people. If he really was looking for the saints' graves, she didn't need to know why to beat him to it.

Ah, there—a gnawing at the back of her mind. She had avoided thinking about it long enough but there was no way around it now. Ammar and Nastia were looking for a saint's grave, and meanwhile she herself knew where one was: in the Thyzak countryside, behind the house she had been born in.

They had buried their mother. Chrysanthi had been too little to form any memory of it, but Rhea and Lexos both remembered. It had always been something to wonder about and something to protect— surely the other Stratagiozis would be shocked if they ever found out that their colleague's consort had been buried instead of burned—but she had never quite looked directly at it. What did it matter? Irini Argyros was dead.

Except it did apparently matter a great deal. Her mother had been a saint, and her portrait, hung in Chrysanthi's head alongside her father's, had been filled in by Rhea's hand. How had she felt, kept away from everyone in that house in the countryside? Perhaps the way Chrysanthi had at Stratathoma, caught between wanting more and wanting very, very much less.

Well, Chrysanthi had all of that now, didn't she? Her family in tatters, but here was the world waiting for her. Less and, she thought as she made her way back toward the fire, very, very much more.

CHAPTER SEVENTEEN

RHEA

The flower had traveled well. Holding it up in the sunlight that snuck through the tent flaps, Rhea could make out the delicate veining that ran through each petal. She could even catch a hint of its scent, although that seemed more like the power of suggestion than anything else.

She had not planned, originally, to take a flower with her, and she'd made it all the way back to where the first violet was tied to a tree without collecting any of them. But something had stopped her there, and without thinking much about it, she'd undone the matching violet ribbon, slipped the flower into her coat, and ridden back to camp. When she'd arrived, and been left alone in her tent while Piros ran to fetch an anxious Michali, she'd tucked it into the pages of a nearby book, eager to get it out of her sight. Just looking at it was mortifying.

Still, she'd packed the book in her things before moving camp, arguing to herself that she might need it—it was an old prayer book, written in Saint's Thyzaki and one of her only sources as to what she was supposed to be doing whenever people came to worship her. When she'd opened it again a moment ago, she'd been surprised to see that none of the violet's petals had come dislodged from its stem.

She twirled it between her fingers before setting it back down on the page it had come from. Where had Falka found this, or any of the other blooms she'd left as little presents? For that matter, how had any of that meeting really happened? Lately it seemed like something come out of a dream. After all, Falka's offer to take away Rhea's gifts was exactly that sort of wishful nonsense. Perhaps a world without her gifts would have been preferable, but for a century they had been, often, the only things keeping Rhea's head above water.

And they would be what saved her again now. She hadn't been privy to the decision the Sxoriza's council had made to move the core of the camp down from the mountain. She'd pretended to know, of course, and told every worried camp follower to trust her, trust their own faith in the cause, but that had done nothing to settle the unease that only grew in her stomach. They were moving south; moving away from Chrysanthi; moving away, worst of all, from Nitsos.

There was, though, one upside to it. Despite the mixing of the seasons, it did seem that some things still held true, and the farther south they got, the stronger the sun and the lighter the mood around camp. That made it a bit easier to bear days of waiting for Chrysanthi, but it also made it even stranger that Rhea herself was still so, so cold. All the time, from waking to sleeping. It seemed to be consistently getting worse, to the point where she'd risen this morning to find her teeth already chattering. Standing out in the wind for hours so that people could worship her had not helped, but neither had a warm meal for dinner. A few minutes ago she'd sent Michali out to look for more blankets; she rose now to peer out of the tent flaps, searching the sprawl of the camp for his familiar figure.

She couldn't see him, but there was Piros, positioned as he usually was just a few yards off. She waved to him and he hastened toward her. Rhea smiled; even though the Sxoriza leadership had soured on her considerably, Piros had not.

"*Keresmata*," he said as he drew near. "Are you all right? Do you need anything?"

He had been so solicitous since rescuing her from Stratathoma. Sometimes, combined with Michali's almost punishing attentiveness, it felt like more than she could take.

"I'm fine," she said. "I was just wondering if you'd heard where we're headed next."

Piros was still not admitted to leadership meetings—his association with her kept him from being invited, she surmised—but he was well liked in camp and had been with the Sxoriza long enough that almost anyone would tell him almost anything if he asked.

Piros nodded and edged closer until they were both poised on the tent's threshold. "West, ultimately," he said quietly. "Toward Agiokon. Although I imagine we'll continue south first."

"And risk passing Rhokera?" A thought crossed her mind; she leaned in, worry tightening in her gut. "We're not trying to unseat the Speros steward, are we? We're not nearly ready, especially now they've got Domina support."

"No," Piros said, "but we'll intersect with some supply lines out-side the city. Athanasios says it's worth the risk." He nodded across the clearing, to where the man in question could be seen speaking to a handful of camp sentries. "I think they're preparing to move on one of the west country stewards. Myritsa, maybe?"

Rhea sighed. She was no expert, but to her it seemed lunacy to imagine that the forces gathered in camps like this one would be any match for a steward's soldiers. They'd had a chance at Stratathoma because of her; it was a mistake to proceed as they were.

"Would he listen to me?" she asked and glanced up in time to see Piros wince. "Is it even worth trying?"

"I think your efforts are better put elsewhere."

She stared ahead, tracing the proud set of Athanasios's shoulders. If the Sxoriza could be said to have a single leader these days, it was him, and though he seemed impenetrable, she'd had practice with men like this.

She was about to make her way across the muddy camp to speak to him when another figure emerged from the woods at the far edge, their arms laden with blankets. Michali, returned from her errand.

"How is he?" Piros asked, his gaze following hers. Rhea thought she saw a sorrow in his eyes and found she recognized it too well to look at it for very long.

"I don't know," she said. "Tired. Restless. He has trouble with what to do, I think." Across camp, Michali had stopped to let a trio of children dart ahead of him. There weren't many here—most families were settled in camps farther out of the mountains—but those that were barely ever gave him a second glance. Perhaps they sensed that he had changed; perhaps they simply had better things to do. All she knew was that it had been different in Ksigori. So many things had been.

She nudged Piros's elbow with her own. "He doesn't speak to you?"

"I don't think he speaks much to anyone," Piros said, before hurrying to add, "Except you, of course."

Except her. Although it wasn't for lack of trying.

"I found a letter in his things the other day," she said. "He was trying to write to his mother—she's back in Ksigori still."

"Now there's someone who could talk sense into Athanasios."

Rhea could well believe it, but it didn't matter. Michali had never sent for her. "He kept starting the letter over," she said. She had put it back carefully, but she could remember the words that had been scratched out, so thoroughly in places that the paper had torn: line after line, a greeting to his mother followed by Rhea's own name, the start of a sentence Michali had each time left unfinished. "It's as if he left his opinions behind in the grave."

Piros did not answer, instead shifting uncomfortably from foot to foot. He never seemed to know what to do when she started talking about what she'd done to Michali. But at least he listened. With Chrysanthi away Rhea found herself aching for that kind of company.

She watched Michali pass Athanasios. To her surprise, the older man held out a hand, saying something she could not hear at this distance. Athanasios alone out of the leadership had, as far as she knew, not approached Michali since that disastrous meeting, so what business did he have with him now?

Maybe, she thought, it was only pleasantries. But after weeks of silence between the two? Rhea did not trust it in the slightest.

"That's odd," she said to Piros, nodding in the direction of the pair still in conversation. "Have you seen them speak like that before?"

"Not in some time."

Michali broke from Athanasios, backing away for a few steps before resuming his walk across the camp. His head was down as he adjusted his hold on the blanket pile he was carrying; he had not seen her yet. Rhea moved to slip back into the tent before he could.

"Thank you, Piros," she said. "I always appreciate it."

"Of course. And if you're still cold under all of those," he said over his shoulder, "we can try to make camp on one of the Rhokeri islands next."

She smothered a laugh and sidled back inside before sitting down at her place by the lantern, its warm light pooling in the folds of her skirts. Not long after, the tent flap rustled—Michali's attempt at knocking—and then lifted as the man himself ducked through. He was carrying that armful of blankets, but an extra portion of food, too, that she hadn't seen, wrapped up in a tatty rag. Rhea tried to ignore the dull pulse of guilt that lingered at her temples like a headache. Whoever had given those things to Michali had given them up freely. It made them happy to keep her comfortable. And in return, she—

Well—

Better not to think about that, she reminded herself smartly and reached for one of the proffered blankets.

"Let me know if that helps," Michali said, dropping the rest by her side. "I think I can rustle up some more, if you like."

"This should be fine." The blanket she wrapped around her shoulders smelled like somebody else's sweat, but it was warm. She tugged it closer.

"Do you think you're ill? Maybe you caught something up in the mountains."

"It's just winter still. That's all."

She eyed him warily as he came to sit next to her. Had he said something to Athanasios? Something about Chrysanthi and her er-rand? She'd kept the truth from him, but he'd noticed that her sister was gone and accepted her explanation—that Chrysanthi had been so ill-suited to conditions in camp that she'd been sent back to Ksigori—with a raised eyebrow and a small smile. It had reminded her of the Michali she'd first met, and it made her wonder now if there was more at work in him than he'd let on. More, perhaps, that he'd shared with Athanasios and not her.

She cleared her throat and asked, "What did he want?"

Michali did not look up from where he was refolding one of the blankets. "Who?"

"Athanasios." As if she could mean anyone else. "I saw him stop you."

"Oh, that? He asked how you were," Michali said. "And he asked if I'd ever traveled through Agiokon before. I think he wanted some advice, but meeting you is the farthest afield I'd ever been, so I couldn't help."

"Agiokon?" That fit with what Piros had said, but it made little sense to her. Yes, the Agiokori had a respect for the saints that the Sxoriza would appreciate, but the city was wealthy, strong, and poised at the intersection of three nations, two of which now were under Domina control. Going to Agiokon seemed to Rhea like asking for trouble. "Did he say why?"

"I don't think so." Michali sat back and slipped one arm around her shoulders, reaching with the other for her clasped hands. "You could ask him, if you wanted. I've known Athanasios since I was a boy." Michali's nose wrinkled. "I think he even courted my mother, when they were young. He's a good man. You can trust him."

She couldn't tell, really, who that recommendation was coming from. The Michali she'd met might very well have trusted Athanasios, too. Rhea shut her eyes, and just for a minute she let herself pretend that it was early winter, that they were back in Ksigori and she had only just discovered what it might feel like to want good things for other people.

Quiet, breath passing between them. Michali's touch was cool against her palm, the gentle pressure of his fingers reassuring. Almost as Falka's had been at the stone table in the woods, the offer she'd made stretched like golden thread between them.

"Elado," Michali said into her hair. "What's this?"

"What's what?"

One of his fingers tapped the back of her hand. "Your mark," he said. "Does it look different to you?"

Her eyes flicked open. "Different?"

"See." Gently, he uncurled her fingers and traced the line of her mark with his own. "It feels hot, no? And there's . . . I don't know what you would say. Feathering? The black bleeding, there, at the bottom."

She peered down at her own skin. If she squinted, she could make out what he was talking about: places where the black was seeping out into the other lines on her skin. They were small, barely noticeable if she hadn't known the shape of her mark better than anything in the world, but they were there.

Rhea's stomach sank, her veins running cold for a breath that stretched on and on, until she blinked hard and said, "I don't see it."

She pressed her palm flat against her thigh. It was not there. There was nothing to worry about.

"Really?" Michali asked. "What about the other?"

He meant her right hand, where she bore a scar that matched her mark, the one with which she'd sealed a new marriage for every season. Quite honestly she'd forgotten it existed; she hadn't touched it since choosing Michali at the end of autumn last. Curious despite herself, she held it closer to the lamp, and—oh—the scar did look a bit red, almost as if it was about to open back up. But these cuts had always healed remarkably well. There was no reason for it to look inflamed.

"How long has it been like that?" Rhea couldn't speak. She could only stare down at the scar, could only imagine the sides of it peeling back to reveal bone underneath. "You haven't noticed any change? Any pain?"

"No," she managed. "No, I haven't."

"It's very small," Michali said, as though that was meant to comfort her. "I'm sure I only spotted it because I pay such close attention."

That was enough to bring her back to herself. "Well, don't. There's nothing different."

She wasn't being fair to him—she knew that—but it stung to be reminded of how his focus had shifted. If a golden thread had stretched between her and Falka at that table, another was tied between her and Michali, this one as black as the clothes she'd worn to mourn him. His sight was so narrow now; his heart was so keenly hers.

Rhea forced herself to take a long, deep breath. She could feel him watching her and knew very well what he was thinking: It was nearing that time of the evening when her matagios would offer her its list of names. Let him think that was why she was on edge. Michali was as familiar with it as she was, although he would never know the pressure that built behind her eyes with each name she refused to speak. At least her nose had stopped bleeding after every list. But then, all that did was make her wonder what toll it was taking now that she could no longer see.

"You might feel better if you try it," Michali said suddenly.

"Excuse me?"

"It's almost time, isn't it?" He leaned in, the lamplight casting odd shadows across his face. "Rhea, this is what comes with your matagios. It's hurting you to refuse it."

She blinked, startled. It unnerved her to hear him suggest it after days of staying quiet. Frankly, Rhea had thought he'd moved on, or remembered, maybe, the sort of cost she would be dooming other people to pay.

"I can't," she said. "You know I can't."

"What I know is that I have seen you sick, and I have seen you troubled. And I love you, so I would like very much for those things to stop."

"Yes, so would I," Rhea said peevishly, "but unfortunately some other things are more important."

Michali sighed. He lifted the lamp from its spot between them and set it aside before rising onto his knees and shuffling closer to her. With both hands, he took hold of hers.

"Don't you think this is a warning?" he said, tapping the base of her mark. "Rhea, you are what is important. You may not like to admit it, but those people out there follow you, and they cannot do that if you—"

"If I what?" She pulled free. "I'm fine."

"You're not."

"I am!" Sometimes when he spoke it felt as though the world under her feet was tilting wildly. "Listen to me," she said. "You wanted the whole federation torn down—a federation built on gifts like this one. But you're telling me now that I should use my matagios and send people to die so I can stop feeling a bit cold?"

"It's not about the federation," Michali protested. "Your gifts come from the saints. You *are* one, Rhea!"

She bit her tongue, holding back the words that threatened to spill out. It was not his fault that he didn't understand. "I don't know," she started slowly, "what death looked like before the saints' massacre. Nobody does. But if it looked like this? If it felt like this? Then they were as bad as the Stratagiozis you hate."

She was expecting some sort of outburst—while he had never claimed to be the sort who knelt in the old churches and prayed, she knew Michali held the worship of the saints dear, if only as a hallmark of his beloved Ksigora. But he only shrugged, his eyes fixed on hers.

"Saint," he said. "Stratagiozi. What does any of it matter if you are not well?"

His words sounded impossibly loud. Rhea's mind filled briefly with the vivid image of an old Ksigoran stone bridge beginning to crack, and then it was gone again.

"I'm sorry," she said. "I have to . . . I'm sorry."

She got to her feet, stumbling slightly, and pushed her way through the tent flaps before Michali could say another word. Out here the sky was dark enough that she could clearly make out the shape of each constellation. Falka's work, and now that she knew that, she could see in it the mistakes: a star out of place in the shape of the huntress, an extra one added to the line of the throne. Falka would learn in time, but if things continued the way they were, she would never have a summer's sky to practice on.

This particular camp had been set up where open ground could be found amongst the trees, which still grew tall and slender here, unlike the greener woods and orchard groves of the west country. Rhea turned and began to pick her way through to the camp's edge and beyond. Somewhere out there, she knew, were sentries, who would not let her stray too far, and Piros was probably watching her from some vantage point she hadn't noticed yet, but she could find a semblance of privacy if she kept to the small paths that wound between the trees, most covered in a thin, unbroken layer of snow.

The first name arrived only moments later. Rhea stopped walking and pressed her back against the nearest tree, her eyes shut, her breathing deep. She had weathered this before; nothing about her argument with Michali needed to change that.

But as the second name coalesced at the back of her head so, too, did a disarming sweetness. He loves you, it said. He only wants you to be well. And after everything you have put him through, can you not give him this one thing?

She had called him back from the grave to stand by her side. Where would he go, if she was not there to lead him?

Rhea opened her mouth. The name waiting there was Trefzan, and it tasted sweet, light as an orange. She longed to sink her teeth into it. To swallow it down.

It wasn't as though people didn't expect to die. It came for most everyone in the end.

"*Aftokos ti kriosta,*" she said. "*Ta sokomos mou kafotio.*"

There. That wasn't so bad. The prayer had been opened and she felt fine. Good, even—thirsty, with a glass of water almost in hand. She cleared her throat and went on. It was only one name. She could stop after that if she wanted to.

"*Aftokos ti kriosta po* Bastia Romano. *Ta sokomos mou kafotio.*"

Light burst behind her eyes, and her mouth watered. It was like the day she had married Michali, like plunging into the lake in the dead of winter and emerging, made new and wide-awake. She could feel her heart thundering in her ears; stopping herself from saying another name seemed nearly impossible. Rhea tasted blood as she clamped her mouth shut.

Had this been what Baba had felt when he'd sat at their dining table to pray? Had he been afraid when he'd spoken his first name, as she was now?

Rhea dropped to a crouch, leaning back against the tree as she willed herself to relax. The rush of Bastia's name was beginning to fade, replaced instead by a heavy bitterness. She scooped up a handful of snow and shoved it into her mouth. Once it had melted, she swished the water around her teeth and then spat it back out. It was pink, spotted with something black.

Whatever she'd spat out was too small to see well. Carefully, she leaned in, dug her index finger under one of the specks, and lifted it to eye level. The substance was dark, barely half the size of her littlest fingernail, and seemed to have layers like the crust of a pita. As the snow around it melted, she could feel its texture, too—soft and fleshy.

Rhea jerked back and staggered to her feet, wiping her hands frantically on her skirt. It *was* flesh. It was—

She'd spat out bits of her own tongue. The black there, specks in the mouthful of water—they were pieces of her matagios.

Her hand shook as she reached into her mouth and grazed her fingertips along the center of her tongue. She could feel the slick of blood there already. Under it, in the place where she knew her matagios sat, her tongue felt soft, as though if she pressed much harder it might turn to pulp.

Her stomach turned sharply. Rhea gagged, nearly choking on her own fingers. Hurriedly, she wiped them in the snow, doing her best not to look too closely at the stain they left behind.

What was happening to her? This, along with whatever was happening to her mark and scar both—was it all because of what she'd done with Michali? Or perhaps it was because of what she hadn't done, in avoiding her matagios for so long. This had never happened to Baba, as far as she knew. His gift had never cost him like this.

Why not? Were there more secrets he'd taken with him when he'd died?

Of course, she thought, scoffing. She should have assumed so from the very beginning. No matter what, though, praying for poor Bastia Romano's death hadn't helped, and now Rhea would simply have to carry it. Another mistake, another life to whom she owed an explanation that she could never give.

She gulped down a mouthful of winter air as a hot panic began to take root at the base of her neck. If her gifts were going bad somehow . . . if they were unable to provide her with the power they'd promised, where did that leave her? The worship she'd claimed from her connection to Aya Ksiga, to her mother, was not enough to protect her in a world like this; in fact, without the gifts of her father, she was not sure she'd survive it.

I wish you were here, she thought fervently, imagining the portrait she'd seen of her mother in that church. I wish you could help me understand.

But her mother was dead. There was nobody she could ask. Nobody who would understand any of this in the slightest, except—

"Falka," she said into the quiet. Falka, who could take gifts for her own, and who had offered to take Rhea's matagios. She had to have some deeper knowledge of their function that Rhea was missing. She was a Domina, and Rhea could only imagine what secrets of the saints that family still kept.

She would ask. As soon as she got back to camp, she would send her hummingbird out to find Falka and request another meeting. And this time, she would be prepared for it.

She kicked some fresh powder over the mess she'd left there on the white ground. Around her the woods were empty—no torchlight and no figures approaching from camp. Thank goodness. She was not sure at all what it meant that this had happened, but she did know that she wanted it kept secret. There were any number of ways that this could ruin things, and not just with the Sxoriza. With Nitsos, too, who might find opportunity in her weakness. No, by the time she got back to camp, she would need to look as though nothing was wrong.

Accordingly, she decided to take a longer route, one that took her farther away before swinging again toward her tent, and as she stepped into the dark, she couldn't help but imagine Lexos walking alongside her. How angry he must have been when he'd realized that their father had lied, for reasons passing understanding, and that he was not the firstborn. If only she could tell him now that he'd been the lucky one, to be without this. But then Lexos had always known better how to hold a weapon. That day in the garden he'd barely blinked before trying to turn the prayer of the matagios against her. Maybe she should try to do as he might have done with this power and pray for the end that Nitsos deserved.

She shook her head, trying to clear it. He had warned her against that, told her that creatures of his could not harm their maker. She did not know if he'd been lying or not, but there were better ways to find out than this. Even if it worked, what did that get her? A death she could not witness, could not claim before the world as belonging to her.

And besides, whether by the choice of its bearer or by its own limitations, the matagios was not an arrow to be fired. She had nobody for guidance, yes, but she had the memory of her father, and for all that he had been willing to do, he had never broken that one rule.

It was so hard, she thought as she made her way back to camp, to be better than Baba. Perhaps she would have to be satisfied with not being worse.

CHAPTER EIGHTEEN

ALEXANDROS

E ttore's feet were jammed into his hip, and if Lexos heard him mutter one more obscenity under his breath, he was fully pre-pared to cut them both off, regardless of how powerful Ettore might be.

The two men were huddled under one of a handful of upturned Domina canal boats, all dry-docked on the lawn no more than ten feet from the canal's main dock. They'd left their own vessel drifting in the water, hoping it would convince their pursuers that they had continued on; whether by luck or by some other gift of Ettore's, it had worked.

He hadn't asked any questions about Ettore's little display, but they were piling up, rattling around in his head to the point of drowning out any other thought. Whatever Ettore had done to lock the gate behind them was not power as Lexos knew it. The Argyrosi had quiet gifts: painting here and mechanisms there. Rhea was the closest they came to anything quite as bombastic as whatever had turned the sluice gate from a fine piece of craftsmanship into a mess of metal. And even though the effects of their gifts certainly reached far and wide, it was still a question of doing something with one's hands. Of making and undoing. The hair Ettore had knotted and the gate—what was there connecting them that Ettore had manipulated? What was Lexos not seeing?

At the moment, he wasn't seeing much of anything, with the hull of the boat an inch from his nose.

"Can you move over?" he whispered. "I want to check the dock again."

"I can look just as well as you can," Ettore said, sounding miffed, but he did at least draw his feet back an inch or two, giving Lexos room to crane his head toward the nearest gap in the hull. Though it was just past dawn, and the light was still thin, Lexos could make out the guard positioned by the palace door across the lawn. There had been a few guard changes in the night, and a boatful of soldiers had gone out down the canal not long ago. They were not back yet; Lexos felt sure that if he and Ettore did not move before they returned, they would both be caught and soon put right back in the house they'd escaped.

"What you did earlier," he said. "With the gate."

He didn't have to see Ettore to know that the other man was raising an eyebrow. "Yes?"

"I don't suppose that might be helpful now, would it?"

"Afraid not." Ettore did not sound at all bothered.

"Right."

The door into the palace appeared to be the only exit or entrance, and the lawn between it and the canal was small enough that even if Lexos could lure the guard to one side or the other, it wasn't likely he and Ettore could make it through the door undetected. And furthermore, who knew what guards might be waiting just on the other side?

He pressed his eye again to the hole, craning his neck to get a better view of the palace walls. They were covered in ivy, thick and glossy. Halfway up, a balcony broke through, white marble against the green. He wasn't sure, but it looked like its glass doors were cracked open.

"Ettore," he said. "How well do you know the palace?"

"Not as well as you might expect."

"So you wouldn't know how populated this part of the building is?"

"I would imagine very, no? I hear my family is quite large."

"Thank you," Lexos said dryly. "You're very helpful."

"What's your hurry anyway?" Ettore asked, yawning.

"My hurry? Oh, I don't know. It might have something to do with the armed guards currently looking for us." Lexos shifted in place as a cramp shot through his calves. "Would you rather stay here? You seem to be quite at home."

"I am as eager as you are to be elsewhere," Ettore said. "But I am waiting for something."

"Care to tell me what?"

"There's a guard I know of that has agreed to assist me."

"A guard?" Lexos pinched the bridge of his nose. Ettore's plan had got them past the gate, and he was more gifted than anyone Lexos had ever encountered; how was it possible that he was also this naïve? "You're trusting a guard to help us?"

"It's not the guard I'm trusting," Ettore said, but that was nonsense as far as Lexos was concerned, and he turned back to the hole in the hull, taking another look.

"There's a balcony a story up," he said. "If I don't go for it now, it'll be swarming with guards, too, before the morning's out." Likely there were some posted there already, but Lexos was tired, tired and hungry, and he wanted very much to not be here anymore. "I'll take my chances," he said. "You can come if you want."

"To the balcony?"

Lexos did not answer, all his attention directed through the gap in the hull, until at last the guard turned to patrol back toward the door. They had to go now—things were bound to only get harder if they waited.

He shoved Ettore's legs out of the way and wriggled toward the stern of the boat, which was only a few feet from where the lawn ended and the marble steps, which led into the canal, began. The slope of the lawn created a gap between the boat and the earth, and Lexos slipped through it now, coming to a crouch behind the curve of the hull. It was so bright out. Already tears were pricking at his eyes, gathering in their corners.

"Come on," he whispered to Ettore and began to run for the palace wall.

The lawn was too soft underfoot. He stumbled, legs aching from being huddled in one position for so long, but Ettore's hand was there, at his elbow, keeping him upright.

"Bit wobbly, are you?" Ettore said, and the laughter in his voice was enough to spur Lexos on toward the ivy.

Not quickly enough, though, to escape the guard's notice. A shout rang through the air, and as Lexos threw himself forward, he saw out of the corner of his eye the flash of sunlight on metal—the guard, his weapon drawn, rushing toward them.

"Go on, if you like," Ettore said. "I'll handle this."

Lexos didn't need to be told twice. He careened into the palace wall, hands already grasping for purchase on the green vines. There was no trellis under the ivy, and for a moment he panicked, sure it would collapse under his weight. But he managed a step up, his boot wedged between two of the vines, and then another, and above him the balcony looked close enough to reach.

Ettore, though, was still below, and there were no screams, no yells for reinforcements, and no clashes of metal on metal. Lexos chanced a look back down.

Ettore stood near the middle of the lawn, and the guard was, Lexos realized incredulously, kneeling at his feet, head bowed. Ettore was smiling, saying something too quietly for Lexos to hear. Whatever it was, it made the guard shudder and gesture oddly, pressing his palm first to his forehead and then to his chest.

"There," Ettore said, louder now. "Carry that *carmiga* home with you."

Lexos bristled at the sound of a word he did not know. It must have been very old indeed to have stymied him—his Trefza was near perfect otherwise.

The guard rose, his knees visibly weak and his expression utterly enraptured. Was it simply the fact of meeting a Domina that had him so awed? It couldn't be. They were everywhere in Vuomorra, and surely it had been no secret that the prisoner in that house had been one of the family.

Lexos swayed a bit as the ivy sagged under him and looked from Ettore to the balcony above and back again. What was he supposed to do now? Just wait here? Or go on?

"Really," Ettore said then, his head tilted toward Lexos. "Thank you so much for your understanding. I can't tell you how much we appreciate it."

The guard blushed. Lexos felt his mouth drop open.

"It's my honor, *patorra*," the guard said. "If your friend would like to come in through the door—"

"Oh, no." Ettore waved a hand dismissively. "He's committed himself to climbing, I'm afraid. I'll join him. He does seem to need a bit of help." Ettore turned to Lexos. "Are you stuck?"

"I— No!"

"I'm not sure I believe him," Ettore said to the guard and then clapped him on his armored shoulder. "Thank you again."

Lexos could only watch, half dumbfounded and half indignant, as Ettore turned away from the guard and came to the foot of the wall, brow furrowed.

"Is there a route you recommend?" Ettore asked.

"Excuse me? What just happened?"

Ettore's smile lessened. Not enough to fall away entirely, but enough that Lexos felt it, as if someone had taken hold of the back of his neck.

"Why don't we discuss that another time?" Ettore said. "You'd better get moving before that vine breaks."

It was humiliating, really, to make the climb with Ettore just behind him, and the guard still watching from his post, but Lexos managed it, finally hauling himself over the white marble railing of the balcony. He waited there for Ettore, catching his breath and peering through the balcony's glass doors.

Luckily, the room looked empty, but the sun glancing off the glass made it difficult to see much beyond a gleaming wooden chair sitting somewhat askew just inside. Slowly, he eased one door open, preparing himself for the likely misfortune of coming face-to-face with another brigade of guards.

Instead there was nobody. Just dark-paneled walls and a matching wood desk that reminded Lexos of the one he'd encountered back at the house he and Ettore had just left. There were a few papers left on its surface, which immediately drew his interest, but before he could go to take a look, Ettore clambered over the railing.

"You know, now that I'm thinking about it," he said, groaning as he straightened his shirt, "we really could have just gone in through the door. That guard was very amenable."

"Amenable," Lexos repeated, disbelieving. "That was . . . I don't know. I don't have the word for it."

Ettore leaned against the balcony threshold, arms folded across his chest. "We can switch to Thyzaki, if that suits you better."

"No, I mean—" Lexos broke off. How far did he want to push? Ettore allowed far more questions than Baba ever had, though of course he only answered them as he chose. And if Lexos didn't ask, simply accepted things as they were, was he showing himself to be a dulled blade, so obedient as to be useless? *"Carmiga,"* he said. "What is that?"

"Ah. That's old Trefza." Ettore frowned, thinking. "I think the closest you have in Thyzaki comes from the Saint's tongue."

Lexos couldn't help glancing over his shoulder the way he might have back at Stratathoma. Baba had hated to hear any talk of the saints, so much so that even on their trips to Agiokon they had never used the word between them. But alongside the worry, anxiousness born of a habit Lexos was not sure he'd ever break, came a cold sort of certainty.

He'd wondered what it meant for Ettore's gift to be as strong as it was. He'd wondered if Ettore might be something other than a Stratagiozi's child. And now he'd seen a man kneel before Ettore in a kind of worship, to receive what Lexos could only assume had been a blessing. A saint's blessing.

His throat felt tight, his mouth dry, but Lexos steadied his nerves and said, "Which one are you, then?"

"Hm?" Ettore had left the balcony and was at the desk now, peering down at the papers spread there. "Which what?"

"Saint." Lexos swallowed hard. "What you did with the gate, what you said to that guard down there. You're not a Stratagiozi, but there's no mark on your hand, either. So that leaves the saints. Which one of them are you?"

For a moment Ettore was silent and so expressionless that Lexos began to doubt himself. But at last, Ettore raised his eyebrows and said, "They all died but one, Alexandros. Take a guess."

"Luco," Lexos said, even as his cheeks went hot. "You're Luco Domina."

The last of the saints; the first of the Stratagiozis, and the founder of Trefazio and the Domina house, which meant—

"But Tarro is the Trefzan Stratagiozi," he heard himself say. "So doesn't he have the Trefzan matagios?"

"Have you ever seen it? Of course you haven't. He hasn't got one. But I'd bet you've never got close enough to tell." Ettore opened his mouth obscenely wide and laid his tongue flat. There was a matagios in the center. It was smaller than what Lexos had seen on Baba (and what Rhea bore now) but it was unmistakable once he knew to look for it.

"And that man," Lexos said slowly. "That guard. He knew who you were?" It would explain the reverence with which he'd knelt and that he'd let them go.

"He did. My family do not like to let anyone know who they keep in that little house, and for the most part that's suited me. But if a rumor spreads through the guards now and then, well . . ." He shrugged, looking quite pleased with himself.

Lexos could imagine what sort of effect a rumor like that would have. A devoted servant of the Dominas might wonder if they were serving the right one, and if Tarro's claim to the Trefzan seat could be legitimate if Luco was still alive. But that in turn begged the question: "Why have they kept you there, then? Why not just—"

"Kill me?" Something gold flashed between Ettore's fingers; Lexos realized he had removed the ring from his pocket and was toying with it now. "I'm a saint. I carved my power from the earth itself, but the matagiosi these Stratagiozis carry? They all came from mine, and from gifts I gave to my children. If I died, who's to say their power would not die along with me?"

"But that isn't how it works."

"Maybe it is and maybe it isn't. Is that a risk you would take?"

Lexos supposed it wasn't. "So Tarro's children—they take their gifts from you?"

"I was very generous with them, for a time." Ettore smiled again, and Lexos shifted uncomfortably; the predatory sharpness had returned. "I am not so generous anymore."

Those gaggles of Domina children running riot around Vuomorra were not marked. Lexos had never thought much of it—his own father had waited for him to reach a certain age before giving him any gifts—but it took on a different shape now. Still, it seemed strange to him that those children were alive at all. The Luco in the stories had cut down his fellow saints to claim their power for himself; why had Ettore allowed those gifts to split apart once more?

"Did you really do it?" he asked suddenly. "Did you really murder all of them?"

"Yes." Ettore seemed to strand up straighter. "Why? Have people been saying I didn't?"

"No."

"Good. Now, I think we've taken enough time for your little interrogation." He reached for the papers spread across the desk and began leafing through them. "Come on, then. Make yourself useful."

Lexos hastened to his side, craning his neck to get a look at the paper Ettore was reading from. Some of it was immediately understandable— Trefza shared an alphabet with Thyzaki—but despite his studies, he still found it tricky to read Trefza without accidentally transliterating it to Thyzaki. Still, he could recognize his own sister's name.

Rhea Argyros and then, farther down, *Ksigori* and *Agiokon.*

Ettore recognized it, too. "Argyros. Isn't that familiar?"

Briefly, Lexos considered lying. It was useless, though; he could tell by Ettore's bemused smile. "She's my sister," he said. "She's—she's the Stratagiozi now. Of Thyzakos. Although only in name. Your family's taken the Thyzak seat."

"Yes," Ettore said, almost gently. "I'm aware."

Lexos blinked. "You are?"

"Did you think I'd been sitting in that house doing nothing? I have a curious mind. I was a scholar before I was a saint, you know."

Ettore looked back at the paper with Rhea's name, seemingly done with this particular part of the conversation, and Lexos felt a muscle twitch in his jaw. Was he angry? Upset that Lexos had lied by omission? Baba would have been.

"Ah," Ettore said to himself after a moment and dropped the page back onto the desk. "I see."

"What? What does it say?" Lexos hoped he didn't sound too eager, but the sight of Rhea's name had set something stirring in him, a restless envy he'd tried very hard to set aside during his tour of the Trefzan countryside. It hadn't served him then to wonder what Rhea was doing with the power that should have been his. Looking at a report on her movements now was an unwelcome reminder that Rhea mattered to the world in a way he did not.

But, he thought, he could again. Lexos was in the company of a saint, and if Falka had been able to take his gift away, maybe Ettore would be able to give it back—or even give him more than he'd lost. The rules he'd followed so carefully under Baba were gone; power did not work the way he'd thought it did.

"That?" Ettore asked. "Drivel, for the most part. People going here, people going there. None of it changes my plans."

"And what are those?"

"Out of the palace, first of all. Then a nice lunch, I think. And after that?" Ettore tapped the paper where *Agiokon* was written. "I owe the city of saints a visit."

So did Rhea, if Lexos understood the report correctly. He skimmed it again, hoping there was more information about what Rhea was doing, but before he could attempt any translation, he found himself caught by the name at the top of the page. The report was addressed to Falka Domina. And when he riffled through the papers remaining on the desk, he found her name scattered across them.

So, this was Falka's study. The knowledge gave the room a new shine, and Lexos turned away from the desk, searching for something else, some other clue as to what she was doing in here, and what she might be planning alongside his brother. Unfortunately, aside from the desk and its papers, the room was as bare now as it had been a moment ago.

"This woman," Lexos said. "Falka. Do you know her? Or is she after your time?"

"I've met her," Ettore said. "Not for long, but enough to see what sort of person she is."

"And what sort is that?"

"Oh, the consummate Domina. Which is saying something, coming from me."

It really was, and Lexos had to agree. If Falka had ever felt uncomfortable or at a loss, he had certainly not been around to see it.

He and Ettore both fell silent for a moment as they shuffled through the rest of the reports. Lexos kept an eye out for any of his siblings' names—he knew Falka and Nitsos had been aligned and might be still—but nothing else seemed to concern them. Faced with sentence after sentence that he could not easily translate, Lexos's attention drifted to Ettore.

He looked perhaps a decade older than Lexos himself did, despite the fact that his life had so far been at least ten times as long. Tarro was younger, but showed more age than this man—than his . . . what? Father? Forefather? That had to be due to Ettore's sainthood, but then that was assuming that Ettore was correct, and that his matagios behaved differently than those that had come from it. Personally, Lexos was not prepared to accept Ettore's word as the truth just yet.

"Do you mind?" Ettore said.

Lexos flinched. He'd been staring, hadn't he?

"Sorry," he said. "I was just thinking—would you like me to call you Luco?"

"There's no need. Ettore is the name my mother gave me. It's nice to hear it again after so long."

It was very strange to think of *the* Luco Domina having a mother, but then it was equally strange to think of him as being still alive, which he clearly was. "Why did you change it?"

Ettore smiled, all teeth. "Most of the saints understood the value in a good title."

"And what about a good second?" Lexos asked. "Did they understand the value of that?"

He didn't know if the saints had kept seconds the way Stratagiozis did now; he didn't know, even, if they'd had children, or if their family lines had died when they had, at the hands of the man in front of him. But it was surely a position Ettore would recognize and taking it would put Lexos right where he wanted to be. He'd led his house and country from behind Baba. He could do it again. He was sure.

"They might not have," Ettore said, "but they're dead, and I'm not. What is it you're offering me, Alexandros?"

"My help." Lexos cleared his throat. "The world has changed since you lived in it last. There are people who would kill you if they found out who you are."

"That's not a change," Ettore said, but he gestured for Lexos to continue.

"I can get you to Agiokon safely. I have contacts with the Devetsi family who hold Merkher now—whatever access you need, I can grant it." Stavra would not appreciate him promising favors that she would have to fulfill, but he could negotiate that with her later.

"And what," Ettore asked, "am I meant to give you in return for such generosity?"

It would not do to ask plainly for what he wanted. Lexos was still learning who he was dealing with, but he knew that much. "Whatever you feel I've earned," he said. "Even if it's only the honor of serving Luco Domina."

Ettore's eyes seemed to sparkle as he smiled broadly. "Why, Alexandros! I hadn't taken you for a saint worshipper."

Lexos smiled back. "I'm not."

Their gazes held for a heartbeat, and another. Lexos could feel the judgment in Ettore's eyes, the balancing of scales. He lifted his chin and drew his shoulders back. Ettore would not find him wanting.

"All right," Ettore said at last. "Yes, all right. You're with me until Agiokon. We'll see then where our paths lead." He clapped his hands together, and with the sound a wave of relief broke over Lexos. Direction, at last. "Right. Shall we?"

"Of course," Lexos said. He cast a glance out to the lawn under the balcony—so far, no more guards had arrived, although that was certainly liable to change. Quickly, he went to the front door of Falka's study and pressed his ear to the door.

"What's in this direction?" he said. "I can't hear anyone, but that doesn't mean we won't encounter more guards. Are they likely to be the sort we can trust?"

"Oh, very much not."

"I suppose we'll just have to hope luck is on our side."

"Well, we could do that," Ettore said, moving toward the wall to the left of Falka's desk. "Or we could go out this way."

Lexos watched as he pressed one of the decorative Domina crests carved into the paneling. With a creak and a low rumble, a section of the wall began to slide back, revealing a passage beyond. It was surprisingly clean and punctuated with spots of pale green light that streamed in through stained glass skylights.

"That," Lexos said, "is a much better idea."

Ettore slipped into the little hallway without a backward glance. Lexos made to follow, but hesitated at the threshold, his eyes fixed on Ettore's figure. As glad as he was to have another chance at a Stratagiozi's power, something about how easily Ettore had accepted him left Lexos uneasy. Ettore had nearly abandoned him back at the house. Why was he so happy now to have Lexos at his back?

Whatever the reason, Lexos would find out and find some way to use it. He'd spent three months out of his element, but he was back now—someone's second again, this time with an edge sharpened by everything he'd lost. And if Ettore tried to cross him, he would feel that edge against his throat.

CHAPTER NINETEEN

NITSOS

The translator he'd enlisted had been reluctant to help, but Nitsos found there was very little that could not be accomplished by combining a polite request with a flash of his black mark. The translator's face had gone pale and her hands had begun to tremble, and after a few days of waiting in his room at the Navirotsk while she assembled the relevant texts, Nitsos had been provided with a very rough translation of the carvings he'd found inscribed on the bottom of the underwater plinth.

It was old Chuzhak, she'd explained, its symbols designed by one of the earliest saints for use in worship and ceremony. Like Saint's Thyzaki, Nitsos had said, but apparently it was even rarer. Most of the records it appeared in had been drowned in the library's lowest chambers as the lake continued to rise. Despite her general dislike for saint worship, Nastia Rudenko had since committed herself to helping the Navirotskovai preserve what they could.

Given all that, Nitsos thought it was ridiculous that the library didn't simply keep a record of the carvings' translation somewhere. His translator had told him, though, that to do so would have been in violation of one of the library's founding principles. And while this sounded like horseshit—and vague horseshit at that—to him, he'd got what he wanted, so what did it matter in the end? Let this be someone else's problem.

The symbols had led him north, up the river that fed the lake currently sinking Vashnasta. The Vitmar was sparsely populated in these parts, its villages dotted haphazardly across the snowy countryside, so Nitsos most often found himself camping alone in the wilderness after a day's march up the iced-over river. Altogether it wasn't too bad, but he was very glad there was nobody around to see him throw his tent down in frustration after one of the pins froze through and snapped.

This morning the sun was more visible than it had been for the past few days, but it was doing nothing to keep Nitsos warm as he tramped onward, his boots making odd, hollow noises against the ice with every step. He'd been told it would be more efficient to follow the river, rather than any of the roads that ran in this direction, and so far that advice was proving correct, although he did have to admit that being so in the open, a lone figure between the banks, made him nervous. With any luck he would not be out here much longer.

Thus far, the river had led him through a little valley, around and between miles of foothills, and today it and Nitsos both had reached the point where those hills turned into mountains, their peaks white with snow in the distance. On either side of the river, stone rose sharply for hundreds of feet, and Nitsos could see spots where handholds had been cut out, or where small caves waited to shelter a stranded climber. Who would actually want to climb one of these cliffs, Nitsos couldn't say—someone at the Navirotsk would know, and he could ask when and if he returned there.

For now, he was focused on a point up ahead where the river curved out of sight. The symbols hadn't contained nearly as much detail as he'd hoped, but the translation had mentioned a spot where the river turned east, something that had been very disheartening during day after day of northward travel. It had also cautioned against anyone following in the procession's footsteps, but that part Nitsos had decided to discard.

Why had they brought the saints' bodies here anyway? Nobody had been able to tell him. The only clue he'd found was an obscure reference to a "source" in one of the additional texts consulted by his translator, but whether that was of the saints' power (unlikely) or of the river itself (more likely) he couldn't say. Whatever the reason, this place he was looking for was meaningful in some way, and if he could find out why, he might have something else to bargain against Zita, and he would take anything to get himself on a more equal footing. Waiting for Baba to give him a second look had been enough dependency for a single lifetime, and he was well into his second one of those.

He pressed on, hoisting his pack higher on his back and turning up the collar on his newly purchased winter coat. That had been one of his first surprises after leaving Stratathoma; it evidently got quite cold elsewhere on the continent. Really, somebody ought to take care of that. He'd have done it himself if he'd been informed before, crafted some sort of contraption on the grounds at Stratathoma to make everywhere else a bit more bearable. As it was, the only thing he could do now was endure it. That, and plan for an even thicker coat next time.

He'd known, of course, that leaving Stratathoma meant losing his gifts. He still had them, yes, and could still build most anything he wanted to, but those creatures carried none of the power that his models had at home. While somebody else—Lexos, primarily—might have been upset to lose access to their gifts after using them for so long, Nitsos was quite confident without them. He'd done what he needed to with Rhea, and their link still protected him from her to this day. Everything else he could manage using the other gifts he'd been given by his father: quick hands, a mind that never settled, and the ability to be forgotten by everybody in the room.

Nitsos rubbed his hands together and shoved them deep into the pockets of his coat, where despite the fur lining of his gloves, they could still feel the chill. He was close now to where the river turned, and it appeared that before it did, it passed through a narrow pinch point where the walls of the ravine nearly met again before opening back up. He would have to make an uncomfortable climb. Nitsos squinted at the rock on either side of the river; perhaps that was what those handholds were for.

With his pack swaying clumsily from side to side as he went, Nitsos began hauling himself up the rock. He'd never had much practice with this sort of thing—Lexos was the athletic one, and besides, all of Nitsos's own work was best done while sitting at a table—and it was only by promising himself that he could stop once he touched down on the other side that he ended up finally tumbling onto the ice once more.

"This is absurd," he muttered to himself. How the procession had made it past while carrying a handful of corpses, he didn't know. Maybe this hadn't been here when they'd made their trek, and the earth had shifted. A thousand years was a very long time.

Luckily, though, there didn't appear to be another obstacle of this sort ahead, and he could see now where the river changed course. It wasn't very wide here and rather than cut a path of its own choosing through the rock, it had given ground to the ravine walls and followed their curve to the east. Nitsos straightened his clothes and continued on, sure to stay alert. He must be getting close now.

After the turn in the river, the translation had only mentioned one more landmark: a white olive tree. According to the translator, this tree was man-made rather than natural, something she had discerned from the particular shape of one of the symbols. She had been confused as to how that might be; Nitsos was not. His gift had belonged to other people before him, and to one of the saints once. Who knew what they might have built?

The sun was nearly at its zenith, flooding the ravine with gold, with a white glare off the snow that gathered in spots where the water met the stone. There were no trees to provide any shade, just some dead moss creeping up from the river and a few other tenacious little plants that seemed to grow horizontally out from the wall. Nitsos spared a thought for how this place must look in warmer weather, the water rushing, the stone wild with greenery, and then spared another for his sister, who was the person to be blamed for the lingering season and the bitter chill. Yes, he'd set her in motion toward Michali Laskaris, but the mess she'd made after Stratathoma belonged entirely to her. Bringing the man back? For what? She'd known him for all of five minutes, and now the whole world had to deal with snow in mid-spring.

Nitsos was in the middle of preparing a list of grievances he had with Rhea when he stopped short, staring ahead. The ravine walls seemed to narrow again, but this time they appeared to fuse into one: solid rock, through which Nitsos could not pass.

He turned around, looked back the way he had come. Had he passed the tree? Surely not.

Warily, he approached the end of the ravine, keeping to the middle of the river where the ice was thickest. There was indeed something strange about the rock wall. It was split by a crevice that Nitsos had not seen at first, hidden as it was behind an outcropping. From a sidelong angle, he could peer through into some sort of natural chamber beyond.

He shed his pack and hung it by its strap nearby before wriggling into the crevice. Immediately, he regretted it. It was damp in here and smelled awful, and he could feel a spear of rock pressing painfully into the small of his back. But there was light, enough to reflect off the river where the ice broke up a yard or two ahead. Nitsos turned his gaze to the task at hand, managing to only get into water up to one of his knees—

No, it was two, he had stepped right off the ice and into the river, and wouldn't that have been mortifying if Lexos had been here to see?

By the time he made it through, Nitsos was soaked, his bottom half with river water and his top with panic-sweat. The warmer air in the crevice had thawed out much of the river, and as he emerged back into cold, he had to clamber out of the water onto the sheet ice. Teeth already chattering, he rubbed furiously at his hands and thighs, trying to shake some warmth back into his body as he examined the chamber he found himself in.

It was surprisingly large, a broad, circular atrium of sorts carved out of the rock, open to the air above. The river filled the space, save for a miniature island that might have once been covered in snow and was now churned earth, holes dug and tracks left all across the island. At the center, undisturbed, stood a great white tree.

Nitsos stared, all awareness of the cold gone. This, he thought, was what the inscription had referred to. And clearly he was not the first to arrive.

The tree was carved from pale stone, and though it held the bearing of an olive tree, it was bigger than any Nitsos had ever seen. The trunk had been expertly sculpted, carved to look just as gnarled and bony as the trees he remembered from Stratathoma, and the sculptor had even managed to give a translucence to the leaves, enough that they were glowing with sunlight.

He approached it slowly, avoiding the all too fresh footprints that crisscrossed the dirt. Here and there, thin white roots surfaced and ducked below the earth again, fashioned as well by the tree's sculptor. If not for the disturbances made to the earth, Nitsos thought they might not have been visible at all.

"Hello?" he called. He had no expectation of an answer, but it was always nice to get a sense of a space, of how it collected voices and scattered them across the air. If they had sung for these dead saints, or if they'd wept, the sound would've lingered, humming in the rock walls.

There was no other sign that such mourning or ceremony had ever happened here. Despite the grandeur of the olive tree, it was accompanied by no banners, no plaques, and no plinths like the one he'd found at the bottom of the cave at the Navirotsk. Instead, it seemed the tree was the only marker anyone from the saints' procession had left behind.

Its visitors had not been so sparing. At the far edge of the island, a pickaxe and a length of rope had been abandoned, and the treads of heavy boots were visible everywhere. People—many of them, by the look of it—had been here not long ago.

Ammar's soldiers, Nitsos thought, or perhaps a brigade of Chuzhaks sent by Nastia Rudenko. It wasn't entirely unexpected. The two had been fighting over Vashnasta and the Vitmar for so long that it really would've been quite depressing if they hadn't thought by now to send anyone into the Navirotsk. What was left to Nitsos was to determine whether or not the previous party had found what they were looking for.

Somehow, he didn't think they had. Apart from the fact that it seemed ludicrous to him to leave the bodies of the saints out here in the middle of nowhere, the tracks their would-be visitors had left behind had no unifying direction. As far as Nitsos could tell, perhaps a dozen scouts or soldiers had arrived here, wandered around in circles, and then walked back out again. They had not crowded around the edge of a grave, or felt their boots sink into the soft earth as they lifted a body free.

Nitsos left the tree, taking a slow measure of the island with careful steps. As he went, he tried to imagine what it must have been like to come here as part of that original procession—a worshipper in grief. Had they feared for their lives back then? Had they worried that Luco Domina might come for them next for daring to mourn the saints he'd killed? Or had he led the procession himself, a last honor given to people he'd known and perhaps even loved?

What did you do, whispered a little voice curled up in the back of Nitsos's head. You left your siblings behind, to live or die or something worse.

Nitsos bit down hard on the inside of his cheek and the voice vanished. It was true; he had not waited to see what might happen to them. He had not marched at the head of their processions. But what did it matter? They weren't dead.

That was the problem with metaphor, Nitsos thought. Eventually, it always fell apart. And he'd had quite enough of power built on it. Rhea and the hummingbird, the sketch he'd abandoned at the Navirotsk—he was bound for better things.

He would go to Agiokon, confer with Zita and with the monks there who knew the history of the saints as well as anyone alive. Let Ammar and Nastia squabble over the Vitmar; let Zita go on thinking he had no designs of his own. While they were busy with their councils and their squabbles, Nitsos would keep following the trail.

CHAPTER TWENTY

CHRYSANTHI

C hrysanthi supposed she had to be grateful in some way for the mess she and Andrija—well, she on her own, really, but she preferred to ignore that—had made at the border between Thyzakos and Amolova. It had taught her just how careful she needed to be while disguising herself, and that meant that when Andrija escorted her to the gate into Vashnasta, the two of them were able to pass through and into the city after undergoing what seemed only an average amount of scrutiny. What a victory, she thought as she followed Andrija up a winding cobblestone street. It was as if she'd been out in the world all her life.

She'd even managed to not be completely knocked off her feet by the sight of the city that morning. She had woken by the banked fire, rolled over toward the lake, and immediately been very glad that Andrija was already up and elsewhere in the camp so that he couldn't see her mouth drop open and eyes go wider than she'd thought possible.

Stratathoma was large, and she'd seen Ksigori on her way through it with Rhea. Not to mention a handful of other smaller cities and towns during their trip across the country. But none of them had been even a quarter of the size of the behemoth that was Vashnasta. Chrysanthi had found herself sitting on her bedroll for minutes on end, gaze tracking from the bottom of the city to the top and back again. It rose for story upon story out of the lake, the bottom portions built from roughly hewn stone before patches of wood began to appear. At intervals across the walls, an ochre Rudenko banner could be seen flying, but each one was obscured by a square of black fabric, indicating, Andrija told her later, that Nastia Rudenko was not in residence.

Relieved, Chrysanthi had let her attention drift, and as she and Andrija had begun their approach, she'd spent the ride trying to pick out one city building from the next. They were so strangely stacked, windows appearing where she would have expected another wall, and though she knew the city had to have been held up by some substantial construction, she couldn't shake the fear that it would simply tip over in a strong gust of wind, particularly given that its founding predated the advent of the Stratagiozis. What could the saints have done to hold up something so great as this?

From within the walls, it was no less confounding. Chrysanthi hurried after Andrija, who was leading both their horses by the reins. Everything here was so close, so covered in soot and dirt, and there were more people passing her on either side than she had ever seen all at once. It seemed there were only so many roads running up the city's spiral, and they were barely wide enough to accommodate a few people shoulder to shoulder, let alone something so luxurious as a carriage. Here and there, Chrysanthi caught sight of little alleys and side streets, but they were built of planked wood, rather than the sturdier stone the main roads could boast, and she could not imagine a scenario in which she set foot on one of her own volition, or one in which she did not get hopelessly lost. There were plenty of signs on every street telling her where she was, but they were incomprehensible, often with some words crossed out or written over.

"Chuzhak and Amolovak," Andrija explained in a hushed voice when they passed a particularly violently edited sign. "You won't find one who can't read the other, but it's the principle."

Ah! Principles. Chrysanthi had heard tell of those.

Andrija led her off to the side soon enough, before they had got too high aboveground. He'd found a small courtyard—a very, very small courtyard—and as she followed him in, he tied their horses to a hitching post that appeared to be only about the length of his hand.

"Perhaps," Chrysanthi said, "we should have left them outside."

Andrija shook his head. "I'd have left them if I thought you could be parted from Lefka."

"She's the best gift my sister's ever given me," Chrysanthi said, immediately defensive, but Andrija apparently had not been needling her, something that she found herself constantly adjusting to. "Where have we stopped anyway?"

"Somewhere to rest for a minute."

"We've barely been awake for an hour."

Chrysanthi caught Andrija's answering eye roll and bit her lip to suppress a smile.

"If we want to find out where your brother has gone," he answered, "we'll need to speak to the people who might know. And I doubt we'll be allowed in to see any of them looking like this."

"Like what?" Finished, Andrija stepped away from the horses, and Chrysanthi hastened after him. "Perfect? Absolutely— No, never mind, actually. I forgot I'm not blond at the moment."

The building just off the little courtyard was an equally small inn, its guest rooms each occupying a single floor. Andrija paid for one with a pouch of Amolovak coin that earned him a skeptical look and a curse or two from the innkeeper, but gold, it seemed, was gold, and soon they were ensconced in a chamber of their own, the walls of which Chrysanthi thought might be held together with beeswax and a wish.

Andrija was still standing by the now-closed door, his ear pressed to it. She looked at him askance as she dropped down onto the narrow bed and felt some hidden knot in her muscles relax.

"Do you really think anybody followed us here?" she asked. "My disguise has gotten very good."

"It's passable."

"And I can't imagine why anybody would come here voluntarily. It's not exactly the lap of luxury." She picked at a loose thread in the bedding. "That said, I will be sleeping in this bed for the next seven hours."

"Are you sure that's wise?" Andrija finally stepped back from the door. "I'm not sure we should spend more than a day or two here, to be safe. No time to waste."

"Rest is not wasted time," she said, swinging her legs idly off the edge of the bed as he set about unpacking their bags with deep, methodical care. "And I don't think you're one to talk."

"You'll thank me for this when your clothes smell less like Lefka tomorrow."

"Maybe, but leave it." She slid off the bed and onto her knees next to him, nudging him out of the way. "I can do it. You packed up this morning. It's only fair."

After a moment, she felt Andrija's body adjust next to hers and then he was standing and taking her spot on the bed. She met his eyes for a moment, amused, before returning to the task, shaking out their spare clothes and setting her paints aside to be put away later in the wardrobe.

"Are you sure you wouldn't rather take a moment here?" she said. "You seem rather comfortable."

He shrugged, flicking a bit of mud off his boots. "You're not in a rush to find your brother?"

"I should be. Only once I do I'm not sure what I'm meant to say to him." It was embarrassing to admit. She had been sent to fetch Nitsos because of her love for him, because of the bond that they'd built together during all those years at Stratathoma. But she knew how to convince him to eat three square meals and how to get him to participate in a conversation—not how to broker a peace neither he nor Rhea seemed to want. "I suppose I need to worry about laying eyes on him first, though."

"Your sister pointed you toward the Navirotsk, yes?" There was a warning in his voice that made Chrysanthi look up, startled.

"Yes," she said. "Is that a bad thing? I mean, I'm sure it's as boring as anything—"

"The library," Andrija interrupted and then waited, as if to offer her the chance to scold him. She did not take it. As much as she usually preferred to be the person talking, even she could admit that she was not the expert here.

"It's protected," he went on. She thought he must be choosing his words very carefully. "It costs quite a lot to gain entrance, and even after that, there are a number of barriers that might stand between us and the information we're after."

"And you don't think they would waive those costs if we simply said we were looking for someone? And not any of their information?"

Andrija's mouth settled into a tight line. Apparently not.

"Well," she said, "what is cost, really? I'm sure I can afford it. I'd even allow you to contribute." She gestured toward his bag. "I know you've got a bit of gold you're hiding away from me. You needn't worry. I only steal from my siblings."

"You're more than welcome to it," Andrija said, but it sounded more like a reflex than anything else. His expression had clouded, and he leaned forward, elbows braced on his knees. "It is not gold, the cost. Still, I would gladly help you pay it. We're not likely to find your brother otherwise."

Chrysanthi was about to ask what the price was, if not gold, but he rose suddenly and went to the door again.

"Regardless," he said, "I think that it's important, still, for you to appear not as yourself. And the Navirotskovai tend to be more welcoming of those who look a bit cleaner than both of us do at the moment."

"I don't know what you're talking about," she said, picking a bit of grass out of her hair.

"There's a bath on the floor above this one. I'll find one of my own in the city."

"You don't want to share my bathwater?"

Andrija shook his head, smiling very slightly. "I'll wait for you by the horses."

He undid the door's flimsy lock and pulled it open, checking the stairwell before looking back at Chrysanthi over his shoulder.

"And be careful, yes?" he said. "We are in no less danger now than we were crossing the Thyzak border."

Chrysanthi shrugged. "At least if I die in this inn I will be clean."

"I would tell you to raise your standards, but I think we both know that for the most part they are already quite high." He paused and then added, "As they should be."

"Indeed." She stood, dreaming of the fresh, hot water that waited for her. "By the horses?"

"By the horses."

Andrija left her then, and Chrysanthi took one last look at the clothes she had taken out of her bags. They were mostly the plain sort, suited for travel, and while she supposed those clothes would do well enough for the library, she had another option: the dress she'd stolen from Rhea before leaving the Sxoriza camp. It was black, diamond patterning stitched across the bodice with black thread. Chrysanthi was very glad its sleeves were long and its fabric was thick; she really hadn't paid enough attention to dressing for the weather when she'd originally packed.

She gathered the dress in her arms, burying her nose in the fabric for a moment. It didn't smell like Rhea anymore, if it ever had. Just of cold, and of something stale. And there were wrinkles in the skirt now that would likely never come out. Rhea would scold her about that when they saw each other next.

That reminded her—she was meant to look for the hummingbird, to send word to Rhea now that they'd arrived in the city. Back at the camp in the Ksigora, Chrysanthi had been desperate to write, desperate to keep her sister close however she could. Now the thought of it left her anxious. She had nothing yet to offer besides news of her own well-being. For once, that did not seem to be the most important thing.

And besides, the hummingbird hadn't even arrived yet. Rhea probably hadn't expected that she and Andrija would make such good time. No, Chrysanthi would write after they visited the Navirotsk.

Despite Andrija's warnings of imminent threat, nobody attacked her while she was in the bath, although she could have used a companion to help her do up the buttons on the back of the dress. Instead, she did as many as she could, and then shook her hair down her back, hoping that would cover the gape of the dress until she could enlist Andrija to help her.

Before leaving, she checked her reflection in the fogged mirrorglass. Her mark had been covered; her hair was dark and hanging loosely about her face; her eyes were a deep brown instead of their proper blue. As different as she looked, she found that she recognized herself quite well.

Outside the air had lost none of its chill. Chrysanthi shivered, wrapping her arms around herself, and continued into the little courtyard toward where Andrija was speaking quietly to Lefka in a conversational tone.

"—a comfortable spot," she heard him saying. "Does it match up to the sort of lodging you're used to? No, I'm sure. That's interesting that you'd— Oh."

"Lefka would prefer it," Chrysanthi said, "if you didn't speak to her in Thyzaki. She's working on her Chuzhak."

"How good of her. What a student."

"Yes, she's very dedicated." Chrysanthi looked Andrija up and down, unable to spot a single difference between this bathed Andrija and the one who had left her an hour ago. "You look exactly the same."

"I changed my clothes."

"Really?"

"Yes," he answered, indignant. "It's just they're another set of the same ones." He fell silent while Chrysanthi laughed, and then he said, "You look . . . not the same."

"You're correct."

"It's nice. The dress."

Chrysanthi smiled brightly. "Thank you. I stole it. Actually, now that you're here, would you mind?" She turned around and swept her hair off the back of her neck. "It's a bit cold with them undone."

Behind her, Andrija made a muffled noise of surprise. It wasn't that there were all that many buttons undone, she supposed, but rather that she had managed to do up an assortment at the top and bottom of the bodice, leaving the middle section flapping in the breeze.

"You can't just—for goodness' sake," Andrija spluttered.

"What was I supposed to do? My arms are only so long."

She heard a slight rustle of fabric, and she glanced over her shoulder in time to see him tugging one of his gloves off with his teeth, brow already furrowed in deep concentration. Chrysanthi smiled; he took everything so seriously.

"Right," Andrija said. She looked quickly away again, fiddling with the ends of her hair. "My hands are cold. Is that—"

"I'll manage."

They both fell silent as he set to work. The small buttons proved troublesome for him at first, but after another moment or two, he said, "There," and awkwardly patted the middle of her back as if she were a horse he had just finished grooming. "Shall we get going, then?"

CHAPTER TWENTY-ONE

CHRYSANTHI

The Navirotsk, Andrija told her as they left the courtyard and ducked back into the crowds, could be entered a number of ways, but most first-time visitors chose the main door, an entrance that apparently was inches away from slipping underwater to join the stories of the building that had once been its first few floors. Personally, she thought everybody in this city would be better off abandoning it in favor of a site that was not sinking slowly into a lake, but these Vashnastaks seemed committed to their current endeavor. Chrysanthi just hoped she got out of here before her room at the inn slipped underwater.

Reaching this entrance required following a side street down to another of the city's main roads, this one spiraling down toward the lake surface. Fewer people were heading in their same direction, and by the time Chrysanthi could see the library's door up ahead, she and Andrija were practically alone on the street. To the left, the city walls were patchwork stone, so solid it seemed impossible that the lake should have snuck through, but it had, of course. The street ended; the lake began, cobblestones disappearing under its surface, and dotted across the water between the street and the library door were a number of floating wooden islands—little barges barely big enough to hold more than one person at a time, and far enough apart that Chrysanthi was not sure she could clear that distance with a single step.

"Excuse me," she said. "Please don't tell me I'm expected to jump."

"I'll help you," Andrija replied. "It's not so bad."

"Have you been here before?"

"To the door. But not beyond."

The door, now that he mentioned it, was imposing, larger even than the doors fitted to Stratathoma, and it was studded and banded with a dark metal, as if to protect against some siege. Ownership of the Vitmar, Chrysanthi reminded herself, had been debated by Chuzha and Amolova for quite a long time, but by the look of the library, designed as if to be a fortress, perhaps that conflict had been going on for longer than anyone knew. Or perhaps something else had happened on these plains, before the lake had swallowed them up.

Andrija began the crossing first, jumping easily to the first island before reaching back for Chrysanthi. She gathered her skirts in one hand and took his offered one with the other. Thank goodness he was so tall, she thought as he guided her forward. Without him, she might have tipped head over heels into the black water below.

The water had risen high enough that only a foot or so of the door's threshold remained dry. When she finally joined Andrija there, she took a moment to straighten her skirts and smooth down her hair. "What now?" she asked. Was there a bell to ring? Someone looking down from a high tower who might see them?

"We knock," Andrija said, and when he did so, it sounded so small compared to the bulk of the fortress that Chrysanthi almost laughed.

Still, it worked; a smaller door, cut into the larger one, opened promptly, and on the other side, a simply dressed young woman was waiting, her eyebrows raised in expectation as she said something in brisk Chuzhak.

Andrija answered before Chrysanthi could even open her mouth, and she would have been miffed if she hadn't heard the word for Thyzaki peppered in. The woman—a Navirotskovai, Chrysanthi remembered Andrija calling these librarians—nodded impatiently and said, "Yes?"

Chrysanthi smiled, happy both to understand and to have an opportunity to deploy her well-honed charm. "Thank you so much for receiving us," she said. "Your city is beautiful. I wonder—"

"What is it you'd like me to do for you?"

Oh. That was a bit abrupt. "We're here to tour your beautiful library."

"I'm afraid that won't be possible," the young woman said. She seemed eager for them to leave, but though Chrysanthi had been expecting a warmer welcome, she was not so easily deterred.

"I have it on good authority that it is, though," she said, inching forward until she was directly in the doorway. Let the librarian try to close the door on them now. "You see, my brother was here, and he told me all about your hospitality."

"Your brother?"

Behind her, Andrija cleared his throat. He'd said it would benefit her to remain in some kind of disguise, but Chrysanthi would do what she had to in order to get into this building. And besides, her experiences with Rhea's old suitors had taught her that her smiles always carried more weight when they came with her name attached.

"Yes," she said. "Nitsos Argyros. Blond, insufferable, about this tall?" For a moment she missed him very terribly. Life was not life without her siblings to make fun of.

The young woman's recognition was instant, with an exhausted sort of annoyance that Chrysanthi remembered from one too many evenings spent calling Nitsos to dinner, only for him to arrive well after the meal had gone cold.

"Right," she said. "I know who you should speak to. Come in."

Chrysanthi followed her into the library's entryway, Andrija at her back. The room waiting for them was in fact not a room, but a landing on a narrow, shadowed staircase. The flight going down was filled with water, which Chrysanthi supposed she should learn to expect in this building. The flight up, meanwhile, was still dry and layered with straw, but steep enough that she couldn't see the floor it seemed to open onto.

"Lovely," she said. "Have you thought about decorating?"

Andrija's elbow connected gently with her ribs, and fine, she would try to be a little less herself, but it really was a horribly dank sort of place. The air smelled of mildew and echoed with the sound of water droplets falling. Hopefully anybody working in the library got plenty of chances to leave, or at least enough visitors to keep things interesting (although given the reception Chrysanthi and Andrija had received so far, that didn't seem likely).

Once Andrija had surrendered his weapons, the librarian led the way upstairs, and as they climbed, the light ahead grew stronger—not warm and flickering, like candlelight, but the sharp, pale glow of a winter sun. This, Chrysanthi found particularly odd, given that the sun, when it bothered to appear, had been so weak all day, but she was not about to second-guess a bit of good weather.

"You said there's someone we can speak to?" she asked as they neared the top of the staircase.

"There is."

She shared a quizzical look with Andrija. Rhea hadn't known of anybody traveling with Nitsos, and Chrysanthi couldn't think of anyone he had willingly spent time with besides herself. But then they emerged onto the next floor, and she stopped thinking about Nitsos at all.

It was a large, open hall, dominated by two long tables that had perhaps once been made of wood and were now so patched with iron that they looked entirely black. Off to Chrysanthi's left, the staircase they had climbed continued around to another flight upward, and she could spot a matching one on the other side of the hall, but doing so required picking it out through the haze of winter light that filled the air, tumbling down through the great hole in the ceiling.

Well, that was probably not the technical term, she thought, but as the librarian led them to one of the tables, she couldn't quite find anything better to describe what she was looking at. It cut through the center of the roof and continued up, up, maybe hundreds of feet into the air, tunneling through structure after structure until it reached the sky. From top to bottom, little spots of light were mounted—mirrors,

Chrysanthi realized, capturing the light from the city's surface and carrying it down to this hall. Now that she knew what to look for, she could spot where beams were redirected, split, sent slicing off through the dark into other rooms.

"Wait here," the librarian said, gesturing to a haphazard collection of chairs at the nearest table that looked as though they'd each been recovered from a different building. "She'll be here shortly."

"She?"

But the librarian had already left. Chrysanthi sighed and chose the most comfortable of the available chairs to slump down in. Andrija sat next to her, his posture stiff and eyes darting as he took in their surroundings. For all that this had been his suggestion, he seemed quite eager to leave.

"So," she said, hoping she could get him to relax even the slightest bit. "Where are all the books?"

"Other floors, I assume."

"I suppose to see them we'd have to pay that cost you were talking about."

Andrija's expression turned grim. "I suppose we would."

"Who do you think we'll be speaking to?" Chrysanthi leaned her elbows on the table before quickly recoiling. The metal was absolutely freezing. "I'd offer some theories of my own, but really I didn't think Nitsos knew anybody."

"No?" This drew Andrija's attention, pulling his gaze at last away from the empty space around them and back to her face, which is where every gaze, she thought, should always be.

"Well, no, of course not. He never left Stratathoma." She leaned back in her chair, thinking over everyone they'd ever had stay with them during Baba's rule. It was, as expected, a very short list. "I mean, neither did I, but I was much more popular with our visitors."

"Of course you were," Andrija said, and she confirmed with a look that he was not teasing her.

"It really wasn't so lonely," she insisted. "Rhea would tell me about the places she'd been, and all the friends she made. And Lexos . . . I suppose he had friends, too, but I never heard." She fell into silence.

It was strange to talk about them like this, as something separate from her life. Sometimes she wondered if she would ever, in fact, see them again, and sometimes she was convinced that if she only turned around, they would be there, Rhea and Lexos and Nitsos, waiting for her to finish whatever she was doing so they might all go home together.

"Chrysanthi?" Andrija said softly. She startled and blinked furiously just in case she was about to cry.

"Yes," she said. "Anyway. I hate it here."

He snorted, shaking his head, and Chrysanthi was intensely gratified when he began to smile.

Footsteps sounded from the staircase on the opposite side of the hall, breaking the little peace between them. She rose from her chair, shaking her hair back and readying herself to make a better impression this time than she'd made on the librarian.

A woman approached them, her gait even and purposeful. She was dressed in the same sort of clothes the worker had been wearing, but something about the way she held herself told Chrysanthi that she was used to much finer fabric. Her brown skin caught the light carried down from the surface, and her black hair was braided in rows, each one threaded through with silver and gold. All in all, she looked like the sort of person Chrysanthi might have tried to flirt with, had she shown up at Stratathoma as one of Rhea's suitors. And really, Chrysanthi still might now if it looked like it would help.

"You're the ones who asked about Nitsos?" the woman said in impeccable Thyzaki as she approached.

Chrysanthi nodded. "My brother, yes."

"Your brother." The woman stopped across the table from them. She seemed to consider sitting down before folding her arms across her chest and remaining right where she was. "I've met Rhea before. That makes you Chrysanthi?"

"It does."

"He said you were blond."

"I am." She lifted her marked hand reflexively before remembering she'd covered it up. "I can prove it to you, but it might take a minute and some water." She grimaced. "I suppose you have no shortage of that here."

"Quite." The woman stared at her for another moment and then nodded. "It's good to meet you. I'm Stavra."

Chrysanthi had heard Stavra's name before on a number of occasions, most of which involved her walking past Baba's slightly open study door in time to hear Lexos updating their father on his latest trip, or preparing for the next meeting of the Stratagiozi Council. Once or twice, Lexos had mentioned her during a conversation over a cup of kaf in the kitchen, the house quiet, the evening late. There had been a fondness in him then that Chrysanthi was unfamiliar with, one that carried none of the exasperation and expectation that she knew her brother felt for his siblings, and that she could hear, sometimes, in her own voice.

What was it, she had wondered, to know people who were not your own blood? To value someone only because you chose to? It had seemed such a bizarre thing to her then. Three months away from Stratathoma had changed that, but still, there was nothing, Chrysanthi thought, nothing like hearing news of her siblings. Nitsos, alive and possibly well even outside the care she'd provided for so long, and thinking of her enough to discuss her with Stavra. It was more than she'd hoped for.

"How is he?" she asked as Stavra gestured for them all to take their seats. "How much did you see of him?"

Stavra met her eyes, seeming to acknowledge her questions, but turned then to Andrija. "And you are?"

"Andrija Tomic." He sounded composed, as stoic as ever, but Chrysanthi could still feel the tension coming off him. Didn't he realize they could relax now? Stavra was a friend.

"Andrija," Stavra said, tilting her head to one side. "That's an Amolovak name, no?"

He shrugged. "It depends who you ask. Amolovak in Amolova. Chuzhak in Chuzha."

"You hear that sort of thing quite a lot in the Vitmar," Stavra replied, "although you don't often hear a Thyzak accent that good on an Amolovak." She returned to Chrysanthi. "Where did you find him?"

"He's a friend of my sister's," Chrysanthi said, which was technically true. "Look, about Nitsos—"

"Let me interrupt. Your brother isn't here."

It wasn't as though Chrysanthi had expected to walk into the Navirotsk and discover Nitsos waiting for her, but still, that was a bit of a disappointment. "Do you know where he went?" she asked. "It's important I find him as soon as possible."

"I'm sure it is," Stavra said, "but I don't know where he traveled after leaving here."

She did not sound as though she was lying, Chrysanthi thought. Still, her family never had, either. "I'm here on an errand," she said. "My sister's, if she asks, but one of my own, too." Andrija made a small noise behind her; she ignored him and went on. "Do you have siblings?"

The corner of Stavra's mouth ticked up ever so slightly. "No, I don't."

"But you know mine. All of mine, actually." Chrysanthi lowered her voice conspiratorially. "You must have seen how hopeless they are alone."

"Some more than others."

Chrysanthi knew without a doubt she was thinking of Lexos. "I'm only trying to bring them all back together. To me. We've lost our father—"

"Lexos," Stavra cut in, "lost you your father."

"Which is why he needs me. Please," Chrysanthi said. "Please help me find my family."

For a long moment it looked as though Stavra had not been moved. Finally, though, she glanced over her shoulder and then leaned in. "He left this behind in his room. They found it under the bedclothes. Hidden, I think, although why he would need to, I'm not sure."

From her pocket, she pulled out a small scrap of paper and passed it across the table. Chrysanthi grabbed for it eagerly. The edges were torn, and the charcoal lines on its surface were faint, but she recognized it immediately: one of his sketches. If he had left it behind, it couldn't have been very important to him; still it was all she had to follow him by.

This sketch was of an insect—a butterfly, now that Chrysanthi had got a better look at it. Most of the body Nitsos had left somewhat to the imagination, but he had taken great care with the shape of the wing and with the markings intended to decorate it, which would be patterned in silver and blue. The sketch was also accompanied by a few words, written in the shorthand of his she'd learned to read long ago: *beaten glass*, read one note, while another specified that Nitsos wanted to use the green of the underside of a leaf in the sunlight.

That, Chrysanthi thought numbly, was the sort of language she used. It was how she had spoken to him so many times, describing the color she was mixing as he followed her about the grounds on a break from his work in the attic. The silver and blue markings on the butterfly even reminded her of the snowflakes she had painted for him.

But she would have seen the sketch for what it was without any of that, would have remembered standing in his clockwork garden one deep summer evening and watching a real butterfly flit past, only for Nitsos to say: "Do you like those? I'll build one for you someday."

And now he was planning to, in a way she had never expected. This—this was hers. As the hummingbird was Rhea's, this little creature was meant to be hers.

Chrysanthi felt her stomach turn. She had known, of course, what Nitsos was capable of. But seeing it here, seeing it meant for her—that was something different. She'd told herself everything would change now that they were away from Stratathoma and their father, but it hadn't. Nitsos was no different from Baba, was he? Were any of them?

"Does it mean anything to you?" Stavra asked. "Nobody could make any sense of it."

If that was true, Chrysanthi had got very, very lucky. She forced herself to smile as she folded up the sketch and slipped it into her own pocket. "Just an idle drawing, I'm afraid. He used to leave these everywhere at home."

Stavra met her eyes, unblinking. For a moment, Chrysanthi could hear her own heartbeat, loud as thunder.

"Too bad," Stavra said at last. "I was hoping I'd be able to help."

"You still can," Chrysanthi said. She could not let Nitsos's trail go cold, not if he really meant to keep on building creatures like Rhea's. What would he do with her under his thumb? With Lexos? And how far would it widen the gulf that existed between him and the rest of his siblings? If she did not find him—and fast—she would never get her family back under one roof.

"You could show me what he came here for," she went on. "I know this place is meant to be very secret and very strict, except I'm already here, and I can't imagine it would be all that much trouble for me to take a little look."

"You can't?" Andrija muttered. "I can."

A flash of discomfort crossed Stavra's face. "The materials he was accessing are not open to the public."

"Oh, don't worry." Chrysanthi smiled. "I'm not the public. I'm Chrysanthi Argyros."

Stavra let out a small laugh, which Chrysanthi thought was rude, as she hadn't been joking. "It really is impossible. The topic alone is more than I can share with you; a word to the wrong person and you could end up like Lexos."

"It's all right. I know about it already." Chrysanthi did not, in fact, but she had a quarter of an idea and just enough bravery (idiocy, she could hear Rhea saying fondly) to speak anyway. "The saints and their graves," she said. "Has my brother gone to find them?"

"No," Stavra answered, but the widening of her eyes told Chrysanthi enough. She was right about Nitsos—and possibly Ammar and Nastia.

Behind her, Andrija's chair scraped against the stone floor, and she caught the shape of him out of the corner of her eye as he began to pace. Was that surprise in his expression? Or disbelief? She remembered how skeptical he'd been when she'd asked about it outside Vashnasta; presumably this was sitting about as well with him as a night in the woods generally did with her.

Which wasn't to say she was enjoying this. There were a number of things about it that set a headache pulsing at Chrysanthi's temples, not the least of which was the fact that following Nitsos to these graves might mean she would have to lay eyes on another dead body. The most difficult of them all to grapple with, though, was that somehow her brother had gone from being a perennial, albeit beloved, nuisance to being someone deeply entangled in the affairs of the continent. She wanted to gather all these Stratagiozis in a room and ask: This is Nitsos, right? We're all talking about the same boy?

"Look," she said, allowing some of her weariness to show through, "Nitsos is single-minded about these things. He would not have left here if he hadn't found something to go on, something to indicate where to find these graves. Is there anyone you can introduce me to? Anyone who can show me what he was researching? I need to know where he's headed."

"You're not the only one," Stavra said, looking a bit annoyed. For a moment, Chrysanthi wondered just how Stavra and her brother had become connected. She had assumed, she realized, that Nitsos had met Stavra through Lexos, but that hardly made any sense. More likely, Nitsos was here on somebody's orders, and Stavra was here on the same. Zita Devetsi, then—Stavra's mother and another Stratagiozi Chrysanthi would need to add to that gathering she'd imagined. "But your brother was using library materials, so what he was looking into won't be available to you unless you'd like to request access."

"I would," Chrysanthi said eagerly. She could decide what to do with him once she got her hands on him. "What do you need from me?"

Stavra's expression softened, and when she opened her mouth next, Chrysanthi caught a flash of something black on her tongue. Was that—no. Stavra was a second. She was not a Stratagiozi; she did not have a matagios. It had to be nothing, just a trick of the light.

"The library does require something in exchange," Stavra said. "Specifically, a person."

Chrysanthi waited for her to continue; she did not. "What sort of person?"

"Any sort, really. You receive access to the bulk of the library's materials, and the library receives a . . . 'guest,' is the word they use. 'Hostage' might be more appropriate." Stavra's mouth twisted with distaste, a flicker of anger lighting in her eyes. "Your provided guest must be a willing one, but that seems to be their only stipulation."

"And for how long does the library expect to play host?" Stavra didn't answer, but her distaste seemed to deepen. Chrysanthi understood and shot a sharp look at Andrija, who had stopped pacing and was watching her, one hand hovering over the empty space where the hilt of his sword usually was. "This is what you were talking about, then?"

"It is."

"But you said it was something you would do. You can't have meant—"

"I said what I meant." Andrija tilted his head. "I most always do."

"Well," Chrysanthi said. "Good for you, then." She could hear the tightness in her own voice, bordering on anger, and it surprised her—confused her, even—but this was not the time to pick all that apart. She swallowed it down and tried to smile just as she thought Rhea would have done in her shoes. Rhea always knew how to make an uncomfortable situation a little bit easier to bear.

"Stavra," she said, "would you mind giving us a moment to discuss? I hope it isn't rude of me to ask, but—"

"There's no need to explain." Stavra stood up. She seemed, if anything, relieved to have been given a reason to leave. "I'll wait for you in the stairwell."

Chrysanthi stood as well, craning her neck to keep an eye on Stavra as the other woman made for the exit. Andrija, meanwhile, had sat back down, his forearms braced on his knees, and was waiting patiently for her. He could keep waiting, she thought. Why hadn't he just told her what the Navirotsk would require from the beginning?

She spent another moment watching the doorway Stavra had disappeared through before wandering away from the table to get a better look at the hall they were in—really anything to keep from having to sit down and speak to Andrija. She did not like being openly angry with people, and she did not have very much practice at it, especially not over things that mattered. But it quickly became very clear that the room had nothing more to offer, so she perched on the edge of the table next to Andrija, folded her arms across her chest, and said, "Would you like to explain yourself?"

His eyebrows flicked up momentarily. "About what?"

"You knew—"

"I told you the truth," he said, and yes, that was correct, but it was not everything. Being Baba's daughter had taught her that. "Certainly I hoped we would be able to find your brother without the help of the Navirotskovai, but we need them. So we'll do what we must."

"It's not 'we' that you're talking about, though."

"No," he admitted easily. "It isn't."

"Then how . . . I don't know why we're discussing this as if it were a serious option. I'm not allowing you to volunteer yourself as a hostage. We don't even know what that means."

The corner of Andrija's mouth twitched. Chrysanthi sighed.

"Oh," she said, "I suppose you do know what it means." Was this another of those things that everybody learned at some point? Everybody except Vasilis Argyros's children, kept ignorant behind Stratathoma's walls.

"It's part of an old tradition," Andrija said. "Before the saints— even during—powerful families would exchange children in infancy. A trade, to ensure those families remained allies. The Navirotsk still trades like that, only it has no children to offer. Just the materials and knowledge it protects."

She didn't care about the practice's origin; she cared more about whether Andrija meant to never see her again. "Can they ever leave? These hostages?"

"No, not while the agreement stands," he said, looking a little amused. "Otherwise it wouldn't—"

"Yes, I see. And you would do this . . . why?"

"I was told to help you find your brother."

"If you knew him, you wouldn't think that was a very good reason."

She squeezed her eyes shut and took a long breath. It was hard enough trying to decide whether Nitsos was worth her own life, never mind someone else's.

He'd had no trouble making that decision, though, had he? Someone had paid this price for him and he was gone, happy to leave it in his wake.

"Stavra is one of these hostages," she said. Stavra's aversion when describing the situation had been too personal for things to be otherwise. The only real question was who had nominated her: Nitsos himself or Zita Devetsi. Dispensing with one's own child seemed a very Stratagiozi thing to do, but Chrysanthi still found that a hard possibility to swallow. That, she supposed, was the fault of her own love for Baba, and his for her.

"She is. And she seems well enough."

"And these other librarians? The people who work here?"

"Mostly volunteers, I would guess," Andrija said. "Many consider it an honor to serve the Navirotsk."

"An honor." She scoffed. "If it's such an honor, why do they need to take hostages at all?"

Andrija leaned back his chair and looked up at her. A lock of his hair was in his eyes; she moved it aside without a second thought, her thumbnail nudging his eyebrow. "I'll be fine, you know."

"That's not my concern. You would be here forever."

"My forever is not your forever."

"Anybody's forever is a long time, all right?" She did not know how he managed to stay so level all the time. The slightest needling could make her snappish, as it was now. "I've seen people give up their lives before. I won't require that from you."

Andrija's brow furrowed very slightly, and she wondered what he thought she was talking about—death, maybe, as had happened to the guard at the Thyzak border. But in her head, there was Rhea's portrait, and there were the nameless consorts she had chosen season after season. Another great honor; another set of people traded in for something else. Chrysanthi had always wondered about the months Rhea's consorts had lived before their deaths, knowing what was coming, when it was coming, and being unable to do anything about it.

"Chrysanthi," Andrija said. His voice was so low; she could practically feel the shape of his words in her own chest. "You are not requiring it. That's the whole point."

He stood up slowly, maneuvering around her and toward the doorway Stavra had gone through. Chrysanthi watched him. Now, now was the time to stop him, to pull him back from this cliff he was ready to walk off for her, but she found she could only stand there and listen to him call to Stavra. How many times had she watched Rhea leave in a carriage, sat alongside a consort who would be dead before the season was out? That had been how things were supposed to go. And maybe this was, too, but it was fast becoming more than Chrysanthi thought she could bear.

As it happened, the process was very simple. Andrija spoke to Stavra quietly in the stairwell, and a few moments later she was coming back into the hall and saying, "Right, come with me, then."

Andrija, though, was nowhere to be seen. Chrysanthi stood rooted to the spot, a franticness beginning to take hold of her as Stavra gestured toward a doorway in the far corner.

"Wait," Chrysanthi said, "where has he gone? You can't just— He—"

"He'll be back," Stavra said calmly.

"I wouldn't have let him go if I knew he was just going to disappear!"

She took hold of Chrysanthi's elbow, pulling her forward toward the door. "I'm not sure that's true."

Chrysanthi felt the sting of it rip through her. It was deserved, she thought, but not just by her. "Will he be safe?" she asked. "Wherever he's gone?"

"Yes," Stavra said, and her expression softened. "The induction . . . it's not comfortable, but it's safe. Now why don't you come with me and make it worth it?"

Chrysanthi cast one last look over her shoulder at the empty doorway she'd seen Andrija disappear through and then hurried on after

Stavra. She was right. If Andrija was going to make this sacrifice, she had to make good use of it.

Which meant—

"Wait," she said. "Stavra, wait. Where are we going?"

"To one of the researchers," Stavra said slowly, as if it was obvious, which Chrysanthi belatedly realized it was. "Just as you asked. Why?"

"Because I think I'd like to see something else." Stavra made a noise of disbelief that seemed involuntary. Chrysanthi ignored it. "I'm sure Nitsos read some ancient text and drew a map in the stars or in the dirt or in some other substance he discovered himself. Why shouldn't he? He's built for that sort of thing."

"And you're not?"

"I absolutely am not." Briefly, she considered charming a Navirotskovai and hoping she could wheedle some information out of them, but the workers seemed, as a batch, immune to that sort of thing. And there were other things she was good at. "I don't suppose the library has a gallery, do they?"

"A gallery? I think so. At the very least there are some paintings in storage, if not hung up. I haven't explored that part of the library yet." Stavra frowned. "And I should warn you that I'm very sure Nitsos never did, either."

"That hardly matters." Chrysanthi nodded to the door ahead of them. "Is it this way still?"

They continued down into the Navirotsk, following small hallways and narrow staircases that grew darker and damper the more they descended. Only occasionally did they pass other librarians (or, she supposed, hostages), but each one was a welcome reminder that this building was in fact inhabited and that Chrysanthi had not somehow slipped off the face of the continent into some sort of dream. The air smelled like wet earth down here, but every so often a breeze carried the scent of food and refuse down from the streets. Sometimes, too, she could hear voices, people climbing in every direction, living packed in beside one another, while here in the library, space enough for hundreds more was going unused.

"How many hostages is this place home to at the moment?" she asked. One more, at least, now that Andrija was here. But she would find some way to get him out of whatever contract he'd entered, for his sake and for hers.

"Not many," Stavra replied before directing them down another hallway, this one lit by torches in addition to the remnants of light that the building's mirror system carried this far. "The practice fell out of favor before our time."

"But you're here." Chrysanthi knew very well why, but she needed to hear Stavra say it. Hopefully it would be followed by some explanation, some hint that Nitsos had not let it happen as easily as she feared he might have.

"I am," Stavra said. "I do what my Ordukamat tells me."

So it had been Zita, then, asking quite a lot of her child, as seemed to be the Stratagiozi way. Chrysanthi could only assume Zita had her own reasons, was moving Nitsos about in her own game of Soldier's Teeth, but that still left the plain fact that Stavra was here, and would be here. For Nitsos, of all people. Chrysanthi was not sure she would ever really understand that.

"Your Ordukamat," she said. "Don't you mean your mother?"

Stavra sighed and quickened her pace until she was a bit ahead of Chrysanthi. "You Argyrosi," she said over her shoulder. "It's always parents with you."

"What makes you say that?" Chrysanthi's heart felt strange in her chest, too quick and too heavy. Did Stavra know what Rhea had told her that first night away from Stratathoma—that their mother, Irini, had been a saint herself? She could not think how that would have happened.

And thankfully, Stavra did not appear to react oddly. "I suppose I should say fathers. That's always been Lexos's preoccupation. How is he anyway? Have you heard news of him?"

"Not lately. The last I heard he was under the care of the Dominas." Before arriving here, using that euphemism had felt comforting. Now, with Andrija under the library's care in much the same way, the words tasted rotten.

"That's what I've heard, too," Stavra said, nodding. "I hope he's well. Will you tell him so, if you see him?"

Chrysanthi could think of a few things she would need to tell him first, but certainly she could add that to the list.

"Anyway," Stavra said as they approached another door, "it's just in here."

The room she led Chrysanthi into looked much like the large opening in that first hall that had let in the sky. Broad, and circular, and reaching for hundreds of feet overhead to a ceiling Chrysanthi could not even see. The walls were hung with paintings, frames almost overlapping in places for lack of space. Landscapes, portraits, all mixed together without much apparent thought for organization. Chrysanthi felt her fingers twitch; she'd never seen so much art in one place. Everything she knew about painting she'd taught herself, and she wished desperately that she were here under different circumstances.

She followed Stavra out onto a latticework of iron that comprised the floor. She risked a look down, worried she would see another hundred feet of emptiness below her, but of course there wasn't. There was only water, inches from lapping at the iron grid floor. If she looked very closely, she could see the shape of submerged ladders and shelves below. This room had once been much taller, much deeper, until the lake had taken it.

Stavra went to a lever near the side of the floor and said, "Just a moment," before pulling it. With a jerk, the floor began to rise. Chrysanthi let out a small shriek.

"Must we?" she asked, feeling a bit faint.

Stavra smiled sympathetically. "It's unusual, but you do get used to it."

Chrysanthi fell silent, watching as the walls slipped by. "I know my brother didn't apologize," she said finally, "so let me. Nitsos should never have expected you to make this sacrifice for him."

"He didn't," Stavra said. "My Ordukamat did."

Right. Chrysanthi gave herself a little shake. Nitsos sat at the front of her mind, but not so for everyone. Even Andrija was probably think-

ing of the Sxoriza and the state of the federation before he thought of
her family.

"I suppose what Nitsos is looking for must be important," she said,
and Stavra nodded. "But I don't understand why anybody cares about
finding those graves. It'll just be a pit full of old bones by now."

"With any luck, you're right."

Chrysanthi gaped at Stavra. That the saints had been buried at all
was shocking enough; she could not begin to imagine what someone
would want with their remains now.

The grind of metal resonated in the emptiness as the iron platform
continued to rise, the sound rattling down Chrysanthi's spine. She
looked for Andrija, about to pull a face to complain, but of course he
wasn't there.

"You said Andrija would be back," she called to Stavra. "When?
Soon?"

"Soon enough. Although he may be somewhat less talkative."

Confused, Chrysanthi tilted her head, but could not keep from saying, "I'm really not sure that's possible."

As they continued to rise through the tower, she found herself
drawn toward the center of the platform, turning slowly in place so as
not to miss anything. The archived paintings were an odd assortment;
Chrysanthi could not tell by what criteria they had been selected. Some
looked to have been done by the same hand, while others had been
damaged so severely by the library's flooding that they did not appear
to have been painted by any hand at all.

"Do you think," she said to Stavra as they rose through the tower,
"that there are any from around the time of the death of the saints?"

"I'd imagine so," Stavra replied. "Although I couldn't say whether
they're displayed here or whether—"

"Wait," Chrysanthi interrupted. "Wait, there. Pull the lever, will
you?"

Stavra did, and the iron grid slowed before jerking to a stop. Chrysanthi moved toward the edge, still wary of falling even though the
grid ran nearly flush with the wall. There was a painting hanging just

above eye level that looked older than the others, judging from the way the paint had cracked and flaked.

"What is it?" Stavra asked.

"A painting," Chrysanthi said, because it was easier to make fun than admit she wasn't sure. The painting's apparent age alone made it worth a second look, but there was something else about it, something more difficult to name.

As she got closer, its subject became clearer. It looked like the base of a mountain, or some stone formation, set in a green valley with a river visible in the background. The sky was striated with pink and blue, a gold wash right at the horizon—dawn, Chrysanthi thought. The painter had diffused the light, found small spots in the greenery to brighten with sun, and even in the river, which could not have been wider than her little finger, there was a sense of motion, of flicker and ripple.

It was familiar, she realized; that was what had drawn her in. She would have painted it just the same, recognized the same silhouettes and guided her brush through the same strokes. A Stratagiozi, or their child, had painted this, and used the very same gift she carried in the palm of her marked hand.

"Are there records kept of each artist?" she asked without looking away from the wall.

"Beyond what signature is on the painting itself, I'm not sure. I would imagine there was a record somewhere, once, but it may be inaccessible."

Chrysanthi pulled her eyes away from the painting for long enough to consider the water some fifty feet beneath them. How much of the continent's history had been obliterated by the lake? And how had the Navirotskovai let it happen? Space in Vashnasta was limited, she knew, and saving the archived work would require displacing something else, but it felt criminal to stand there on the iron grid with centuries of art drowning below.

"Let's hope this one is signed, then," she said. She took another step closer to the painting and the grid beneath her creaked dangerously; she couldn't see the mechanism it was hanging from somewhere high above, and that was probably for the best given how dilapidated things appeared to be in the library.

"Why that one in particular?" Stavra asked.

But Chrysanthi could barely spare any attention to listen to her. She was entirely focused on the painting, searching the corners for some set of brushstrokes that might be out of place. She'd thought that as she approached the scale of the painting would reveal itself to her—the frame massive from edge to edge, the stone mountain contained within its borders as tall as Chrysanthi herself. But no: It was as small as it had looked from the other side of the grid, an oddity among the other paintings hung on the wall. And there, tucked neatly in the lower right corner, was a bit of writing, inked in gold with a finer point than any of the other brushstrokes.

"Stavra," she said, "can you read that signature? I don't know its alphabet very well."

"It's old Trefza. Under all the flourishes anyway." There was a pause and then Stavra cleared her throat. "I only see a few letters. I think, transliterated, it would be L and D."

A Stratagiozi who had once held her own gift, with those initials? There was only one candidate.

"You asked me why this one," she said. "Because Luco Domina painted it. That's why."

"No, he didn't."

"But you said L and D." Chrysanthi reached for the signature, stopping just short of touching it.

"Some artist has the same initials." Stavra shrugged. "I imagine it's happened a few hundred times over the last thousand years."

"I'm sure you're right, but it isn't just that." How could she explain about the light, about what it meant to recognize in someone else's art the work she'd spent a hundred years learning to do? She would have tried to relate it to Stavra's own gift, but she didn't know what that was, and it felt rude to ask. "Here," she said instead, pointing to the bottom of the frame where something was written in a language she did not recognize. "Can you read this?"

Stavra came to stand next to her and leaned in, squinting. "Sort of. It's Trefza, but . . . archaic, I suppose would be the word for it. Like the letters in the signature. Not Trefza as it's spoken now."

"Trefza as it might have been spoken a thousand years ago? By Luco Domina?"

Stavra smiled gently, shaking her head. "Perhaps. In any event, I think the best translation would be that it says, 'Rest.'"

"Rest?" From its placement on the frame, Chrysanthi supposed that it was meant to be the work's title. And yes, the scene certainly looked peaceful enough, but was that what the first of the Stratagiozis had meant? Or was it something more?

Nitsos had gone looking for the saints' graves. He'd read his books and consulted his maps and found something to send him hurrying out of the library. But if history was to be believed, Luco had been the one to kill those saints. Why shouldn't he have been the one to bury them? To lay them, as had been the custom at the time, to rest?

"Stavra," Chrysanthi said, "where do you think this is?"

"What do you mean?"

"The mountain and the river. I don't know where that is. Do you recognize it?" There came no immediate answer, and when Chrysanthi turned to see why, Stavra was looking at her in dumbfounded silence. "What?"

"That's not a mountain. It's a rock."

"I mean, yes, but—"

"It's the base of the spire." Stavra frowned, incredulous. "Have you really never been to Agiokon?"

CHAPTER TWENTY-TWO

RHEA

She and Falka decided to meet within the city limits, and while at the time of planning it had seemed like a ridiculous risk to take, now, as Rhea sat in the back of a farmer's cart clattering toward Rhokera, it seemed the only possible option. Meeting outside Rhokera would have found her and Falka standing out in the open on one of the vast, dry plains that surrounded the city, and all of Rhea's insistence on secrecy would have been for nothing.

Still, there was something that went against instinct about this. The cart was getting closer to Rhokera's main gate with every minute, and over that gate hung the Domina banner. If one of Tarro's guards caught her here, she would soon be joining her brother as their prisoner. But Falka had guaranteed that she would protect Rhea while she was here, and as unwise as it was to take something like that on faith, being wise had never got Rhea anywhere before.

"Are you sure about this?" a voice said, low in her ear, and she sighed.

Michali. She'd been unable to convince him to stay behind with the

Sxoriza caravan, camped some twenty miles outside of the city, hidden where the forest continued down onto the plains. The council of advisors had some destination in mind—whether it was Rhokera proper or somewhere else, Rhea didn't know, but she had stopped pretending that she might ever get a real answer out of any of them. Wherever they did end up, the council would ask her to stand at the head of the camp and accept worship, and she would do it, but until then, her time was her own as far as she was concerned. Or rather, hers and Michali's.

"Yes, I'm sure," she said. She and Michali were both dressed in the dustiest, most ragged clothing they could find (the camp had quite a selection available), and Rhea thought she looked unremarkable, but more importantly unidentifiable, like this. Anybody looking for her would be looking for a Stratagiozi's daughter, for a saint come back to life. Right now she looked more like a farmer inches from death.

"But what makes you think you can trust this woman?" Michali inched closer to her. "Give me a real reason. Not this nonsense about 'one daughter to another.'"

"That's what it is, though." She couldn't explain it any better. Falka was a Stratagiozi's daughter—she knew what it was to see your father consumed by something other than yourself, and she knew, too, what it was to search for your own power in whatever your father had cast off. Her offer had been genuine up there in the mountains that day; Rhea truly believed that. And she believed it, too, that Falka would protect her, would get her in and out of the city safely.

That said, she had been very careful not to let Michali hear Falka's name. As far as he knew, Rhea was here to meet some lesser Domina, and not Falka. Falka, who had been a Sxoriza operative until she'd betrayed them that day at Stratathoma. Rhea could picture it, how incensed Michali would be if he found out who she planned to see.

Or maybe he wouldn't mind at all. Maybe she was thinking of the Michali she had met and married. This one, the one she'd raised from the earth, seemed content to take her at her word and, rather than asking questions, only reached for her hand. She sighed and let him take it.

The farmer whose cart they had ridden in on left them outside the gate, and among a crowd of other people they passed through it, shoulder to shoulder with a collection of families that, judging by their clothes, had come up to Rhokera from the southernmost reaches of Thyzakos. There were a number of habitable islands a ways out from Rhokera harbor still considered to be within the state's borders, but Rhea's scouts had told her that supplies out there were running thin and had been for the last few decades of Baba's rule. They had never been wealthy, never drawn Baba's attention as someplace he could exploit; accordingly she had never married anyone from the islands, and if she was honest, she wasn't sure her father's many maps of Thyzakos had included them. She could not be surprised or even angry now that many islanders had come north to the mainland, drawn by the promise of food and work under the new Domina rule.

Evidence of that rule was everywhere. Not just in the banner that hung over the gate, but in the partial veils she could spot on more than a handful of passersby, and in the snatches of Trefza she could hear as she led Michali through the first square. The Speros family, who had been stewards under Baba, was still in charge; from what she'd heard, they'd been all too happy to cooperate with (and benefit from) the Dominas. But their influence had clearly weakened, and Rhea wondered what someone passing by would say if she asked them what state they lived in now.

Falka had told Rhea to steer clear of the Speros compound and make for the harbor. Luckily, Rhea had been to Rhokera a number of times in her old role as Thyspira, and she knew the way. Instead of following the main thoroughfare right to the water, she kept herself and Michali to the side streets—nothing wider than two men, and most of them simply staircases leading down the hillside that helped shield the natural harbor below.

It was summer-warm here—even Rhea's deepest winter could do little to change that—and all around, leaning out of windows overhead or sidling by on the pebble-paved street, people were dressed in simple, loose garments, their tanned arms bare to the sun. She felt silly, dressed as warmly as she was, and more than that she was beginning to sweat. It would be mortifying if Falka saw her like this.

With a furtive glance around her, she ducked into a little alleyway and pulled her hood down. Immediately, Michali's hand closed around her wrist.

"What are you doing?" He was sweating, too, his face alarmingly pale, but his hood was still drawn up despite the heat.

"It's fine," she said. "Nobody here is giving us a second glance."

"They might now." He brushed his thumb along her cheek, her lips. "They'll recognize you, *kora*."

"I don't think they will," she said, hoping her voice still sounded fond. "Nobody knows my face as well as you do these days."

They continued on down the steps, past a woman selling woven belts out of her kitchen window and past a tiered courtyard where a kafenio had been set up, little tables and chairs playing host to collections of people drinking kaf, sugared and frothed and poured over Ksigoran ice.

Would Falka be waiting for her at one of these tables down by the water? Would they sit and talk as Rhea had not allowed them to in the woods? Certainly not if Rhea showed up with Michali a few feet behind her. She'd planned to lose him at some point after getting through the gate, but they weren't far from where the hill began its steepest drop, and there he was at her elbow, as he always was.

Be kind, she reminded herself. He loves you.

She had been so staggeringly grateful for that love a season ago. She had held it tight to her chest, trusted it to keep her afloat on strange new waters—to do more than that, in fact. And when it hadn't, when she had found herself kept out of another room, staring at the backs of people she was meant to stand alongside, it had felt like Michali's fault. Without him, she wouldn't have been here in the first place.

A twinge in her right palm pulled her focus away from Michali. The scar there, a match to the mark she still bore on her left hand, had broken open at one end some days ago, the skin around it flaking and peeling. It had not yet begun to bleed, and with any luck it wouldn't pick today to start. Still, just in case, she'd bandaged it, too, both of her palms now covered in plain linen. Unlike most of Michali's suggested precautions, this one she'd thought was a good idea.

"Remind me," she said, waving him forward. She preferred when he walked next to her, rather than a step behind. "You've never been this far south, right?"

His answer was a stern look—a simple farmer from the outskirts of Rhokera certainly had been this far south before—but finally he relented and shook his head. "No, never."

"And the sea. You've never seen it?"

A flush seemed to rise on Michali's cheeks, though she knew he would deny it if asked. That, at least, had not changed after his time in the grave. "I have, thank you," he said. "At your own house."

Ah, right. She'd met him on the veranda at Stratathoma. Sometimes she forgot. It seemed to belong to an entirely separate person.

"But you could see the Trefzan coast on the other side of the gulf," she said. "This is different."

"One seems much the same as another," he said stiffly. They continued for a moment before he added, "Lots of people haven't seen the sea, you know."

"I'm sure."

"In fact, it's perfectly natural, when you live somewhere so remote as Ksigori—"

"Oh, now who's risking detection?"

"And the lake is nearly a sea anyway."

Rhea raised an eyebrow, suppressing a smile. "Nearly a sea?"

"It's very large."

"I've seen it."

"Well, then you know."

She nodded contemplatively and broke apart from Michali so a young man could dash between them, clearly on some errand. "I think," she said when they'd rejoined each other, "that you're in for a bit of a surprise."

Up ahead, the street dipped again into another staircase, and instead of hewing close to its edges the buildings split wide, opening a view down to the lower section of the harbor.

"Why?" Michali asked, his brow furrowed.

"The sea is very large, too."

His subsequent expression—deeply skeptical, only a hint of his ever-present fondness remaining—made Rhea's heart lift for a moment before sinking deep into the pit of her stomach. That was the Michali she'd first met. As good as it was to see him, it was also a reminder that he was so much harder to find now.

She turned away from him and hurried on. There were too many people at the crest of the stairs to get a good view of what was below, so she stepped off the street and into a little bakery whose other exit opened onto another street running parallel. Michali followed her through, ducking a loaf of bread as it was tossed to a waiting customer.

This second street was farther removed from the main thoroughfare and not nearly as crowded, which meant Rhea had no trouble finding a spot on the public veranda that served as an overlook for the harbor before narrowing again to another flight of stone steps. The ocean and sky were both a deep blue, one reflecting the other so perfectly that for a moment it was difficult to tell what she was actually looking at, but quickly the view came into focus: the harbor bristling with masts, cradled by the hillside, and the sea reaching out endlessly beyond. Gulls were wheeling overhead, their cries distant, almost mournful, and Rhea could taste the salt off the water.

"See," she said to Michali. "It's a bit bigger than your lake."

"I suppose." He lifted one hand to shield his eyes from the sun, and then after a brief study of the scene before them, turned to her and plucked at a lock of her hair. "You're curling more."

"Michali."

"It's very sweet. I like it."

She bit her lip, holding in an unkind response. He loved her; he was only complimenting her. It did not matter that she wanted to tell him to look, look at the ocean, at the swell of the waves, at one of the fishing boats coming into the harbor. To look at anything, as long as it wasn't her.

"Where is your Domina meeting us?" he asked, still tugging lightly on the ends of her hair. "There must be thousands of people down there."

"I think she'll find us."

Falka had in fact given more specific instructions in another of her letters, but that, Rhea kept to herself. Sending the hummingbird back and forth between them had been a secret she'd relished keeping, even if it had meant delaying any contact with Chrysanthi. Her sister would understand and was probably only just arriving at the Navirotsk anyway, where Rhea had promised to send the hummingbird to meet her. It had taken off the day before, and though Rhea knew she could not reasonably expect it to be back already, that didn't mean she couldn't feel nervous about it.

"It *is* very beautiful," Michali said next to her. He had looked at last at the sea before them, one hand lifted to shield his eyes from the sun. "More peaceful than the view from your house."

For a moment Rhea could hear the crash of the waves, muffled and familiar as they had been through Lexos's bedroom window. "Oh, I don't know," she said. "I suppose there are different sorts of peace."

There was something about the look on his face that sat uncomfortably behind her ribs. A sadness, almost, made all the more unusual by the fact that for once, she didn't think it had anything to do with her.

"Is that what it felt like?" she asked before she could think better of it. "When you died?"

His recoil was immediate, if slight. She had never found him overly easy to read—had never had time, really, to learn how before everything changed—and so she was left to watch anxiously as he gazed out at the ocean for a moment longer.

Finally, he shook his head. "Not in so many words."

"In what words, then?"

"Why do you want to know?" His gaze slid to hers, hardened and sharp. "Why now?"

"I'm not sure," she said, which was true in essence. "That's . . . You're right to ask. I'm sorry."

Her answer seemed to sit poorly with Michali. The corner of his mouth twitched; his eyes narrowed. "I climbed out of the grave three months ago and you're asking me today. Here." He let out a low laugh. "It felt like nothing, Rhea. Nothing. I was dead. I don't even remember it happening."

"Right," she said. "Of course." What had she expected? That he had dreamed? Or lain awake there under the snow waiting for her to come for him?

She had seen his body the day he'd died, the emptiness of it. And she had seen it the day she'd pried his coffin open, ready to kneel by his side and pray for whatever more she could get of him. Nothing was right. He had been gone, gone completely, until the very moment her prayer had worked and he'd opened his eyes. Not nothing, then, but something. Someone.

She didn't want to ask, but she had opened this door, and she owed it to him now to walk all the way through. "What about when I called you back?" she asked. "How did that feel?"

He sighed. She could see him softening, and whether it was because of his love for her or the weight of the subject at hand, she would take it.

"Like waking up too early," he said, "when you've been up too late."

"Did you—" She swallowed hard. "Did you want to go back to sleep?"

"No," he said hurriedly. His hand came up to cradle her cheek, all his earlier anger gone. It never lingered these days. "I was so happy to see you. Believe me, my love, I am always so happy to see you."

"Good," she said, smiling, and was relieved that she meant it. "I want so much for you to be happy, you know."

"I know. And I am. It's only that I'm tired, sometimes."

"Like waking up too early," she repeated, and he nodded before drawing her in close and kissing her forehead, right where she might have marked herself with blood if she was preparing to bless her worshippers. She let her eyes fall shut, leaning into him even as the sting of guilt began to eat at her—it would be harder to leave him behind today, after this.

"Now," he said once he'd pulled away. "Enough of this. Let's keep on, yes? It's a long way down."

Most anybody coming up from the harbor took a separate path, riding one of the city's provided donkeys on a track of beaten earth that cut up the middle of the hillside, so the stairs down to the sea were packed with people all heading down together, so many of them carrying some assortment of goods that Rhea found herself cheek to cheek with a basket full of salted fish. There were so many people that she wondered if she could slip ahead of Michali and disappear into the crowd, but before she could inch ahead of the basket of fish and its attached bearer, Michali had grabbed her hand and laced their fingers together.

"This is mad," he said in her ear. "Even at its busiest I never saw Ksigori like this."

She made a small noise of agreement and urged him forward with her, all the while looking for some opening to drop his hand, or better yet, let someone step between them. The closer they got to the water, the higher the guard presence would be, and while that could certainly be useful, it was a risk she didn't yet know if it was worthwhile to take. If she ended up in Domina or Speros custody, she wasn't sure she would ever get out again.

She waited until they were almost to the water, at a point where the stone steps flattened and widened for a moment before narrowing again for the last descent to the harbor. There was a patrol of Speros guards overlooking the crowd on either side, each positioned on a small wooden platform. Rhea tugged on Michali's hand as they approached, slowing them enough that the crowd behind them was forced to part.

"Keep pace," Michali whispered. "The guards—"

"It's fine," she told him.

She took a deep breath, squeezed Michali's hand once in apology, and then swayed to the right, knocking her shoulder against her neighbor's.

"*Sigama*," she said immediately and stepped back, directly into the person behind her. Already a rumbling was beginning around her; already she could see one of the guards peering in their direction.

"Get your girl off the street if she can't keep her feet," another man nearby snarled and jostled her sharply, forcing her to stagger forward again and drop Michali's hand. She let the momentum carry her farther, stumbling twice before catching herself on the back of the woman ahead of her, who let out a startled cry. As Rhea straightened, she saw, out of the corner of her eye, a guard step down from the wooden platform and start toward her.

"Hey," Michali called, but the crowd had already closed between them. Perfect. She nodded toward the approaching guard, pulling an apologetic face, and then, before he could get any closer to her, turned her back and began picking her way out to the edge of the crowd, angling so she could create more space between her and the guard.

The little alley, when she reached the entrance, was so cluttered with shops that she only needed to get a few yards down it before she could no longer see the crowd over her shoulder. As soon as she could, she took an offshoot to the left, and then another in the opposite direction, weaving a path away from Michali and the guards. The guards would give up looking for her quickly, but Michali would not be so easily deterred, so after a few minutes she ducked into a shop that sold some typical Rhokeri clothing and emerged again wearing a loose white dress that left her arms bare and looked much like what most people on the street were wearing. She'd also bought a hairpin carved from a Rhokeri shell to keep her hair back; nobody in this area was selling the veils the Dominas were beginning to popularize, and Michali would recognize her whether the bottom half of her face was covered or not.

She continued down a set of stairs so steep it was no wonder they were not in much use, until she arrived, finally, at the harbor base. Ahead of her, colorful fishing boats rocked at their moorings, people unloading baskets of fish and sea sponges. Over the tang of salt in the air she could taste something else—orange, and honey, and the lifting snap of goat's milk yogurt.

Somewhere in this harbor was a boat that belonged to Falka Domina, a boat she was meant to find and board before Michali could find her. She had better get to finding it.

CHAPTER TWENTY-THREE

RHEA

She had expected Falka's boat to be much more like the ones at the far end of the harbor—hulls of varnished timber and sails like a great bird's wing. Instead, she found the flag Falka had told her to look for on a fishing boat painted sky blue, its shoddy rigging tied with bells that clinked gently. The flag itself made her roll her eyes: a violet flower, exactly the sort that Falka had tied to a tree up in the Ksigora, on a field of white.

The gangplank was already down—Falka was expecting her—but Rhea stopped at the edge, peering into the water below. A handful of little fish were flitting here and there, catching the sun before vanishing under the boat.

"Hello," she said to the nearest one.

"Hello," said Falka, and Rhea jumped.

The other woman was standing on the far end of the fishing boat, leaning out from behind a stack of cage traps with one hand braced on the rigging overhead. She, like Rhea, had disguised herself somewhat as a local, her hair up in a simple horse's tail, her own dress a deep wine color that set off her olive skin.

"Feel free to board when you've finished speaking with the fish," she said, smiling. "I hear they're not very good for conversation."

She disappeared then, back behind the cages. Rhea took a moment to wait for her blush to recede before climbing the gangplank and following the deck of the boat until she'd reached the bow.

Falka had, as was apparently her habit, laid out a very nice meal for the both of them. On a white blanket there were baskets of grapes and other fruits, along with a large block of white, crumbly cheese seasoned so beautifully that Rhea's mouth immediately began to water. Falka was already sitting on one side, her legs drawn up under her; dutifully, Rhea took her own seat across from her.

"This is lovely," she said. "Thank you."

Falka's delight in the compliment was evident. She began making Rhea a plate, arranging each new delicacy just so, and something about the eagerness with which she moved made Rhea wonder, for the first time, if Falka perhaps did not have anybody else to play this sort of host to.

"Well, you made quite the trip to get here," Falka said. "I thought I might make it worth your while." She handed the plate to Rhea and then snatched one of the grapes off it and popped it into her mouth. "Where is your consort? He was with you earlier, no?"

Rhea stiffened. "I thought he'd enjoy exploring the city for the afternoon."

"Ah." She tilted her head, considering Rhea sharply. "A shame, to not have a chance to see an old friend. But then Michali Laskaris probably no longer considers me one after that nasty business at Stratathoma."

"You mean your betrayal—"

"Yes, yes, my utter betrayal of the Sxoriza, et cetera, et cetera. You don't really think it was only due to me that they weren't successful that day, do you?" Rhea opened her mouth; nothing came out, and after a moment, Falka shrugged. "No, I'm sure your consort is enjoying his day out. And I can't say I'm not glad to have you all to myself."

Rhea met Falka's eyes for a moment before shying away, her right hand clenching to a fist. The movement did not escape notice; before

Rhea could blink, Falka had reached across the blanket and taken hold
of her wrist.

"You're hurt," she said.

"What? No, I'm . . ." Rhea trailed off, staring at her bandaged
palm. The scar underneath had begun to bleed, it seemed, and a red
stain was now visible on the bandage itself. "It's nothing," she finished.
"An old wound."

Falka's fingers hovered over where the bandage had been tied off.
"Do you mind?"

"Oh. Yes, that's fine."

She held still as Falka untied the knot and began to undo the wrapping. With every layer peeled back, the bloodstain became larger and
larger, until at last the bandage fell away and the scar itself was revealed, completely broken open and welling with fresh blood.

"It wasn't like that this morning," she said. "The blood, I mean. It's
been . . . not right for a few weeks now."

"Not right?" Falka was still bent over her hand, hair hanging over
one shoulder. "This scar matches your mark, if memory serves."

"It does."

"And the mark? Does it show anything like this?"

Rhea swallowed hard. In principle she was not sure how wise it was
to be honest with anyone these days, especially Falka, but in actuality
she had come here, hadn't she? She had already unwrapped one hand.
It seemed pointless to leave the other covered.

She undid the bandage quickly, wincing when the movement pulled
at her scar and sent a few drops of blood scattering onto the blanket.
"Sorry."

Falka waved a hand. "It isn't mine. I borrowed it from one of the
Sperosi." She grimaced. "Horrible man. He deserves it."

"Kallistos?" Rhea asked, choking back a laugh.

Falka looked up, a delighted surprise in her eyes. "Yes. The very
same."

"I take back my apology, then."

"As you should." She nodded to Rhea's marked hand. "Right,
come on."

Perhaps it was the glare of the sun off the water, or the pleasant chatter from the fishermen on either side of Falka's boat, but whatever the case, Rhea did not hesitate in tipping her left palm toward Falka, her fingers relaxing under the other woman's touch.

Falka's head was bowed over Rhea's hand, and both of her own were wrapped around Rhea's wrist; for a moment Rhea floundered, wondering what she was meant to do while Falka conducted her examination. Should she say something? Lean in to look alongside her?

"Ah," Falka breathed, her thumb pressed firmly in the center of Rhea's palm. "I see."

Rhea knew what she had noticed—the feathering around the edges of the mark identifying her as Thyspira. It had gotten worse lately, seemingly in tandem with the scar on the opposite hand, and her very bones ached sometimes, pain radiating down the spindles of her wrist. Had it been this way for Baba? She didn't think so. He'd have made sure his children all knew what he suffered on their behalf.

At last, Falka made a sound of disapproval and sat back. "I'm sorry," she said. "It isn't fair."

"What isn't?" Rhea held up her marked hand. "This? I'm not sure fairness ever had much to do with it."

"Of course not," Falka replied, a bit snottily, but then she sighed. "I mean that your father's attitude toward both saints and Stratagiozis had the effect of leaving you quite in the dark."

"I know what I need to do," Rhea said, although that was almost never true.

"You don't." Falka took a moment to look over her shoulder, likely checking the other fishing boats for eavesdroppers. "You are the Thyzak Stratagiozi, Rhea. There are things you should know, by rights. But you've been hiding away in the mountains instead of—"

"Instead of what? Getting myself captured like my brother?"

"Instead of learning what you've got on your hands." Falka cracked a sly smile. "Literally, in this case." She waited, giving Rhea a chance to laugh.

Rhea did not take it. "These gifts have been under Thyzak control for centuries. I am not sure what I could learn about them that I haven't already."

"Yes, but what came before those centuries? Think, Rhea. Time passes."

"You don't say."

Falka hummed appreciatively, and Rhea felt herself relaxing. She leaned back against the stack of cage traps behind her and began re-wrapping her hands. She was looking down at the cracks in her skin, considering dipping her scarred hand into the ocean to wash out the cut, when Falka said, "Where are your people moving to now?"

"Nobody's quite told me," Rhea said absently, "but it seems to be Agiokon." That was what Athanasios had asked Michali about back when they'd been in the Ksigora, and the path they'd taken since had held true to it.

"Is that so?" Falka sounded so pleased that Rhea went still, her own eyes fixed on the bloodstain on her bandage. Had that been a secret? Yes, of course it had. Just because Rhea and Falka were able to spend time peacefully together didn't mean the groups they served weren't opposed.

"I don't . . . It might be there," she said. "It might not be."

That sounded pathetic even to her. Falka very kindly did not press further. "If it is," she said, "then I'm glad. It's where you ought to be."

"Why do you say that?"

"I didn't, if anyone asks." She reached out, tapped the edge of Rhea's bandage gently. "But that's a problem. One you should learn more about, and one you should get sorted. By somebody, if you won't let it be me."

"And the monks at Agiokon can help me with that?"

Falka plucked an orange from one of the dishes of fruit she'd laid out and began to peel it. "Who said anything about the monks?"

Rhea had never been to that city herself, but as far as she under-stood it, Agiokon and the monks were inextricably linked, the people living each day in the shadow of the great rock towers and the monas-teries perched on top. What else could there be for Falka to refer to?

At least, she thought, it was some kind of guidance. Even advice as vague as that was more than Michali had given her since he'd died.

"All right," she said. "If I assume you're telling me something worthwhile, something valuable, I am still left to wonder why you're telling it in the first place. The Sxoriza are set against your family. And moreover, just weeks ago you offered to take my gifts from me. Why should you want to help me with this now?"

"It's a sight better than my other options." Falka looked at her, serious for a moment before returning to her orange. "And besides, if your gifts get the better of you, I might be deprived of a lunch companion."

"Is that what I am?"

"I hope."

Rhea felt a spark light in her chest. Anger, she thought, tinged with something else she could not identify. "You say that, but you're the same person who betrayed my people."

"Are the Sxoriza your people? Really?" Falka popped out a section of fruit and took a bite. "You're a fool if you trust them, you know."

She ignored that and pressed on. "What for? I mean, yes, I know you took Stratathoma, but you could have had the same if you'd kept to your word."

"First of all," Falka said, leaning forward, "I don't think that's true, and second of all, I don't think you do, either. What is it you'd like to say to me, Rhea?"

"I—" She found herself faltering, but Falka only waited, her gaze intent. Rhea took a deep breath. "I was counting on you," she said. "I didn't know you, and you didn't know me, and it isn't as though I find it difficult to understand, really. But I was counting on you."

"Ah." Falka's expression softened, and when she spoke next, she sounded almost tentative. "I'm sure you would never make such a mistake again."

"No," Rhea said, smiling somewhat against her will. "Never."

"Can I ask, though—"

"I'm sure you will regardless of my answer."

"Is it what you wanted it to be?"

The question caught Rhea off guard. It was so plainly asked, and Falka was watching her so openly, with no indication that she expected it to be a difficult thing to answer.

"What do you mean?" Rhea asked.

Falka gestured broadly. "The Sxoriza. Your consort. The path you've put yourself on. Everything, I suppose."

Rhea took a moment to stare out over the ocean, to lick the salt from her lips. It would be wise to say yes; Falka was still her enemy, and any fracture Rhea laid bare was something she might try to use for her own gain. But Falka knew about the hummingbird, had used it to summon Rhea in the mountains. She knew that as much as Rhea had been the one to choose the Sxoriza, it had been Nitsos who sent her out Stratathoma's door headed for the Ksigora, and that despite Nitsos's reassurance that he had not decided everything else for her, the question of where Rhea had ended up and what she wanted was not a simple one at all.

"I don't know," she said finally. "I wanted . . ." But how to finish? She'd wanted Michali; she'd wanted her mother; she'd wanted to be the sort of person whose heart beat for other people. All of that had soured the second she'd understood just what Nitsos had done. Was she really the woman who had stepped away from her father and toward another way of thinking? Would she ever have done it alone? Thinking about it too long gave shape to something inside her body, something gnawing and slick with guilt, with rage. It was much easier to resent Michali and chafe at the bonds the Sxoriza kept her in than to look that thing in its glistening, Argyros blue eyes.

"I see what you mean," Falka said, and Rhea looked back at her, quite ready to tell her there was no way she could possibly understand, but the rueful smile on Falka's lips stopped her.

"You do?"

"In a manner of speaking." She tilted her head, frowning a little. "I'm sure there's quite a lot about the particulars that I have no grasp of, but there's a certain air we breathe, I think. A certain kind of person we become."

She was avoiding some very particular words, Rhea thought—

"powerful," and "lucky," and perhaps "doomed"—but it was a comfort to hear, all the same, and the space between them felt, suddenly, like it was filled not with salt off the water but with honey, as though Chrysanthi's sunlit paint had spilled over them both.

"I suppose you have to go quite soon," Falka said. "Your consort must be looking for you."

Rhea looked over her shoulder to the stone flat of the harbor. Opposite the boat's mooring, a kafenio was serving fresh juice. Farther down the promenade, two children had climbed atop one of the city's donkeys, and the one in front was whispering into its ear.

"I can spare another minute or two," she said. Just a minute more. Then she would go find Michali, they would go back to their tent, and she would bring up his conversation with Athanasios again, just to be sure that they were indeed headed to Agiokon. But until then, she would let Falka add a fresh slice of bread to her plate, pretending there was nothing waiting for her onshore.

CHAPTER TWENTY-FOUR

CHRYSANTHI

She was given the option of spending the night at the Navirotsk in one of their guest rooms, but she could think of very little that appealed less to her than that, so instead, as dark gathered in the sky above Vashnasta, Chrysanthi found herself back at the inn, perched on the edge of her bed and staring at Andrija's things where they still sat at the foot of the wardrobe.

Stavra had said she would see Andrija again shortly, but when Chrysanthi had asked if, before leaving, she might be able to speak to him, the answer had been quick and decisive: certainly not. She was reassured that tomorrow he would be finished with whatever rites the library was putting him through as a new hostage, but that did very little to keep a nervous twitch from making a home in her. They had been traveling together for nearly three weeks, the two of them, and while that was not very much of her life, or in fact of anyone's, it was the most—the only, in fact—time she had ever spent away from Stratathoma, from family, from what she knew. What she knew right now was Andrija. And it would not do to leave him here, stuck inside a promise he never should have made.

She would simply have to find a way to get him out.

She was up early the next morning, having slept poorly, and remembering what the approach to the library entrance had required, dressed not in the gown she had borrowed from Rhea but in a combination of her traveling suits and one of Andrija's spare shirts—this way, she reasoned, she would have something left of her own to change into should anything go wrong.

This proved wise, as she made it only to the first of the small floating barges that served as a bridge to the library entrance before slipping and tumbling head over feet into the water. She surfaced with a sputter, her soaking hair plastered to her face, her clothes billowing around her, and held tightly to the nearest platform to keep herself afloat.

Some yards away, the door to the library opened with a creak, and a Navirotskovai poked their head out. "I heard a noise. Is someone— Oh."

Chrysanthi lifted a hand and waved pathetically. "Hello."

"Do you need help?"

She took a few shallow breaths to ready herself before lunging toward the next barge, aware that her clothes might prove heavy enough to drag her into the deep if she wasn't careful. "I should be fine." The wake from her sudden movement sent a splash of water directly into her mouth. It tasted, in a word, revolting. "Actually, would you mind not going back inside just yet?"

The librarian proved more patient than Chrysanthi thought she would have been in a similar situation and did indeed wait until she had floundered her way to the stone threshold of the library door. With an only slightly suppressed sigh, they reached down and extended a hand to her. She took it gratefully and, once standing again, began to wring out her clothing and her hair.

"I guess I needn't bother," she said, smiling. "It's quite damp in there already."

"Damp?" came Stavra's voice from just inside the open door. "You're a bit more than damp."

"I try to look my best for you."

Stavra stepped closer and lifted a lock of Chrysanthi's sopping hair. The dark color on it had faded, leaving some blond to peek through in an odd pattern. "I'm honored." She dismissed the librarian then and led Chrysanthi inside, back up the stairs to the first hall, with its large opening to the sun. The weather was better today, and the mouth of the tunnel was almost painfully bright.

"What can we do for you today?" Stavra asked, staying well away from Chrysanthi as she continued to shake off water.

"I'm sure you won't be surprised to learn that I am here to see Andrija." She leaned toward Stavra, beckoning the other woman forward as Stavra wrinkled her nose. Yes, the lake water smelled terribly, but what did Stavra want her to do about it? "I won't allow you two to remain here," she whispered. "Hostages, guests—whatever you call it, it isn't right."

Stavra kept still, only a momentary flash of worry crossing her face. "Our contracts are not to be taken lightly. Neither, more important, are my mother's orders." This close, Chrysanthi could see that she had been right the day before—there *was* something black on Stavra's tongue, right where a matagios would have been. But it was not a matagios at all. Rather it was a stud of blackstone, pierced through the center of her tongue. Chrysanthi winced and lifted a hand to her own mouth.

"Yes, yes," Stavra said, "that's how they mark what is theirs."

"Like a matagios?" That belonged only to the Stratagiozis as far as she knew. What meaning did it have to the librarians, that they would mark their prisoners so? "Did it hurt?"

Stavra looked at her for a moment as if she was quite stupid. "Of course it did. But this isn't what I'm worried about."

"Oh, what can a library really even do to you? They've got books and paper and nothing else. We'll walk right out of here."

"They have a bit more than that," Stavra said, "but it isn't even the power of the library itself, necessarily." She looked nervously around the hall; empty as it was, she still pulled Chrysanthi toward the staircase on the opposite end and into a little alcove. "I was ordered here by my Ordukamat. If she finds out I've left, disobeyed her—"

"You can tell her you weren't disobeying her. You were obeying me." She offered her most winning smile; Stavra did not seem impressed. "Right. I do understand. But she can't really expect you to spend the rest of your life here, can she?"

The corner of Stavra's mouth twitched, but when Chrysanthi looked for the resentment, the anger that she knew would have been obvious were it one of her own siblings standing in Stavra's place, there was nothing. "She'll call me home when it's time. I don't know when that will be, or how she will negotiate for it. But I trust that she will."

"You do?" She couldn't imagine ever saying something like that about Baba. Yes, she'd been her father's favorite, such as it was—it had been hard to ignore the fact that he never spoke to her in the way he did to her siblings—but she hadn't been a fool, and only a fool would trust Vasilis Argyros to look after them.

Stavra, though, was unwavering. "I do. As much as I appreciate that you want to get me out"—and she smiled, genuine and small and wise—"I'm where my mother means for me to be. That has always been all I need to know." She nodded toward the second staircase, gesturing for Chrysanthi to go first. "I'll take you to your friend now. He's not far."

Andrija's room was only two levels down from the entrance hall, but the difference was stark; the light had to be coaxed down from the main shaft, and by the time it reached Andrija's guest quarters it had lost some of its sharpness, turned mellow and rounded as if cast by a flickering candle. Chrysanthi thought longingly of her paints sitting back in her room at the inn. Light like this was always so tempting. She could imagine it now: Andrija sitting patiently before her as she painted some sun onto his hair.

"Here," Stavra said, stopping in front of one of the doors off the corridor. "Take your time, but do be aware, I won't be far. They wouldn't like you left alone."

Chrysanthi knocked right away, not bothering to wait for any sort of privacy from Stavra. "Andrija? It's me, it's Chrysanthi." She heard a scrape in the room of wood against stone, and then the door was opening abruptly. On the other side was Andrija, hair tied back and shirtsleeves rolled up, blood crusted at the corner of his mouth. Chrysanthi felt her nerves ease at the sight of him. He was all right.

"I hear you've got a new piece of jewelry," she said, breezing past him. "Let's see it, then."

Slowly, he shut the door behind her and turned to look at her, a frown etched deeply into his brow. "Are you—" he began, but cut himself off with a wince.

"Don't worry about talking," she said. "I imagine it's quite sore, and anyway, you never seemed to want to say much before. This should be business as usual for you."

His eyes narrowed, but he otherwise ignored her. "You're dripping," he said slowly.

"A misstep earlier. It doesn't matter."

"Did you find what you were after?"

She nodded. "What Nitsos is looking for is in Agiokon. He may be on his way there already." She explained then about the painting, about Luco Domina's initials in the bottom corner, and finished, "If I can head Nitsos off at the pass, get him back to Rhea before he gets in any deeper, at least there's some chance the Argyrosi can get out of this mess clean." Andrija opened his mouth before appearing to think better of whatever he meant to say. That would not do. "What? What is it?"

Andrija went past her to his cot, where his black jacket had been discarded. He began to unroll his shirtsleeves. "I don't know your brother. You do." He grimaced, biting his cheek. There was a roundness to his accent today; she could hear him speaking around the blackstone studding his tongue. "All the same, I get the sense he is not easily dissuaded from completing his goals."

"Maybe." She moved closer to him, reaching up to brush the dried blood from his cheek. "But I'm very persuasive."

Andrija looked gravely down at her and did not answer.

"Besides," she went on, "if I can't convince him to come back to the fold, as it were, you can just truss him up like a piece of game and toss him over the back of your horse. That's another sort of persuasion."

"I can't leave here," he said, his voice quiet. "I will help find you someone else, someone to—"

"Absolutely not."

"Vashnasta is full of hired hands. It won't be difficult."

"You're being very silly right now," she said, aware that there was a sort of hysteria held in every word just waiting to be let through. "You're coming with me. I won't have it any other way."

"Chrysanthi," Andrija said helplessly, and she only just resisted the urge to clap her hand over his mouth.

"Listen to me," she said. "I am the youngest child of the Argyros family, I am my father's favorite, and as a rule, I get my way. I will not let you be the exception. Do you understand?"

He sighed and shut his eyes for a moment. She waited for him to smile, or better yet laugh, but instead there was a resignation about him as he looked at her again and nodded. "You know if I'm caught, I'll be killed," he said.

"I assumed."

"And if I return to Vashnasta, I'll be killed."

"Yes, yes."

"You don't seem concerned."

"I'm not." She leaned in. "I do not mean to let us be caught. And I certainly do not mean to ever come back to this wretched place once we're gone."

"And that means I won't, either?"

Chrysanthi's voice caught in her chest for a moment. She could feel herself beginning to blush. "Exactly," she said, ignoring her embarrassment. "Now will you please help me think of how we're going to get out of here?"

Stavra had, in the entrance hall, seemed to think there were ways in which the Navirotskovai could deploy some force, but Chrysanthi had yet to see anyone who might count as a soldier or a guard. It seemed to her that the librarians relied more on the building's odd design and constructed defenses to keep its hostages in check. But Andrija did not agree with her eventual suggestion that they simply walk out the building's front door, and so they were sitting together on his cot, her knee knocking against his as he thought in deep silence and she fidgeted ceaselessly.

At last his hand came down on her knee for a moment, settling her. "You're making my teeth rattle."

"Sorry." He wasn't having too much trouble speaking, all things considered, and the swelling could certainly have been worse. Still. She did not like that he was in pain, and she liked even less that it was because of her. "Stavra said her tongue hurt."

"I'm sure it did."

She stole a sidelong glance at him, at the clench of his jaw and the tightness in his shoulders. She couldn't tell if by refusing to speak about his own blackstone he was trying to spare her any discomfort, or if he was upset with her. She wouldn't blame him if he was. In fact, she thought she would almost prefer it—she knew better how to respond to anger than to devotion.

"Maybe there's some bargain I can strike with the head of the library," she said suddenly. "I know you and Stavra would both say it's not as simple as asking for you to be released, but has anyone tried? Has anyone ever just asked?"

"Chrysanthi—"

"I'm very persuasive."

"I don't think it's a question of persuasion. You—" He made a very small wounded sound, one hand pressed to his cheek, and swallowed what Chrysanthi assumed was a mouthful of blood.

"Oh, just take it out," she snapped.

A knock came at the door, hurried and loud. It opened immediately after, revealing Stavra, who sidled in and slammed it shut once again, her back pressed up against it.

"I'm sorry," she said. "I don't mean to disturb you. But you need to get out of Vashnasta right now."

Chrysanthi got up, exchanging a nervous look with Andrija. "What's happened?"

"Nastia Rudenko is in the city."

"And?" Nastia was the Chuzhak Stratagiozi, and the woman currently in control of Vashnasta, at least by all official accounts. Certainly she was someone Chrysanthi had decided she would rather not cross paths with at the moment, but Vashnasta was large. They could stay out of her way.

"She's coming here. Someone must have told her your brother came, because she's asked specifically to see any current hostages—anyone who might have paid the cost for him." Stavra looked harried, and her marked hand was trembling. "The two of you need to leave immediately. She cannot find you."

"Why not? We're all Stratagiozi here, and I'm no friend of Ammar's, just as she is not." For a moment, unbidden, the image of the border guard rose at the front of her mind, his blood on the floor and his calloused hands grasping hers. She blinked. "I don't see why we can't have a lovely chat between us."

"I do," Stavra said. "We're not all Stratagiozi here, Chrysanthi."

Chrysanthi stepped to the side, slotting herself in front of Andrija. "If they try—"

"Not him. You. My mother's arrangement with your brother is out of bounds, and Nastia will no doubt be furious when she sees I'm the one who bought him access, but I am still the Devetsi second. I'm protected. She cannot kill me without losing my mother's support, something she dearly needs to keep Ammar at bay. But you?" Stavra shook her head. "You are the daughter of a deposed house. You have your mark, but no power to go with it."

Nothing she could offer Nastia in exchange for her own safety; nothing to protect her. "I see," she said. "I suppose we really should be going, then."

"I can get you to an exit. But from there?"

"An exit is more than enough," Andrija said from over Chrysanthi's shoulder. "Thank you, Stavra."

Chrysanthi stood, dazed, as Andrija shrugged on his jacket and began buttoning it up. He'd been relieved of his weapons, and everything else was back at the inn. His spare blade. Her clothes. Her *paints*.

Lefka. They would be able to go back there, right? They would— How had it all happened so quickly? She hadn't even had time to write to Rhea. The hummingbird would arrive to fetch her letter and find her gone. What would Rhea think?

"*Elado,*" Andrija said in her ear, and she jumped. He had taken hold of one of the buttons on her jacket, the fabric of which was still heavy with water from her fall. She stared down at his fingers—index and thumb balanced gingerly as though he was afraid of touching her. "Do these up, yes? It's cold out."

But Stavra did not lead them outside. She led them, instead, deeper and deeper into the library, far deeper than she and Chrysanthi had gone on their trip to the gallery. The halls here were dark and narrow, and after yet another descent down yet another staircase, Chrysanthi found she could barely see a foot in front of her. She kept waiting for Stavra to stop, to say that she had only been joking, or to at the very least produce a torch of some kind, but they continued, Andrija's presence at Chrysanthi's back the only thing keeping her moving forward.

Soon, water began to gather on the corridor floor, each step splashing Chrysanthi's ankles. Her boots were soaked through, making her feet ache with the chill, and someone's teeth had begun to chatter, although the sound carried so strangely that she could not tell whose.

"Where are we going?" she asked. "I imagine if we go much deeper we won't have any air left."

"Quiet," Stavra whispered. "We're not far now."

A few minutes later, the passage began to widen, a warm orange light appearing as a pinprick in the distance. Chrysanthi startled at the feel of a hand on her elbow—Andrija's as he drew alongside her. It remained there, warm and steadying, as they sloshed onward.

"Are you all right?" he said, his head bent low.

She ignored Stavra's scolding look and nodded. "Just cold. That's all." Though it was too dark to see Andrija's face, she could tell he was looking at her still, unconvinced. She sighed and said, "What about Lefka?"

"Ah."

"She's tied up at the post. No water, no food."

"The innkeeper will look after her."

But that wasn't good enough. "Isn't there someone you know? Someone you can write to and send to fetch her?"

A pause, and then Andrija cleared his throat. "I can try."

"Thank you. She—" Chrysanthi's chest clenched painfully. She cleared her throat. "Rhea gave her to me."

"I know." His hand slid down the length of her arm to grasp hers tightly for only a moment before he let go entirely. "They'll both be all right."

The light up ahead was getting stronger now, though still some ways away, so Chrysanthi fell silent, Andrija following suit. It was torchlight—that much became clear quickly—and it carried down the corridor toward them, reflected on the surface of the water. But the water had, oddly enough, gotten shallower, and Chrysanthi realized that this corridor was running uphill, at such a slight degree as to be almost unnoticeable. That was strange; she'd expected they would be delving deeper into the city.

"When we reach the end of the hallway," Stavra said over her shoulder, "stay back until I wave you forward. There will be at least two Navirotskovai in the chamber beyond, if not more. I'll get them to clear the way ahead and keep them distracted while you make a run for it." She stopped short, turning to examine Chrysanthi and Andrija. "I should've asked: Can you swim?"

"Yes," Chrysanthi said proudly, just as Andrija asked, "What for?"

"You'll see," answered Stavra. "To sum up: Swim down. That's as much as I know."

Chrysanthi shot Andrija a skeptical look, but he seemed unbothered. "I understand," he said. "We'll wait for your signal."

They kept on, until at last the chamber at the other end of the corridor became clear. From their vantage point a few yards back from the mouth of the hallway, Chrysanthi could see a window cut into the stone wall, iron bars across it, and a person standing behind it in another, smaller chamber filled with stacks of paper. In the main room, another librarian was pacing back and forth in front of a large door opposite the hallway opening. Two people, then, and no more. They'd got lucky.

Stavra held up her hand, bringing them to a halt, and together they all drew back into the shadows by the corridor wall.

"Right. You know what to do?"

Chrysanthi nodded. "Yes, we do. Thank you, Stavra. Really."

"Don't thank me yet." She looked back down the hallway over Chrysanthi's shoulder, something like alarm registering briefly on her face. "I'm sorry for how this turned out. But I *am* glad we got to meet. Now be quick, all right? And be as quiet as you can."

Stavra straightened her drab library clothes, pushed her braids back over her shoulders, and put on a smile—a process Chrysanthi recognized and had seen her own sister perform herself, although Stavra's smile showed more strain than Rhea's would have in a similar situation, which Chrysanthi found charming. Then, with a deep breath, she strode into the chamber ahead.

The conversation she had with the first Navirotskovai was entirely in Chuzhak, but at least judging by Stavra's posture it seemed to be going well enough. Chrysanthi watched Stavra gesture toward the door as her voice took on an almost embarrassed tone. The librarian laughed in response, but neither made a move toward the large iron door beyond them.

"Our clothes will weigh us down," Andrija said, so quietly that to hear him Chrysanthi had to lean back until her head brushed his chest. "Don't fight it. Let it help you."

She had not fully considered what the necessity of swimming implied. It hit her now like winter's first cold, numbing and slow. The city was being swallowed by a lake, and they were down in the bowels of it now; where else were they meant to go? "Andrija—"

"It's all right," he said. "If Stavra is sending us down, there will be a way out. Do not panic." In the chamber, the librarian was still talking, but finally began using a ring of keys to unlock the door. Chrysanthi's heart was racing, but Andrija continued: "Begin breathing very deeply, right now. From the center of you, not your chest."

She could hear him doing the same in the silence that followed. Shutting her eyes, she worked to match her breath to his. He was right. They could trust Stavra's advice. There was a way out of here. And he would not leave her, as she had not left him.

When she opened her eyes again, the Navirotskovai had finished unlocking the door and started opening it, something that apparently required all of their body weight. Chrysanthi narrowed her eyes and peered through the widening gap; yes, there was some sort of pool there, lit by torchlight that showed, too, the raw rock walls of a cave. She knew there was no way to tell from here, but still, the water looked terribly deep.

Stavra stepped through the doorway and spoke in Chuzhak, before crouching and snatching up something Chrysanthi could not see (and something she suspected did not in fact exist in the first place). After she had straightened, she opened her palm, displaying a bit of metal that glinted in the torchlight. An earring, perhaps, that Stavra had carried here with her.

The librarian laughed again, gesturing toward the window where the second Navirotskovai was poised and watching. Chrysanthi stopped listening, focusing instead on her breathing again. Stavra would wave them forward when it was time.

But as the Chuzhak receded into the background, and the quiet in the corridor pressed in close against her ears, Chrysanthi stiffened and twisted to look behind her. She wasn't sure, but she thought she'd heard some noise, some splash in the water. Another librarian? Or maybe a rat, upset at having its home disturbed by so many guests. She nudged Andrija and nodded toward the far end of the corridor, only to find he was already alert, already staring back into the dark.

The sound came again. And again, and again, this time with a more metallic ring. The library workers wore only fabric and leather—nothing that would create a sound like that. No, Chrysanthi had seen enough in the Sxoriza camps to conclude that this was armor, clanking in time with its wearer's footsteps. Whoever was coming toward them was armed, and not alone.

"Chuzhak soldiers?" she asked Andrija.

He nodded, looking grim. "Nastia never travels to the Vitmar without them."

"Which means?"

"That we can't afford to wait for Stavra."

Back in the chamber, Stavra had managed to maneuver the first librarian toward the window, where she was now chatting with both, but she had not signaled yet, and as she nodded toward a plain door cut into the wall that Chrysanthi had missed on first look, Chrysanthi understood why; she wanted both Navirotskovai out of the chamber before she waved them through. If nobody saw, nobody could ever tell Nastia where they had gone.

Oh well. At least they would still have a head start.

"Ready?" Andrija said.

"Yes."

They ran. Chrysanthi's boots slipped on the wet floor, and all her deep breathing was a distant memory, but still she sprinted for the pool ahead, the shouts of the librarians ringing in her ears. Andrija had his hand fisted in the back of her jacket, and as she stumbled, he hauled her back to her feet and shoved her ahead of him. Almost there now.

She careened through the still-open door and, without a second thought, dove into the pool.

Immediately, the urge to surface again clutched at her, but then Andrija's figure sliced into the water, and she stroked down into the black, following him. Down, through feet of emptiness, toward the floor of the lake, where some sort of stone plinth sat at a slight angle. Chrysanthi fixed her eyes on it, her lungs already begging for air she didn't have.

Finally, they arrived at the lake floor, where ancient, now flooded corridors split off to the left and the right. Chrysanthi risked a look up at the surface—an armed figure could be seen overhead, their silhouette warped by the water. She and Andrija had to continue, no matter what.

Andrija had swum toward one of the corridors, so she took the other. Light, she told herself. Look for light, or for an air pocket at the very least. She was still looking when something tapped her leg, and

Andrija swam up alongside her, his hair drifting in the water as he shook his head.

Only one way forward, then. Chrysanthi began to swim, her muscles straining, her vision blurry. Forward, she thought, just push forward, and as the stone plinth disappeared behind her, she imagined the painting Luco Domina had left in the gallery. A stone tower, a river held by a green valley, and sunlight draped over it all by an artist's hand. She would be there soon enough.

CHAPTER TWENTY-FIVE

ALEXANDROS

Lexos had thought that nobody could possibly be worse to travel with than Baba, but Ettore had proved him wrong. It hadn't even been that long of a journey—two days to cross the gulf before continuing overland for another four to Agiokon—but every possible element of that trip had been mortally offensive to Ettore: the food, the lingering snow, and the accommodations (although Lexos did agree that traveling as a stowaway in the bottom of a trade vessel had been less than ideal). Now that they were out of Trefazio and into Merkher, Lexos expected that they would have a bit more freedom to move, but he was not at all hopeful that Ettore would become a more agreeable traveling companion.

The worst part was that Ettore was always in good spirits. All of his complaints were conveyed with the widest of smiles. Just that morning, after they'd crawled out of a stall in an inn's half-empty stables, Ettore had thrown his arm over Lexos's shoulders, kissed him on the cheek, and said, "Alexandros, I'm afraid if we spend another night in one of these tragic little boxes, I will begin the next morning by breaking someone's neck."

"You won't do it the night of?" Lexos had asked, now quite accustomed to this sort of thing.

Ettore had laughed and said, "Well, I'd want *some* sleep first."

As strange as it was, Luco Domina did need rest. Of course Lexos had known that the Luco of the histories was a man like any other, but to witness it, even after living alongside Ettore in that prison of a summer house, still left some part of his mind whirring in confusion. Luco Domina was a figure of legend, of story, and he was also the person who kept Lexos up at night with his whistling snore, leaving Lexos to stare up at the stars and pretend he did not miss stitching them in place.

They had then stolen two of the innkeeper's horses—"liberated" was the word Ettore had used when he'd suggested it—and after a morning's ride, shivering all the while in the unseasonable chill, they were just coming to the outskirts of Agiokon, the city's rock spire rising in the distance. Lexos remembered the last time he'd arrived here, bound for the Devetsi house after making a ruin of things in Vuomorra. It seemed not much had changed, except that this time, his father was dead, his gifts were gone, and he was riding behind one of the most irritatingly charming people on the continent. The only person who might be able to give Ettore a run for his money, he thought, was Chrysanthi, and he hadn't the first idea where she was. She was alive, he hoped. Happy, too—he supposed that would be nice.

"Alexandros," Ettore called. "Keep up, please!"

Lexos urged his horse forward, brimming with dread. The closer they got to Agiokon, the less time he had to truly endear himself to his new friend, and so far, he didn't think he'd made much progress. Since their conversation in Falka's study, Ettore had begun to more freely reference the life he'd left behind, but every new detail he let slip only served to make Lexos feel more inadequate. How was he meant to help a man who'd corrected his Merkheri pronunciation over breakfast and then begun to reminisce over the creation of Merkher itself? The most Lexos had been able to muster had been a fairly pathetic offer to feed Ettore's horse.

No, Lexos did not ever like to admit that he was in over his head, but he rather thought the jig was up in this case.

And to make matters more complicated, Ettore was still frustratingly close-lipped about what was waiting for them in Agiokon. At least he had confirmed that it was not another saint left living, thank goodness.

"Well?" Lexos asked as he drew even with Ettore. He might as well try again. "Is it the monastery we're heading for?"

"The what?"

Lexos pointed to the silhouette of the rock spire in the distance. "There's a monastery on the top. Saint worshippers. Keepers of ancient texts."

"Are you calling me ancient?" Ettore asked, with what Lexos hoped very much was a mock frown.

"I've been there many times," he said, "and—"

"Have you?" Ettore interrupted. "What about the rest of your family? Was it a little trip you all took together? Taking in the sights of another age?"

"No. Just myself and my father."

"Your sister didn't go with you? She inherited your matagios, but she didn't travel with your father?" Ettore cocked his head. "I thought she would have been the elder of the two of you."

Lexos wasn't sure why Ettore was curious about this, but any interest in him seemed to be a good thing. "She is," he said, and wasn't that a bitter thing to say? "But Rhea and I were twins at birth."

"That's an odd way of putting it."

"Is it?"

"Yes, unless you've stopped being twins in the interim. Are you very similar, then?" Ettore asked. "They say it's often like that."

Lexos thought of his sister, of her hand in his as Baba reprimanded her. Of the two of them out on the grounds on a summer morning, Rhea's joy at being home again so pure he could feel it in his own heart.

"No," he said. "No, we're not alike at all. Look, about the monastery. If that's where we're going, I can show you how to get in. It's difficult, but—"

"That's very kind, but it won't be necessary."

Lexos had a hard time believing that. Agiokon was a lovely city, but if all Ettore wanted to do was enjoy a nice meal and a bit of sunshine, they could've stayed in Vuomorra.

Whatever Ettore's reason, it was not for him to argue. His job was to get Ettore where he wanted to go, and then maybe—maybe—Ettore would see fit to give Lexos something in exchange for his service. A position at his side, or better yet, power of Lexos's own. He missed it so bitterly that sometimes he could barely breathe.

Unlike many of the other cities scattered across the continent, Agiokon was not walled—everything its earliest builders had needed to protect, they had put up on top of that tower of stone—and so there was nobody to give either Lexos or Ettore a second look as they rode past farms and between houses that were growing more frequent the closer they got to the city proper. Despite the lack of guards, Lexos kept his head down, afraid that someone would recognize him. He'd been here often enough, visiting Stavra and her mother, Zita, before every Stratagiozi meeting.

Was Stavra here? Where had she gone after that day at Strata-thoma? He'd written to her as soon as he and Ettore had got clear of Trefazio, told her he would soon be in a position to pay her a visit, but thus far she had not answered. It was true that she had not been able to save him at Stratathoma, but she had got as close to it as possible, and she was the only person he considered reliable on perhaps the whole continent. If she'd been able to help—

There was no point in wondering. She hated him now, or did not trust him, or very simply was not reading her mail; whatever the case, it changed nothing about Lexos's current his situation. His closest and only ally now was Ettore, who had just leaned down in his saddle to steal an apple from a farmer's cart heading in the opposite direction as they passed. He took a bite from it before tossing it in Lexos's direction. Lexos caught it without much thought, recoiling from the wet cling of Ettore's saliva. With a wince, he held it by the stem at an arm's length.

"No?" Ettore asked. "Too good for a bit of fresh fruit?"

"I prefer to pay for what I take."

Lexos had hoped this might inspire some reflection in Ettore; instead he burst out laughing. "Do you? And you paid for your gifts how?"

"Blood," Lexos replied, annoyed.

"Yes, but it was only a very little bit." Ettore sighed, looking wistful. "I much prefer gold."

Lexos thought briefly of the ring he knew was still in Ettore's pocket, of the braided hair hidden inside and what Ettore had made it do. So far Ettore had made no further use of his gifts, but that did not keep Lexos from spending every night wondering what else he might be capable of. Saints' gifts seemed of a different sort than those held by Stratagiozis in the way that water was purer when drunk straight from a mountain spring. Maybe, after Lexos had got some sort of power back from Ettore, he could find a spring of his own.

Another cart was approaching; Lexos pulled his horse to the side of the road, off into the snow. The valley was wide here, its floor dominated by sprawling farms and fields of flowers. There was none of that today. Instead of sweeping green plains and the hum of activity as early crops were planted, there was only white, the mountains in the distance, and the sky brutally blue overhead. And yet the cart approaching was laden still with fruit, as if it truly were spring. It made his mouth water to see everything so fresh.

He eyed the apple he still held. Ettore's bite was not too big, and besides, Lexos was not the one who had stolen it. Why deny himself a bit of food?

He shut his eyes and took a bite, quite ready to savor the sweetness— that is, until something moved against his tongue. He shrieked, spitting the apple out onto his horse's neck. There, inching its way through the yellowing flesh, was a worm.

"Perfect," Lexos said, shaking it off onto the road below and tossing the rest of the apple over his shoulder.

CHAPTER TWENTY-SIX

CHRYSANTHI

After days following Andrija through the Vitmar on foot, and another few clutching his waist as she sat behind him on a horse as it cantered south, Chrysanthi had been something beyond delighted to topple into a proper bed. She'd fallen asleep still dressed, and it was late in the morning now as she slowly came awake. She rolled over with a groan, pressing her face into the bedclothes. They smelled like soap, so strongly that she could taste it, but after a week carrying the stink of horse and sweat, she couldn't bring herself to mind.

They'd left their money behind in Vashnasta and only got this room because Andrija knew someone in the city and had a favor he could call in. She'd spared a moment to wonder how it was possible he knew so many people when he hardly ever opened his mouth, but it seemed part and parcel of the quiet he kept regarding the life he'd lived before the Sxoriza. And, curious as she was, she knew how it felt to split yourself in two, a before and an after. Her before had been left behind at Stratathoma and waited now within those great stone walls. Where had Andrija left his?

With a sigh, she wriggled over onto her back and sat up, rubbing at her eyes. "You snore," she said to him, having no real idea of whether that was true, but when she'd finally wiped the haze from her eyes, she realized she was alone. The blanket Andrija had slept under on the floor was folded up neatly on the foot of the bed, but the man himself was nowhere to be seen.

Chrysanthi scrambled to her feet, her mouth dry and her heartbeat suddenly too loud in her ears. Had Nastia's men found them? Had he been carried away in the night? No, no—she was still here, the paint washed from her yellow hair and from the black mark on her left hand. Anybody who took a good look at her might know what she was, but she had been left behind.

The door swung open at that moment, and Andrija stepped through, two rolls of bread held in one hand and a waterskin in the other. "You're up," he said, turning to shut the door behind him. "I brought— What is it?"

She shook her head and hoped very much that her cheeks weren't visibly red. "Nothing." How utterly embarrassing; back at Stratathoma she'd been so comfortable being alone. Now even a mere minute in her own company was enough to curdle that comfort into something more like panic. "Are those for me?"

"One of them is," Andrija said, smiling a very little bit. He came to sit on the edge of the bed, and she tucked her legs under her, holding out a hand for one of the rolls. "I got one with raisins and one without. I wasn't sure what you'd like."

"Always something sweet," she replied. He nodded, and Chrysanthi let herself imagine that he was making note of it.

"There was something else, too," he said, "something I saw on my way back in." He went to the window, throwing the shutters back. In through the open space came Rhea's hummingbird.

Chrysanthi's heart leapt. She held out one hand toward the bird, and it chirped as it landed on her index finger. It looked only a little worse for wear, with grime and dirt speckled across its blue wings. Its tiny metal claws were cold with the winter chill. How far had it traveled to find her?

"Hello," she said to it softly. She could hear her own breath catching, her voice trembling. "I'm very glad to see you."

She was gladder still to see that a strip of parchment was tied around one of its legs. Word from Rhea. It had to be. "Hold still," she said and undid the knotted twine holding it in place. Released of its duty, the hummingbird spread its mechanical wings and flitted off to sit on Andrija's shoulder.

"Oh," he said. "All right."

Chrysanthi unrolled the piece of parchment eagerly. It was barely as tall as her littlest fingernail, but long enough to have been wrapped around the bird's leg many times. Even so, the handwriting that covered it looked cramped, as though the message had barely fit.

> *You did not write. Are you safe? I travel next to Agiokon.*
> *Meet me here, with or without what I sent you to retrieve.*

Chrysanthi let out a choked laugh. The hummingbird had gone to Vashnasta, just as Rhea had promised it would. And when it had returned without any message, thankfully, she had sent it back out again. It was more than Chrysanthi could have hoped for already, never mind that her sister had summoned her to the very place she had just arrived in. Was Rhea already here? It seemed possible.

"Do you have anything I can write with?" she asked Andrija. "Some charcoal, maybe?"

He did not, but he procured some from the innkeeper without much trouble, and some minutes later the hummingbird was whizzing back out the window with the parchment scroll retied to its leg, a reply from Chrysanthi scratched onto the back of Rhea's original message. They would have to wait for her response, but until it came, Chrysanthi could investigate the base of the rock spire. Whatever she found there might be enough to make up for having failed to fetch Nitsos himself.

She got up, making for where her boots were lined up by the door. They were crusted with mud still, from their climb out of the lake at Vashnasta, but at least they were dry. For days as they walked south from the city she'd heard the squelch of water with every step.

"Do you need something?" Andrija said suddenly.

"Hm?" She slipped on one boot, wincing as it scraped against a fresh blister.

"If you want something more to eat, I can go back out."

Chrysanthi looked up at him as she moved on to the other boot. "No, I'm full." She wobbled slightly; Andrija reached out to brace her, but she'd already straightened back up. "Why? Do you want something?"

"No."

"All right." They stared at each other, the air suddenly awkward in a way it had never been before. She cleared her throat. "Are you ready to go, then?"

Incredibly, she thought Andrija might be beginning to blush, but he did not flinch. "Go where?" he asked.

Was he being purposefully obtuse? Or was he trying to make a joke? Much as she applauded the decision to branch out into new forms of expression, she didn't think now was the time.

"I told you about the painting," she said, tilting her head. "The base of the tower? It's the whole reason we came here." He opened his mouth, and she waved him off. "Yes, and to get away from the Chuzhak soldiers, but we could've gone anywhere to do that. We came here because of what I saw in the gallery." He did not reply, and his stillness set an unease stirring at the back of Chrysanthi's mind. He was always like this, but something was different. "Andrija, is anything wrong?"

"No. I just think it might be wise to wait here for your sister to respond. That's all."

"It could be days before we hear from her," Chrysanthi said. "And we have something to do in the meantime. You don't want to come see the sights with me?" Even when she smiled up at him, he didn't soften. If anything, he might've got a bit more dour. Chrysanthi moved without thinking and tapped his nose twice with her index finger. Andrija's expression flickered at last, and his eyes widened. "Come on," she said. "We're almost there. On our way, let's have a nice walk in a new city."

"I've been here before," he said darkly as she backed away, but he followed her out of their borrowed room, his gait so closely in tandem with hers that their shoulders brushed with every step. She said nothing about it, nor about the way he checked behind them more often than he ever had before. He would tell her if there was anything to truly worry about, and meanwhile the stone spire of Agiokon was getting closer. Only a few hours more and she would find the graves that Luco Domina had hidden at its base.

CHAPTER TWENTY-SEVEN

ALEXANDROS

Lexos and Ettore said little else between them as they continued into the city, the expanse of the farms giving way to houses of increasingly better construction, interspersed with shops. This was all very familiar to Lexos—he'd come this way so many times—but Ettore kept looking around them with an almost violent curiosity in his eyes. Lexos was still not sure how long he had been imprisoned; clearly, though, it had been long enough that the world had become something new and intriguing.

At the moment Ettore was particularly entranced by the decorations hung up in the street. Lanterns, not yet lit, hung from ropes strung across the street some feet overhead, and between them dangled dried flowers and strips of colored fabric in reds, blacks, and blues. Ettore reached up as they passed under one of the ropes and yanked down one of the black strips, peering at it closely.

"What's all this for?" he asked Lexos.

"I'm not sure." It was not, as far as Lexos knew, any particular holiday in Merkher, and he assumed the decoration wasn't in honor of the Devetsi family, being that none of it was proper Devetsi gray. Likely just the locals making their neighborhood a bit more pleasant. "Did you really have to tear that down?"

Ettore ignored him, and if possible, his examining gaze grew even sharper. Before Lexos could ask why, he had pulled his horse to a stop and swung down out of the saddle, the black strip of fabric still clutched in his hand as he strode across the street.

Lexos eased his horse to a halt alongside Ettore's. "At this rate," he grumbled, "I will die of old age before we make it there."

Ettore stopped in front of a merchant's stall offering an odd assortment of talismans, bolts of fabric, and vegetables. He appeared to say something—whatever it was, Lexos could not hear—and the merchant manning the stall replied, gesturing to the decoration in Ettore's hand and then toward one of the talismans for sale. Without looking over his shoulder, Ettore beckoned Lexos toward him.

"What is it?" Lexos called. No response, of course, because Ettore must have known that he would, after a moment, relent, dismount from his horse, and cross the street, which he did.

"This kind fellow was explaining," Ettore said once Lexos had arrived next to him, "that the decorations were put up in honor of this week's nameday."

Ettore looked quite smug about it, but Lexos froze. That was troublesome. Long ago, certain days had been dedicated to the celebration of certain groups of saints, one that extended, too, to children born on those days. Though nobody had bothered outlawing them specifically—surely the outlaw of saint worship had been enough—he'd thought it was pretty well understood that they were not to be celebrated, even here in Merkher, in the shadow of the monastery.

The merchant, however, seemed not at all worried about sharing details of this supposedly outlawed practice with strangers, particularly one as interested as Ettore. At Ettore's request, he began to show—and attempt to sell—the talismans he had on offer, wooden pendants carved with little portraits and hung on leather cords. The first talisman, painted red, honored a saint Lexos had never heard of, while the second was a vivid blue and was associated with a saint that he'd seen depicted in much more detail up in the monastery. The third, though, was in black, and though the carving was simple, just the shape of the portrait's eyes was enough to make Lexos's heart beat painfully fast. He flinched, only barely managing not to snatch it out of the merchant's grasp.

The merchant did not appear to notice; Ettore definitely did.

"This one," he said in Merkheri, tapping the black pendant. "Who is it?"

"Ah," the merchant replied. "That's Aya Thyspira."

Of course it was. Of course. That was just Lexos's luck. Rhea, wherever she was, had fashioned herself into this travesty. What would Baba have thought, if he'd been alive? And what was Rhea thinking now, making herself into a saint? Wasn't Stratagiozi enough for her?

It would have been for him. He would have made proper use of it; he would have found a way to restore the Thyzak seat to its proper glory.

Ettore and the merchant were still conversing, and when he forced himself to listen to them again, he was relieved that they had not lingered on the subject of Aya Thyspira. Instead, the merchant was asking Ettore about his accent.

"Trefza?" he said. "Traces of Chuzhak in there, too, though."

"Trefza," Ettore replied, a bit rueful. "I hope my Merkheri isn't too bad."

"Not at all."

He practically invented the language, Lexos wanted to say, although he'd been gratified, earlier in their trip, to notice that Ettore shared some of the linguistic quirks Lexos himself had picked up in his studies, as though he was accustomed to speaking an older dialect of Merkheri.

"Well, as lovely as these are," Ettore said, tapping the black pendant, "I find myself without any gold, but thank you so much for satisfying a traveler's curiosity." He looked to Lexos. "Can you tear yourself away?"

Lexos thanked the merchant, and before long he and Ettore were on horseback again and heading deeper into the city. Rather than riding ahead, now Ettore seemed intent on keeping level with him.

"He said she was a new saint," Ettore told him after a few minutes of quiet. "Aya Thyspira." Lexos nodded but said nothing. This did not deter Ettore. "Thyspira is a familiar name, though. Stratagiozi in origin, no? And if memory serves, that particular role has belonged for some time now to a member of your family. Is that right?"

"Do you need me here to carry on the conversation or are you happy to have it with yourself?"

"You said your sister is the new Thyzak Stratagiozi." Ettore flashed a smile at Lexos. "You left out the fact that she now calls herself a saint."

Lexos stiffened. "It didn't seem important."

"I hope that's a lie. It doesn't speak well of your intelligence, otherwise." Ettore paused, as though something had just occurred to him. "How did the two of you become familiar with the saints anyway? It was my understanding we'd been outlawed."

"You have. We . . ." Lexos trailed off. His mother was dead, and so was Baba; Baba could not get angry with either of them now for disobeying him. "Rhea and I learned from our mother," he said. "She was one of your worshippers."

"That's lovely," Ettore said. "She sounds like someone I would have enjoyed meeting."

They continued riding then, and while Lexos supposed he was grateful that Ettore had chosen not to press further, their exchange had left him unnerved. What else did Ettore know, and who had been passing him this information? Perhaps the same person who had sent Lexos to join him, but then Falka had her ally in her father, Tarro. What would she need with anyone else?

These questions would have to wait, though, as the street was quickly becoming too crowded for horseback. At last, when they could go no more than two feet at a time without drawing dirty looks from some passersby, they both pulled to the side and dismounted. Lexos slapped each horse on the flank and sent them trotting back the way they'd come.

"Right," he said, turning to Ettore. "Agiokon proper. So where do we go next?"

Ettore pointed into the distance, where the rock spire rose into the sky. "That way. And no, not your little monastery."

"What, then?"

"The tower itself, Alexandros. There's an entrance built into the base of it."

He began walking again as if that was everything Lexos needed to know. Against his better judgment, Lexos hurried after him.

"An entrance to what?"

"I have not survived this long by being too free with my secrets," Ettore said. "You will just have to wait and see."

CHAPTER TWENTY-EIGHT

RHEA

Rhea stood in Agiokon's main square, looking up at the rock spire as it blotted out the sun. So, she thought. Somewhere up there was what she'd come here for.

She still had not worked out what Falka meant in directing her to the city—any further pressing she'd attempted during their meal together had been rebuffed—but it seemed silly, standing here, that she hadn't considered coming sooner. This was a saint's city, even though these days it pretended not to be. The monks who lived in the monastery still worshipped people like her.

Had they heard of her? Did they keep a portrait of her there? Perhaps there was still one of her mother, Aya Ksiga. Lexos had never told her much about the monastery, and she had never asked, which she regretted, but she could do better now—soon she might have a chance to see it herself.

First, though, she had a chance to see Chrysanthi. Rhea had written to her sister as they'd come north from Rhokera, expecting that it would take some time for Chrysanthi to make her way to Agiokon from wherever she'd followed Nitsos to, but her answer had come back only that morning: She was here already. Now, the two were planning to meet in the square. If everything went to plan, Chrysanthi would be with her again in a matter of minutes.

How different would she be, Rhea wondered. Would she be able to recognize Chrysanthi without the trappings of Stratathoma surrounding her? They'd carried some of their old wealth and status with them up in the Ksigora, but out here they were nothing but a pair of women who knew less about the workings of the world than they ought to.

"Do you see her?" she asked. Next to her, Piros searched the crowds of people flooding the square, his height an advantage that Rhea did not share.

"Not yet," he said.

"Maybe she got lost."

"She has Andrija with her." Piros rested a comforting hand on Rhea's shoulder. "I trust him to get her here."

It was far more likely, Rhea thought, that Chrysanthi would be getting Andrija here. She could picture it, Chrysanthi hauling her bodyguard around the city with a beatific smile while he wished for a quick and merciful death.

"Why don't you sit down?" Piros said, gesturing to the table they'd claimed at a nearby kafenio. "I'll tell you if I spot her."

"I really should—"

"I told Michali I would take care of you." Piros's expression grew stern. "Sit down and order something to eat. You're looking pale."

It was not the warning carried in Piros's words that sent her back to her seat; rather it was the memory of what she'd left behind in the Sxoriza camp that morning. Michali had not protested her departure. He had not even come along to say goodbye. In fact, since finding her in the harbor at Rhokera, he'd hardly spent more than a handful of minutes in her company.

She supposed she couldn't blame him. It had been callous of her to leave him behind, knowing he would worry for her safety. And to make matters worse, she hadn't been able to bring herself to apologize, not when doing so would've required admitting that she'd left him on purpose. Instead, she'd led him back out of the city, let the crush of the crowds keep him from getting too close to her. When they'd arrived back at camp, he'd finally said: "You got lost, then?" And she'd been a coward. All she'd been able to do was nod.

At least he hadn't seen her with Falka. That would have turned an already uncomfortable situation into a catastrophe, and she couldn't bear the thought of anything ruining the peace she'd found on the deck of that little fishing boat.

Well, not peace, exactly. She was not quite so naïve anymore as to pretend that Falka had no designs of her own, designs that were probably working against Rhea's. But still. A bit of sun, and some good food, and the company of someone who did not look at her with quite so much expectation. That had been a gift.

With a sigh, she took a seat at the kafenio table and ordered some flatbread, along with seasoned oil to dip it in. She was rarely hungry these days, but everybody here seemed to be picking at something or other, and it was important she not stand out too sharply. Still, as necessary as her anonymity was, she found herself chafing at it. It wasn't as though she'd wanted to announce herself to the whole city—she knew the sort of danger that would put her in—but it felt wrong to pretend to be something other than she was. Especially here, in the shadow of the monastery.

The square around her reminded her of the one she'd seen in Ksigori, by the site of the church, only here it was the rock spire that held the place of honor. Here and there in the city crowds she could spot people peering up into the sky and lifting a hand in some gesture of respect toward the building perched more than a thousand feet above.

She'd been able to see from the Sxoriza camp that the city pressed up against the base of the spire, but it had remained some abstract image in her mind until she'd laid eyes on it herself—the gargantuan stone, the breadth of it nearly incomprehensible this close, butting up against the city square, its scale comically different. The bottom ten feet or so of the pillar were covered in layers of graffiti, most of it in the alphabet that Merkheri shared with Trefza and Thyzaki, and some enterprising street artist had drawn a landscape on one section in colorful chalk, and was now using it as a backdrop to perform a puppet show for a gaggle of children.

None of these people, she thought peevishly, looked equipped to help her with whatever was happening to her gifts. Part of her wanted to march up to the rock pillar and, absurdly, knock on it as if it were a door that might open, but the rest of her was too nervous to make any moves at the moment. What if she climbed up the spire and found the monastery door and asked for the help of those who lived inside, only to be turned away? What if they saw, instantly, that she was not the saint her mother had been? That she was something else, something neither here nor there?

These monks worshipped true saints, not a beggar's choice like her, not somebody who could not even keep from spitting shreds of her own matagios out of her mouth.

"No sign of her," Piros said, sitting down opposite her. "But I was starting to get a few looks from the owner of the kafenio, so I'll get up again in a moment."

Rhea made a small noise of understanding, but she had not taken her eyes off the spire. "Do you know," she said suddenly, "that I never came here?"

Piros raised his eyebrows. "Really?"

"When I was Thyspira. When I was the other Thyspira," she amended. "I married so many times. Hundreds of times. But never to an Agiokori, even when they sent their finest."

"Was that by your design?"

"My father's. It was his preference that I not honor Agiokon with my choice. He said the city had enough power already." She squinted up at the monastery, imagining for a moment that she could see someone waving down to her. "I think really he just didn't want me near the monks."

He had known what she was—what all four Argyrosi were—and he'd kept that secret from each of her siblings equally. But he'd gone to greater lengths to keep Rhea from knowing she was his firstborn. For the first few months with the Sxoriza, she had written that lie off as Baba being Baba, doing what he always did and keeping information in reserve to use as leverage in some game they had not yet begun to play. Since then, though, enough had happened that cracks had begun to form in her understanding both of her gifts and of the man who had given them to her. Perhaps he had kept her out of certain things to spite her. Perhaps he had been afraid.

"I'm sorry," she said, "but I really don't think I can sit here any longer. Can't we go look for my sister?"

"It'll be easier for her to find us if we stay in one place."

"You stay, then. I'll go."

She was almost to her feet when Piros's hand closed firmly around her wrist. "You are not the sort of person who can leave behind her guards as often as you do," he said, his voice low enough that only she could hear. "Please, Thyspira. Sit back down."

Rhea felt her pulse begin to beat at her temples in the way that it had so often in Baba's house. Piros, she reminded herself, was not trying to scold her. He wanted her to be safe.

So had Baba, in his way, but before Rhea could begin to argue with Piros—or herself—she heard her name, called across the square by a voice she knew better than her own.

"I heard something," she said. "I think she's here."

Piros let go, and she whirled to face the direction the voice had come from. There, pushing through the crowd, was a young woman, tall with yellow hair that caught the winter sun. Behind her followed a man dressed all in black, his shoulders broad and his steps measured despite the eager pace of his companion.

"Chrysanthi," Rhea breathed.

She could tell the minute Chrysanthi spotted her: Her sister's eyes went wide, and she smacked Andrija with the back of her hand before taking off in Rhea's direction. Rhea sidestepped a pair of merchants and emerged into the square proper just in time to hold out her arms before Chrysanthi careened into her chest.

She was warm—that was Rhea's first thought. Rhea was always so cold, but Chrysanthi felt like the high point of summer, like a night in a proper bed with a well-tended fire. Rhea locked her arms around her sister's waist and let out a long breath.

"You're here," Chrysanthi was saying in her ear. "You're really here."

"I am." Rhea stroked her hand down the length of Chrysanthi's hair. It was as soft as it had been when they were children; for a moment Rhea was back in a little bedroom in a house in the country, peering down into a crib at a small, pink infant. "Everything's all right."

Chrysanthi sniffed and said, very wetly, "I lost Lefka."

Rhea's heart collapsed in on itself, sweet and painful at once. "It's all right."

"But you gave her to me."

"I know." She pried herself away from her sister, holding Chrysanthi at arm's length. Did she look different? Not older, but then they never did. Her eyes, though, shone with tears, and her cheeks had gone splotchy. "My goodness, *koukla,* you'd think we'd never been apart before."

"It was different this time!"

"It was," Rhea said and cupped Chrysanthi's dear, dear face in her hands—a face which twisted immediately into a childish grimace.

"What is that?" Chrysanthi said, pushing Rhea's right hand away. "Did you just wipe something on me? Really?"

"No, I—" She broke off. The scar on her unmarked hand, the one that would not fully heal. She had bandaged both hands before coming into the city, but the scar had opened and bled through the linen. The stain was fresh enough that it had left a matching print on Chrysanthi's cheek. "Sorry," she said. "It's nothing."

"You're bleeding," Chrysanthi said. "Do you usually bleed?"

Moments ago she had been so glad to have her sister back; now Rhea thought it was past time for Chrysanthi to be on her way again.

"I said it's nothing. Come on, we're in the way of people."

She led Chrysanthi toward the edge of the square, where Piros and Andrija had found each other and were standing side by side, equally vigilant. Briefly, she imagined the four of them sitting down at that little kafenio table and ordering lunch as though it weren't a great stroke of luck that they'd all arrived here safely.

"We're fine," Chrysanthi said as they reached Andrija. "I told you it would be fine."

"I know you did," Andrija said. "And yet."

Rhea had never got to know him all that well, but she thought that a single glance at him now told her enough. She'd been right to let Chrysanthi choose him as her companion; in fact, she rather thought Andrija would have gone with Chrysanthi anyway, chosen or not.

"We should get out of the square," Piros said, "before we draw any more attention. And then we can discuss the outcome of your errand and what to do next."

"Yes," Rhea said, but Chrysanthi said, "Just a moment," and began undoing the bandages around Rhea's right hand.

"Excuse me," Rhea said. "Do you mind?"

"I do, actually."

Rhea tried to pull free, but Chrysanthi always got the better of her in things like this. Already, the bandage was half off.

"Chrysanthi," Andrija said, "Piros is right. We really should go." He looked to Rhea, eyes apologetic as Chrysanthi continued to wrestle with her right arm. It took everything in Rhea to maintain her composure. "We saw Domina banners on our way here. Tarro is in the city, if I'm not mistaken, and I think it's best that you two not meet."

"Quite. I— Chrysanthi, if you don't stop— Don't touch me!"

The bandage came loose and fell to the ground. Rhea shut her eyes, a swell of anger sweeping through her.

"Rhea," Chrysanthi said, "what is this?"

"A cut." She pulled her arm free; Chrysanthi put up no fight, not as Rhea cradled her hand to her chest, nor as she backed away. "I told you not to touch me."

Slowly, her sister nodded. There was a new confidence to her bearing now, which was odd—Chrysanthi hadn't been lacking in it before—but for all her poise, the look on her face was so unsure that Rhea felt it like a hit to her stomach. The anger drained out of her. Chrysanthi had been Baba's favorite, yes, but he'd left his mark on her just as he had the rest of them.

"I'm sorry," she said. "I didn't mean to be— Let's get off the street, yes?" She smiled, the shock of seeing Chrysanthi again faded enough that she could think of what it might mean if her sister had completed her errand. "You can tell me all about what you found."

She could feel Andrija and Piros watching her, both of them waiting for Chrysanthi to respond. Her sister hesitated, mouth half open.

"Please?" Rhea said. Nitsos. She just needed to get her hands on Nitsos, and all of the uncertainty of the last few months would be worth it. "I've missed you very much."

Chrysanthi's eyes softened, and there, that was her littlest sibling. That was the girl she'd come back to season after season.

"All right," Chrysanthi said. "I have a lot to tell you."

They left the square together, Piros leading the way toward an inn he'd found with rooms for rent some blocks away. Andrija brought up the rear, and though Chrysanthi seemed quite used to his presence, Rhea found it a bit unsettling. As glad as she was that Chrysanthi had a dedicated protector, she was not used to being around people for whom she was not a priority.

She'd meant to leave Chrysanthi to herself until they reached the inn, but as they passed another block of shops, some decorated for the upcoming nameday, Rhea could not help herself.

"You didn't find him, did you?" she asked.

"Nitsos?" Chrysanthi nodded to Piros. "I think we should probably wait to discuss that."

"It's all right if you didn't." Rhea wasn't sure if she really meant that, but if it got Chrysanthi to just say, flat out, what had happened, then it was fine. "We'll sort it either way."

"Chrysanthi," Andrija said from behind them. Rhea held up a hand, silencing him.

"Is he nearby, do you think?" she asked. "You were already here when I wrote to you, so I thought—"

"Chrysanthi."

"What?" Chrysanthi asked.

Andrija lifted a hand, gently ushering her to one side. Rhea followed suit, tracing the line of his gaze.

"Is that him?" Andrija asked, but his voice sounded dull to Rhea, dull and very far away, because half a block to the east was a man—a boy, really—stopped at the intersection between the main thoroughfare and a side street. He was peering down at something in his hands, and then he finished with it and stuffed it into his trouser pocket before looking up.

Blond curly hair. Eyes whose color could not be mistaken, even at a distance. All Rhea could hear was the thunder of her blood.

Nitsos fucking Argyros was in Agiokon.

CHAPTER TWENTY-NINE

ALEXANDROS

Ettore guided them in a wide circle through the eastern side of the city, toward the northern side of the rock spire. Lexos had never seen it from this angle—the approach taken for Stratagiozi meetings curled up and around the western mountainside—and the size of it was overwhelming. How could he ever have stood atop it and done anything but panic?

Still, there were plenty of other things to draw his attention away from the mammoth stone tower: people, food aromatic enough to make his mouth water, and most distractingly, more evidence of saint worship that (bafflingly) included his sister. There were fewer talismans on display at the shops they passed, and there were no decorations hung overhead, but it was enough to set a chill running down Lexos's back.

He quickened his pace, catching up with Ettore. "We can't be far, can we?"

"No, not far."

Ettore beckoned Lexos onto a side street, and after another block's travel they emerged again onto a road that was paved with ancient cobblestones. Unlike most of the others they had encountered so far, this one ran dead straight. It must have been part of the city's first iteration, laid into the earth before the rest of the city had time to sprout up in the valley.

Lexos peered ahead of them, trying to get a good look at where the street led, but it was so narrow that even two people walking shoulder to shoulder ahead were enough to block his view. The stone spire was off to his left now and much closer than he had realized. Looking up to the top made something crack in his neck.

"Was it a particular saint your mother worshipped?" Ettore asked suddenly, and the sound of his voice was enough to make Lexos jump. Since leaving their horses behind they'd spoken very little between them, other than whatever few words it took for Ettore to direct him here.

"I don't know," he said. "I don't think it was you, though."

Ettore pressed a hand to his chest. "You wound me."

"You'll live."

"I will," Ettore agreed. "But I'm curious. You and your sister—did you like what your mother taught you?"

"Did we like it?"

Ettore stopped short, leaving Lexos to nearly collide with him. "Did it mean something to you? Your sister calls herself a saint now. I find I'm wondering why."

So am I, Lexos thought. He had no good answer for Ettore. Maybe their mother's instruction had meant something to Rhea, but more likely, it had been so long ago that she didn't remember it.

"After our father . . . I don't know," he said. "You'd have to ask her."

"Maybe I will."

Now there was a disastrous pairing if Lexos had ever seen one.

They continued down the road, its stones underfoot more ancient than even the buildings that lined it, until most everybody traveling in the same direction had peeled off onto one of the side streets, making for one of the busier blocks and smaller markets that were tucked here and there in this part of the city. Ettore kept them moving forward, and gradually Lexos began to assemble an image of what lay ahead.

The blur of green and gray sharpened into trees laden with fresh spring leaves growing between stone arches and beyond stone walls. Ettore led Lexos under the first arch and onto an even narrower path, its uneven surface tiled with black-and-white mosaics.

"This used to be the center of the city," Ettore said, gesturing to the shaded path ahead. "The northern side of the spire. Agiokon has shifted, though, over the years. Can you hear that?"

They paused under a nearby lime tree and Lexos shut his eyes, listening. There, the sound of hundreds of voices, chatter drifting on the wind.

"The square is just on the other side of the spire," Ettore explained. "But I would reckon most Agiokori haven't been this way. The money's moved south."

As they continued on, their path began to join with others, all of them funneling any visitors closer to the spire. Lexos examined the greenery around him, looking for anybody else who might be wandering the grounds, but they were empty—almost eerily so. He could understand, though, why the average person might feel more comfortable staying clear of a place so long devoted to the saints.

Most markers of that old worship had been altered or simply worn down with time, but he could see the remains of them still, carved on the underside of the arches he and Ettore walked through. Portraits, much like those on the pendants they'd seen earlier, with their heads scratched out, their etched features chiseled away. Zita and Stavra, Lexos knew, did not care nearly as much as Baba had about saint worship, but it seemed the allowances they made for the monks above did not hold for the grounds below.

"Are any of these you?" he asked Ettore as they passed under an arch left more intact.

"Not these, no." Ettore pointed to one of the faces. "Actually, I think that one was meant to be, but they haven't got my chin right."

At last they emerged from the trees onto an overgrown patch of grass that pressed right up against the base of the spire. Lexos looked from side to side; this close, the spire was big enough that he couldn't see where it began to curve.

Ettore had stopped walking and was eyeing the spire with a frown. "It looks different," he said.

"It's a rock that's been here for more than a thousand years. I very much doubt that."

"Rock," Ettore said primly, "erodes. And anyway, that isn't what I mean. Has nobody been tending to the trees?"

He led Lexos to the right, trailing his left hand along the spire as they walked. Lexos watched for a few moments before hesitantly extending his own hand and doing the same; he didn't want to miss another of Ettore's tricks. But instead of pulling the gold ring out of his pocket again and fussing with the dark braid stored inside, Ettore simply stopped in his tracks when they'd gone a little ways into the overgrowth and said, "Here we are."

Keeping his left hand pressed to the stone, Ettore reached with his right across the rock face, inching his fingertips along as though he was feeling for an edge of some sort. Lexos couldn't make out any identifying mark on the stone, and certainly nothing that looked like a destination to which one might arrive, but he'd had enough of Ettore ridiculing any questions he asked, so fine. He would stay silent and let him do whatever he was doing.

After a few moments more of examination, Ettore dropped his hands before leaning in and pressing his thumb to a seemingly random point on the stone face. Somewhere within the spire, something clicked, and Lexos heard a sound so familiar that he half expected one of his siblings to step into view—gears whirring and clockwork machinery grinding to life.

A perfectly rectangular section of the rock, only an inch or two taller than Ettore at his full height, began to recede into the spire, leaving a shadowed doorway in its wake. Lexos stole a sidelong glance at Ettore. He'd seen Nitsos's work in the Domina palace at Vuomorra and, more specifically, in Ettore's prison. Was this another collaboration between his brother and the Domina family?

It couldn't be, though. Everything here was far too old, from before the Argyrosi had ever come into their gifts. And Nitsos, for that matter, had been so invested in their father's good opinion of him that he would never have involved himself with a bastion of saint worship like this. More likely, some previous holder of Nitsos's gift had done this work.

Ettore stepped into the dark of the spire, and Lexos followed. Just inside the doorway was a small, square chamber, its walls too deeply in shadow to make out. The floor, though, was covered in grass much like the outside, the green of it still strangely fresh. It was real, though, not like the glass and wire creations Nitsos had made in his garden back at home.

"Out of the way," Ettore said. "The door needs to close." Lexos could not see him, even in the shaft of daylight that carried through the still-open doorway, but there was something about his voice that unnerved him, something determined and rough. Maybe it was just the way the sound carried in this little room.

He stepped to one side, aware suddenly of the tracks running through the grass that carried the door back and forth from its threshold. Very much like Nitsos's work, indeed.

The door began its return journey, the squeals of the gears grating against Lexos's ears. Behind the door, cut into the opposite wall, was a matching opening, and through it, a stone staircase descended into the black. He stared, trying to gather every bit of detail he could about it until the stone door slid home with a thud, and the last of the light was gone.

Silence, and then Ettore cleared his throat and his face appeared, lit with a glow too pale to be torchlight. It was coming, Lexos realized, from something in Ettore's hand—small and round, but not the ring. This looked like one of the dials Nitsos made for his siblings, trackers to count the passage of time, only instead of a clock face, it held a mirror, the surface of which had been painted with light. More saintcraft, a combination of gifts worked into an object that made its Stratagiozi counterparts look like child's play.

Ettore began to descend, the light off his pocket mirror seeming to amplify as he went. Lexos, as he was very used to doing by now, trailed behind, but slowly, so that he could take a better look at where he'd found himself. Like the arches they'd passed through outside, this staircase appeared to be ancient and was decorated with likenesses of the saints. But where the portraits outside the spire were all defaced in some way, those etched into the stairs themselves and carved into the walls were intact. One he recognized from the talismans on the outskirts of Agiokon. Another he thought looked quite like Rhea, but was not her at all.

They continued down for what felt like a very long time. The air grew increasingly damp and pungent—like something green and gritty, Lexos thought, as if stone and herbs had been ground together in a mortar and pestle—and the winter chill that existed outside the spire seemed unable to penetrate to here, where they were climbing down into the earth.

Did the monks know this was here, a thousand feet underneath them? They had to, Lexos thought at first, but then it was entirely possible that the saints themselves had constructed this place and never bothered telling their worshippers above.

He wiped the sweat from his brow and continued on. The staircase ran in a spiral, curving around a column of empty space in the middle that he could not see the bottom of. Like Ettore ahead of him, he was making sure to keep close to the outer wall, his shoulder almost pressed against it, but still the prospect of the drop that might be waiting there over the edge of the stairs was enough to make him dizzy, the dark swimming in front of him.

It was because of this dizziness that he almost didn't notice when they passed the first doorway. Simple, crooked, cut into the rock as if by a dull knife. Once he understood that it was not, in fact, some trick his eyes were playing on him, the sight of it staggered him. It had been odd enough for him to understand that this staircase had been dug down into the ground, and that it was clearly leading somewhere, but the idea that there were other rooms—hallways, perhaps, or even another staircase just like this one, leading deeper—felt like too much for him to understand.

Of course he had always known that the continent had been just as vast as it was now during the time of the saints. But how strange, Lexos thought as he kept after Ettore, to remember that there were layers of earth under every step he took, names and lives stacked thick like paper.

Suddenly the dark thickened, and the beacon of Ettore's mirror ahead disappeared. Lexos's heart jumped into his throat. Breathing quickly, he pressed his palm to the wall.

"Ettore?" he called. His voice echoed, suggesting a size to this stairwell that Lexos would rather not think about. Had Ettore slipped and fallen? Dropped without a word?

He had not, as was immediately made clear when the glow of sunlight reappeared, silhouetting Ettore's head as he leaned out through another doorway, this one below Lexos by at least two spirals of the staircase, on the opposite side of the chute.

"This way," he said.

Lexos resumed his descent, moving as quickly as he safely could. "I don't suppose you would consider slowing down, would you?"

"You're welcome to turn back if this doesn't suit you."

"No, thank you," Lexos replied, and Ettore stayed where he was, waiting, but Lexos was all too aware of the other man's impatience. He'd come here intending to make himself indispensable to Ettore, and instead here he was, entirely dependent on him for light and a way out, among other things.

Once he had reached the threshold, Ettore stepped aside, gesturing for him to go through. The mirror had been left in the room that waited beyond, balanced on a cairn. The chamber it was illuminating was simple, huge stone slabs expertly joined, but its opposite wall featured another doorway, and through it Lexos could make out another room. In it stood the shape of something strange: a white olive tree.

It was made of stone, he realized as Ettore led him into the second chamber, a pale sort he had never encountered before. Though at first the dark had made it difficult for him to determine its scale, as he got closer it became clear that the sculpture was only a foot tall and perched in the middle of the room on a waist-high box carved from the same white stone.

Ettore threw out an arm suddenly, catching him across the chest. "Hold on," he said and then crouched low, aiming the light from his mirror across the floor. The dust was thick, almost plush, and undisturbed. Satisfied, Ettore snapped the mirror shut.

"Excuse me," Lexos said, and then he heard a shuffle as Ettore moved before the air turned sharp with the scent of a spark; seconds later, a torch mounted on the wall flared to life. He sighed. "Have there been torches this whole time?"

Ettore ignored him and moved toward the box. Lexos decided to let him do whatever it was he'd come here to do. In the meantime he would wait by the torch, just in case.

Ettore took hold of the tree, the muscles in his forearms standing out as he tried to move it off the box. Finally, after a few moments without success, he made a sound of disapproval and straightened up. "Come here," he said to Lexos. "It's heavier than I remember."

Lexos approached. From this close, he could see that the tree and its base formed the lid of the box. Ettore had said nothing about what might be inside it, but given his Domina name, Lexos had assumed they were here to fetch an obscene amount of gold. Looking at the box now, that didn't seem to be the case.

"Ready?" Ettore said. Lexos nodded.

Together, they grasped the tree by its trunk and pulled. With a horrible, grating noise, the lid began to move. Lexos felt a muscle twinge in his back and swallowed a complaint. Ettore was not in any sort of mood to appreciate it; he hadn't been since they'd got within a hundred yards of the spire.

Beneath the tree-adorned lid was a dark, hollow space. Lexos held the lid as Ettore reached into the box. With a muffled groan, he began to lift something out.

It was an urn, made of some sort of metal, and it was smaller than the size of the plinth suggested—maybe the length of Lexos's forearm at most. Ettore set the urn down on the floor and knelt by it before popping the top off. Air rushed through the broken seal with a hiss. From his vantage point over Ettore's shoulder, Lexos couldn't see what was contained inside, but whatever it was, Ettore's satisfaction with it was palpable.

"Good," he said. "You can shut the box now."

Lexos did as he said, with some difficulty. "What's in there?"

"Some old friends," Ettore replied. He reached into the urn and came up with a handful of fine white powder, letting it sift between his fingers. "I confess I'm quite pleased to see everything in order. It's been a very long time."

A gnawing sort of dread was beginning to burrow its way up Lexos's spine. He didn't have much experience with tombs, but he'd seen bodies burned, and seen what could be left behind. "Ettore," he asked, "where are we?" He cleared his throat and ventured further: "Who are they?"

Ettore did not answer, but he didn't really need to, did he? Their faces were everywhere in this place, etched into the walls, the floor. The saints had to have been laid to rest somewhere—Lexos knew that they were here, ground to dust and poured into the urn that Ettore was now sealing back up.

How long had they been here? And what, he wondered, did Ettore want with them?

"Right," Ettore said, and Lexos folded those questions up, to be considered once they were out of this place. "I'd carry this up myself, but you look like you're a bit stronger than I am, much as I hate to admit it. Do you mind?"

At last, something he could do for Ettore, something to make himself useful. "Of course."

He had just taken hold of the urn when a strange vibration ran through the stone wall, juddering up through his hand and into his shoulder. He recoiled immediately. A trap sprung somewhere? Perhaps the staircase had shifted, or there were more tricks to this tomb that Ettore was keeping hidden.

But Ettore said, "What was that?"

"I thought you—"

Ettore shook his head. Together they held still, both listening intently. Nothing, no change in the air, until Lexos heard a bit of loose rock drop from the chamber ceiling and land on the floor with a clatter. Another followed, and then another, and as Lexos looked up, the ceiling began to shake. Somewhere above, something rumbled, the sound reverberating in the empty stairwell.

"How far down are we?" Lexos asked. When he faced Ettore again, the other man was grabbing the torch.

"Do you have the urn?" Ettore asked. He looked grim and there was a feverish gleam in his eyes. Lexos nodded. "Good. Follow me. Now!"

"Why?"

"We have to get out. The tower's coming down."

CHAPTER THIRTY

CHRYSANTHI

One moment Rhea was there next to her; the next she was halfway across the street. Beyond Rhea, Chrysanthi could see who she was moving toward: their brother, head lifted to stare at the stone spire.

Of course Nitsos had figured out where to come next. Chrysanthi had hoped that she and Andrija might have beat him here, but he'd been too quick and too far ahead. And now Rhea was charging after him, the sense gone from her so completely that there was nothing left to do but follow suit.

"Wait here," Chrysanthi yelled over her shoulder. "We'll be back!"

If Rhea confronted Nitsos now, it would all be over. Every dream she'd ever had of pulling her family back together, gone up in smoke. With Andrija calling after her, Chrysanthi threw herself into the throng of passersby, elbowing her way through a small nameday celebration before breaking into a run. Nitsos was already out of sight, but she could still catch Rhea if she hurried.

She emerged onto the street Nitsos had taken. It cut a straight line to the spire and the surrounding square, and was busy enough that all

Chrysanthi could see were the faces of strangers. Finding either of her siblings in this mass of people seemed impossible. How had they moved so quickly?

Despite the urgency pounding through her veins, she forced herself to breathe. Think, she told herself. Think.

Ignoring the protests of the corner shopkeeper, Chrysanthi climbed onto a crate of produce to get a better vantage point. From this angle, she had an unobstructed view nearly to the square itself. And it was because she was looking for her family, because she was staring so intently at the view ahead, that she noticed the first explosion—a burst of red and orange about halfway up the tower of rock.

It looked so small from this distance that she wasn't sure what she was seeing. Was it part of a nameday celebration? Some sort of display? But soon after, another explosion followed, and cries of horror broke out across the street as the supports holding up one of the monastery's many cantilevered verandas crumbled and fell.

Nitsos, Chrysanthi thought, stunned. Was this his doing? Was this why he'd come?

Brickwork and stone dropped through the sky, little specks of black against the blue. The veranda began to topple over the edge of the spire only moments later, taking what looked like half the monastery down with it. The crowd on the street watched in an eerie silence, until behind Chrysanthi, someone let out a scream.

People began to run, voices thick in the air. Chrysanthi was knocked hard in the shoulder by someone and stumbled off the crate, falling to her knees on the cobblestones. Pain streaked through her as her palms tore against the rock. Before she could gather her wits, a man pulled her to her feet. He said something in Merkheri, pushing her back the way she'd come, but she shook him off. Rhea—where was Rhea?

Where the street had been busy moments before, it was mobbed now. Chrysanthi could hear the shout of someone being trampled up ahead; behind her, a child had begun to cry. Surely Nitsos and Rhea would've turned back. Surely she would spot them rushing toward her, all their enmity forgotten in the face of whatever had happened at the top of the spire. But they were nowhere to be seen. And the longer she stood here, the more she found herself pressed against the shop wall behind her. She lifted one arm, trying to break some space for herself in the flood of people, only to be knocked back another step.

"Rhea?" she called, desperate to hear an answer. None came. Chrysanthi scrubbed at the tears that had begun to wind down her cheeks. She had just found her sister again. They would not be parted now.

She ducked the elbow of a fleeing woman and clambered over a merchant's upturned display table. There, behind the other shop stalls that lined the street—an open path, if she kept out of the street proper. She started forward, breath coming quick and shallow.

A few blocks on, she still had yet to spot either Nitsos or Rhea, so she paused to take another good look at the spire. The air around it was clouded with dark smoke, but so far the rest of the monastery seemed stable. She could only imagine, though, what sort of wreckage waited at the base of the spire. There had been so many people there, so many shops and buildings all directly under the falling debris. Who would have wanted to do that kind of damage?

In the distance, dark hair and a black coat—someone still heading toward the spire, against the flow of the crowd. Chrysanthi couldn't be sure, but it was enough to send her pushing across the street. Somebody going in the other direction caught on her jacket; she shrugged it off and left it behind.

She'd made it three blocks closer to the main square when the ground underfoot began to shake. Slowly, but stronger every second until she had to throw herself against a nearby wall to keep to her feet. Then, the boom of another explosion, and a great crack, the likes of which she'd never heard before. Chrysanthi flinched as a rush of heat buffeted her, sweeping out from the spire. When it had cleared, she squinted up at the monastery, afraid that another section of it had been destroyed, but there was no change. And besides, the sound had been far louder this time, almost as if it had come from ground level.

She swallowed hard, a cold fear clutching at her throat. It took all of her will to start moving again, to continue after her siblings, but she had to. Find her family; get them out. Those were the only things that mattered now.

The street grew emptier as she ran, chest heaving, legs aching. She passed someone collapsed by the side of the street, and someone else came staggering toward her, bleeding from a nasty wound at the temple. Chrysanthi made to help them, but all they could do was repeat a phrase in Merkheri that she couldn't understand. She let them go and kept on.

The street widened a few blocks from the square itself. Chrysanthi stumbled to a halt, bracing herself on a deserted shop's wall as she strained to catch her breath, to ignore the sounds of people screaming. She lifted one arm to cover her mouth with her sleeve; dust was so heavy in the air that even through the fabric she could taste it, could feel it turning to paste in her mouth.

From here she at last had an unobstructed view of the base of the spire, but it looked strange, as though a blackened mouth had opened just above the ground. She rubbed at her eyes, blinked hard, but the shape remained, and she could see, too, that the square was littered with huge chunks of rubble.

The last explosion—it had blown the base of the spire wide open. She stared at the spread of destruction, the ash staining the square and the gaping crack in the remains of the spire. Only an hour before it had been impossible to imagine that anything could touch something so large, so ancient, but now she traced the shape of the crack and realized that it was changing, and that it was not people she heard screaming, but the stone. The crunch of rock grinding to nothing, the scrape of great slabs breaking loose, all of it so loud that she could practically feel it pressing down on her shoulders. And there, silhouetted against the gray haze, her siblings. They were too far. She would not be able to reach them in time.

"Rhea!" Chrysanthi yelled. "Nitsos! Run!"

Her brother could not hear her; he was kneeling in the wreckage, checking the pulse of a corpse. And Rhea was approaching, one hand outstretched as she called Nitsos's name.

Chrysanthi stepped forward, only to reel back as another hail of stone came tumbling down from above. Didn't they understand what was happening?

"Nitsos! The tower! Rhea, please!"

Somebody grabbed Chrysanthi around her waist and began to drag her backward. She kicked hard, nails biting deep into their skin, but their grip only tightened. Andrija, she realized and felt a pang of relief even as she tried to get free of him.

"We need to go," Andrija said in her ear. "Now."

"I can't. I can't leave them. I have to—"

Another explosion ricocheted down. Chrysanthi let out a cry, shrinking against Andrija. He hoisted her off her feet and she let him turn them away from the square. In moments, he had them braced under the arch of a shop doorway, her back pressed to the stone as he cradled her head with both hands.

"Hold on," he said. She shut her eyes. The tower had begun its collapse, and there was nowhere left to run.

CHAPTER THIRTY-ONE

CHRYSANTHI

She could feel Andrija shaking where her hands were gripping his shirt. She could taste the smoke in the air. It was so quiet; no, it was louder than anything she'd ever heard. Chrysanthi opened her eyes.

"Are you hurt?" Andrija said. His shirt had been white once; it was gray now, and when she drew herself away from him, she could see the outline of her body in the dust coating him.

"I'm all right," she said. Over them, the archway was still intact, and the rest of the shop looked as though it had survived, although many of its wares were destroyed. Maybe, Chrysanthi thought, nothing too bad had happened.

The thought vanished as soon as she stepped outside. The noon sunlight had been dimmed. Everything appeared to her as if through a fog; even the air itself felt rough, scraping through her as she breathed deeply to calm herself. The buildings in this neighborhood had been all but flattened, leaving half walls and crumbled ruins behind, and the street was almost impassable, littered with debris. A massive chunk of stone had driven deeply into the earth; still the bulk of it remaining aboveground was taller even than Andrija.

And in the square, there was—

Nothing. An absolute emptiness where the famous Agiokori spire had been only minutes before.

Chrysanthi's eyes began to sting. Whether from dust or tears she wasn't sure, but Andrija's mouth twisted with concern. "I don't know how stable any of this is," he said. "We should leave as soon as we can."

Stable? Why should she care about that? The spire was gone. People—there had been people up there, in that monastery. People down below. How many of them were dead now?

"My sister," she said. "My brother. They were up ahead."

"I think we know what happened to them," Andrija replied, his hand insistent at her elbow. "Please. Please, will you come?"

Voices began to slice through the quiet. A woman crawled out from the collapsed kafenio across the way and called for help; someone was trapped farther in.

"See?" Chrysanthi said. "See? She's all right. And we're all right. Rhea and Nitsos—"

"This could have been an attempt on their lives," Andrija cut in. He looked his usual stern self, but this time Chrysanthi could see everything underneath: the fear, the confusion, and the barely contained panic. "Or on yours. I need to get you somewhere safe."

She understood that. Really, she did. This was probably some Stratagiozi's work, aimed at ridding the world of the last few remaining Argyrosi. But she could not leave her family. And Andrija would follow her if she went ahead. She knew that.

"I'm sorry," she said and started picking her way through the wreckage. Sure enough, she'd only made it over one slab of the spire before she could hear his footsteps, rock crunching under him as he climbed after her.

She headed for the last place she'd seen Rhea. The rubble had fallen heavily here, obliterating shop stalls and kafenios. Chrysanthi could make out crumpled bodies, some crushed beneath the stone and some beginning to stir. There an intact teacup, dotted with red enamel; here the catch of sun on a broken window. And there—

She gasped, her heart seizing in her chest. There was a hand, reaching out from under the rock just ahead of her. Unmoving and pale, emerging from a black sleeve, palm up.

"What?" Andrija asked. "What is it?"

"A mark," Chrysanthi breathed. On the extended hand, a black line arcing from index finger to little finger. She knew that mark as well as she knew her own. Rhea.

She dropped to her knees, scrabbling at the stone, but she wasn't strong enough to move much of it. A moment later Andrija joined her and nudged her out of the way. Chrysanthi felt for a heartbeat on her sister's wrist as he began to move the rocks covering Rhea's body. She was cold. Cold and unresponsive.

"No," she said. "You're fine."

She kept saying so, over and over as Andrija cleared away the stone. It didn't look so bad, right? Rhea had fallen near the wall of a building that was only partially damaged. Perhaps she had taken refuge inside and only come out after the worst of the collapse, just as Chrysanthi and Andrija had.

Chrysanthi clutched her sister's hand tightly, the black of Rhea's mark peeking through the knot of her fingers. Something . . . there was something odd about it, now that she was this close. The edges were not as she remembered them, and the color seemed to be spreading through the lines and whorls on Rhea's palm, as though it were ink on paper.

She thought of Rhea's bandaged right hand, of the scar there that had bled through its wrappings. What had happened to her? And why had she not told Chrysanthi about any of it?

Later. She would ask Rhea when they were out of this place.

"Almost," Andrija said as he levered a jagged bit of stone away from Rhea's head. There was a large wound oozing blood on her jaw, and her face was pockmarked with little cuts and scrapes, but Chrysanthi let out a burble of nearly hysterical laughter when she realized that her sister, unbelievably, was breathing.

She scrambled over to keep Rhea's head steady as Andrija cleared the rest of the rubble. The fingers on her scarred hand looked badly broken. Chrysanthi could only assume her body was bruised to the bone. Still, she was Rhea; she was alive. That was all that mattered.

Chrysanthi folded over and pressed her forehead against her sister's. "Rhea, please," she whispered. "Please, wake up."

Finally, Andrija was finished. He stood over Chrysanthi and her sister, keeping watch back up the street even though this block was deserted. "Don't move her," he said. "If she wakes, we'll get her out of the street."

"*If* she wakes?"

"You never know." Andrija nodded at the wound on Rhea's temple, which Chrysanthi refused to look at closely for fear she might get a glimpse of the inside of Rhea's skull.

"What happened, Andrija?" she asked instead. "How could anything bring the spire down?"

"I don't know."

"I've never seen . . ." She trailed off. She'd never seen anything at all, had she? Fleeing Stratathoma, traveling to Vashnasta—as new as it had all been, what was any of it compared to this? None of it had taught her what might be done with a Stratagiozi's powers. None of it had made her afraid of the mark on her left hand.

"Chrysanthi," Andrija said suddenly. "Your sister."

She looked down just in time to see Rhea draw a long breath. Her eyes fluttered open, darting wildly before they locked onto Chrysanthi. Her body relaxed just barely, recognition washing over her face. "*Koukla,*" she said, her voice horribly rough.

"Don't," Chrysanthi said. "You've been hurt. But you'll be all right. We'll get you help."

Rhea began to laugh, only managing a few seconds before it turned into a hacking cough. Something dribbled out of the corner of her mouth. Chrysanthi wiped it away, ignoring its deep red color.

"Don't move too much," she said. "I can't tell how badly you're hurt, so—"

"Nitsos?" Rhea asked. Her eyes were lit with that cold sort of eagerness that Chrysanthi had come to recognize back in the Ksigora. "Did you catch him?"

"I— No. No, I didn't." She glanced toward the spire, toward the square that had, only an hour before, been bustling with life. Now, all those people were gone forever, along with whatever she and Nitsos had been racing toward.

Rhea was trying to move, and it seemed as though both her legs were still working, but she was far too weak to do much of anything. Chrysanthi kept the heel of her palm pressed to Rhea's chest; if her sister got up now, she couldn't imagine she'd manage to keep standing for long.

"Easy," she said. "Easy, you have to—"

"I have to get up." A tremor ran through her; Chrysanthi heard her breathe in sharply. "He was only just ahead of me."

Andrija exchanged a skeptical glance with Chrysanthi. Just ahead of Rhea did not bode well for Nitsos. The destruction wrought by the spire's collapse was worse closer to the base.

"Well, you survived," Chrysanthi said impulsively. "He might have, too."

The set of Rhea's jaw made Chrysanthi worry, for a moment, just what outcome she was hoping for. "Go look," she said. "You have to find him."

Chrysanthi had insisted the same thing to Andrija; hearing it now from her sister, she understood it for the impossibility it was. Nitsos was dead.

But what did that change, really? She had wanted so many times before, back at Stratathoma, to stop caring for Nitsos, to stop comforting him after a bad loss at Saint's Grave with Baba and to stop poking her head through the little doorway that led to his wind-up garden. She'd never been able to then and she didn't think she could now.

"Wait here with her," she said to Andrija. "I'll be right back."

Despite his protest, she turned and began to make her way toward the spire. Rhea had fallen only a handful of blocks from the square, but the distance seemed like miles now. People had begun to return to the street, some so untouched by the dust and grit that it was obvious they'd come in from the outskirts to help. Already, some of the rocks had been cleared, and a handful of bodies had been uncovered. Chrysanthi caught sight of someone's bare ankle, punctured through with bone, before she looked away, sick to her stomach.

She couldn't make sense of the way in which the spire had collapsed; there were bands of clear space where almost nothing had fallen and other sections that were barely passable. A stranger helped her climb up a stack of debris that had once been the upper floor of a building; another pointed her around a spot where the square had split from the impact. Most structures that had bordered the space had been razed by the falling rock. Beyond, the very base of the spire was intact, but it seemed to have sunk on its northern side, as though the earth had swallowed part of it. Even so it still loomed perhaps a hundred feet over the ruined square, across which a growing number of survivors were scattered.

Chrysanthi looked from figure to figure. None of them were Nitsos. If she found anything of him, anything at all, it would be more than she could expect. The spot where she'd seen him last, kneeling over a victim of the first explosions, was now obliterated. And she couldn't imagine him so much as flinching when the tower had collapsed. Not if he knew what she did; not if he knew where Luco Domina had interred the saints. He wouldn't have run for safety. He wouldn't even have considered it, not when there was something to be done.

She stopped on a slab of rock, its surface startlingly flat. The more she saw of the wreckage, the more it appeared as if the spire had simply come apart at a set of seams nobody had known it had. Layers of rock compressed over the ages, come undone. That seemed to her like Stratagiozi work, but she couldn't fit it together very well with those explosions she'd heard—a Stratagiozi would likely find brute force like that beneath them.

No amount of understanding would change what had happened, though. Nitsos's body was here somewhere, but the rubble was so thick, and there was blood on the stone, blood everywhere. The people here would be digging bodies out of the ruins for years.

Someday they would find him and wonder who he had belonged to. Tomorrow, she would mourn him, mourn the years they had spent alone together in that great stone house. But today her sister was alive, and she needed help.

"I'm sorry," she said to her brother and left the square behind.

CHAPTER THIRTY-TWO

RHEA

S he had not expected to wake. Frankly, she almost wished she hadn't. She could feel her heart beating throughout her entire body, thrumming in time with the burn that radiated out from her broken hand, and her head felt too light and too heavy at once. Judging by the destruction around her, though, she supposed she qualified as lucky.

Andrija shifted his grip on her waist, squeezing a particularly tender rib. She gasped but clutched at his arm in case he tried to pull away. He'd taken great care moving her off to the side of the street and helping her to her feet. Now he was the only thing keeping her upright.

"You think he's dead, don't you?" she said hoarsely.

"Your brother?" Andrija looked down at her, and she nodded, instantly regretting it when a wave of nausea crashed over her. "I do, yes."

Rhea felt the words settle in her gut, empty and cold. Everything she'd done since leaving Stratathoma behind had carried that wish inside it—to meet Nitsos again, this time across a battlefield she controlled. To see him dead for what he'd done to her. So hadn't that wish come true, if Andrija was right?

It hadn't. None of this was what she'd wanted. Nitsos gone, not even at the hands of some other person he'd wronged, but crushed into nothing under ancient stone? She refused to accept that. Yes, she could see what had happened all around them, and yes, Nitsos had been closer to the spire than even she had, closer to the worst of the destruction; still it seemed impossible that he had not used some trick of his to escape.

He was her brother. An Argyros. He was simply not allowed to die this way. And if Chrysanthi had only done what she'd been sent into the world to do, Rhea would not have to stand here and wonder whether or not he had.

"Did you ever get close to him?" she asked Andrija. "In Vashnasta, or after?"

She could practically hear him deciding how much to tell her. "I don't know," he said at last. "Not close enough, regardless."

Indeed. "Well," she said, "thank you for looking after my sister. I know it couldn't have been easy carting her halfway across the continent."

"It wasn't. But not because of her."

Rhea was a little bit startled to realize that he might have actually meant it. There was a softness about the line of his mouth that looked out of place; it faded as soon as he noticed her watching, and she turned away. She could not imagine Chrysanthi paying someone like Andrija much mind, but maybe her sister had changed out there in the cold. Stranger things had happened—were happening now, in this city. And all she could do now was stand here and wait for Chrysanthi to come back.

She shut her eyes as her head began to ache again. The dark of her sight burst with purple, with blue. When would she have a moment to rest? She thought of Michali, and what he'd described to her as they'd looked out at the ocean in Rhokera. The weariness in his voice, because she'd woken him too early. Because she'd woken him at all. She understood that now better than she ever had before.

"There she is," Andrija said in her ear. Rhea's eyes flew open, finding her sister immediately as she came toward them. Chrysanthi's hair stirred in a low breeze; a new layer of dust clung to her skin. And she was—

"Alone? Why is she alone?" Rhea asked. "Where's Nitsos?"

Andrija called to Chrysanthi: "Are you all right?"

Chrysanthi nodded, and Rhea felt Andrija's body relax. Something began gnawing at the base of her spine, something feverish, angry, and hurt. She had barely survived the tower collapse, but that didn't matter to Andrija or Chrysanthi, did it? They thought Nitsos was dead; they thought it was time to move on. And they didn't care that this was the only thing she'd ever asked of her sister—one thing in a hundred years of keeping her safe and well.

"Well?" Rhea demanded. "Did you find him?"

Chrysanthi hurried over, stepping out of the way as a group of young people carrying a stretcher ran past, toward the square. "No," she said. She was flushed and avoiding Rhea's eyes. Embarrassed? Ashamed? Good. She ought to be.

"Then we'll all go," Rhea said. "I'll show you where I saw him last."

"I saw him, too. I knew where to look. It isn't that." Chrysanthi swallowed, her throat bobbing. "I'm not going to find him, Rhea. He's dead. His body . . . the square . . . he's just gone."

No. No. Chrysanthi had simply not looked hard enough.

"Fine. If you won't do it, I will." She pushed at Andrija's arms where they were clasped around her waist. "Let go of me." Nobody moved. "Right now."

"Rhea," Chrysanthi said, "we need to get you help. You can barely stay upright."

"I don't care." She reached up and grabbed a handful of Andrija's hair, ignoring Chrysanthi's cry of protest. "Let me go."

He did as she said. But Chrysanthi was right—she could not stand—and she dropped immediately to her knees, her broken hand cradled against her chest. Her ribs felt as though they'd cracked in half; maybe they had. A dizzying, liquid pain spread through her chest.

With a deep breath, she ignored it. Nitsos was alive somewhere, trapped under the rock just like she had been. If she could not make it to the square, she would start looking here.

She grabbed the nearest chunk of stone, tugging at it with all her strength. All she could manage was a few inches of movement before her grip slipped and she nearly toppled over backward.

"What are you doing just standing there?" she snarled up at her sister. "Help me find him."

Another look passed between Chrysanthi and Andrija, one that made Rhea want to claw Chrysanthi's eyes out. What right did she have to look concerned for her? This all could have been avoided. It was Chrysanthi's failure. Chrysanthi's fault.

Chrysanthi knelt down opposite Rhea, but she did not begin to dig through the rubble. "There's no Nitsos to find. I mean, look at this place."

"I survived."

"I know. I'm so grateful you did."

"So he must have, too. He's not supposed to die like this, Chrysanthi. It's supposed to be me who does it. You were supposed to bring him home and then I—" She broke off as Chrysanthi's face twisted with confusion. What wasn't she understanding? Nitsos could not die this way. She would not allow it. And besides, he had proven himself to always be a step ahead, to have strings tied to all of them they'd never noticed before. He might have even engineered the collapse himself. Actually, perhaps they were right to suggest that he wasn't here anymore. He might have known to flee the square before the tower fell.

"Andrija," she said, "will you help me up? He might be off in those buildings, or he could have already left. We should be looking for his trail."

"Rhea," Chrysanthi said, "please. Let me help you."

"I don't need your help." Rhea reached again for a piece of rock; this one was easier to move. "I had your help and it did nothing."

For a long moment her sister was silent. It was just as well. There was nothing she could say that would make any of this better. The only thing that would help would be Nitsos, here and alive in front of her, so that she could kill him herself.

Finally, Chrysanthi leaned toward her. She was so close that Rhea could feel the warmth of her body, but her figure was somehow soft at the edges, and Rhea found she couldn't quite focus her eyes properly.

"I wish he were alive," Chrysanthi said. "I never saw it the way you did, and I really thought that we could all find our way back to . . . I don't know. To each other, I suppose." She took a long breath, and when she spoke again, the earnestness in her had disappeared. "But I saw the kind of work he can do, and I know what you told me, and maybe it's for the best that it ended this way. Maybe you can be free of it now."

"Free?" Rhea recoiled. There was no such thing as freedom anymore—that's what nobody seemed to realize. Nitsos had undone her that day in the garden. Everything she'd ever built for herself was his; every choice she'd made that she was proud of was nothing at all. Even if he *was* dead, she would never be free of that. "You have no idea what you're talking about."

"I know something about it," Chrysanthi said. "More than I did when you sent me out in the first place."

That wasn't saying much, Rhea thought bitterly. Chrysanthi had never understood that all the beauty in her life was paid for by her siblings—no, not by her siblings, but by Rhea herself. Rhea had saved her back at Stratathoma. Not just on the day of the sacking, but every day before then, too, and that should've been enough to put her on her knees looking for Nitsos from the moment Rhea had opened her eyes. Rhea never even should've had to ask—Baba never had. His children had taken his word as the law it had been.

Perhaps he'd had the right of it. And here she was, names gathering, unspoken, at the back of her mind, her mark and matagios gone to rot in her body. She was doing this all wrong.

"I said help me," she told Chrysanthi. "Or do you no longer respect the word of your Stratagiozi?"

Her sister's mouth dropped open. "Rhea—"

"Well? Do you carry the matagios?"

There was no answer. Chrysanthi looked at her as the quiet between them grew. What was that, that flicker in Chrysanthi's expression? Fear? Rhea would take it as long as it came with obedience.

"Oh, Rhea," Chrysanthi said at last.

Not fear, then, but pity. She could feel it pressing down on her, as heavy as the tower rubble, and her chest began to tighten, breath going shallow and quick.

"Andrija!"

Someone was calling to him from back up the street. Rhea turned to look, and it was Piros, hurrying in their direction followed by two Sxoriza guards and, of course, a furious Michali.

"Thank goodness," Chrysanthi said.

Rhea pressed her shattered hand to her forehead as hard as she could stand and shut her eyes, focusing on the pressure, on the pain. Not now. This . . . it was too much. Could she not ever be alone, not ever find a way forward that did not eventually drag her back into a mire of bullshit? All that was left for her now was finding where Nitsos had gone. She would stay here; she would turn over every stone in this city; she would find nothing, wouldn't she? Only bones, only bodies, only—

"Rhea?" Chrysanthi said quietly. "Rhea, are you all right?"

Michali's voice rose over hers, but he was nearly incoherent. All she could make out was her name, over and over. She kept her eyes closed, let herself pretend he was not so near, until she felt him collapse next to her and his hands stroke over her hair.

"What happened?" he was saying now. "Are you hurt? Your hand, you—"

"She's all right," Andrija answered, "considering."

Michali cursed, and Chrysanthi said something admonishing, and Piros was talking, too, all of it noise, noise, and they were right, weren't they? About Nitsos? She could barely form the word in her mind but the truth of it crept through her all the same. Nitsos with his head staved in, Nitsos with one eye burst by a spear of rock, Nitsos not even knowing she was just behind him, and even if he had, would he have cared? He was like Chrysanthi; he'd never been afraid of her. Nobody was. They prayed and they worshipped and they trusted that she would help them because they did not know who she was, and what she could do, and that despite everything, she was her father's daughter.

Rhea folded in on herself and began to scream. Wordless, rough and failing, the sound pressing in. She could not stop, not even as the effort of it shook through her, wrung her out until she gagged.

Nitsos, she thought, and felt a strange heat wash over her, down from the black spot on her tongue. Nitsos, come back. Please, come back.

Bile stung her throat; she choked it down, struggled for a clean breath as she tasted blood. The world around her seemed to warp, her vision pulsing. And then: pain, everywhere, red and clutching. She felt a horrible, wet tear as the mark on her left hand burst. It ripped a gaping line down her palm, through her wrist. Her skin split like wood under the blade of an axe. Underneath, blackened muscle and dull white bone.

Rhea stared at the wound, breathing hard. She imagined digging her fingers into her own body, taking hold of her bones and pulling them out. Maybe it would hurt less that way. At least it was quiet now. Had it always been quiet?

"Rhea?" someone said. She ignored it and spit out a mouthful of something soft. But it came again. "*Mala,* what happened?"

Slowly, she lifted her head. Chrysanthi was still there, kneeling with her. Her eyes were wide, and her face had gone ashen.

"Rhea," Chrysanthi said, "did you do that to yourself?"

She looked back down at the mark—at what it had turned into. "I don't know."

"Are you . . . are you all right?"

For a moment, Rhea had felt lifted out of her own body; now she slammed back into it all at once. The world around her looked wrong, too bright and too large.

"I don't know why," Michali said next to her, "but it's not bleeding."

Chrysanthi leaned in to get a look at Rhea's arm. "We should be grateful for that. Andrija?"

"I'm here."

"We need to get her to the Sxoriza camp."

"No," Rhea said. "No, I don't—"

"I know you want to stay here and look for Nitsos, but that's just not an option right now." Chrysanthi stroked Rhea's hair back from her face, her hand clammy against her cheek. Rhea flinched away. "Everything will be fine. It's over now, all right?"

She felt on the edge of laughter. Over? Nitsos was dead—a door had been closed—but everything went on. That was the problem. Here was the world; here was her body; and every second there was something pressing at every inch of her. Sleeping or waking, there was never any peace. Chrysanthi didn't understand, did she? She liked that, the sound and color. She didn't carry each day like a bruise. And if Rhea had to look at her for a moment longer, she thought she might scream again, and this time never stop.

"I brought horses in as far as I could," Michali was telling Chrysanthi, "but they're a ways back still."

"Carry her, then. I'll be right behind you."

Rhea took a shuddering breath as Michali lifted her up. "No," she said, when he'd got her on her feet. "Not you."

Chrysanthi looked up at her, confusion rippling across her face. "What?"

"You're not coming with me." Something clicked in the back of Rhea's head. This was the right thing. She'd given Chrysanthi a task, a chance to show that she could understood what Rhea had been through. And she had failed. The gap between them would never be bridged. She stepped away from Michali, a mad strength coursing through her. "You can stay here, or go wherever you like, but not to the Sxoriza."

"But why?" Chrysanthi scrambled to her feet. "You're not thinking properly," she said, looking stoic despite the tremble in her voice. "You're hurt, and you need water, and rest, and looking after. We'll go together."

"Not this time."

"Of course we will." Chrysanthi smiled, but she had started to cry, whether she knew it or not. The sight of those tears winding down her cheeks lit an ugly little fire in Rhea. What did Chrysanthi have to cry about? What, really, had she lost? Her mark was still there, still perfect; she'd never bled for it. Not for a single thing.

"I'm with you," Chrysanthi said. "Always, always, no matter what."

"Then where were you?" Rhea interrupted. Her voice was ragged, every word more painful than the last, but she had to say it. "Where were you when our father sent me off to marry with a knife hidden up my sleeve?"

Chrysanthi jerked back as if Rhea had hit her. Her mouth was working but no sound was coming out, because of course she had nothing to say, no defense to make. She had never really been there. Rhea had always been alone.

"I was barely twenty," Rhea went on. "Barely twenty and I carried our family on my back every day after that, and instead of helping me you would tell me how much you envied me."

"Rhea—"

"Which part was it that you envied, *koukla*? Marrying someone who is already dead? Or coming home every season just to hear Baba tell you again how you've failed?"

"I was a child," Chrysanthi said, but she did not sound very sure. "I didn't . . . There was nothing I could have done."

"You've held the sunlight in your hands." Rhea shook her head, her heartbeat roaring in her ears. "Don't tell me what you could and couldn't do."

For a moment it was quiet between them. Across the square, a woman began to wail, her body slumped over something hidden within the rubble. Rhea felt the rush begin to leave her, a numb sort of certainty taking hold in its wake.

"We're going," she said to Michali. "Leave your men here. I want Nitsos's body found."

He nodded and passed the order on. She didn't care how long it took, or if those guards never left this square again. Even dead, Nitsos could not be underestimated. That was a mistake she wouldn't repeat.

Piros and Michali both came toward her, and despite how much she wished she could move under her own power, she knew better than to fight for it now. Michali's touch was cold as he lifted her off her feet, and he began to climb back toward more level ground.

"Rhea!" Chrysanthi tried to hurry after them, but the rock shifted suddenly under her feet, sending her crashing to her knees. "Wait!"

"I told you to find me Nitsos. And he's dead."

"I know, but I'm your sister."

She was clearly reeling and Rhea pitied her—she did—but she had been protected from the world for too long. "He was my brother, and look how that ended up." She shrugged with her one uninjured shoulder. "Keep Andrija if you like. But the Sxoriza isn't your home anymore."

"The Sxoriza?" Chrysanthi's voice cracked. "You are, Rhea!"

Chrysanthi could offer her all the pretty words she liked. Rhea had heard enough of those to last her lifetimes.

"Let's get back to camp," she said in Michali's ear and was gratified when he immediately began to move again. If he was going to insist on loving her, she would find a way to put it to use.

Chrysanthi remained where Rhea left her, tears streaming freely now as Andrija rested a hand on her shoulder. Rhea could admit, as she took a last look at her sister, that she was glad he'd stayed with her. He would keep Chrysanthi alive, and that was still what Rhea wanted. Chrysanthi safe, and Chrysanthi happy. Just as long as she didn't ever have to see her again.

CHAPTER THIRTY-THREE

CHRYSANTHI

She was faintly aware of Andrija's hand sliding up to the back of her neck, and of Piros saying something to her before he followed Rhea and Michali. One of the Sxoriza guards knelt near her feet and began digging through the rock. Should she say something? Did they even know what Nitsos looked like?

Andrija's grip tightened for a moment, reassuring. "Come on," he said. "Let's get somewhere safe."

Chrysanthi couldn't think. Rhea was there, she was leaving, she was . . . "I have to go with her."

"We can try to rejoin them another time." Andrija ducked to catch her eye, and the sight of him, of someone familiar, brought some of the feeling back into Chrysanthi's fingertips. "Right now, the most important thing is that we not be here."

He was right. She didn't think she could bear it a moment longer. "Yes," she said. "We can go."

He led her back through the city without another word. She expected that they would return to the room they'd occupied that morning, but instead he steered them toward the southeastern part of the city, beyond the radius of the damage from the spire's collapse. As they walked, they passed houses the injured were being ferried to, and spots on the city walls where lists were being formed, names of the living and dead written in charcoal on the stone. Chrysanthi remembered the stone slabs in the square and averted her eyes—she was sure that one of her kind was responsible for at least part of this. It felt unfair, almost, for her to participate in the mourning of it.

It was still early in the afternoon when Andrija nodded to a deserted storefront, its door left swinging open and half its wares smashed on the floor, and said, "There." He'd been looking over his shoulder the whole way, which she'd written off as habit—surely nobody here cared about following her when so much else had happened—but he was not content to simply get them off the street and instead escorted her through the shop's main room into a tiny storeroom at the back.

With the door cracked, there was enough light for Chrysanthi to see as Andrija flipped an empty wooden carton upside down. "Sit down," he said. "You look about ready to faint."

"I'm fine."

He nodded and leaned back against the wall. On one of the shelves, there was the tinkling of broken glass as something fell over.

"And you?" she asked suddenly. Why hadn't she asked sooner? "Are you all right?"

"Well, the hole in my tongue hurts a bit still," he said, and Chrysanthi smiled despite herself. He had a particular way of speaking when he was trying to make her laugh—a tentativeness, under everything else, as if he'd only recently learned it was possible.

"I'm sorry you had to be there for all that," she said, sighing. Andrija made a sound of dismissal, but she meant it. Rhea, become cruel as she collapsed in on herself, as she fashioned Chrysanthi's devotion into a weapon of her own—it wasn't how Chrysanthi had ever wanted to see her sister. Now it might be the last thing she saw of her ever again.

"Do you know what happened?" he asked. "Have you heard of anything like that before?"

Chrysanthi shook her head. "I suppose that doesn't mean it's never happened before, but . . ." She trailed off, the image of Rhea's wrist tearing open hovering too closely. "I just don't know what I'm meant to do now. I'd never left home before Rhea brought me to the Sxoriza. I don't have anywhere else to go."

"There are options. Favors I can call in on the Chuzhak side."

This was enough to make Chrysanthi chuckle. "You've always got favors ready, don't you?"

"My mother's family is there," he said good-naturedly. "If nothing else, I can get you to a warm bed."

It was, she thought, an indication of how wrong everything had gone that Andrija would willingly share a personal detail with her. "Maybe," she said, "but surely we can find one closer."

"Probably." He ducked down, catching her gaze. "I mean it, you know. There are things we can do. I've even heard there's a Domina girl in the business of collecting marks for herself. Maybe she can take Rhea's, if that would help."

"Collecting marks? That sounds . . ."

"I know," Andrija said. "Still. It'll be all right. We'll sort it out."

Chrysanthi shut her eyes to avoid the earnestness in his. It was one thing to joke about his family; it was another to realize that he meant it, and that he was planning to be at her side even now that their task was impossible to complete.

"I'll sort it out," she corrected, her voice hoarse, and when she looked at him again, he seemed confused. "It can't be you, too, Andrija. It was too much already in Vashnasta. You shouldn't have—"

"You needed me to."

"I could have found another way. You aren't beholden to me, and not to Rhea, either. I know she put me in your care, but you don't need to follow her orders like that."

Andrija stepped closer and crouched in front of her, his forearms braced on his knees. "It isn't orders."

"You're right." She remembered how she'd stood to the side as people knelt to worship Rhea. Had he been one of them? She had never seen him in that line of camp followers, but then, she'd never looked for him. And she'd never asked him about it, even after learning what Nitsos had been searching for. But he kept so many things private; his worship of Rhea and the saints would certainly be part of that. "Faith," she amended. "I'm sorry." The corner of Andrija's mouth twitched, and his knuckles brushed the back of her hand as he shifted in place, but he said nothing, so she offered him a wry smile. "I imagine there isn't much you wouldn't do for her."

He shrugged minutely. "Maybe. Maybe not. I don't care for hypotheticals." She let out a soft huff of laughter. "I can find somewhere safe for us, and we can wait for your sister to change her mind. Or we can go do more of your sightseeing. We can even find you some more paints."

She thought of them packed away in their room at the inn in Vashnasta. Even though they would be only ordinary paints in someone else's hands, she hoped that someone had found them and put them to use.

She was about to answer Andrija when a noise from the shop front sent them both jumping to their feet. The start of another collapse, Chrysanthi thought, or Rhea come back to say one last horrible thing, but she forced herself to breathe slowly. It had only been a creak of the floorboards.

"It's nothing," she said, touching Andrija's arm lightly. "Just the building shifting."

"That's not quite true," a voice came from the outer room. Andrija immediately stepped in front of Chrysanthi, and she stumbled back, knocking into a propped-up broom that clattered to the floor. "Sorry, sorry," the intruder said. "I didn't mean to— Are you all right?"

Andrija drew a short knife from inside his jacket and pushed the storeroom door farther open. It was not far enough for Chrysanthi to see who had come into the shop, but the light from outside fell across Andrija's face, and she was relieved when he seemed to relax, if only a very little.

"We're fine," he said. "You've been following us since the square."

"I have." The intruder sounded sheepish and very young. Chrysanthi inched toward Andrija, craning her head to try to get a glimpse. "Was it that obvious? I've never done it before."

Chrysanthi watched Andrija roll his eyes, and then he nudged the door the rest of the way open, revealing a lost-looking boy no older than fifteen dressed in fine gray clothing. His hand was raised, as if he'd been in the middle of waving, and he had a bit of acne on his cheek that looked particularly inflamed.

"Hello," he said. "So sorry to bother you. But my mistress would like to speak with you."

"Your mistress?" she said. "Who is that?"

The boy looked down at his clothes and then back up at Chrysanthi before cocking his head. Next to her, Andrija whispered, "That's Devetsi gray."

And that meant that this boy reported to Zita Devetsi, Stavra's mother and the ruling Ordukamat of both Merkher and Agiokon.

"Are you sure she wants me?" Chrysanthi asked. From what Stavra had said (and been careful not to say) in Vashnasta, Zita had been familiar with Nitsos, and had in fact been his benefactor. Perhaps Zita had sent this boy to find the yellow-haired Argyros wandering through town, and he had got confused and followed the wrong one.

"That's what she said," the boy insisted. "Can you hurry, do you think? I've got to be back to muck out the stables."

Your city has been destroyed, Chrysanthi wanted to say, but she did not think it would move this boy very much at all. He was young enough that he likely did not grasp the full meaning of what had happened in the square. Neither did she, if she was honest; if only she had his excuse.

She looked up at Andrija, who nodded back at her slightly but did not otherwise move. He would go if she did, she thought, but it was her answer to give.

She'd never met Zita, and knowing that the other woman had ordered Stavra to make such a sacrifice at Vashnasta did not leave her excited to change that. But she was adrift here, all her moorings cut and Rhea gone. Why not hear what Zita had to say?

"I'd be happy to join your mistress," she said. "Lead the way."

CHAPTER THIRTY-FOUR

ALEXANDROS

Before today, Lexos had not thought of himself as lucky. The disintegration of his allies in the Stratagiozi Council, the loss of his gift, not to mention the tour across Trefazio as a political prisoner—those would not have happened to someone with a bit more good fortune. But here he was, alive and mostly well even after a thousand feet of stone fell out of the sky, so he would have to reconsider.

Being within the spire itself had been to their advantage. They'd felt the tremors in the rock early enough that as they emerged from the tomb of the saints and began to run, the sounds of the square on the spire's other side had still been raucous and cheerful. Lexos couldn't forget how the laughter had turned to screams as he fled.

Even Ettore had seemed rattled. He'd tugged them into an alleyway on the north side of Agiokon, staring into nothing as they both caught their breath, the urn they'd come to retrieve left behind below the earth. It had been many long minutes before he'd mustered a smile and said, "I know where we'll go. Somewhere safe, where we can think."

That had sounded as good to Lexos as anything, and he'd followed as their path led them back around toward the southeastern side of the city, expecting to end up at a little hut on the outskirts, or in an open room at some out-of-the-way inn.

Instead, they were now ensconced in a nicely outfitted, windowless sitting room built into the foundation of the Devetsi house, one Lexos was fairly sure even Zita Devetsi herself did not know existed, if the well-hidden access tunnel had been anything to go by.

"There," Ettore said, "finished." Lexos turned from his examination of the room to see that Ettore had tucked a blanket over the large divan. "Don't forget: no boots."

It was, he'd said when they arrived, important not to damage the furniture with the grime they carried on their persons from the spire collapse. It had apparently all been quite expensive.

"How did you even get any of this down here?" Lexos asked. "Didn't anyone notice?"

"Please," Ettore said. "I built this place and this house long before there was any Merkher to speak of."

"Really?"

Ettore sat down and began peeling off his boots. "Agiokon was Trefzan once. Everything was. So why wouldn't I have kept quarters here?" He paused for a moment, considering. "I suppose I do have to commend the Merkheri for their good taste. It would have been tragic to let a house like mine go to waste."

Lexos tried not to look too interested. Ettore never shied away from his questions, but he was quite able to keep from answering plainly when he wanted to. It seemed best to Lexos to approach things from as slanted an angle as possible.

"Where else did you keep houses, then?" he asked, taking a seat at one end of the divan.

"Oh, everywhere," Ettore said. "One in what you call Prevdjen now. I imagine it's gone into quite a state of disrepair. One in Legerma, if memory serves. A good four or five in Vashnasta over the years. They kept sinking."

"What about in Thyzakos?"

Ettore snorted. "Your little backwater? No, I'd seen quite enough of it, thank you."

"What do you mean?"

"I kept hearing rumors after I'd taken hold of things," he said. Lexos supposed that was one way to describe massacring all of the other saints. "People said I'd missed one, and she was somewhere in the east, in those mountains."

Rumors of a saint survived? Was that why he had been interested in Rhea? Did he think it was her? Lexos could ease his mind on that front, at least.

"Horseshit, all of it," Ettore went on. "But I do like to be thorough. I saw enough of that horrible place to tide me over for a great many lifetimes."

"So Stratathoma was not yours, then?"

"Strata—" Ettore leaned in, a delighted smile tugging at one corner of his mouth. "I'm sorry, but have you named your house something that quite literally means 'Home of the Stratagiozi'? How quaint."

"I didn't name it," Lexos replied stiffly. "And besides, it's very nice. Or it was, anyway, before your family got to it." He'd heard nothing of what it must be like now. Perhaps the Dominas had handed it over to one of the steward families, or maybe Tarro had ordered it razed. If that was the case, Lexos would have liked to see them try. Stratathoma would certainly put up a fight.

Ettore's expression had darkened, and he rose to his feet, leaving an outline of dust behind him as he went to a cupboard on the left-hand wall. "I can claim no responsibility for what Tarro has been doing," he said. "Much as I might like to—he's done well to position Trefazio as strongly as he has. But he makes his own plans and has done for quite some time."

He opened the cupboard and leaned in. Lexos listened to him mutter quietly as he rummaged inside for a minute before emerging again with a bundle of cloth in hand. "These will no doubt be stale enough to break our teeth," he said, returning to the divan, "but perhaps we'll manage a bite or two before they do."

"I'm game to try," Lexos said, although he regretted it as soon as Ettore unwrapped the cloth to reveal a stack of biscuits that looked as though they'd already been eaten. He took one anyway, holding it awkwardly in his lap. "Don't you want any?"

"I'm waiting to see how successful you are with yours."

He attempted a bite; the biscuit did not give. He thought he heard a bone crunch in his spine.

"Never mind, then," Ettore said. "I really should have had somebody looking in on this place. That's the sort of thing that slips your mind, I suppose."

Lexos placed his biscuit back on the pile. "You mentioned Tarro," he said. There was a contemplativeness about Ettore right now, an openness that he was eager to take advantage of. "What is it that passed between you two? You're the founder of his family, the source of his power. Why has he treated you so poorly?"

Ettore raised an eyebrow. "You've asked me something like this before."

"I have."

"My first answer did not satisfy you?"

Lexos leaned in, confident as Ettore began to smile. He had passed some sort of test, he thought—seen the right door to open and was now walking through. "I have learned," he said, "that you do nothing that does not serve you. And that includes sitting in Tarro's prison for a handful of centuries." Ettore said nothing, but his smile grew. "Who is he to you? I've heard grandson, great-grandson. I don't think that's right, though."

"It isn't."

"He's your son."

"The oldest," Ettore said. "There were four, once. Boys like you. I gave them almost everything, in time. The sky, and the earth, and the sea. Even death, to one of them, although I admit I can't remember which."

It was strange to think of Ettore as a father, but then, Lexos supposed he did not have the best point of comparison in his own. "What happened to them?" he asked. "Are they in Vuomorra still?"

Ettore waved one hand dismissively. "They went the Domina way, in the end," he said. "Died, and made new matagiosi for new nations."

"But why—" Lexos broke off, trying to find the right way to ask what he wanted to. Ettore was a saint, had power that operated by rules so ancient they seemed not to exist. Why had he let his strength be diluted? "Why share with your children at all?" he said after a moment. "Why willingly give up your own power and then, when they died, not call their gifts home?"

"Is it giving up power for a general to stand at the back of an army?" Ettore asked. "Is it giving up to let others be cut down first?"

"I don't understand. Cut down by what? Did you fight—"

"It's a metaphor, Alexandros," Ettore said, sighing exasperatedly. Lexos flushed. "When I carved my gift from the earth, it did not go peacefully. Nothing does." A flash of anger crossed his face, tinged with something more like sorrow. "And from the moment I swallowed it down, it has been trying to return home. Earth to earth, sea to sea."

"Return home?" Lexos had spent much of the journey to Agiokon wishing for a break in Ettore's relentless smile; witnessing it now only made him uneasy.

"You will not have felt it," Ettore said. "But your father will have. And your sister now. Corrosion, almost, like rust on a blade. Bearable enough when you have only a small piece of the whole, but when I had killed my fellow saints, when I gathered all their gifts and fit them together with my own, it nearly ruined me."

Understanding broke over Lexos, clear as a winter morning. "So, you divided it back up. Handed it out to your children, and their children, and new families besides, to make what you kept easier to carry."

"I stopped, eventually, once I could stand it again. But the Thyzak matagios—your sister carries a piece of power that has hardly changed since I gave it to one of my sons almost a thousand years ago. A piece that wants to return home very badly."

Was it that piece that had made Baba the man he was? Difficult, and brittle, and . . . Lexos didn't bother wondering further. Baba had been like that before the matagios, and he would have gone on that way if there'd been an after. What Ettore was talking about was something else.

"Well, that sounds uncomfortable," he said, tracing the line on his palm his mark had once followed. "I suppose I should be glad I escaped it."

"Indeed."

"Is that what you want, then? To escape it?"

"Oh, don't be silly."

"But if it works the way you say it does—"

"There are ways around it," Ettore said. "Ways that died with my fellow saints. But I may finally be able to learn them."

Old secrets from people long dead. And Ettore had taken him here to Agiokon, but not to the monastery, where the monks kept old texts and records. To a tomb far below. To the remains of the saints themselves, which he and Ettore had failed to carry out with them. What use would their powdered bones be to anyone, except—

"You've heard," he said slowly, "of what my sister did in the Ksigora?"

Ettore grinned, eyes narrowed. "Why do you think I left Trefazio now?"

Lexos felt an answering smile form on his lips, one born of utter absurdity. Luco Domina, broken out of a prison of his son's making, searching for a way to resurrect the very people he had murdered. How was it that this was not the strangest thing that had happened today?

"You can't get to them now, though," he said. "To their bodies, I mean."

"Yes, well, I wasn't the one who dropped that urn."

Lexos could not feel sorry for it. It had been too heavy; keeping hold of it would have killed them both. Ettore knew that just as well as he did, which was perhaps why he sighed and relented, saying, "A minor setback. I suspect that was somebody's attempt to make things more difficult for me, and for anyone else looking for those graves. One of the Stratagiozis, most likely, although I'd rule out Zita and my son both."

Lexos thought of Milad and Nastia, neither as new to power as Baba had been but children, almost, compared to the ancient houses of Domina and Devetsi. He could imagine how threatened they might find themselves by a symbol of the saints, and how much sense it might make to one of them to destroy it. Still, why leave the saints there at all? "Why didn't you just keep the bodies in Vuomorra with you?"

"It didn't suit me at the time to build a memorial to my enemies in my own city," Ettore said, "but I did love them, and they deserved some honor. I gave them what I could."

Oddly enough, Lexos thought that he meant it. After all, he'd gone to the trouble of having them cremated in accordance with a custom that had not existed when he'd taken power.

"But take heart," Ettore went on. "Agiokon may be a lost cause, but I am not out of options just yet. We'll be leaving here soon, and we can start thinking of how best to find your sister."

Lexos winced inwardly. If that was what it took, though, to keep him at Ettore's side, to keep him this near to the center of the world? He would accept it. Nobody knew better than he did how to reach into Rhea's heart.

"How soon is soon?" he asked. "Are we waiting for something in particular?"

"Our guide. She shouldn't be too much longer. I imagine it's the mess in the city that's slowing her down."

"She?" Lexos couldn't help imagining Stavra, coming down from the house above them and throwing open the door. He'd been angry with her after Stratathoma, but all that was gone. It would be so nice to see her face.

"Yes," Ettore said, eyes flicking open. "My daughter."

Lexos choked on a bit of his own saliva as he drew a sharp breath. "You didn't mention a daughter."

"She's my youngest." Ettore sounded fond, almost loving. He had taken hold of his gold ring and begun twirling it around his little finger.

Lexos remembered the braid of hair inside, which Ettore had used in their escape from the house. A memento, he realized, for a child Ettore still loved. "Actually, I believe you've met her."

"What?"

"Yes." A smile split wide across Ettore's face, and Lexos knew a second before he said it, a pit opening in his stomach. "Dark hair. Tall. She goes by Falka."

CHAPTER THIRTY-FIVE

CHRYSANTHI

Zita's house was not all that far removed from the site of the spire, but it had been entirely untouched by the collapse. As Chrysanthi waited in one of its beautifully appointed sitting rooms, she found herself staring out the windows, looking for any sign in the street beyond that what she'd seen in the city square had actually happened. But whether by the power of Zita's gifts or by pure chance, the yellow Devetsi house and its surrounding district was beautiful, and whole, and surprisingly busy with people going about their usual errands.

The boy had deposited them in this room with the promise of tea and a light lunch. When it had come, the apple fragrance wafting from the glass kettle had been enough to make Chrysanthi's mouth water, but the thought of actually taking a sip (or having a bite of one of the miniature pitas that had been artfully arranged on a blue tray) made her ill.

Andrija appeared to have no such qualms and had tucked in immediately. After swallowing four or five of the little pitas, he was now sitting on a heavily embroidered divan and very studiously stacking the remaining handful on top of one another. He didn't look up even when a door opened somewhere down the hallway that led to this room.

It was odd. He'd been tense in the morning, even bordering on nervous, but where she'd only felt more and more on edge since the collapse of the spire, Andrija was more settled. She supposed she could understand that; in a situation like this, there was only so much that could be done.

Chrysanthi returned to the divan and sat next to him, her leg bouncing rapidly. At least he'd chosen to sit facing the door.

"What if this was a terrible idea?" she whispered suddenly. "We spent all that time in Amolova hiding from Ammar's people, and then Nastia in Vashnasta . . ." She buried her face in her hands for a moment before jumping to her feet again and making for the window. "Maybe we can climb out this way? Zita probably doesn't even know we're here yet."

Andrija's pastry tower fell. Without a reaction, he began to build it once more. "She was your brother's benefactor," he said. "And she sent an errand boy to fetch you, instead of someone more like me." He paused, one tiny pita cradled in his palm. "From everything I've heard, if we could be received by any Stratagiozi, I'd choose her."

"Not my father?" Chrysanthi said wryly.

"Not your sister, either."

She waited for him to crack a smile, but he did not appear to be joking. She'd called it faith earlier as they hid in that back storeroom, faith in Rhea that kept him at her side, but perhaps she'd been wrong. Perhaps it was something else.

"What filling is the pita?" she asked, hoping it would keep him from noticing the blush spreading across her cheeks.

Andrija pointed to the one at the base of his newly built structure. "Cheese. Then onion. Then cheese. And so on."

"I like that you alternated."

Footsteps began to approach from the far end of the hallway, and moments later a woman rounded the corner. She was dressed in elegantly cut trousers and a matching blouse, the pale color of which set off her dark brown skin, and her hair was twisted back into long braids, each woven through with gold.

Chrysanthi watched her approach. This was clearly Stavra's mother; they shared not only a physical resemblance but an air of stillness as well. Suddenly it made sense entirely that the Devetsi house had remained untouched.

"Welcome," Zita said in perfect Thyzaki as she neared the doorway to the sitting room. "Thank you so much for joining me."

Chrysanthi elbowed Andrija. Together they stood up, and because she knew Andrija would not be smiling, she made sure to smile wider to make up for it.

"It's my pleasure," she said. "You have a lovely home."

Zita sidled across the threshold, her hands in her pockets. There was a grace to the way she moved, an effortless ease that Chrysanthi recognized, viscerally, as something her father had long tried to emulate. He had never been successful, though—the Argyros name held none of the security that Zita Devetsi wore about her shoulders.

"Please, sit." Zita gestured to the divan and took her own seat opposite them in a low armchair. "I've been trying to think—I've met your brothers both, but I think I must have met your sister, too, although I can't quite remember when."

"That's odd," Chrysanthi replied. "We tend to make a significant first impression." She cleared her throat quietly, hoping her discomfort was not too obvious. "I wondered, actually, if you meant to summon one of the others."

Zita nodded. "I might have, on a different day." She looked at Chrysanthi for a long moment before offering a sympathetic smile. "I'm sorry about Nitsos."

Chrysanthi felt herself falter. She blinked rapidly, focusing on the warmth of Andrija's leg alongside hers. "Thank you," she said. "He . . . Thank you." She had argued so much with Rhea over whether he was dead at all that Zita offering her even this much comfort made her throat go tight. But the task of mourning him felt impossible with so many questions left unanswered. "How is it that the two of you met?"

"We were introduced through a mutual friend." Zita began to pour the still-steaming apple tea into three of the accompanying cups, white with blue enamel designs circling them.

"Who was that?" Chrysanthi asked. She had not been aware that Nitsos had any friends.

"Tarro," Zita said. She set the glass kettle back on its table. "Do you know him? I always expect that everybody does."

Chrysanthi drew in a long breath. "I'm familiar, yes, though I've never had the honor." But Nitsos had? Nitsos had met Tarro Domina? She'd spent entire afternoons trying to get him to eat half of a sandwich and all the while he'd known Tarro Domina.

"Well, your brother had done a bit of work for him, as it happens, so he came highly recommended. I thought he might prove up to a new challenge." Zita handed one of the cups to Chrysanthi, who cradled it tightly, even as the heat burned her palms. "He was uniquely positioned, your brother. People recognized his last name, but never his first." She took a sip of tea and swallowed delicately. "It's a position I think you might share. That's what I wanted to speak to you about."

Chrysanthi raised her cup to her lips and drank deeply, buying herself a moment before she had to react. Zita's evaluation of her wasn't strictly an insult, but it didn't feel good, either. And neither did the prospect of stepping into her brother's recently emptied shoes, particularly when Zita had yet to be clear about what that would entail. Still, she had nowhere to go, no family left that would take her in. Whatever Zita was offering, she was in no position to refuse it out of hand.

"I followed him here from Vashnasta," she said. "While I was there, I spoke to your daughter." Zita nodded. This was clearly not a surprise to her. "So while I think I know what you'd like me to do—what you'd like me to find for you—I'm not entirely clear as to why."

Zita leaned in. One of her braids fell forward over her shoulder; without taking her eyes from Chrysanthi's, she pushed it back again. "It is a commonly held belief," she said, "among people of my station that the remains of those who preceded us have a certain value. Well, I say commonly held. That was not true until twenty or thirty years ago, but—" She waved one hand. "The particulars of those debates are not relevant between the two of us quite yet."

Chrysanthi nodded politely, all the while digging through every memory of Baba that she had left. What had he been like thirty years ago? A difficult man, certainly, just as he'd always been, and exacting, and stern, but she thought he had been warm, too. And though that had certainly faded, she could not remember exactly when, or even be sure that warmness had ever existed outside the constructed world of her memory. If Baba had been part of Zita's debates, they had not marked themselves in any way she had noticed. And he had never gone back to their old house, to where her mother was buried. Surely if he'd understood the value Zita was placing now on any remains of the saints, he would have made something of the fact that he'd buried one himself. If, that is, he even knew who he'd married.

"What matters," Zita went on, "is that my fellows and I have agreed for some time now that acquiring the remains of the saints is of importance. We found what we thought to be their gravesite not long ago, but either the bodies had been moved, or they had never been there to begin with." She folded her hands in her lap and then said carefully, "Since then, it's been difficult to reach a consensus. I thought we had time to negotiate, but after what passed with your sister near the turn of spring, I'm not sure that we do."

"My sister?" The turn of spring—that had been Michali's raising. Of course Chrysanthi had known that bringing him back would change things, and she'd seen the proof everywhere: snow lingering on the ground, flowers blooming already dead. But she hadn't realized that it might register with the other Stratagiozis in any real way beyond displeasure. "Why? What does her consort have to do with you?"

"Besides this unfortunate season we're having?" Zita raised an eyebrow. "Lovely weather, truly."

Chrysanthi could feel herself blushing, but she refused to acknowledge it. "Yes," she said, "besides that."

"You Thyzaks," Zita said. "Your matagios is particularly powerful. I've often wondered how the Domina line managed to let it go. But I suppose they ought to be glad they did." She tilted her head, her gaze turned knowing and sharp. "It's a heavy burden, death. Most people find it hard to carry, but what your sister did with her consort will have only made it more so."

Hard to carry? Chrysanthi carefully schooled her expression. Was that meant to describe what had happened to Rhea in the street? Chrysanthi had watched her sister's flesh shred itself open. If Zita had seen what she had, she would have called it something different.

"Why," she asked, "does that matter to you?"

Zita glanced at Andrija, and Chrysanthi tensed up for a moment, afraid she would ask him to leave. But she needn't have worried, as Zita only offered him his own cup of tea and turned back to her.

"The matagiosi have always been linked," she said. "They came to us from the same man. While at one time they may have been something like siblings, with the way the lines have re-formed over time, I might call them now something more akin to rooms in the same house." She smiled, as if she'd amused herself. "Separate, in many things, but when you light one room on fire . . ."

"Yes, I see." Chrysanthi took another sip. "I didn't realize that's what Rhea had done."

"I'm not sure she has, either." Zita frowned, focus drifting very slightly. "Nor am I sure that the rooms were not already a bit on fire."

"Excuse me?"

"All of which is to say that we need to help Rhea, you and I, if we're to have the time we need to understand this." Zita reached out and squeezed Chrysanthi's knee somewhat sympathetically. "She was given something she wasn't ready for. It isn't her fault."

No, it wasn't, but that didn't make what it had set off in Rhea any easier to swallow. The way she'd spoken to Chrysanthi, the way she'd clutched at the idea of Nitsos's survival and gone so empty as it had slipped away—that was not the burden of the matagios. That was their father. Months dead, and still alive in every breath his children drew.

Chrysanthi set down her cup of tea. She was in over her head here. And it seemed to her there was a very simple way out, if only Zita and the other Stratagiozis were willing to take it.

"You're all worried about what might happen to your gifts," she said. "Why not get rid of them? We've heard about that Domina girl. Just let her collect your matagiosi and it all goes away."

"Even if that were something of interest," Zita said, "Falka Domina hasn't been seen in Vuomorra in weeks. I'm not sure where her allegiance lies these days."

"So find her and ask."

"We cannot always rely on Domina goodwill, Chrysanthi. The other nations in this federation need options of their own."

"Yes, all right, but what—" Chrysanthi broke off, embarrassed at the impatience in her voice but unable to swallow it. Stavra had avoided this question; she would not let Zita do the same. "What options do you get from a pile of bones? They're dead. The saints are dead."

"But when they lived, they did not live as we do." Zita leaned in, a fervent light in her eyes. "These graves might tell us how to keep your sister's fire from spreading."

Chrysanthi fell silent. Irini Argyros, saint turned general's consort, was buried in the Thyzak countryside outside their old house. Could that gravesite give her the same answers Zita had wanted from the spire? Maybe, but Zita had had centuries to learn, to formulate the right questions, to even begin to know what she was looking for. And meanwhile all Chrysanthi could imagine herself doing was wandering the house's grounds, wondering where precisely her mother's grave could be found. For an instant she considered telling Zita everything and doing what she'd always done—let someone else find the way forward. But she was not so much of a fool as to trust another Stratagiozi, one she had only just met. And besides, it felt wrong to tell someone who was not her family. Irini was theirs, despite the secrets she had kept.

"So," Chrysanthi said. She'd been quiet too long—she would save all that to think about later, when she was not in front of Zita. "What do you want me for, then?" She nodded toward the window, to where there was no sign of the spire's collapse aside from the gray dust beginning to cloud the air. "I can't make it past that wreckage to find them. I can't do anything like my brother could, either."

"I know," Zita said. "I asked you here because you are Rhea Argyros's sister. She calls herself a saint these days, and I wonder if she might have knowledge of her predecessors the rest of us do not. It's my hope that you will find out and report back to me and, if possible, serve as something of a grounding influence for Rhea while you do."

Chrysanthi felt her mouth twitch violently, and her stomach rolled. No doubt Zita had been informed of what had happened in the square between her and Rhea. Whether Zita's words now were hopeful or cruel, she couldn't tell. Regardless, she had no wish to hear any more of them. Her legs aching under her, she jerked to her feet. Andrija rose alongside her.

"I don't think I can help you," she said. "Not with your coalition. Certainly not with my sister." She looked down, realizing she was still holding on to her cup. "Oh. This is yours." Zita watched her set it down on the table. She did not move as Chrysanthi backed away, bumping into the divan and nearly knocking over the vase on its side table. "Thank you for having us. I'm sorry about . . ." She floundered. "About your city."

Zita nodded. "If you change your mind about my offer, do let me know. You can consider it standing."

Andrija replied with something in Merkheri—she would be more surprised, at this point, to find a language he didn't speak—and Chry-santhi was happy to let that be the last of the conversation. Quickly, she made her way toward the door and started down the hallway, Andrija following closely behind.

"It was a generous offer," he said as they neared the house's central atrium.

"It was."

They passed two servants dressed in Devetsi gray heading in the opposite direction. Andrija watched them go and, when they were out of earshot, said, "But I don't think it is the only way to help your sister. If that *is* what you want."

What could she even say to that? Of course it was. Rhea was what had kept her on the back of that horse, riding into the mountains from Stratathoma, and what had kept her from leaving those mountains for anywhere warmer. And whether she was kneeling in the ruined square screaming at Chrysanthi, or burning silently and brightly, as if a room in a house with five other doors, she was always, always an immovable portrait hung over the mantel in Chrysanthi's head.

Chrysanthi did not need Zita and her saints' graves to help Rhea. She had one of her own.

CHAPTER THIRTY-SIX

RHEA

I t was an afternoon in late summer, and Nitsos had decided to learn to swim. He'd announced his intent that morning, the four of them together at the breakfast table for the first time in a season, and it had been such a surprise that Chrysanthi had choked on a mouthful of kaf. They'd held Stratathoma for a number of decades then; all the while Nitsos had adamantly refused to even so much as visit the stone beach at the base of the cliff.

But they had the day ahead of them, and the water, Chrysanthi said, was still warm enough to be tolerable, which was why, some hours later, Rhea was standing at the edge of the sea, Lexos by her side as they watched Nitsos wade in. Chrysanthi was the most natural swimmer of them all—she was already in up to her neck, one hand reaching above the waves to beckon Nitsos forward.

"Be careful," Rhea called. "Both of you. I mean it."

"Yes, if you're drowning, don't hold on to Chrysanthi," Lexos said. "I'd rather just you die than both of you."

Rhea smacked his shoulder. "You'll scare him."

"No, I won't. He doesn't get scared."

Yes, Rhea thought, he does, but it wasn't in a way Lexos would ever recognize. Nitsos toiling away in his attic workshop for hour after hour, day after day—what was that, if not fear? If not the desperate worry that, were he to stop moving, he would discover Baba was right?

Or maybe Nitsos didn't think like that at all, and Rhea was just frightened enough for the both of them.

"Still," she said to Lexos, "you could have at least smoothed out the tides a little."

"I offered. He said no."

"Of course, but you should have done it anyway."

Nitsos took another few steps into the water. It was lapping at his hips now, almost to the waist of his trousers. He'd left his shirt behind him on the beach; Rhea's heart had done something odd in her chest when she'd seen Chrysanthi's attempt at patching up a hole in its left elbow. It should not have been Chrysanthi's job to look after her brother. It should have been Rhea's. But she was so often gone, and when she came home, it was to a pair of younger siblings she loved very dearly and knew very little.

"Come on," Chrysanthi cried. She had ducked under the surface, and her hair was water-dark, slicked against her neck. "You can't learn from there!"

"Don't rush me," Nitsos said. "I'm acclimating."

Rhea could see the tilt of his shoulders, the slight turn of his head, and wondered if it was worth sending Lexos back to the house so that Nitsos could relax. Whether because he held too closely to them to see it, or because he simply didn't want to, Lexos seemed to have no real sense of how deeply he impacted his younger siblings. They fell into step behind him, watched his conversations with Baba with envy and with awe.

Well, Rhea amended, Nitsos did. Chrysanthi had yet to give any indication that she cared too much one way or the other.

"All right," Nitsos said at last. "I'm doing it. I'm going under."

Chrysanthi stopped floating on her back and came closer. "Ready?"

"Don't count."

"I wasn't counting."

"I'm saying don't start counting."

"For goodness' sake," Lexos muttered.

Rhea took a half step toward Nitsos, easing a bit in front of Lexos. "Take your time," she said. "And come right back up."

"He's just seeing how it feels," Chrysanthi said, flicking water in her direction. "You don't have to get all worried."

"I'm not worried, I'm just—"

"I'm doing it," Nitsos said. Without another word, he dropped into the ocean. The water closed over his head; for a moment, his form held strangely still, and then, as Rhea watched, it vanished entirely.

"Nitsos?" she said. "Nitsos?"

Next to her, Lexos looked on, nonplussed. "What is it?"

"He was just there. And now—Nitsos?"

She turned wildly, searching the clifftop for his silhouette before peering out across the waves. Had the current pulled him out? "Chrysanthi, did you see where he went?"

"Where who went?"

Enough. Rhea made for the water, but Lexos took hold of her. "You can't," he said. "We haven't taught you how yet."

But Rhea could see it in her mind's eye, Nitsos's body carried by the waves only a few feet from where she stood. Whatever had happened, he needed help.

"Nitsos," she called. "Hold on!"

She pulled free of Lexos and plunged into the water after him. Cold and dark, nothing but the sea and her outstretched hand, and then—

She was awake—

—in a tent, in a Sxoriza camp. Overhead the canvas bowed and flexed as rain drummed down. Rhea gasped, coughed; immediately a pair of hands came to rest on her shoulders.

"You're all right," Michali said. "You're safe."

She shut her eyes again before his face could appear looming over her. It had been days since the tower, days since she'd left Chrysanthi in Agiokon, and still the feeling of it had not faded—that sense that everything around her was too much to be looked at directly.

"Your brother again?" Michali asked.

She cleared her throat. "Yes."

"I'm sorry."

It was not always the same dream when she slept, but it was always him. Some memory of her family gone wrong and empty. Sometimes she expected to see him there at her side when she woke, called back to life by her gifts. It had happened with Michali. Why not again?

The answer came as it always did: pain that crept in at the edges of her mind, stemming from the wound at her wrist. Her power had failed her, had flared hot and guttered out fast, as though she had wanted Nitsos back more than her body could bear. Maybe if she could find his remains she would have a better chance at it. She had to try.

"Come," Michali said. "We should change your bandages while you're awake."

She let him prop her up, aware of a twinge in her side. The other hurts she'd taken at Agiokon were still there, still fresh and in need of mending, but she hardly felt them. What difference did they make, as long as she was alive and Nitsos was not?

Michali crawled around to kneel in front of her. "This one first," he said, his head bowed as he reached for the bandage around her ribs. She lifted her right arm so he could begin undoing it. He'd wrapped it a hair shy of too tightly; though her ribs immediately began to complain about the lack of support, it was noticeably easier to breathe without it.

"Any news?" she asked.

He did not look up. "Piros says we'll be here for another few days. Nobody seems quite sure where to go next. Everything is still settling."

"That's not what I'm asking about."

Something stirred in Michali's expression—discomfort, maybe. "I know," he said.

"Well?" He never liked to talk about this, but she couldn't bring herself to care. "Has anyone found Nitsos's body yet?"

"No."

"Are they looking? Are they—" She broke off with a gasp as Michali's hands, cold and dry, brushed against a tender bit of skin.

"They're doing what they can," he said, clipped. "Nothing you can do will make it go any faster. You just need to rest."

He knew why she wanted Nitsos's body—not just proof that he really had died, but something to call him back to—and she could see how that weighed on him. He'd told her he'd been woken too soon; it must've rankled him to see her willing to do the same to someone else. But he didn't understand. Nobody did. Nitsos had been the horizon, the point she had spent every second since leaving Stratathoma moving toward. Now there was only a road stretching ahead of her, endless and aimed at nothing at all.

And she should have been glad, she knew, that she'd survived. The tower collapse had been dangerous enough, but there was the question, too, of what Nitsos's death meant for her, as his creature—more than that, as his Stratagiozi.

It was hers now, wasn't it? The gift he'd carried on his palm. When he'd died, it had returned to the matagios it had come from, which now sat on her tongue. Perhaps that was why she hadn't died when he had. For all his threats in the garden at Stratathoma that day, he'd never counted on her having the matagios.

What would he think, to see her with his own gift under her power? If she wanted, she could go home to Stratathoma and build a creature just the way he had. A new Nitsos, maybe, or Baba, or—

Michali braced one hand against her side, and a panic woke in Rhea's mind, dizzy and hot. Or Michali. She'd already used Nitsos's gift, long before it had come to belong to her. She was no better than him—except, she thought, in one way. She had loved Michali, once, and she very possibly still did. She did not think her brother could ever have said that about her.

Michali began winding the new bandage around her ribs, bringing his face close to hers as he passed the bundle of linen around her waist. She fell silent, willed herself to feel warmth unfurl in her chest the way it had so easily a season ago. His lashes, dark and long. His mouth, teeth worrying at his bottom lip as he worked. Tentatively, she leaned forward and kissed his cheek.

He did not move, so she stayed there for a moment, her forehead brushing his temple. With her eyes shut she could pretend they had only just married, just climbed out of that freezing lake in their drenched wedding clothes. What if she'd fallen in love with him sooner? Maybe it would have had time to root more deeply in her chest, deep enough to keep the bitter season from reaching it.

"Almost done," Michali said at last. When he wrapped the bandage on its next pass, he was farther from her than he had been.

There was still the dressing on her arm to change, but Michali sat back after finishing with her ribs and held one of his spare shirts out to her. "I don't want to tire you," he said. "We can do the other later."

"No, it's all right. I feel I haven't been this awake in days." She slipped the shirt on over her head, the smell of it a little stale. "Visit with me."

Hesitantly, he crossed his legs in front of him, his hands folded in his lap. A little bowl nearby held candied nuts, and somewhere behind her, Rhea knew there was a jug of warmed wine, but neither she nor Michali moved to sample either option. He ate very little—he had done so since she'd raised him—but since Agiokon, or perhaps a little before, she, too, found that there was something unappetizing about the texture of most food. It seemed to fall apart on her tongue, and just the thought of it sent her tumbling, for a brief, overwhelming flash, into a different Sxoriza camp, one where she'd clutched her stomach and spat up mouthfuls of her own skin.

"I wanted to thank you," she said when it had faded, leaving her here again, across from her glum-looking consort. "You've taken very good care of me."

Michali nodded. "Someone had to."

That was rather unlike him. Nervously, Rhea licked her lips and couldn't help pulling a face at the spoiled taste left there. What had she eaten last that—ah. The kiss.

"I know you would've wanted to go with me," she said. "Especially . . . well. After Rhokera."

He made a small sound that could've been a scoff. "I've stopped considering things in terms of what I want." When he met her eyes, there was a terrible sort of blankness in his own. "Haven't you?"

Rhea reeled back. That seemed uncalled for, to her. Yes, she'd left him behind and treated him a bit poorly, but she'd just had a building collapse on top of her; perhaps he could stand to be a bit more forgiving.

"Please," she said. "I'm trying to talk to you. To apologize. I want things to be better for us." She paused, leaving room for him if he chose to speak, but he seemed determined to let her lead the way. "I think it's that I've been afraid to bring you with me to these places," she went on, swallowing down the shape of Falka's name. "There are things that need doing, sometimes, and your priority is my safety, and my life, but it isn't always possible to . . . to do things the way you might like to, I suppose."

Michali nodded slowly. She could practically see him chewing through what she'd said, working each word from beginning to end. Finally, he leaned forward. "I thought we stopped lying to each other a season ago."

"I—" Rhea felt her cheeks go hot. "I'm not—"

He waved one hand, looking away. "Fine."

"No, Michali, really."

"I wish you would realize you don't need to do any of this," he said. He sounded exhausted, and the roughness of his voice, new since his return from the grave, seemed to thicken. "You have things you want; you have plans you do not share with the other Sxoriza. And you keep them from me, too, because you think I am still—"

"You *are* still Sxoriza," Rhea interrupted. She could not bear to hear him claim otherwise. The Michali she had married had been willing to die for this cause, and he had done it, too. When she'd woken him, it had been so he could live for it again. "If I keep things from you, it isn't because of that, but you are."

"I'm not." His face crumpled, and his hand trembled violently as he reached toward her for a moment before recoiling. "You called me back, Rhea. Your voice. Your gift."

"What does that matter? I called you back, yes, but I called all of you."

He shook his head. "I had these strings in me. To Ksigori, to my mother, to the Sxoriza. Until I died, and they were cut, and now that I'm here again, they're all of them knotted around your wrist."

How could she argue? He knew, and she knew. Rhea cradled her head in her right hand, her broken fingers alight with pain. "I'm sorry," she heard herself say. "I didn't know it would be like this."

"If you had, would you have left me to rest?"

Something about his voice sounded strange; when she looked up, he was crying, wretched gray tears trailing from his dark eyes.

He wishes I had, she thought. We could have buried ourselves together.

"Is there anything for you here?" she said.

"There's you," he answered. "You, only you're running from me, and you're lying to me, and you hate the sight of me—don't tell me you don't, because I know. Because I love you, Rhea, I do, but I hate the sight of you, too." He screwed his eyes shut for a moment, as if it cost him something dear to go on. "You took something from me. And you don't even want what's left."

"I do," she tried, but it only made him flinch.

"I looked for you for hours in Rhokera," he said. "Hours, and then I saw the boat you boarded. I saw who you met there."

Rhea thought she might throw up. It hadn't been anything, her meeting with Falka. Not . . . not what . . . It was nothing for him to worry about, except that she'd left him behind, and she'd spent that day laughing alongside someone who wasn't him, and she hadn't felt sorry even once.

She stared at him helplessly. What could she say to him now? She'd thought she had the excuse of being the only one out of the two of them to understand that things between them were altered. But of course he knew what was happening to him, and of course it hurt, much the same way it hurt her to move through the life she had designed when she'd expected that the old Michali would be at her side.

"I just wanted you back with me," she said at last, her voice small and quaking. "I didn't know."

She kept her eyes down as Michali moved, rising up onto his knees and shuffling toward her. His touch was gentle when he took hold of her injured arm and turned it palm up, fingers ghosting across the bandage there. The wound that radiated from her mark was still not bleeding, but on occasion it leaked a gray liquid that reminded her of the tears he had wept.

"How does it feel today?" he asked. "Better?"

It was some kind of forgiveness, an offering made to her. Rhea wanted more than anything to accept it, but she couldn't. He hadn't given it freely. The choices he'd made, the words he'd spoken—even if he'd chosen them himself, with no thought from her, they weren't truly his. She'd called him back, and he'd come, and now she was always there at the front of his mind. Love didn't matter; she had built her own little hummingbird.

"Rhea?"

"I feel sick," she managed, and she did, but her stomach was empty, and it only cramped viciously. "I think I need some fresh air."

She couldn't move very quickly yet, but Michali was kind enough to let her struggle to her feet alone. He said nothing as she passed, and when she looked back from the threshold of the tent, he had not moved.

Outside the air was heavy with cold. They'd camped in an abandoned orchard, stunted fruit trees caught somewhere between bare and blooming, and the rain flattened the dried grass as Rhea started down the path toward the rest of camp. There was another ring of tents here, this one inhabited by Athanasios and his like, and at the center burned a fire large enough to withstand the rain. Rhea eyed the faces of those gathered there as she approached, increasingly dissatisfied until she realized: She was looking for Chrysanthi.

It wasn't that she regretted leaving her sister back in Agiokon.

Chrysanthi needed the push, needed to understand what it cost for the Argyrosi to carry on in a world that had shattered everything they'd held dear. But that didn't make it easier to forget the look on her face as she'd stood there amidst the rubble of the city. Especially not when Rhea felt as though the same thing had happened to her—Piros and Michali and Athanasios standing in the shadows, watching her flounder now that her purpose had been stolen from her.

Where was Piros anyway? She'd hardly seen him since the spire, aside from one visit that had come so close to their arrival here in camp that she could barely remember it. Most everything before this very morning seemed washed over in black and fog.

She ducked between two tents, wishing she'd taken a coat with her before leaving Michali. It was cold here—not as bad as the Ksigora, but still distinctly out of season—and the rain had soaked through her borrowed shirt. Over her shoulder, perhaps a mile down the empty aisles of the orchard, the house this land had once belonged to stood empty. She was not sure why they hadn't camped inside, but she had to admit, she was glad they'd stayed clear of it; the sight of it unnerved her a little. It looked too much like that first house the Argyrosi had shared. The house she'd fled when she was small, her arms wrapped tightly around her twin brother's waist as they rode into the dark.

"Aya Thyspira?" someone said. She jumped; Piros was coming toward her, his hand outstretched. She backed away before she could help it.

"I'm fine," she said, though he hadn't asked. "Who do I speak to about Nitsos? Michali didn't tell me."

"Oh, I don't—" Piros looked sidelong at the people waiting by the fire. Rhea vaguely recognized them, but could not recall their names. "Let's get you somewhere warm." He gestured toward a nearby tent. "We can talk more privately there."

"I asked a question."

"I know," Piros said quietly, stepping between her and the fire, "but it's not one I can answer for you just like this, Rhea."

She wiped the rain from her eyes. "Why not?"

"Because these people think you're a saint, and you don't look like one today." Immediately, he looked apologetic, but she had heard enough.

"I'm alive," she spat, "after all of that. That makes me saint enough."

"You're right. Of course you're right. I'm sorry."

"If you want to speak in private, you had better have something good to say." She turned on her heel and pushed into the closest tent, disregarding Piros's cry of protest. This tent was one of the largest in camp, and judging from the papers and maps scattered across the makeshift desk, it belonged to Athanasios. Rhea almost turned back, hardly eager for another scolding, but the man himself was absent, and Piros was already close behind.

"I really am sorry," he was saying, Thyzaki pronunciation slipping as he hurried on. "You know how deeply I respect what you've done for this organization."

"Calling it an organization is being charitable."

"Rhea—"

"If I've done so much for you, why can you not do this one thing for me?" Her anger had a rotten tang to it—Piros was not the right target—but she found she relished it just the same. "Find Nitsos. I told you where he was when he fell. I should have had his body in front of me yesterday."

"It isn't that simple," Piros said. "You saw how the square looked after, and even if they did find him, we're days out from the city. It will take time."

Rhea turned away, unable to bear the earnestness written across his face. He did not mean to upset her, and he was right. The square had been demolished, and though they hadn't gone too far from Agiokon, there was more distance now to cover. But if she allowed for Piros to be right, she had to allow for Chrysanthi, and if she allowed for Chrysanthi, then that meant that leaving her had been—

She bit down hard on the inside of her cheek, blood coming quick. She'd given her sister a gift, she reminded herself, and she could do the same now for Piros, by letting things rest between them. He was hardly the only person involved in delaying the retrieval of Nitsos's corpse.

"And him?" she asked, approaching the desk near the far wall of the tent. "Athanasios?"

"What about him?"

"Does he understand how important this is?"

"I . . ." She could practically hear the frown in Piros's voice and knew that if she looked over her shoulder, she would see him rubbing reflexively at his beard. "I'm not sure anybody could."

The desk spread before her was layered thick with parchment, most of it waterlogged and curling at the edges. Rhea plucked idly at the top sheet—a map of Agiokon, appearing to focus primarily on the shopping district that had surrounded the base of the spire. Athanasios would never have a chance to see it. All of that was buried now, just like Nitsos.

What had he wanted there anyway? Shepherding the Sxoriza out of the Ksigora and across Thyzakos to the meeting point of three countries, none of which were particularly welcoming—why take the risk? Rhea could remember watching him ask Michali about Agiokon, but there had been no reason attached, had there? Or had she forgotten?

No, she thought dimly, she hadn't, but she had forgotten something else, something Andrija had told her in the square where she'd met Chrysanthi: They'd seen Domina banners on their way in. Tarro had been in Agiokon, too.

It wasn't so unusual, she supposed, for two powerful men to find themselves in the same place at once, especially if that place was Agiokon. It was one of the continent's oldest and most central cities and drew plenty of visitors for all sorts of reasons. Perhaps it had been a coincidence, or perhaps Athanasios had planned to make an attempt on Tarro's life somewhere in the Agiokori alleyways.

Still, a cold point of dread had formed in the pit of Rhea's stomach, and she began to search through the rest of the papers covering the desk. A supply order here; a report from a Sxoriza outpost there; letters from people she did not know, and one from someone she did— Michali's mother, Evanthia, reporting on her consort Yannis's management of the Ksigora. Nothing to tell her why the Sxoriza had come so far west. Wasn't that a bit strange? Shouldn't there have been some evidence, some record of Athanasios's intentions? Or were they here for a reason so secret he could only share it with a select few?

Tarro Domina was a reason of just that sort. And Piros would have had to be one of the few.

"Where's the rest?" She whirled to face Piros, her ribs throbbing in protest. "What have you hidden from me?"

Piros's mouth dropped open. "Hidden? Nothing, no, I— What is it you're looking for?"

"Tarro was in Agiokon," she said, "just at the same time we were."

"Yes, I think I've heard that he was." Piros came closer and reached for the desk, raising his eyebrows as if to ask for permission. She relented, stepping aside. "Have you found some reference to him?"

No, no, she hadn't, and that was the point. Athanasios would know better than to let this sort of plan be so easily discovered. "Did you know?" she asked instead. She could feel an echo of pain rolling up her right arm, coming, oddly enough, not from the wound on her wrist but from her broken fingers. She ignored it; rest would come once she had sorted all of this out. "Did you know about the tower coming down, or Tarro, or even Nitsos being there? Any of it? What did he tell you about Tarro?"

It happened then, in Piros's eyes—one moment she was his superior and the next she was a sick child refusing to stay in bed on a nice summer's day.

"I think," he said, "it would be better for us to get you back to Michali."

A haze of anger swept across her sight, warping the edges of Piros's form, and with it came the sort of acceptance that had followed her for a hundred years. All of this—everything since leaving Stratathoma with Michali that day two seasons past—it had changed nothing. She was not a saint and not true Sxoriza—no, she was something else to these people, something that felt so familiar it was both incredible and inevitable that she had not realized it sooner. An Argyros. A Thyspira. Built to be traded, to be used, to be a knife in someone's belt.

Athanasios had brought the Sxoriza here, but more accurately, he had brought her. Because now that she had the Thyzak matagios, she was just the sort of thing Tarro might want. Who knew what Athanasios meant to bargain for? Official recognition for the Sxoriza and an independent Thyzakos, perhaps—Athanasios might have realized that he could never truly hope to topple the Dominas and Trefazio with the resources he had. And in exchange, Rhea turned over into Domina hands. A ship sailing into Vuomorra harbor, Rhea dressed in Argyros blue and matagios black at the prow so everyone could see whose banner she served now.

What was she meant to do? Let it happen? Find some way to make it serve her? But how? Lexos might know, she thought sullenly, but he wasn't here, and if Rhea did not look after herself now, there was nobody left who would. Certainly not the Sxoriza, and not Piros, who was looking at her with wide, uncertain eyes.

She had to go. That was all that was left to her. The spire had fallen; Chrysanthi was gone; Nitsos was dead. Rhea could not stay here another second.

"All right," she said, her voice on the edge of breaking. "Yes, all right. I'll go rest."

"I can escort you," Piros started, but she shook her head. As often as she had relied on him before, she could not trust him now to help her. Not if he'd known what Athanasios had intended for her.

"I'll be fine," she said. "Thank you. You've been very kind to me."

It had been true through winter, through spring. And she would miss him for it after she was gone. But she left him there in Athanasios's tent, one hand lifted to shield her eyes as she stepped back out into the rain. In the distance, she could see the orchard house, its dark roof breaking through the trees. She had fled once, from a house just like it. Her arms wrapped around Lexos's waist, their horse breathing hard as they made for somewhere safer. It would be harder without him, harder to ride alone, but she would do it, and this time she would never turn back.

CHAPTER THIRTY-SEVEN

CHRYSANTHI

The problem in visiting her mother's grave was that Chrysanthi did not remember where it was. She knew that it had been on the grounds of their country house, and she knew that the house was not terribly far from Stratathoma. But she had been so young when they'd left, only a few years old, and enough time had passed since then that when presented by Andrija with a map of western Thyzakos, all Chrysanthi could do was stare and say, "Well, this is certainly something to think about."

They had gone back to their room at the inn following their meeting at Zita's house, and after searching for a day and a half, they'd found a pair of horses whose riders seemed to have perished in the spire collapse. The waiting had left Chrysanthi itchy and anxious, but Andrija insisted—they had barely any money, and he refused to steal, which she supposed she approved of.

It had been easy enough at first to simply aim for the west country. She'd been so confident that just the sight of Thyzak orchards and meadows would jog something loose in her memory, and she would guide them home as if she were one of Nitsos's scouting birds, coming—

That was a poor analogy, not in the least because it hadn't happened that way at all. A day's ride into the countryside, Chrysanthi was still as confused as ever.

She bit down hard on the inside of her cheek and stepped away from the map Andrija was holding. They'd been following the road for their first day of real travel, at times encountering other carts and riders, most of whom were heading to Agiokon, unaware of what had happened there. But today they would have to decide whether to stay on the road, which curved to the east toward the middle of the country, or to break from it and ride into the trees.

"I think you *do* know," Andrija said. "What does your instinct say?"

"My instinct says I should never have left Rhea," she snapped, but he didn't even blink. He must be used to it by now, she thought. She hadn't been the easiest person to deal with since the spire—she knew that—and she was at once grateful and mortified that Andrija had been there and understood why.

He nudged the tip of her boot gently with his own. "What else does it say?"

"I don't know," she said, throwing up her hands. "That the road takes us in the wrong direction. There was never anybody passing by, at home. My father served someone, but we never . . . they never . . . It was like it was only us. In the whole world."

She'd cherished that feeling for a long time, conjuring images of herself wrapped in her mother's arms, though she had never been able to remember her face. Years at Stratathoma had ruined that, as she'd come to understand that the walls her father built were not to keep his children safe, but to keep them in. And now that she knew the truth of her mother, she was forced to wonder: Had Irini wanted that for them, too? A saint in hiding—of course there had never been anyone to visit, never any new banner on the horizon. And so there had been nobody there to protect them from Baba.

"All right," Andrija said. "We can always turn around, you know. If you think you've got it wrong."

"I don't want to waste time."

He nodded, folding the map back up. "Are we hoping to beat some-body there?"

"Maybe." She wasn't sure how many other people knew what her mother had been. Just Rhea, she thought, but there was always the possibility of a nasty surprise. "I'm not sure, really. I just want to be quick."

"Then we'll be quick."

Andrija had been quiet with her since the spire—well, even quieter, really—but always there, always listening when she thought of some-thing else she wished she'd said to Rhea. And he hadn't asked her why they were heading south for her childhood home, something she was infinitely grateful for. How was she meant to explain it? It had made sense when Zita described her own interest in the saints' graves, but now, miles removed from the calm of Zita's sitting room, all Chrysan-thi really knew at this point was that she wanted to stand between Zita and her mother. Between the other Stratagiozis and the woman Baba had killed. Explaining that to Andrija and exposing herself even fur-ther as someone completely out of her depth was not an attractive course of action.

She mounted her horse again and waited for Andrija to spur his forward, wincing as a blister on the inside of her knee popped open. Her body had begun to ache terribly on the ride south from Agiokon, as though the tension she'd carried there had only just found its way into her bones, and she'd already been fragile to begin with, skin still new and muscles untried from years in her father's house. On the jour-ney from the Ksigora to Vashnasta she'd told herself it would all be over in a little while; now making that promise seemed foolish. Yes, maybe they would find the house by the evening, and she would sleep in a bed that was somehow still perfectly made, and nobody would ever require anything of her ever again. More likely she and Andrija would spent ten or twenty nights wandering the countryside without getting any closer to what they were looking for.

They rode on, away from the curve of the road, until the sun had dropped below the horizon, the sky above fading purple. Though

Chrysanthi was anxious to keep going, she gave in when Andrija pointed to a little grove in the distance—orange trees just starting to blossom. It reminded her of where she and Rhea had set their camp with Piros that first night away from Stratathoma. She'd been terrified, but she'd had Rhea by her side, and she would have followed Rhea anywhere then.

Chrysanthi pressed one hand to her chest, her heart twinging underneath. Could she say that anymore?

"There isn't much to eat," Andrija said once she'd left her horse to graze and ducked into the grove.

She sat down opposite him where he was clearing a place to build a fire. These trees had grown too close together for any of them to reach the height and breadth they'd been meant to, but as sad as that made her, being underneath their branches was like being held. A sharp, green scent poured off the flowers overhead, and the earth lay gently over the twist of the roots, rumpled like bedclothes come morning.

"I don't mind," she said. She hadn't thought they'd had anything, really. "I'm not hungry."

Andrija nodded to the bag he'd had buckled to his horse's saddle. "At least have some water."

She fished the waterskin out before relaxing back against one of the orange trees, watching Andrija as he set about starting the fire. He'd shed his jacket once they stopped riding, and his hair had gone lank and grimy, some of it falling out of the knot he'd pulled it back into. She knew hers probably looked even worse and thought longingly of her paints. What would she add, if she had them here? A blush to her cheeks, although she already had a sunburn, or a sliver of light in the depths of her eyes. Then a bit more pink in the sky, and a wash of red for the fire that was now starting to spark. And for Andrija—no. She would leave him as he was.

Finished with the fire, he sat back, pulled his knife from his belt, and began to sharpen it. He'd left his sword in Vashnasta, and while for somebody else that might have rendered them less capable, and less dangerous, Chrysanthi was very sure that none of that was true for him. Wherever he'd learned to wield a blade, it had not been with the Sxoriza.

She drew her knees up, resting her folded arms on top of them. "You'd been to Agiokon before," she said. Andrija looked up, eyebrows raised, the fire throwing strange shadows across his jaw. "To Vashnasta, too."

He waited a moment and then said, "Was that a question?"

"And you speak perfect Thyzaki—"

"Passable."

"No, really. Perfect." He pulled a face—barely a grimace, but even that much was unusual from him. "Thyzaki, Amolovak, Chuzhak, Merkheri."

"You're being generous," he replied. "Amolovak and Chuzhak are only pretending to be different languages."

"How did you learn all of that, though? Just by traveling?"

Andrija shrugged. "You pick up what you need to."

"Yes, but I've had years and years of lessons and I don't speak anything half as well as you."

"Except Thyzaki."

She rolled her eyes, smiling. "Except Thyzaki." She let silence unfold between them, warm and comfortable, and then relaxed more deeply into the curve of the tree. It was odd; as sure as she was that she was safe with him, she was equally sure that he was lying to her. The languages, the arms training, even the way he was so comfortable listening and giving nothing away—they were a set of skills that suited a particular kind of person. Somebody in the Sxoriza had to have known about his history. It must have been why he'd been assigned to her in the first place, and why nobody had protested when she'd asked to bring him along with her when she'd left the Ksigora.

But he had never pushed her, and so in turn she wouldn't pry, as contrary as that was to her nature. She hoped, though, he would tell her about it all someday. Where he'd grown up, what had happened to make him leave wherever he'd been and come join a small, ragtag movement in a country that wasn't his. If he'd left any family behind.

The weight she felt settle on her shoulders at the thought of her own family must have shown on her face, because Andrija cleared his throat and, without meeting her eyes, said, "She'll be all right."

Chrysanthi tipped her head back against the tree and sighed. "Do you really think so? Or are you saying that to be nice?"

"I really think so."

A lump rose in her throat; she swallowed, blinking against a sudden swell of tears. How could he sound so confident when he'd seen exactly what she had become in Agiokon? When he'd heard the tear of skin from skin as Rhea's arm had split open? "Why?" she asked, her voice rough. "She's got nobody left with her. Just Michali, and I don't think she'll listen to him even if he does try to help."

"She has you," Andrija said before glancing up at her. "Doesn't she?"

"Of course she does."

"Then she'll be all right."

It would be lovely to leave it there and to enjoy the rest of the night by the fire, listening to Andrija hum as he cleaned his knife. But they were ignoring the real question, and that wouldn't do them any good if the answer ended up being what she was dreading it would be.

"What about me?" she asked. She could feel the shape of her mark as though it were burning. So far it had not begun to feather and bleed as Rhea's had, but she knew that could very well change. "What happened to her, whatever it was—what if it happens to me?"

Andrija's expression softened. "It won't."

"But—"

"I won't let it."

Something sweet and lifting spread from the center of her, winging out along her shoulder blades. He couldn't possibly promise that, but here he was, looking at her across the fire, his eyes solemn and warm. Just as they had been in that Agiokori storeroom, their bodies close enough that she'd felt his every movement as her own.

"Is that your faith again?" she asked, smiling at the memory. "Serving my sister?"

She expected another demurral, another answer that was not quite an answer, but this time his hands went still on the hilt of his knife, and he said quite plainly, "No. It isn't her at all."

Chrysanthi blinked, her mouth going dry. She'd wondered that herself, but to hear it from him? Was that—was she meant to—

"Well," Andrija said after a moment, "you should get some rest."

As he returned to his work, Chrysanthi felt herself blush. She'd been quiet too long. He probably thought she didn't care now, although that was assuming he'd actually been looking for some kind of response.

She sighed. If they'd been in her father's house, she would have known how to read him; she would have known what they were holding between them. But he was not the sort of person she had much practice with. The Argyrosi ran hot, summer and spark at the core of even Nitsos, while Andrija reminded her more of those places up north where the Dovikos pooled, held still for a breath before rushing on. Maybe she was misunderstanding him, and he hadn't meant anything by it at all. She was happy for his company either way.

When her eyes started drifting shut some hours later, she came around to his side of the fire and accepted his offered jacket. It was already quite late, and with any luck it wouldn't get much colder before sunup, but she was not above taking advantage of his kindness just in case. She'd done the same during their trip south from Vashnasta and had got used to stretching out a yard or two away from Andrija. Tonight she hesitated and then eased closer, waiting for him to protest before lying down next to him.

"Comfortable?" he asked as she pulled his jacket up to her chin.

"Not in the slightest."

"Of course."

She turned onto her side and shut her eyes. After the flurry of the last few days, it was difficult to accept that there was nothing left for her to do today. All she could do was sleep and hope that some memory of the old house resurfaced overnight. Meanwhile, Andrija would stay up for some time more, looking after the fire and making sure they were safe.

His jacket was pleasantly heavy where it fell across her shoulder, the fabric double-layered, if not triple, and smelled surprisingly inoffensive given how much wear it had seen. She gathered it close to her, eyes blinking open when her hands encountered a pocket stitched into the lining. There was something inside: a bit of parchment, edges frayed.

Chrysanthi went still. What was he keeping here, so close to his heart? A letter from his family? Or from a partner he'd left behind and promised to come back to?

Slowly, slowly, watching in case Andrija looked away from the fire, she began to unfold the parchment, dismissing the little voice at the back of her head that was trying to say something about privacy and respect. You did away with those things when you had siblings, she told herself; if Andrija hadn't wanted someone to read whatever this was, he would've destroyed it.

The parchment had been torn at the bottom, and it was only partly covered in ink. Chrysanthi could not read most of it—the text was in Amolovak—but the script was simple, angled forward and very neat. She had never seen Andrija's handwriting before, but if this was his, it looked just as she'd expected.

So, not a letter from a sweetheart. She wouldn't pretend not to be pleased about that. She peered more closely at the parchment, straining to make out any word she recognized in the firelight. Amolovak and Chuzhak used a mostly unfamiliar alphabet, and to make matters worse, not every letter functioned the same way in both languages. As much as she'd tried to learn during her travels, she had no idea how to begin picking out words. There didn't even appear to be a name at the top.

Maybe she would make Andrija translate it for her in the morning. He would frown at her, and tell her how she wasn't supposed to go through people's things, and then he would do as she asked.

She was doing her best to slip the parchment back into its pocket without moving when she noticed one particular string of letters near the beginning of the text. The first of them was capitalized, and the rest—well, she wasn't sure, but she thought that, if sounded out, it might have spelled "Agiokon."

Andrija shifted, stretching one leg out in front of him. She shut her eyes tightly and hoped the fall of his jacket hid the parchment well enough. The quiet continued, only the snap and sigh of the fire to break it.

It didn't necessarily mean anything, did it? A small mention of Agiokon—that was nothing. Agiokon was a big city. It had been an important place long before the fall of the spire; it would be for a long time after. Why shouldn't he write about it, whether in his notes or in a letter to somebody?

"If you like," Andrija said suddenly, "I can read it to you."

Chrysanthi's stomach sank. Of course he had noticed her rooting around in his things. Was that anger in his voice? She almost hoped it was—anger, she knew how to handle.

She sat up slowly, pushing her loose hair behind her ears. He was watching her, but with none of the indignation she would have expected if she'd been caught in Lexos's room. Instead he sounded resigned, as though he'd known this was coming and been dreading it the whole while. Only Chrysanthi had no idea what "this" was. Surely the letter was nothing serious. In fact, why even bother with letting him read it aloud? As long as she said nothing, they could continue on as they were and leave this as some small secret tucked in the pocket of Andrija's jacket.

But so many had lost so much at Agiokon. If he knew something about what had happened, she owed it to every last person who had died alongside Nitsos to hear it.

"All right," she said. "Read."

Beyond the border of the grove, one of the horses whinnied impatiently. Andrija cleared his throat. "'South from the library,'" he started. "'Agiokon and the spire intended. Your friends—'" He paused for a moment. "'Friends' is not exact. It's more . . . never mind. 'Your friends have sent the younger brother in search of the same.'"

Chrysanthi drew a sharp breath. This was a report on her and on Nitsos. Andrija had been making note of their every move. Immediately, she thought of each mistake she'd made since leaving the Ksigora—how mortifying to think he had written them down, marked them against her. But worse than that was every question she'd had about who he was that she had swallowed out of kindness, hoping Andrija would tell her himself. She'd been so naïve. He belonged to someone else.

But who? His report had obviously not been to the Sxoriza and, furthermore, hadn't been sent at all, if he still had it, so she had to ask—

"Who? Who are you writing to?"

Andrija held up a hand. "There's some more." He hadn't looked at her since he'd begun reading, but he did now, and she felt the strength of his gaze ripple over her skin, as though she'd stepped too close to a fire. Was he sorry for it? For ruining this? Or had he simply been waiting for it, so that he might be free of her again? Better for her to know, even if it hurt.

"Fine," she said. "Go ahead."

He nodded, bending again over the note. "'The city will be full, is always full. Let me close the door for you. There is nothing more that need be done.'"

That seemed to be it; he set the note down on the dirt in front of him almost deliberately. Chrysanthi suspected that he was trying to make her feel more at ease—his folded hands a promise that he would take up no arms against her—but it had the opposite effect, serving more as a reminder of the strength he carried with him, weapon or no. She'd seen it in him every day of their travels as he rode alongside her, or dragged her out of the lake in Vashnasta, or carried her on his back for the last mile of a hard day as they made for Agiokon.

She had trusted him then. Trusted him, and all the while she'd been nothing more than a task to complete.

"My question still stands," she said. She could hear her own voice trembling—whether with hurt or something sharper, she didn't know. "Who is that letter for?"

Andrija didn't flinch. "The Korabret."

So: Ammar Basha, the Stratagiozi of Amolova. Chrysanthi couldn't really say she was surprised—the note had been in Amolovak—but it still cost her something to hear it from him. Everything they'd done together, every new border they'd crossed. Even the stone studded through his tongue; she'd told him not to and he'd still volunteered, and of course he had, if that had been his order from the Korabret. Of course he'd devoted himself to her like that, to keep himself by her side. To lead her so that she might lead him to what Ammar and the other Stratagiozis were fighting over.

Still: He hadn't sent this particular letter. She reached for it, waiting for Andrija to stop her, but he made no move. She snatched it up and examined each word, turning over in her head the message he had read aloud.

He'd meant to let Ammar know about their trip to Agiokon and about Nitsos's eventual arrival there under the employ of Zita and Tarro, but more than that, he'd suggested that Ammar not take any action in Agiokon. So was it Ammar, then, who'd collapsed the spire? Against the advice that Andrija had never, in fact, really given?

"Why did you keep this one?" she asked. "It was your job to report back, no?"

"It was." Andrija swallowed hard, his throat bobbing. It was the first sign she'd seen of true discomfort, and it made her want to reach for him, to reassure him as she might have done a day ago, but she couldn't. "I sent a different version instead. The same, until your brother, but nothing more."

No word of caution about Agiokon, and no offer to handle things personally for Ammar. "And this?" she asked, holding up the letter.

"I couldn't bring myself to throw it away."

"You couldn't bring yourself to send it, either. Did you know what he would do?" She could hear the hope in her own voice, hated it even as she held it close. "When you told Ammar where we were going."

There was only one answer, wasn't there? Andrija was no fool. He had to have considered that Ammar might take action on a dangerous scale, and he'd chosen to send that letter anyway.

He shook his head—barely, perhaps without realizing it—and his hands clenched tightly into fists. "It doesn't matter," he said. "I sent it either way."

Yes, she thought. You did.

They stared at each other, silence growing heavy between them. For once, Andrija was the one to look away. Whatever shame he felt, Chrysanthi could not hold it for him, no matter how much she wanted to, no matter how well she knew the weight of it. In a way Rhea had been right. She had been content to be a child in her father's house, to let things pass her by, but that had never felt like Andrija to her. He knew the world, lived in it, bled and breathed just like those people buried under the Agiokori rock. To know he had let that pass—to know she might have, too, in his place—

She leaned forward, ignoring the cold sinking in her stomach. "How many people died?"

"I don't know."

"How many wounded?"

"I don't know."

"How many—"

"I don't know," he interrupted, the muscle that jumped in his jaw almost as unnerving as anything else she had ever seen. She watched as he gathered himself. "I tried to count," he finished quietly. Chrysanthi thought she might cry.

Instead, she got to her feet, her legs half numb under her. She staggered at first before bracing herself against the nearest of the orange trees. An odd sort of buzz had started at the back of her head, and everywhere she looked, the flickering shape of the fire seemed to stamp itself onto the dark, but it had become very clear to her: Whatever came next, she couldn't stay with him anymore.

She bent to pick up the bag Andrija had traveled with and took out one of the two waterskins, tossing it to Andrija before she could change her mind. "That's yours. I'll keep the rest."

"You mean to go on alone?" Andrija scrambled up, a sudden gawkiness about him. "You can't."

"I have to." She slung the bag over her shoulder; it wasn't as heavy as she'd worried it might be. "How much have you told your Korabret about this? About where I'm going?"

"Nothing," Andrija said quickly.

He ducked to catch her eyes, and she let him. She had nothing to feel guilty about. "Your word doesn't count for much."

"I know. You have it anyway."

She hoped he was telling the truth, but she couldn't count on it. Safer to assume that more of Ammar's men would be following close behind her, if not Andrija himself. More than that, it was possible Andrija had not been alone in the Sxoriza. There might be people still, people close to Rhea who served another Stratagiozi.

It was even more important now that she be quick to find her family's house.

Chrysanthi began to gather her things. She would leave Andrija with his horse, his jacket, and his knife. The water would keep him for a few days, and there were enough farms scattered throughout the countryside that she didn't feel too badly about keeping the rest of their food for herself.

A cursory look around their little campsite told her she'd got everything else of value. Well, almost. There was, though, one more thing she could take from Andrija before she left.

"Ammar is looking for these graves just like the other Stratagiozis," she said. "Did he ever tell you what for?"

Andrija had listened to Zita's explanation without batting an eye. She'd assumed that had been his characteristic composure, but perhaps it had been something else: familiarity.

"Not quite," he said. "And it wasn't him. It was his second."

Chrysanthi couldn't help scoffing. Was this how he'd justified lying to her? Threading everything through little loopholes like that?

"But she said something," Andrija continued. "She said they would be the end of the Stratagiozis."

"What is that supposed to mean?"

"I don't know. Really. That's all she ever told me." He shifted his stance, hand flexing at his side as if desperate for something to do. "He is looking for the saints, yes, but not to find them. To make sure that nobody else does."

He looked so sincere, and she could hear it in every word—how hard he was working to tell her anything at all, in defiance of whatever loyalty he'd sworn to Ammar. It made her want to reach for him, to draw them both back into the moment that had lived and died by the fire only hours before. He'd lied to her, but he would never have hurt her. Everything he'd done, every decision he'd made since leaving the Ksigora had been to keep her safe.

But she was almost certain that that was only true because she'd never told him about her mother. If he'd known why she was going home now, and who was buried on the grounds of that old house, he might have decided differently.

She gathered herself, lifting her chin and shaking her hair back. "I know that I can't keep you from following me," she said. "But I'm asking you not to." Andrija stepped forward, a pained twist setting deep in his brow as he opened his mouth, but before she could tell him not to argue, he had shut it again.

"Right," she said. "Goodbye, then."

She turned on her heel and pushed through the orange trees before she could regret it. Her head felt half empty, her lungs too tight. The horses were waiting a few yards away; she could not remember which was meant to be hers, and with the sound of Andrija moving not far behind her, she went to the nearest one.

She buckled the bag she'd taken from Andrija to the back of the saddle and had swung up into the seat when she realized too late she'd chosen the wrong horse. The stirrups were far too long for her legs, and to fix it she'd have to dismount again, all with Andrija standing right there, watching her.

She froze, reins clutched in one hand, the other poised uselessly over the edge of the saddle. Finally, Andrija took a half step forward from where he'd been lingering by the edge of the orange grove.

"Here," he said. "Let me."

He approached her slowly, and her horse shuffled under her as her grip on the reins tightened. It settled, though, when Andrija laid his hand on its shoulder, and he began to adjust her stirrups.

He managed the right-hand stirrup without touching her. Every movement deliberately slow to give her time to lift her foot out of the way. Still, she could feel the warmth off his chest where he almost brushed against her knee, and she found herself fixed on the hand he dragged across her horse's chest as he came around to adjust the second stirrup. This time she left her boot where it was.

"Chrysanthi."

She flinched, embarrassed. Surely he had noticed her staring. "Are you finished?"

"Yes, but— Chrysanthi," he repeated, more insistent this time.

She looked down. He was so near now, his chin tipped up, the blue of early morning wound through his hair. She wondered, for a moment, what he would do if she pressed her palm to his cheek.

"The Korabret sent me to the Sxoriza," he said.

"I know."

"But he didn't send me to you."

Her breath hitched; she did not move, and neither did he. If she hadn't found that letter—

If she'd stayed in that storeroom with him, ignored Zita's messenger, and let him lead them somewhere new—

"I'm sorry," she said. "I just don't know what to do with that."

Andrija's face seemed to fall, and Chrysanthi looked away, toward the open country ahead. With a gentle kick from her heels, her horse surged into motion. Andrija did not call after her.

She supposed what he'd meant, she thought as she rode on, was that following her had not been his assignment. He'd chosen her himself, chosen to follow her once and every day after.

And really, didn't that only make everything worse?

CHAPTER THIRTY-EIGHT

ALEXANDROS

The fourth day after the collapse of the spire saw Lexos sitting on a veranda overlooking the gulf, a hot cup of kaf in one hand and a fresh slice of bread in the other. They'd arrived at Falka's Merkheri summer home—she had a summer home, he thought enviously for the thirtieth or fortieth time—the night before, and in the daylight now he was able to properly take in the view: deep blue water, a white stone promenade, and colorful fishing boats moored all along it, their hulls shaped into exaggerated curves. Across the water was Trefazio, but for the moment Lexos was pretending it did not exist. The only things that mattered were this beautiful morning and the fact that he'd been able to wash his hair before getting dressed, and both were made better by Falka's absence.

Their reunion under the Devetsi house had been wonderfully brief, given the need for a quick escape, but during their travel north to this house, Falka had been unavoidable. Lexos had thought he might just lie down and die if he had to see another of her smug smiles. He was perfectly capable of realizing just how thoroughly he had been played on his own; he did not need her help. Because of course it had been her idea to send him to her father's prison so that he might help Ettore escape.

"So glad I could help," Lexos had sneered when she'd brought it up, and then he'd tried to storm off, except they'd all been sleeping in the same shabby rented room, and there had been nowhere to storm off to.

Now, though, he had his own room, and he did not have to look at his own mark on Falka's palm. He did, however, still have to think about his needle and thread and his tidebowl sitting somewhere in this house, ready and waiting for her use, but for the moment the morning sun was pleasant and his kaf was just the right side of too hot. He took a long sip before tilting his head back, the wrought iron chair under him pressing into his aching muscles. He'd thought that both he and Ettore had made it out of Agiokon unscathed, but as the days passed, his whole body had begun to cramp painfully as the tension he'd been holding finally released.

His relative peace was disturbed when, a few minutes later, a knock came at his bedroom door. Lexos groaned and rose to answer it.

"Yes?" he called. "Who is it?"

"Do open up, Alexandros. If I have to keep carrying this much longer, it'll end up on the floor."

Hurriedly, Lexos pulled the door open. On the other side stood Ettore, dressed in a set of pale pink linen summer clothes and carrying a tray laden with fresh fruit. Without another word, he breezed past and made straight for the veranda.

"Good morning," Lexos said. "Have you been up long?"

Ettore was already seated by the time Lexos joined him at the little table. A trio of gold rings glinted on his left hand as he reached for Lexos's mug of kaf and took a sip.

"Too sweet," he said and set it back down.

"How? I haven't put anything in it."

Ettore gestured to the empty chair opposite him. Lexos sat down gingerly. A muscle in his back twinged; he covered his wince by reaching for one of the figs on the tray, only to discover that a bite had already been taken out of it.

"Sorry," Ettore said when he noticed Lexos putting the fig back. "I got peckish."

"It's all right."

"It's the sea air. It stirs the appetite."

Lexos followed the line of Ettore's gaze out across the promenade below. It was busier now than it had been when he'd woken, but it was still relatively empty; more people seemed to be out on the water, in little boats or swimming off docks that drifted in the wind, moored loosely to the shore.

"Was this house one of yours, too?" he asked.

"Like in Agiokon?" Ettore shook his head. "This one's a new acquisition. I asked Falka to find somewhere nice. And I've always liked this part of the coast."

"I can see why."

"Can you? I thought you Argyroses preferred the dark, brooding cliffs and that sort of thing."

"It's 'Argyrosi,'" Lexos muttered, but he supposed he was lucky Ettore was willing to conduct their conversations in Modern Thyzaki and not the Saint's he seemed to know better. "We were not always at Stratathoma, you know."

"That's right. Your father took his seat maybe a century back, no?" Ettore reached for the kaf again and took a sip before unceremoniously spitting it back out. "It's still too sweet."

"Of course it is. Nothing's happened to it since you—"

"Where were you all before that, then?"

It was, Lexos thought, incredibly odd to sit here discussing family history with Luco Domina, particularly in light of recent events, but Ettore looked genuinely interested, and though other aspects of his charm had worn thin over their travels together, there was very little so alluring as the last of the saints wanting to know what you had to say.

"The west country," Lexos said. "In Thyzakos. We had a bit of land from the steward my father served."

"And your mother was there with you? The saint worshipper?"

Lexos raised an eyebrow. "I thought your interest was with my sister."

"Oh, it is. But I'd like to know anyway. I've found it hard to discover much about your mother."

"I— You've been asking?" Who had Ettore been pressing for information and for what possible reason? Irini Argyros had lived an ordinary life until she'd died at the hands of a terribly ordinary man. And it had all happened so long ago that even Lexos, her oldest child— second oldest, he corrected himself bitterly—could not remember her face.

"At first it was just a passing curiosity," Ettore said. "But do you know, Alexandros, how unusual it is that I find it difficult to learn more about a person?"

"I mean, if you've tried to send one of your informants to speak to my mother's corpse, I can see where you'd have found trouble."

"Well, at least for the moment, yes," Ettore said, an uncomfortable reminder of how he hoped to use Rhea. "But it isn't only my informants I rely on. I have quite a talent for this sort of thing myself."

"Oh?" Of course Ettore could manage to say something like that and sound only matter-of-fact, rather than entirely full of himself. "And where did you acquire that? I wouldn't think you'd have had much spare time—"

"What with all my murdering, yes. Don't forget, though. Just as you were not always at Stratathoma, I was not always Luco Domina." Ettore leaned back in his chair, eyes gone distant. "When I was a boy I spent quite a while in Vashnasta. There is a library there. You might have heard of it."

"The Navirotsk."

"Yes. It was my home for some time. Mine, and also home to a number of others."

He fell silent, but there had been a weight to his words. A sense of added meaning.

"Who were they?" Lexos asked.

Judging from Ettore's widening smile, that was just what he'd hoped Lexos might say. "Saints, before we were saints. Where do you think we got the idea for the matagios?"

Something shuddered to a halt in Lexos's head before slowly ticking forward again. Of course the first saints had not always been such, but it had never occurred to him to wonder much about how they'd ascended, if that even was the right word. He had been more concerned with their fall, and with wondering how long it would be before the same thing happened to Baba.

"You were all . . . librarians?"

Ettore threw back his head with a bark of laughter. "We absolutely were not. We were students. And we were young, and we had nothing else to do but read and listen and learn. Although it wasn't everybody, mind you. Only four or five of us. Maybe six. The rest came later, although I couldn't say how long it took. To be honest with you, I forget the details. It's quite a responsibility being the only one left."

"By your own design," Lexos said, and Ettore nodded amiably.

"You're right. I shouldn't complain."

Another knock came then, at the bedroom door, but even as Lexos got up to answer it, the door swung open and Falka came through. Her hair was loose, and her clothes were so identical to Ettore's that Lexos nearly burst out laughing. As if she hadn't been clear enough about her wish for him to leave.

"Good morning," she said, gliding across the threshold onto the veranda.

"By all means," Lexos said dryly, "come right in."

"I'm afraid I don't have time for pleasantries," she said, but still she reached for one of the nectarine slices near the rim of the tray and took a bite. "It's good news, though, which is something of a relief after the last few days."

"Well?" Ettore asked.

"It's her," Falka said. "I've got a line, if I move now."

That was about Rhea, wasn't it? Lexos sat up straight, a low hum of panic setting him on edge. What did Falka mean?

"How direct?" Ettore sounded no more interested than he had a moment ago, but still, Lexos could feel the importance of the question in the way Falka lifted her chin before answering.

"More direct," she said, "than this." Without meeting Lexos's eyes, she nodded toward him.

Oh dear, he thought. That wasn't very good at all.

"Hold on," he said, "hold on," but he could think of nothing else to say, not as Ettore rose from the table and dusted his palms off on his trousers.

"That's a shame," Ettore said. "I did hope we had a longer road to walk together."

"But——" Lexos stumbled to his feet, finally finding his words. "Where is she? What do you mean, direct?"

"I don't think that's anything you need to worry about," Falka said coolly. Lexos really could not believe that he had ever thought her impressive, or worthy of his admiration. He had never in his life met someone so annoying, and he had met all of his siblings. But she didn't matter; she was not the person whose mind he needed to change.

"You'll need me," he said to Ettore, who had started for the door. "I can still help you."

Ettore stopped. "That might be true," he said, "but all things considered, you haven't done much of that yet, and I've been just fine without it. So you'll understand if I don't bring you along, won't you?"

"I'm sure he does," Falka said. "We should be away, actually, so if you don't mind——"

"Of course."

Ettore turned, falling into step alongside Falka as they left the veranda. Lexos could not believe it was happening like this. So quickly, with seemingly nothing he could do to stop it. Well, not nothing. He had one arrow left to fire.

With a deep breath, he called out: "You've told me a lot about your plans."

"Oh, come now," Ettore said, sighing. "Let's not do this."

"You've told me about all the things you know that the Stratagiozis don't." Lexos lifted his chin, all the steadiness he'd learned as Baba's second brought to bear. "Did you want that kept private?"

But Ettore was not Baba, and Lexos was not a second anymore, and he knew, even as Ettore's expression turned pitying, what he was about to hear.

"Do you really think anybody would believe you? You, claiming to be in my confidence? You're a child, Alexandros."

"I'm not. I've seen a hundred years."

Ettore waved him off. "You don't know a thing. I mean, really: What is an Argyros? What power do you come from? What mark do you carry on your hand? Why would they ever believe I wanted anything to do with you?"

Lexos curled his fingers around his blank palm, a blush burning across his cheeks. "They might," he said. "They know me."

"But they also knew your father, and . . ." Ettore grimaced. "From what I understand of him, he might not have made a very good impression. Look, I really don't see any need for us to part in anger. In fact, Falka?" He waved her over, and she obliged. "See if one of your servants will pack Alexandros a bundle of fresh clothes before he goes. Surely we have some we can spare."

With that, Ettore slipped off the veranda and out the bedroom door. Falka was close behind, sparing a single glance over her shoulder before she was entirely gone, and Lexos was left alone.

He felt his jaw drop slightly, and his body swayed forward, as if to follow. This couldn't be it, could it? It had happened so fast. One minute he and Ettore had been talking about the Navirotsk, and the next, this?

But along with his shock came a humiliation so deep he could barely stand it. What had he expected? He'd let himself sit back, let himself follow Ettore's guidance instead of truly distinguishing himself. Ettore kept what served him and shed what didn't, and Lexos had allowed himself to become the latter.

"*Mala,*" he said and held his head in his hands. He'd never been backed all the way into a corner before—there had always, always been some way out, even that day at Stratathoma. But it wasn't even a corner that he found himself in now. It was just him, alone on a veranda with absolutely nothing in front of him aside from the beautiful view.

A line to Rhea. What did that mean? And would his sister be in any way equipped to handle it? He'd thought he would be, and look how wrong he'd been. No, if he had not been able to get by alongside Ettore, there was no chance for Rhea.

He gave himself a shake. Her fate was not bound to his anymore. Ettore could try to get what he wanted from her, but like Lexos had, he would find that counting on Rhea Argyros was only asking to be disappointed. And now Lexos was free to do whatever he wanted. And that was a good thing, wasn't it?

Lexos's optimism, however, was quick to fade when, only a few minutes later, a servant arrived at the door and very politely turned him out of Falka's house. He was told that any number of inns in the area would be happy to accept him as a guest, provided he could pay the required sum. That, unfortunately, was something Lexos was very unprepared to do.

He was unfamiliar with this part of Merkher—most of his visits to the country had been limited to Agiokon—so after accepting his eviction with as much dignity as possible, he found a spot on the promenade and sat propped up against a nearby merchant's discarded boxes, his feet dangling over water. Perhaps, he thought, he should swim out to one of the floating docks and hope that he might drift out into the open ocean. At least that would solve some of his problems (while, granted, posing a whole host of new ones).

He had been there for the better part of the day when a shadow in the shape of a man fell across him and a loaf of bread landed in his lap. Lexos grabbed for it before thinking to look up; when he did, he was greeted not by Ettore, come to apologize for their spat earlier, but by a different familiar face: Michali Laskaris, who looked somehow even more despondent than he himself felt.

"Oh," Lexos said. "I have to tell you, you're not who I was hoping to see."

Michali's face remained impassive. "I know just how you feel."

He was dressed improperly for the weather, in a set of clothes that would've been better suited to the deeper winter of the Ksigora. There was a slightly alarming amount of sweat visible on his forehead, and his skin was so pale as to invite questions about whether or not he was entirely alive. Which, Lexos reminded himself as he got to his feet, was appropriate to ask about the Laskaris boy.

"Well," he said, "you're the one who found me." He lifted the loaf of bread in a mock salute before taking an aggressive bite. "What can I do for you?" he asked with his mouth still full.

"You can come with me," Michali said. "There's a conversation that needs having." He eyed the promenade around them, looking distinctly uncomfortable. "Not here, though."

Lexos swallowed his bite of bread and then took another. He'd spent maybe a minute or two total with this man—everything else he knew came from Rhea, or from other sorts of secondhand reporting. Was any of that enough to warrant trusting Michali now?

No, he thought, but he didn't really have a wealth of other options.

"Right," he said. "Lead on."

They went through the seaside city, south along the promenade and then inland, toward one of the city's small, provincial squares. Michali said nothing as they walked, not even when Lexos nearly got knocked into the water by a passing courier. He hardly even looked over his shoulder to make sure Lexos was still there. Perhaps he was hoping Lexos might change his mind, or he knew that Lexos had nowhere else to go. Whatever the case, when Michali did eventually nod toward a simple wooden door leading to an equally simple wooden house, Lexos was right behind him and followed him inside dutifully.

The house was clearly lived in—a pair of badly patched winter boots sat neatly by the door, and the idea of someone bent over them, needle in hand, lodged under Lexos's ribs—but whoever usually occupied it appeared to have made themselves scarce. Waiting in the front room, rising from a plain, lopsided divan, was a man Lexos had never met before. Tall, broad-shouldered, wearing a solemn look that seemed, even at a glance, ill-suited for his face.

"Thank you for coming," the man said. "I'm Piros Zografi. I'm a friend of your sister's."

"Which one?"

Piros seemed to freeze for a moment. "I'm sorry?"

"A friend of Rhea's is very different than a friend of Chrysanthi's."

Neither of Lexos's new companions replied, apparently not in the mood for a bit of chat. Lexos wasn't, either. He could hear a sharpness in his voice; just like Baba, he thought. Some fun with one's live meal, before you swallowed it whole.

"Anyway," he went on, "you'll know who I am if you've invited me here. What for?" He stepped around Michali, who had gone very still just past the threshold, and sat down on the divan Piros had just vacated. "You're Sxoriza, aren't you? I'll tell you, the Sxoriza are not very fond of me."

Michali and Piros exchanged glances. "I'm aware," Piros said, and that was odd, wasn't it? Everything Lexos knew about the Sxoriza put Michali higher in rank than this Piros, but Michali had been the one sent to fetch him and was stepping back now into the shadows, his face gone somewhat empty.

"I don't come as a representative of the Sxoriza," Piros said, drawing Lexos's attention back to him. "I'm here on your sister's behalf."

"Really?" Lexos raised an eyebrow. "Because she's not very fond of me, either."

" 'Behalf' is maybe the wrong word." Piros took a seat in the armchair opposite Lexos. "It's true that she doesn't know we're here. But after what happened at Agiokon, we thought this was necessary."

"Agiokon? You were there?" They had to mean the collapse. By now the news had reached even the farthest edges of the continent.

"We were," Piros said.

"And Rhea? Her, too? Is she—" Lexos forced himself to stop talking. Yes, his concern for her was habitual, but unwelcome. She had pushed aside everything he'd ever done for her; the tie between them was broken. Her pain did not belong to him anymore.

Piros cleared his throat. "That's a difficult question to answer, to be honest."

Well, all right—that was fair enough. And if Ettore and Falka were heading off to pursue their line to Rhea, Lexos felt he could be reasonably sure that she had not, in fact, died at Agiokon. He leaned back, stretching his legs out in front of him.

"I'm sure the collapse was quite a lot for her," he said. "Give her a few days. She'll be fine."

"It's not the collapse, actually," Piros said. "It's what happened afterward. She had . . . a bit of an outburst."

Another look between Michali and Piros; what did Michali have to say about this anyway? When Lexos glanced over at him, he was as impassive as he'd been moments ago, with only the slightest hint of anger in the furrow of his brow. Lexos could understand that; Rhea had probably told him all sorts of unpleasant things about him.

Still, whatever those things had been, they were not enough to keep Piros from leaning forward. He looked viscerally uncomfortable. "Something's changed, since raising Michali. She isn't well, and it's only getting worse."

Would he ever, ever be able to get rid of the tug in his chest at the mention of some misfortune for her? Probably not, but he could at the very least keep anyone from realizing that link still existed between them—anyone, including Rhea.

"I'm still not sure why you're involving me," he said. "Are we finished here?"

Piros opened his mouth, but before he could say anything else, Michali cut in.

"Her mark," he said. "It doesn't look right anymore."

Lexos had been about to get up and head back out into the city; this, though, drew all his momentum out of him. A wash of cold fell over him, gathering at the base of his spine. "What do you mean?"

"I'm not sure how best to describe it," Piros started.

Michali cut in: "I am." He held up his left hand, gesturing to where Rhea's first mark, Thyspira's line, lay. "The black seems to spread. Ink in water." He lifted his right hand. "And the scar bleeds. Day and night, it bleeds. Not to mention—"

"She needs some help," Piros interrupted, but Lexos waved him off.

"Not to mention what?" he asked. "Her matagios?"

Michali shrugged, but there was nothing careless or disinterested about the burn of his gaze. "The same, I think," he said. "I would guess that whatever she did to call me back, it cost her. But we don't know. She needs help from one of her own."

Lexos nodded slowly. That much he certainly believed. But everything he'd heard from Ettore was ringing in his ears: the particular weight of the Thyzak matagios, something even Ettore himself did not want back just yet. What he wanted Rhea to do for him, and how he had left Lexos behind only hours before to make it happen.

Maybe if he'd had the matagios, things would not have happened this way. Maybe he would not have found it so hard to bear. But it had gone to Rhea, and yes, all that had been Baba's doing, but she had cherished it, branded it onto her very identity. She had stolen from him; he would not now help her escape the consequences.

"I don't think there's anything I can do for you," he said. "Rhea's not much for my company these days." He held up his own hand, the palm blank as it had been since Stratathoma. "And I'm hardly an expert in this sort of thing anymore."

"That's actually why we wanted to speak to you," Piros said. "You lost your gift, and you seem—well, you seem fine."

Piros's words slipped under Lexos's skin, nestling like little vipers. "Fine" was not at all what Lexos had wanted for himself. He had been meant for so much more, and instead he was here, so far down on his luck that his rejection by Ettore was as close as he'd come to power lately.

"We thought," Piros went on, "that that might be something worth exploring for your sister. How did you lose yours? It was my understanding that losing gifts like that usually involves—"

"Dying? It does." Lexos tamped down on the urge to get up and leave, or at the very least smack Piros across the face. "I thought you knew all about my situation."

"Reports varied," Piros said. He at least had the courtesy to look embarrassed. Meanwhile Michali had barely blinked.

"Well, my particular situation will be of no use to you." Lexos got to his feet; he was finished with this. "My gifts were taken by someone who I think wants even less to do with you than I do. Besides, if you think my sister would let you scrape the black from her tongue, you are out of your mind. We're Argyrosi. We don't do that."

"What your sister does or doesn't do is a mystery at the moment," Michali said darkly. "She's gone."

"Gone?"

"She left a Sxoriza camp not long ago. We don't know where she went."

Lexos couldn't help a snort of laughter. "You don't know where she went? Your Aya Thyspira? Nobody was keeping track?"

Piros's tanned cheeks went surprisingly pink. "It was an oversight."

"I'll say." An oversight that Ettore and Falka were now poised to exploit.

"But she's your sister," Piros insisted. "And we thought you might be able to find her."

Lexos pinched the bridge of his nose, squeezing his eyes shut. He was so, so sick of people coming to him for that. Always to find Rhea, and never for what he could do—what he could still do, thank you very much, with or without a mark on his palm. At least he understood what Ettore wanted with Rhea, ludicrous as it seemed to him. What did these two want her for? To bring her back to the Sxoriza so that somebody could try to take her gifts from her?

If anybody was going to do that, it would be him. The grievances they held between them were not for anybody else to solve. And that matagios was not for anybody but an Argyros.

"I appreciate you asking me," he said. "It's always nice to be included. But I'm afraid our conversation is finished."

Piros stood up, one hand fluttering toward Lexos before he thought better of it. "Finished?"

"I can't help you. You obviously can't help me. So I'm not sure what else there is to say."

Lexos had almost reached the door, Piros left in stunned silence behind him, when Michali took hold of his arm. The other man's grip was too cold through the fabric of Lexos's shirt.

"You really won't do anything for her?" Michali asked. "She's your family. And she's out there alone."

"That's not my fault, is it?" But he softened at the look in Michali's eyes. It was one he recognized—the fear of knowing part of his own heart was out there, unwell and in danger. Of course Michali wanted to do something about it. "She'll be fine," he said. "She's looked after herself before, and she will again."

He sidled through the door before either of the others could stop him. But while he'd felt caught in a haze after being left behind by Ettore, he felt a purpose now beating in his chest, because he'd lied to Michali: Rhea would not be fine. She had built a whole world for herself around that matagios and the line on her palm. If they were crumbling now—if they were anything less than the power she'd imagined for herself—she would crumble with them. He knew that she thought she'd changed, left behind their lives at Stratathoma, but he could see the truth, could see the way she had left being Thyspira behind only to slot sainthood in its place. And he was the only one who could understand.

They'd raged and they'd hurt each other, and they would surely do it all again, but she was his sister. More than that, she was an Argyros in power, with a matagios on her tongue. And if Lexos had to comb through the rest of the continent to find her before Ettore and Falka did, well, at least it was something to do.

As for what he would do when they met, he would decide that later. Protect her, protect the Argyros line, and help her back to the sister he had always loved so dearly. Or kill her himself, and let the matagios pass to him.

CHAPTER THIRTY-NINE

RHEA

For lack of a better option, Rhea went south. The first day's travel got her across the border into Thyzakos; the second had, thus far, taken her into the beginnings of the west country, until she'd come to a dead stop in the middle of the road after realizing that if she went any farther, she might end up on the route to Stratathoma. Feeling quite dispirited (not to mention tired and hungry), she'd tied her horse to a dried-out beech tree and was at the moment in her second hour of sitting by the remains of someone else's abandoned campfire, trying to decide what to do next.

Perhaps it had been unwise to leave the Sxoriza without any plan. Well, really, there was no perhaps about it; it had been unwise. But if she'd stayed there any longer, who knew what deal she might have found herself bound up in? At least this way she was holding her fate in her own hands—never mind that one of them was split nearly in half.

She shifted uncomfortably on the ground, cradling her injured arm across her chest. It hurt more now than it had the day before, but there was very little she could do about that. Aside from the bandages she'd taken with her, she'd only managed to steal a bit of food and water before she'd slipped out of camp. Soon she would need to find somewhere safe to replenish, and that was a tall order. Nowhere seemed all that safe, particularly after Agiokon.

"You'd better eat some of this grass," she said to the horse, who was decidedly not as nice as Lefka. "I won't be giving you any of my food."

Still, despite her own hunger, the idea of eating any herself did not feel very appetizing, not with the ache of her injuries refusing to fade. She eased backward, twisting the cord that kept her hummingbird tied in a bundle at her waist until she could rest comfortably against the trunk of the beech tree.

"I'll let you out in a little while," she told the hummingbird and shut her eyes. Some peace and some rest—that was all she wanted.

Unfortunately, now that she was paying attention, she could hear in the distance the rattle of a carriage, growing nearer with every second. This road was not a secret, but Rhea had encountered so few travelers on it all day that the noise had her scrambling to her feet and off into what cover the trees could provide. With her luck it would be Michali and Piros come to fetch her, or even Lexos. He, at least, she might be somewhat glad to see, if only because of how wrong it felt that he, presumably, did not know their brother had died.

But the carriage that came into view was much too nice to belong to the Sxoriza or to Lexos. While it had been decorated simply, its lacquered doors and gold trim were enough to make clear how much it had cost its owner, not to mention the condition of the horses pulling it—perfect, with not a fleck of sweat on either one's hide.

Rhea flinched into the shadows, hoping to avoid the driver's gaze. Her own horse was still visible, but with any luck this fellow traveler would continue on, instead of—

Right, they'd stopped, and the door was opening. "Thank goodness," a new voice called. "We've been trying to catch you since sunup."

Rhea shut her eyes and waited for some sort of surprise to fill her; nothing came. When she opened them again, there was Falka Domina leaning out from the black carriage, looking neat and somber in a matching traveling suit that could have been taken out of Rhea's own closet at Stratathoma. Resigned, she stepped back out onto the edge of the road.

"Hello," she said flatly. "Well, you've caught me." Less than two days on her own, and here she was again. At least Falka was Falka—understanding in ways Rhea had never expected, and a lot easier to look at than Piros or Michali, with their matching expressions of misplaced concern.

"I wouldn't say 'caught,'" Falka replied. Above her, the driver had already climbed down from their post and stepped politely away, off to the opposite side of the road. "It's not like that at all. I just wanted to see you."

She grinned, pretty and sharp. It stirred something in Rhea—of course it did—but she was too exhausted to muster anything up in return.

"You've seen me," she said. "What else, then?" She could tell what this was; no matter her mistakes, she always knew when someone wanted something from her. Falka would find herself disappointed, just as Michali and the Sxoriza had all been, and Baba before them.

For a heartbeat the world around her seemed to sway. She blinked, gone cold and hot, only to find Falka had stepped down from the carriage and was already at her side.

"Are you all right?" she was asking. "I heard— No, let's get you sat down first. Come on. It's comfortable inside."

Rhea put up no fight as Falka guided her toward the carriage and helped her in. The benches were both well padded, with enough blankets piled on one side to withstand even the deepest Ksigoran cold. Rhea shuddered as she sank down onto the right-hand one, her body unused to the comfort.

Falka left the door open behind them as she climbed in after and took a seat opposite Rhea. "Did you ride with anything? Rations?"

"I did, but—"

"I'm sure it wasn't enough," Falka said, grimacing. Rhea let the impulse to defend the Sxoriza's supply chain rise and fall. "I've got plenty here anyway. And you need something to get your strength up."

She rummaged through one of her own bags before straightening with a fresh end of bread and a canteen. "The water first. Don't drink it too quickly."

Rhea accepted the canteen and took a sip. Falka watched her intently. "What?" she said, when she'd swallowed.

"You just look awful, that's all."

"I have your advice to thank for that."

"Agiokon." Falka leaned in, her knee pressing against Rhea's. "Yes. Wasn't that something?"

"That's one way to put it."

Falka paused, a frown creasing her brow. "You didn't think that I had a hand in it?"

"No," Rhea said. She took another sip of water, suppressing a shiver. "It didn't seem to suit you."

"That's true. I do prefer something a bit more subtle."

"Like laying a path of flowers through the middle of the woods?"

Delight sparked in Falka's dark eyes. "Exactly like that."

How long ago that seemed now. How much had changed since they'd come face-to-face in the Ksigora, and since Rhea had rejected Falka's offer. It stung to think of how sure she'd been then that her gifts would be what got her to Nitsos, when really they had not even been enough to bring him back.

"I don't understand," she said. Her voice sounded muffled, distant, but Falka only nodded for her to continue. "What happened with the spire, I mean, but . . ." She held up her right hand and watched Falka's mouth drop gently open as she took in the heavy bandages visible at the cuff of her jacket sleeve. "I suppose you've heard all about this by now."

"All about what?" Falka asked. "Were you hurt?"

"In a manner of speaking." Rhea knew it would have been easier to just show her, but she'd had enough of that for now. Chrysanthi in the street, Michali in their tent together—she wanted someone, just for a second, to look her in the eye. "It's got worse since you saw it last."

"I don't doubt it."

"Maybe I should've let you when you asked."

Falka went very still. "Let me what?" she asked. She sounded almost nervous. Rhea had never heard that in her voice before.

"Take the mark," she said, all too aware of Falka's nearness. "Like you offered to in the woods. Although I think you'd have quite a job in front of you, getting it all out."

Falka made a soft noise—appreciation, maybe, or more likely dismay. "Does it hurt very badly?"

"Yes," Rhea said, "only it doesn't bleed. Not the new bit." And then, when Falka offered nothing else, she continued into the quiet: "I wish, sometimes, that it would."

"What for?"

She didn't know how to answer that. Not really, not in a way she could carve into sense. It wasn't as though she hadn't suffered for trying to call Nitsos back. Anybody could see as much. But if she could not bring these gifts to bear—if they would not work for her as they had before—if her power in this world was not what she'd bargained for—

She wanted to feel it, in everything. She wanted all of it, from the bruise to the blood to the bone.

But Falka was looking at her, listening to her, and as well as they understood each other sometimes, Rhea was not sure she could count on that for this.

"Oh, just to give the bandages something to do," she said and was proud at how airy she sounded, at least until Falka reached across the gap between them and took Rhea's marked hand in hers. Her skin was cool; or rather, Rhea was warm, too warm, and caught entirely by the way she could see Falka weighing her words.

"You'd think that I would know quite a lot about these," Falka said finally, tapping Rhea's bandaged mark, "given what I do. But I don't. Not more than . . . well, not more than I learned from my father. I can't help you the way I'd like to."

Rhea let out a wry laugh. "I didn't ask you for help. You're the one who found me."

"I know," Falka said, "I did." Her gaze drifted from Rhea's, and her shoulders tightened briefly before she seemed to come rushing back to herself. She dropped Rhea's hands, pressing herself back against the carriage wall. "You should go, actually."

"What?"

"Take the bag with you. There's food and water enough to get you wherever you're heading."

"I don't know where I'm heading," Rhea said. That was probably a mistake, but she was too confused by Falka's apparent rejection to care. "What's happened just now? We were—"

"Don't go north," Falka interrupted. "East is fine, I suppose. Farther south, too, but just . . . not where there are Dominas."

"There's a Domina here."

"That," Falka said, her jaw tight, "is my point. Do you know someone called Ettore?"

Should she? Rhea knew there were things she'd missed from Sxoriza meetings and reports, but as far as she could remember, there'd been no mention of that name. "No, I don't think so."

"He's a Domina elder. He's sent me here to bring you back with me. He thinks he can help you, but—"

"Help me? With this?" Rhea held up her marked hand and, when Falka nodded, felt an eagerness wake under her ribs. Was this someone who could help her bring her gifts back under her control? "Is he with Tarro?"

"No. No, they're not . . ." Falka's discomfort was striking, and if Rhea hadn't been curious to hear more before, she certainly was now. "He and your brother were imprisoned together. He's as much with Tarro as Alexandros is."

That, Rhea thought, spoke either very well or very poorly of this Ettore, and she could not decide which. But none of this spoke to why Falka was telling her now to go.

"So you're offering me this man's help," she said slowly. "But you don't want me to take it?"

"Yes," Falka said, through gritted teeth. The dark of the carriage clung to her, gathering in her hair, and her palms were flat against the bench.

"Why not?" Rhea leaned in. "You don't think it will work?"

"I don't know. Truly, I don't. But, Rhea, if you stay—" Falka cut herself off. Her eyes met Rhea's so plainly that the world around them seemed to shudder, as though it had kept moving while Rhea had stopped short. "I can't offer you this again. Either you take this now and I never saw you, or you come with me."

Rhea swallowed hard. She had left the Sxoriza over their Domina connection, and though it was a different Domina, and a different deal, she couldn't be sure they were different enough. But if this Ettore could get her gifts working the way they had with Michali, maybe none of that mattered. Maybe it was enough that she was not going into it alone.

There was Falka, who would stay at her side, who cared enough to break her own word and offer her a way out. Falka would not disappoint her like Piros; she would not burden her like Chrysanthi, or serve as a reminder, like Michali, of all the wrong she had done.

"If I come with you," she said, "do I have to stay with my horse, or can I ride in the carriage?"

Falka let out a bark of laughter. "Yes, yes, you can drive it if you'd really like to. Rhea, are you sure?"

Her cheeks were flushed, and a lock of hair was beginning to escape the knot it was tied up in. Rhea watched it tumble down to brush against her throat.

"Very sure," she said.

"Good."

But from the look in Falka's eyes, they were both talking about something else, and Rhea found she could not breathe. Falka leaned across the space between them; for a moment they stared at each other, a rushing in Rhea's ears, and then she was pressing forward, Falka's hand already buried in her hair and her name already whispered— once, twice—before she caught Falka's mouth in a fumbling kiss.

She had been shy, sometimes, with Michali. Afraid that he would see the heart of her and draw back, realizing his mistake. And he hated her now, for asking so much of him, for holding him so close. But Falka knew what she was, and she was here anyway—already that close, with her lips pressed to Rhea's jaw.

It wasn't long, though, before leaning too far into Falka's body sent a bolt of pain streaking up Rhea's own. She let out a muffled groan, and immediately Falka braced her, helping her straighten back up against the carriage wall.

"Sorry," Falka said. Her white shirt had come untucked, and Rhea could see where her hand had left a smudge of dirt on the collar. "Are you hurt?"

Rhea laughed. "Are you really asking that?"

"Right." Falka sat back, her marked hand lingering on Rhea's knee. There were more lines inscribed across her skin than there had been when they'd met in Rhokera and in the Ksigora. So many new gifts under Falka's control, but Falka had let Rhea keep hers. "If you're sure, then why don't we get you out of here?"

Minutes later, after they had loaded everything into the carriage and told the driver to bring Rhea's horse along, Falka settled onto the bench at Rhea's side and let out a long breath.

"We'll meet Ettore at an inn a few hours north," she said. "The road's fairly flat between here and there. You should be able to get some rest."

Rhea did not think she would be able to sleep for a long while, not with Falka next to her, but she only nodded and closed her eyes. With one hand, she took hold of Falka's; the other she left resting protectively on the hummingbird in its cloth bundle, tucked between her hip and the carriage door.

Overhead, the driver could be heard climbing back into position. Any second now they would be on their way to somewhere new, to someone who might actually be able to help her. She had not felt so relaxed in weeks, or perhaps not even since she'd left her father's house to go marry Michali.

"Rhea?"

"Hm?"

"I wanted to tell you: I'm sorry about Nitsos. I didn't know him well, but I liked him."

Rhea supposed she ought to have felt angry, or at least upset to hear his name, but what point was there in it now? She would learn how to summon him home; she would have the confrontation she'd been denied. Everything else could wait.

"I'm glad someone did," she said and knocked twice on the carriage ceiling with her right hand. "Drive on."

CHAPTER FORTY

RHEA

For all the wealth evident in the carriage and the status Falka had hinted that Ettore held, the inn he'd apparently picked was a bit laughable. Rhea supposed he hadn't been spoiled for choice—this part of Thyzakos was sparsely populated even in a good year—but the bedroom she was waiting in would have barely fit the tent she'd shared with Chrysanthi inside it.

Falka had told her that Ettore would be just a minute, and though that had been more than several minutes ago, Rhea was glad for the time to herself. Her decision to go with Falka had seemed natural when she'd made it; what unnerved her now more than anything was that it still did. If she had learned anything at Agiokon, it was that the people she'd been surrounded by had nothing more to offer her. Michali, Piros, Chrysanthi—they'd understood even less than she had. If Ettore could give her any guidance at all, she would consider this alliance well worth it, and that was saying nothing of what had passed between her and Falka.

Rhea felt a blush beginning on her cheeks and turned away from the lit fireplace, pacing toward the window to get a breath of cool air. She refused to meet this man looking like a flustered child.

Not long after, the door swung open, and Falka came through. Behind her strode a man perhaps a head taller than Rhea or Falka, his dark hair cropped close and a smile already creasing his tanned face. The green of his coat was too deep to qualify as Domina green, but he was, quite plainly, another Domina; in fact he looked so much like Falka that Rhea could have sworn she'd met him before, and she wondered briefly if they, like her and Lexos, were twins.

"Rhea," Falka said, "this is—"

"Ettore," the man interrupted. "It's a pleasure. I can't tell you how long I've wanted to meet you."

"That's very kind," Rhea replied. She could always count on her manners to carry her through, even when most of her was focused on trying to parse out the way Falka was watching Ettore, attentive nearly to the point of anxious.

Not a brother, then. Rhea had never paid either of her brothers half that much attention.

"You look as if you could use a rest," Ettore was saying. "The sooner we finish chatting, the quicker we can get you to a good meal and a warm bed. Did you come with anything? Luggage? Carriage? No?"

Rhea blinked. "No."

"Perfect, then. Falka, if you would?"

Falka shut the door behind them while Ettore kept on chattering, hardly seeming to require an audience. His Trefzan accent was a little stronger than Falka's, to Rhea's ear, but his Thyzaki was practically perfect.

She frowned; she should have asked Falka beforehand. Was it rude of her to expect both Dominas to speak Thyzaki with her? Should she have been attempting Trefza? Hers was serviceable; nowhere near as good as their Thyzaki was, but perhaps they would appreciate the effort.

"You come to us from where?" Ettore said, dropping into one of the armchairs by the fire. "Remind me."

She took the chair opposite him. It was the most comfortable she'd been in weeks. "The Sxoriza," she said, sighing. "I'm not sure where they are now, but when I left they were just across the border in Merkher."

"Oh," Ettore said. He looked a bit taken aback. "I meant, 'Where's your family from?' That sort of thing. But all right." He glanced up at Falka, who had come to stand at his elbow. "The Sxoriza. Should I know what that is?"

"At least one Domina does," Rhea answered, even as Falka shook her head. "They tried to trade me to Tarro in exchange for a bit of temporary peace."

"I'm not sure that's right," Falka said slowly. "They're a regional power, if that. Tarro wouldn't need to bargain—"

"Whatever the case," Ettore interrupted, "I'm so sorry you had to bear all that. It's lucky you've found us, eh?"

It certainly seemed so. She knew, if Lexos had been here, that he would have scolded her for trusting Falka and this stranger so readily, and for sharing so much. But the worst had already happened to her. Besides, if he hadn't wanted her to throw her lot in with strangers, he shouldn't have tried to use the matagios against her back at Stratathoma, something he might have forgotten by now but that she very much had not.

Actually, she thought, hadn't Falka mentioned something about Lexos knowing Ettore? Rhea sank more deeply into her seat, weariness pressing on her shoulders. She didn't particularly want to ask, but it seemed only polite. "I hear you've met my brother," she said. "I suppose I should extend my condolences."

Ettore smiled. "Alexandros isn't such a bad sort. In fact I was quite enjoying his company until very recently."

Rhea shot a look at Falka, who was avoiding her eyes. How recently was recently? "What happened?" she said, returning to Ettore. "Did he lose his charm?"

"Nothing like that. We've simply parted ways."

"What do you mean?"

"Just what I said."

"Is he all right?" she asked, despite herself. "Where did you leave him?"

"Somewhere up the coast," Ettore said, waving his hand. Rhea tucked the information away, just in case. "It's a nice town. Good for a little break now and then. You might go there once we're done. I think you'd find it refreshing."

Rhea tried not to let her frustration show. After all, it was not with either of the Dominas, but with herself. Falka had presented this as an offer of help, and Rhea had been so tempted by the promise of some kind of comfort that she hadn't bothered to ask what would be expected of her in return. And of course something would be, but Rhea was not sure she was in any state to follow through. Her gifts were not performing properly, and any sway she'd held as Aya Thyspira was too tied up in them to be counted on.

"Once we're done with what?" she asked. "Falka never quite said."

Falka, to her credit, blushed, but Ettore did not appear to notice. "Didn't she?" he said instead.

"We don't have to do this now," Falka cut in. Since arriving at the inn she'd retreated somewhat, but now—perhaps conveniently—she looked quite concerned. "You're tired. You've been through quite a lot."

Ettore ignored her. "What did she tell you?"

"That you could help me." Rhea lifted her marked arm. "With this."

"That's quite a lot of bandages you've got there."

"It's quite a wound."

Ettore grimaced, looking a bit ill. "Poor thing. Well, you can tell me the details later. I'll be very curious to hear, and I'll help you if I can, of course, but before any of that, I'd like to know a little more about what you did."

"What I did?"

"Yes, the back-and-forth with your consort. It's quite a feat." He smiled, and there was an edge, a threat hidden inside, that Rhea found so familiar as to be almost comforting. "Even in my day, we wouldn't have been so bold."

"Your day? When was that?"

"About a thousand years ago," Ettore said. Rhea leaned back very slowly. She knew as well as anyone what that implied.

"So, that would make you . . ." she started, and Ettore nodded.

"Luco Domina," he said. "I'll spare you the story."

Rhea blinked. She'd expected some obscure saint's name—another like Irini, who'd managed to escape Luco's blade—but then, if her mother had lived so many years past the massacre, why should the man behind it not have lived, too?

"It's true," Falka said into the quiet, and Rhea shook her head. She didn't need to hear anything else. She was familiar already with this sort of thing, and Ettore certainly looked the part, his Domina blood clear enough and the vague markers of age on his face in line with what Rhea remembered of her mother.

That said, she was not without questions. And she had to wonder, too, how much this man knew of her own history. Was it just word of what she'd done with Michali that had drawn him to her? Or did he know who lay buried on the grounds of their family's old house?

"I won't ask much of you, to prove it," she said. "I don't think Falka would lie to me, and she strikes me as very difficult to mislead. But perhaps you can answer something for me." She folded her arms across her chest as best she could. "I was fairly unfamiliar with the saints until I arrived in the Ksigora. They taught me there about one called Aya Ksiga. Do you know that name?"

Ettore smiled wistfully, as though he was calling up a memory. "I do. I knew the woman herself as well."

"There's something of an argument amongst those who worship her now. Some people say that she died along with the rest of the saints during your massacre. Some people say she died by her own hand, to keep from dying by yours."

"Are you asking me which?" Ettore looked pleasantly surprised. "I expected a test a bit more rigorous than this."

She shrugged. "It's what I'd like to know."

He considered her, the silence between them stretched thin. Rhea could feel Falka's eyes on her, but did not look away from Ettore, who finally nodded to himself and said, "I don't know, I'm afraid. And I looked for her for quite a long time. I think sometimes she might have died long before I ever took up my sword. I'm not sure if that answer will satisfy you, but it's the truth."

"Well, it's not one I'll be passing on to her faithful," Rhea said. "It suits me, though."

"You've taken quite an interest in her, have you?"

"It comes with the territory," she said. "Literally."

"Ah," he said, offering her a tight smile in place of laughter. "Is that why you styled yourself after her, then? It must help that you look very much like her. And your brother says your mother had a soft spot for my sort." For a moment his smile seemed carved out of stone, and his stare narrowed. "Irini had the most striking eyes."

The sound of her mother's given name ricocheted through Rhea, and it took all of her composure to keep from reacting. Of course, that had to have been Ettore's design. She could tell that what happened next hung on how she answered him. And while she didn't know what it would mean to him, to learn of her mother's identity, it had served her well so far to keep that a close secret.

"Maybe so," she said. "But I got mine from my father."

"Vasilis Argyros," Ettore said, almost fondly, and the tension evaporated as if it had never existed. "Now there's a man I wish I could have met. You didn't want him back, too?"

"Don't be rude," Falka said, but Ettore continued.

"No, really. Once you've raised one, what's a few more?" He laughed, loud and unreserved; Rhea flinched. "That is what I wanted to speak to you about, though. About who you might be able to bring back next."

"I don't—" Rhea's surprise caught up with her, her throat going dry. She had spent a season with the Sxoriza, who dealt in arguments, in logistics, in scouting reports and supply stores. Whatever Ettore wanted from her, she had expected it would be of that sort: a favor she could ask of someone, or a door she could leave open, the way she had at Stratathoma last winter. And instead it was this—the one thing, really, that she was sure she could not do.

"Who?" she asked. "What for?" Maybe there was some other way she could think of to get Ettore what he wanted.

"Oh, we'll sort all that out," he said. "And it won't be quite as simple as it would have been before that nasty bit of business at Agiokon. But really, I'd like the chance to speak with some of those I've left behind." He nodded to her bandages, which had slipped a little; Rhea realized the very edge of the wound at her wrist was visible, the skin there dull and curling.

"I think it's something you could benefit from, too." Ettore's voice was quieter now, with a depth to it that might almost have been sympathy. "I understand you're in some pain."

She did not answer. It was too difficult to explain that the pain was the very least of it.

"You shouldn't be," Ettore went on. "These gifts cost something to keep, yes. Corrosion, I called it when your brother and I spoke. But that is not corrosion. That is . . ."

He trailed off, not seeming to know how to finish. Rhea knew how very well. It was failure, what had happened to her. It was mutiny; it was disobedience. Her gifts, refusing her the power she was owed.

But it had not been like this for Baba, not to this degree. She'd assumed as much, and now Ettore had confirmed it. Whatever the matagios had done to Baba, he'd been able to hide it. If not for Lexos, he might have even survived it.

Was she weaker than her father? Or had the matagios become more difficult to bear? Perhaps it had recognized some wickedness in her, something it felt required to punish. But more likely all this was just her own failing. A burden anybody else would have been able to lift.

She'd resolved, back in the Ksigora, not to be like her father. In this, at least, following his example might have done her some good.

She cradled her injured hand in her lap. "Why, then? Why only me?"

"I'm not sure. It's possible this sort of thing is only a matter of time for anyone with a matagios. Or perhaps you've asked too much of yours."

Rhea thought of trying to raise Nitsos and felt her cheeks go hot. She'd had no idea it wouldn't work, no idea she'd been left so weak after Michali. But as far as she could tell, nobody outside the Sxoriza had heard of her latest attempt.

"Whatever the case," Ettore said, "I think we can learn something from the old saints. It seems to me that something has been lost. Like a translation of an old text, from language to language until the true meaning of it is gone. I see it everywhere. The languages I grew up speaking. Your Saint's Thyzaki. And now you and I talk, and we sound like this." He tapped his own blank palm with his index finger. "Now these gifts take more. They require a sacrifice we never agreed to make. And I'm not expecting any of my old friends to know exactly what to do, but I think I'll get a lot closer to finding out what that is if I can speak the language I was born to, for a time."

"But why do you care what happens to me? None of it affects you."

She was worried Ettore would take offense at being asked a blunt question; instead it seemed to roll off him. "That's true," he said easily. "It will, though, when I take everything back, so I'd like to get it sorted before I do that."

For a moment Rhea was back in the Ksigoran woods, sitting across the stone table from Falka and watching her trace the line of Lexos's mark on her palm. Falka had been serving Ettore then—the marks she was gathering were not for her, in the end, but for him.

But what was their plan? That every Stratagiozi and their child would simply line up for a peaceful transfer? Falka had already been more successful than she'd had any right to be, but once she tried for the Stratagiozis themselves, she would find her task much more difficult.

Rhea looked back and forth between Falka and Ettore, but they were watching her, one more patiently than the other, seemingly unaware of the impossibility of what they were suggesting. "Look," she said, "I don't know how much you know about the current Stratagiozi Council, but these are not people prepared to give up the thing that keeps them in power, no matter what it might be costing them."

"That's fine. I don't need their permission before I take back their marks." He leaned forward, and Rhea was aware, suddenly, of just how much he had seen and how much he must have lived through to be sitting in front of her now. "I do not want any of you to suffer. I'd like them all back, to spare you that. But more than that, I don't want a pack of children carrying weapons they do not understand, particularly when those weapons were mine to begin with. So I will do with them what I like."

"Will you be taking mine?" Rhea did not know whether she was eager or afraid. Maybe, without the matagios and mark both, the wound on her wrist would begin to heal. But where would she be meant to turn then? Who would she be? Just Rhea, a garden vine with no trellis left to keep her upright.

But she needn't have worried. Ettore eyed the poorly bandaged wound on her right arm. "No, I think at the moment I'm quite happy to leave it with you."

Rhea snorted. "You're very kind."

"I am, aren't I? And while you've got that top of mind, I will re-extend Falka's offer." Ettore got up from his armchair and came to crouch by the side of Rhea's. On somebody else, it might have looked like begging, but the nearness of him made her feel small, like a child speaking to her father before bed. "We can help each other. I really do believe that, Rhea. I can make your gifts easier to carry. You only have to let me."

It was, she thought, just about the nicest thing she'd ever heard. Some rest, and some help, and a bit of reprieve? All in exchange for helping Ettore learn things that would help her, too. The only problem was the possibility that her gifts were beyond repair.

She would have to keep that secret, at least for now, and no, that was neither smart nor wise, but she was past the point of caring. Ettore was offering to help, to guide her forward in the way her mother might have done, if she'd still been alive. The way Baba had when she was very young, and the way she'd dreamed, sometimes, that he might again, if she could just prove herself worthy of it.

Maybe she could have it again. Ettore Domina, his hand on her shoulder and his plan laid ahead of her, a path so much easier to follow now that she didn't have to find it herself. The mark before the feather-ing, she thought. The scar before the bleed. Maybe this was finally her chance to get everything right.

"All right," she said. She had already come this far. She would go a little farther. "Yes, whatever I can do to help. Whatever it is you need."

Ettore beamed and rose to stand, the firelight lending his eyes a dangerous gleam. "I'm so glad you said that. Because before we get to raising the dead, there's someone in Vuomorra who's overstayed his welcome. And I'd quite like your assistance in getting him out."

CHAPTER FORTY-ONE

CHRYSANTHI

Chrysanthi hoped very much that Andrija had not been following her since they parted ways; she'd traveled what felt like the entire breadth of Thyzakos ten times over searching for her family's house, and now that she'd found it, she was fairly sure she'd ridden past it once or twice before.

That said, she could hardly be blamed for missing it. All she remembered of her former home was the shape of the building from one specific angle, and as it turned out, the house and grounds both were entirely overgrown, with the house's silhouette obscured. Standing where she was now at the southeastern corner of the building, her horse munching contentedly on a patch of weeds behind her, it was difficult to match anything up with the scraps of memory she'd retained (or hoarded from Rhea's kymithi).

"Well, we're here," she said to the horse, who ignored her. "I suppose I should go inside."

Of course, that meant finding a door, which was easier said than done. Two appeared to have been boarded up, while another was blocked off by a particularly hardy growth of ivy. Chrysanthi wandered farther along the wall, eyeing the house's façade. There—a window, the glass coated in dust and the wooden crosspieces rotting. She stared at it for a long moment and waited for some memory to spark at the back of her head. But nothing came, so she approached the window and, with a deep, fortifying breath, smashed in the glass with her elbow. The noise of it scared her horse some yards away, and she could feel that already her arm had begun to bleed. Ignoring it, she set about clearing the rest of the glass from the frame.

It took a few more minutes to complete entirely, but soon enough she had a good view of the room she'd opened a way into: an expansive pantry, lined with shelves that looked to be still stocked with jars and little burlap sacks.

"I'll be right back," Chrysanthi said to her horse and then climbed through the window.

The pantry's ceiling was generously high, and each of the five rows of shelves reached almost to the very top. As she turned in place, taking it in, she found herself coughing; the air was thick and smelled stale, like the oldest stores of grain that they'd kept at Stratathoma. It seemed highly unlikely that anybody had been here in quite some time—perhaps even since the Argyrosi had left. Even the walls were peeling, flakes of green paint collected around the edges of the room.

Chrysanthi approached the nearest shelf and reached for a jar that was filled with something granular and black. Peppercorns, by the look of it, and when she popped the lid off the jar, the strength of the spice was nearly enough to make her eyes water. The next jar she opened contained a handful or two of rice that had kept well enough to be eaten. Her stomach rumbled loudly, and she thought of the food she'd taken with her upon leaving Andrija, most of which was already gone. This was a welcome sight; she would have to do a more complete inventory of the pantry later and determine what she could use.

The door out to the rest of the house proved difficult to open, but after a bit of effort and a bit more cursing, she managed to pop it from the frame. Beyond, a kitchen lay waiting, cobwebs covering most of the cookware that she could see. Chrysanthi stood in the threshold, staring at the square wooden table that dominated the far side of the room.

She must have sat there once, maybe watching her mother cook or sharing a meal with her siblings, but reaching for that moment only left her empty-handed. Not for the first time, she wished that one of the twins was here with her. They would likely remember this place, would feel *something* at the sight of it fallen so deeply into disrepair. It wasn't fair that she did not.

Leaving the kitchen, she turned left, into a long hallway. Her mother's grave was out in the ground, but without any precise sense of where, she knew she could spend the rest of her life—however long that might turn out to be—looking for it. And though she knew now from Rhea that her mother had not planned to die in the manner she had, she could still hope that there would be some hint here to direct her. She did not remember arriving at Stratathoma so long ago, but everything she'd called hers there had been new since Baba's title. Nothing old, nothing carried over from this house. Had Baba simply abandoned everything? The house seemed too empty for that.

But other people had obviously found their way in over the years. There were footprints in the dust every so often, and no doubt she would find food stores that had been depleted, or valuables that had been taken. She did not care about any of that—the house had been empty, so why not let somebody make use of it?—but she did hope that whoever had taken shelter here had not disturbed whatever personal effects her parents might have left behind. Papers of Baba's, or old belongings of her mother's that he hadn't had the heart to destroy.

The hallway led her to a formal dining room, through which she could see a sitting room straight ahead and another chamber to the right that had apparently been cleared of furniture. Chrysanthi went on straight, eventually arriving at the end of the house, where a narrow spiral staircase led upstairs. As she climbed, the air seemed to freshen and grow cooler. She remembered, for a moment, the warmth of Andrija's jacket around her shoulders. But she had no need of him now. And if he'd wanted to stay at her side, he should have been honest. She would have forgiven him; she would have helped him. She was almost sure of it.

Once at the top of the stairs, Chrysanthi found herself at one end of another hallway. This one was wider, and every one of the doors off it had been left open, allowing blades of sun to slice through. There were four rooms, two on each side. Without looking, Chrysanthi knew: These had been her and her siblings' rooms.

A lump stuck in her throat. She tipped her head back, staring at the ceiling and blinking furiously to keep her tears from falling. She missed all three of them so much, and it had been easier to bear when she'd had Andrija next to her, but she was alone now. Nitsos dead, and Lexos gone, and Rhea . . . She didn't know, did she? She might never know.

With a sigh, she gathered herself and barged into the first room before she could think better of it. It was mostly empty: a little cot with the bedding removed, an upended table that had clearly been built for children, and a mobile of carved wooden birds hanging from the ceiling over the bed. Nitsos's room, she thought, judging by the size of the bed. The window overlooked the north side of the house, and if Chrysanthi craned her neck she could see the bank of a small pond.

The next room had to have been her own. There was a crib against the far wall, and a chest at its foot was open, revealing a stash of toys inside. Chrysanthi thought about going in, about picking through the toys and finding something she could keep, but though this room had belonged to a Chrysanthi, it was hard to believe that that had been her. None of this felt anything like her room at Stratathoma, which she had known so well she could have sketched it with her eyes shut. Instead she stayed where she was, eyes tracing the floral shapes that someone had painted across the walls. She could imagine herself asking for that sort of pattern, but the colors were a milder sort, nothing like the blood colors Baba had always favored. This, she supposed, was something she could call her mother's.

She backed out of the room and went on to the next. One of the twins had lived here, although it was difficult to tell which. This had been emptied out entirely, with not even a bed or a wardrobe remaining. What was left over, however, was a string hung from end to end of the window, to which were pinned bundles of dried herbs and flowers. They were so old that most of them had crumbled almost to nothing, leaving only stems behind. But some were intact enough that Chrysanthi could identify what they had been—some lavender, some yarrow, and some therolia, a flower that as far as she knew did not grow in these parts. She'd seen it arrive in the tithes the stewards sent to Stra-tathoma, from somewhere in the north if memory served (although everything about her arrival here was telling her it often did not).

She approached the window, taking in the view of the orchard be-yond before focusing on the most complete of the herb bundles. If they were indeed from the north, then it stood to reason that her mother had brought them here and hung them in her children's rooms. Well, was it all of them? Not hers, and not Nitsos's, and a quick glance into the remaining room told her not that one, either. And of course they could have been lost to time, but these remained. This child, granted something special by their mother. Chrysanthi had no reason to, noth-ing but her own suspicion, but she would have bet all the money she'd ever laid eyes on that it had been Rhea.

None of her old toys had felt right to take, but this did. Gently, she detached the herb bouquet from the string. It still held a very little bit of its fragrance, and it was heavier than she'd expected. After a close examination, she was surprised to discover why: Knotted in where the herb stems had been bound with twine was a blackstone stud. It re-minded her of the sorts of gems she wore in her ears sometimes, but this one had a longer pin, and the clasp was a mechanism she did not recognize.

The stone, though, that was familiar. She'd seen it on Stavra, and on Andrija, marking their tongues like a matagios of their own.

What was this doing here? As far as she understood, it would have belonged to a hostage of the library, but Baba had never been one, and while there was certainly a lot she didn't know about her mother, she didn't think Irini had been one, either. She'd been a saint; she'd carried her own matagios. She wouldn't have worn something like this, would she? And even if she had, hanging it in her daughter's room like some sort of talisman did not make sense. Not to Chrysanthi, at any rate.

She pulled it loose from the bouquet and pocketed it. Understand-ing her mother would have to wait until she'd found her; nothing here seemed like it would help her do that.

She made her way back down the hallway, the bouquet held carefully in both hands. She could feel some part of herself trying to surface—small, and young, and terrified, just as she'd been when she'd left Stratathoma—but it simply would not do. She had work to do here. And she had the beginning of an idea of how to get started.

Her parents' bedroom could be found in the southwest corner of the house, through a series of doors and down a separate corridor. As she stood at its window, keeping the bed itself at her back, Chrysanthi had a view of part of the orchard and the grounds beyond, which were now overgrown with tall grasses and clover.

She lifted her hands, framing the view. Where her left thumb met her palm, there grew a particularly crooked apple tree. Another, near the tip of her index finger. On the right, she marked a patch of dead grass that hovered above her thumbnail.

These, she thought, would be the boundaries of where she would begin digging. Because there was no way Vasilis Argyros would let one of his family out of his sight—not even once she was dead.

CHAPTER FORTY-TWO

RHEA

Rhea was only vaguely aware of the ship's rocking as she lay on her bunk. She had stayed belowdecks since the previous night, avoiding any sliver of sea or sky through the gap between her cabin porthole and its cover. Falka had warned her that they would be passing within sight of the cliff on which Stratathoma was perched, and Rhea thought even a small glimpse of that house might be enough to make her physically ill. As it was, the mere mention of it had put her in a foul mood that showed no sign of stopping.

She would feel better, she told herself, once they were in Trefazio, once she had truly left her old life behind. Not an Argyros now, but a Domina—that was what Ettore had said to her the night before as they spent a long, slow evening on deck, Falka sitting nearby while Ettore sketched a constellation Rhea could not find in the stars.

"That means you don't need to worry ever again," he'd said. "How does that sound?"

Lovely. It had sounded lovely. It still did, but Rhea worried it wasn't meant for her, or rather, that she was not meant for it. If she could not be happy now, when would she ever be? All she'd had to do for the past three days was to wake up in bed next to Falka come morning and go to sleep when it got dark, and even so she lay awake, knowing that the moment she did drift off, a new nightmare would take hold. A family argument over dinner fallen quiet as her siblings began, one by one, to choke on their own blood, or Chrysanthi, turning away from her easel, her eyes painted over with a depthless black.

Falka, very generously, said nothing when Rhea woke each night, sweat fresh on her brow and a cry in her throat. Rhea was beginning to feel like more trouble than she was worth.

The door to the cabin opened and Rhea caught a whiff of figs and salt, and something sweet—Falka, stepping into the room as if summoned by the thought of her.

"Rhea? Are you awake?"

With a sigh, she pushed herself up to sit and shifted to the side until she was leaning up against the wall. Her hair was down, the roots slick with oil, and her own mouth tasted foul as she cleared her throat. Falka, meanwhile, looked fresh as ever, her Trefzan-style gown swaying with her steps.

"Ettore sent me to fetch you," she said. She'd explained to Rhea before their departure about her actual parentage, not to mention Tarro's, and Rhea had done her best to look as though it was the first time she'd ever considered what it might be like to be the direct child of a saint. "He says we'll be there soon." One of Falka's eyebrows ticked up almost imperceptibly as she looked Rhea over. "Do you want help finding something to wear?"

"What's wrong with this?" Rhea asked, her voice rough from lack of use. She was wearing one of Falka's shirts, her legs bare under the blankets. Across the room, her old clothes were drying after another round of washing them in the sea.

Falka came to perch on the edge of the bed. She'd been understanding, accommodating—she allowed Rhea the moments of regret that sent her pacing around the cabin at all hours of the night, and then welcomed her back to bed as if nothing had happened. Rhea felt a pang of guilt watching her now that eclipsed any regret over betraying Michali, if that was what she'd done. Falka deserved better: an equal. Rhea wasn't sure she was equal to anything at the moment. But it didn't stop her from rising onto her knees and closing the distance between them.

"We've passed Stratathoma, then?" she asked. "Where does that put Vuomorra? East or west?"

"Today? Neither," Falka answered. "Today Vuomorra is dead ahead."

Ettore had outlined the vaguest of plans to Rhea—dock in Vuomorra harbor, take one of the city's canal boats up to the city proper, and then use both Ettore's particular knowledge and the access afforded to the public to get into the palace and to Tarro himself. Honestly, Rhea was relieved to leave the planning and striving to other people. Everything she wanted lately, she failed to reach.

She shuffled closer, slid her palm along Falka's cheek, and drew her down. Better, she thought, to focus on what she already held in her hands.

Falka squeezed her wrist gently before kissing her cheek and standing back up. "Not until you wash your hair, I think."

"We're on a ship," Rhea snapped. "I'm not wasting fresh water to—"

"Would you like to keep talking? Or would you be quiet and let me do it for you?" Falka had gone to wait next to a chair on the opposite side of the room, only a few feet away. Beside it, a washing basin was waiting, the water inside tilting with the movement of the ship.

How long had that been there? Aware of a blush heating her cheeks, Rhea busied herself straightening the bedclothes before reluctantly sliding to her feet. "You don't have to."

Falka nodded to the chair and said, "Yes, I know. If we start now your hair will be dry by the time we arrive."

Rhea sat down and tipped her head back, shivering as Falka began to wet her hair.

"Easy," Falka said. Rhea realized that her hands were clenched into fists at her sides, nails cutting into her palms. "You don't have to do a thing."

Her eyes fell shut. She let the press of Falka's fingertips against her scalp lull her into a daze. When, some time later, Falka began to pour the cold water over her hair, Rhea opened her eyes again to find that the sun had passed overhead and was now throwing long, honey-sweet shafts of light through the western porthole of the cabin.

"There," Falka said. "Wring that out and then get dressed. I left some clothes on the bed."

Thus far on their journey Rhea had not minded wearing Falka's clothes, but the fabric felt too rough on her skin as she put on the suggested green gown, gold studs running from neck to hem in perfect lines. She'd enjoyed dressing like this once. Today, even doing up the buttons felt like it was asking too much of her.

She left her hair down to dry and started out of the cabin, up the stairs to the deck. Already, she could hear Ettore speaking to someone, his cadence always so expressive that she often felt she understood him even when his Trefza was too fast or too archaic for her to translate.

Falka met her at the top of the stairs. She was meant to be seen in the sun, Rhea thought, watching as Falka looked over her shoulder to listen to Ettore. The dark shine of her hair, the rich olive of her skin—thank goodness their paths had continued to cross after that first meeting in the Ksigora. It had not been nearly enough.

"We're almost there," Falka said, turning back toward her. "Ettore's asked to speak to you when you're ready. I told him you weren't feeling well, but—"

"I'm fine." Rhea took Falka's hand for a moment. "Thank you."

She crossed the deck of the ship toward the bow, where Ettore was deep in conversation with the captain. The sails overhead were a deep green, emblazoned with a white olive tree. Ettore's symbol, Falka had said. Or, more accurately, Luco's. There was such a reverence in the way the people around him treated him. Not the same one Rhea had received from the worshippers in the Sxoriza camps—something older and more innate. As though Ettore were part of the continent, as constant and beloved as land itself. For all her followers, Rhea had never inspired anything half so meaningful.

He broke away from the captain as he noticed her approach. "There you are!" he called, switching to Thyzaki as he always did when she was near. "Come and join me."

The Trefzan coastline was closer now than it had been the last time she had been above decks. As the ship continued on, she could make out places where the water went shallow and clear, and a few beaches, some sand and some stone. There were houses, too, little hamlets dotted along the shore. Rhea could not be sure when she'd last been to Vuomorra, but if memory served, the approach had looked much like this.

"Good afternoon," she said as she drew alongside Ettore. "You look as though the trip's been treating you well."

Ettore nodded, his hand lifted to keep the sun out of his eyes. "I get along well anywhere. But it's true; I do love a good sail." He pointed to the nearest hamlet. "I grew up someplace much like that, you see. You learn to swim before you learn to walk."

"We could drop anchor," Rhea said, only half joking. "Row ashore and decide we've arrived home."

"We could." Ettore's smile turned sharp. "But I've got my sights set on Vuomorra."

"Falka says we're not far."

"Indeed. Have you been?" He didn't wait for her to answer. "I didn't see much of the city when I was leaving with your brother, but it seems Tarro has made it quite the destination. Clean streets, beautiful parks. I'll have to make sure it lives up to his standard."

"Under you, you mean?" Rhea shifted uncomfortably. It was too hot for this dress and the sun was in her eyes. "I didn't realize you wanted his seat," she said. "You didn't mention it when we met."

"I did think it was a bit implied," Ettore said, and she felt, for a moment, unbearably foolish. "If I hold Vuomorra, I hold all of my son's power. His alliances, his money. And I'll need all of that to bring the other Stratagiozis to heel."

Rhea looked away, across the water. A season ago she would have been able to gauge his words properly. As it was she couldn't tell whether he was offering her the truth, or something else. Was it even her place to wonder?

"So what is it you need from me once we arrive?" she asked. "I can't make Tarro my consort."

"What a match that would be," Ettore said, laughing. "No, I would like for you to make use of your more recently inherited gift."

Despite the warmth of the sun, Rhea felt a coldness begin to spread from the center of her chest. The prayer. He meant for her to use it, to say Tarro's name. He could have no other meaning.

She had considered it, of course. Baba had never been entirely clear whether their matagios was incapable of such a thing or whether it was simply not to be done, and in the absence of an answer, the possibility of turning that prayer into a weapon lived in a little box at the back of her mind, one she opened every now and then just to look at how it gleamed in the light. But she had sworn not to use it, if she even could. She would have to find a way to refuse Ettore without leaving herself too vulnerable.

"I'm not sure I can do what you'd ask of me," she said carefully. Her predecessors had let rumors spread about their matagios's capability for a reason, and she knew it was part of what protected her now—the fear that she might turn it against anyone who tried to take it from her. It was safer if Ettore thought it was her own hesitance keeping her from using it.

But he didn't seem to see her hesitance as much of an obstacle. "As much as I appreciate your honesty," he said, leaning in as if to share a secret, "I would appreciate it more if you would try."

"You don't really need it to be me that does it, though. If we're going to Vuomorra, what's stopping you from taking a more . . . physical approach?"

"Oh, nothing, I suppose. But anyone could take a knife to Tarro Domina's heart. I am not trying to be just anyone." Ettore nudged her, his elbow sharp against her aching ribs. "Say you'll give it a go. What harm can it do, eh?"

Could she afford to protest any further? She had done nothing yet to prove her use to him, and if she dug in now, he might regret their agreement. He might leave her in the harbor and go on without her. Falka would follow, because of course she would, and Rhea would again be right where she always ended up: alone and afraid.

"All right," she said. Anything to keep that future from being hers. She supposed she ought to worry more about what might happen amongst the federation with Tarro gone, but it was so difficult to imagine it working at all that the whole thing felt more like a joke she was telling herself than a promise she was making. "When would you like me to? Now?"

Ettore turned to the horizon, where Vuomorra would shortly come into view. "No," he said. "I should like to look my son in the eye one more time before he goes." His hand landed on her shoulder. "Now why don't you take a moment and enjoy the sun? I'll call you when it's time."

She needed no further encouragement, especially with Falka waving from the deck rail, two mismatched glasses of wine in her hands. Rhea drifted toward her, already reaching for the glass of white. She had resented so much the Sxoriza's way of setting her aside. All that waiting. All those closed doors. This was different, or perhaps *she* was. Whatever the case, she had endured quite enough, and if all she had left to her now was a sunny afternoon and a cool breeze, she would do everything she could to enjoy it.

CHAPTER FORTY-THREE

RHEA

Even this late in the day, the public hall in Tarro's palace was nearly full. Rhea had been here before as Thyspira, but she'd never seen it from this particular angle: stuck at the back of a crowd that showed no sign of dispersing, unable to see the dais at the front that usually held at least a handful of Dominas.

"This way," Ettore said in her ear, nodding toward the colonnade along the right-hand side of the hall. It was measurably emptier there, and while she was eager for the space, if only to keep her injured arm from being jostled, she was worried it would only give someone room to spot them. She supposed she would have to trust that the Trefzan half-veils Falka had distributed would do enough to hide their faces.

With hers sticking awkwardly to the corner of her mouth, she followed Ettore and Falka through the crowd and into the colonnade. It was darker here, the torches still unlit despite the nearness of evening. Down the colonnade, closer to the dais, a smattering of people was gathered in front of one of the portraits hung at intervals along the wall. One of them turned to look at her; she lowered her gaze, letting her hair fall across her face. Aya Thyspira was not well known here, but she could not afford any surprises.

"Are we ready?" Ettore whispered. He was, generously, still speaking Thyzaki. "You're prepared?"

She nodded and felt Falka take her hand. "Should we come with you right to the front?" They'd left a pair of hired guards near the entrance to the hall, and though Rhea knew very well that Ettore could handle himself, it made her nervous to think of him approaching Tarro alone.

It did not, however, make Ettore nervous. "Wait for my call," he said. "I'd like a moment with Tarro first."

"What makes you think he'll give you one?" Rhea asked. She hadn't seen, yet, if Tarro actually was here—although judging by the size of the crowd alone, it seemed likely—but Tarro had proven himself canny enough to stay in power for this long. She could not imagine him willingly letting Ettore near.

"He will hope," Ettore said, "that he can convince me to leave this hall and go somewhere his subjects cannot see. But they're not his, are they? They're mine, and I'd like very much for them to watch you do what you do."

He slipped away before Rhea could think of anything to say in response. Mouth half open, she watched him wind through the people filling the hall, until Falka's grip on her hand tightened for a moment, reassuring.

"I know it seems mad," Falka said. "But he generally does know what he's doing."

Rhea pressed in closer to Falka, narrowly avoiding a passerby. "He's not the one I'm worried about."

Falka said nothing, but Rhea could feel the weight of her gaze as they made their own way forward, keeping to the colonnade. She was too observant to not have wondered before at Rhea's nerves over this task. Rhea could only imagine what conclusions she was drawing now.

They drew to a halt where the colonnade ended. From here, Rhea could see over the heads of the remaining rows of people to the dais at the front of the hall. It was crowded with Dominas, most of them wearing Tarro's preferred shade of green. She glanced down at her borrowed dress, suddenly all too aware that it matched the coat Ettore had been wearing when she'd first met him. Like father, like son, she supposed.

"Not so far," Falka said, pulling her back a few steps. "They can't see us before it's time."

"Do you know them?" Rhea nodded to the group on the dais. From what she understood about the Dominas, she'd assumed Falka's family were far too numerous for her to know any of them by more than name.

"Some." Falka kept one hand lifted to her half-veil, making sure it stayed in place. "And the rest will know me, regardless. Tarro will have told them to watch for me."

"Did he know you weren't his child?" Something occurred to Rhea that had not before: "Did you?"

Falka made an exasperated noise. "No, and yes, although not at first, but is this the time for that?"

"All right."

"I mean, really."

"I was only wondering."

"Well, there you are, then," Falka said, and Rhea thought she could see a hint of a smile through the other woman's half-veil. "Oh, look. He's near the front."

Rhea turned in time to see Ettore emerge from a cluster of Trefzans at the front of the crowd. He stepped aside as one of the many vendors scattered through the hall passed by, then began to approach the dais. There were guards positioned here and there, particularly around the back of the dais, but none of them moved to stop him— just as Falka and Ettore had predicted. It was tradition, they had explained, that guards not interfere with the family's dealings, particularly in public. One Domina died so often at the hands of another that anybody trying to protect the family would almost certainly wind up dead as well.

Rhea understood the concept, but watching Ettore approach the steps up to the dais now, unapprehended and unquestioned, it seemed absolutely ludicrous. Those were Dominas up there—did Tarro feel no impulse to protect them?

Ettore stopped at the foot of the steps. A few of the gathered Dominas had noticed him, but they did not appear to recognize him. Next to Rhea, Falka had gone tense.

"Is Tarro here?" she said. "I don't see him."

"I don't know." Rhea craned her neck, trying to see around the front row of Dominas. "There's a cluster near the back, but it could be just more of the same."

One of the Dominas on the dais leaned down and said something to Ettore, who grinned back. Rhea hadn't noticed much of a resemblance before between him and what she remembered of Tarro, but there it was in his smile. Father and son. As Ettore started up the stairs, he glanced over his shoulder, searching for a moment before finding her and Falka. She caught the near-imperceptible shake of his head. No Tarro. Not yet.

Luckily, they did not have long to wait. A few minutes later, Rhea heard a set of doors open from behind the dais, and though she could not see who had entered, she was fairly sure it was Tarro, judging by the way the crowd immediately fell quiet and parted down the middle. Sure enough, the man who came bounding up onto the dais was dressed in pale green, his blond hair pushed back and his expression genial and welcoming. The people gathered around Falka and Rhea began to cheer and call out; Tarro stopped at the edge of the dais and waved to them.

Where was Ettore? He had been speaking to a small group near the front, but she'd lost track of him. What if she missed his signal?

"It's so lovely to see you all," Tarro called to the gathered Vuomorrans from the dais. "Thank you for coming!"

"Ettore," Rhea said, turning to Falka. "I can't find him. We need to—"

"I've got him. It's fine. Keep your eyes forward."

"What?"

"Don't draw Tarro's attention." Suddenly, her hand was tight around Rhea's wrist, careless of the wound there. "Look. Ettore, to the right."

There he was, almost entirely hidden where he'd crouched to speak to a pair of younger Dominas. They were both laughing as he spoke, his expressions exaggerated as though he was telling a story; meanwhile she could see him watching Tarro, his position shifting slightly as Tarro moved.

"The prayer takes a minute," Rhea said to Falka. "I know you know that. But just—"

Falka slid her fingers down to tangle with Rhea's. "You don't need to worry. All you need to do is say the words. The rest is up to us."

Rhea shut her eyes, breathing deeply as she recited the matagios prayer in her head. Even with no name slotted in, the words were heavy and humming, eager to be spoken. It would work, she told herself. The prayer wanted to be spoken; what name she gave it wouldn't matter.

"Out! Out! Everybody out!"

Rhea's eyes flew open. Tarro's voice cut through the air; he stood on the dais stairs, arms outstretched, and he was looking right at her. No, not her. At Falka.

"Out the doors at the back of the hall," Tarro yelled. "You're all right, but for everyone's safety, we need you to leave."

The crowd began to move. Slowly at first, but faster and faster as people started to scream. For a moment Rhea was back at Agiokon, following Nitsos against the tide through a throng of people fleeing for their lives. And then Falka was dragging her toward the dais, and Rhea was in Vuomorra again.

"What's going on?" she breathed. "Falka, what—"

"He recognized me. We have to hurry."

Rhea looked back over her shoulder, only to see that the doors at the back of the hall were shut. Nobody was getting out. Ettore's men, she thought, the ones they'd left at the entrance. It must have been them keeping the doors barred. Whatever came next, Ettore had wanted people to see.

The guards at this end of the hall had split, some rushing toward the back doors and some to the dais. A handful of Dominas pushed down the stairs, blocking Tarro from view. By the time they'd gone, he had retreated to the dais, one hand held out toward Falka as she continued to approach, taking Rhea with her.

"Don't," he said. "Falka, get back. We've had our differences but I don't see why we can't find some middle ground. Whatever that man has told you—"

"It's not about anything like that," Falka said. Trefza, quick and fluid. Rhea would have to pay close attention. "It's about what's best for us. For everyone."

"You have no idea what's best," Tarro said. "There is so much you don't understand."

The hall's doors were still shut, and the cries echoing in the air were louder, more desperate. Rhea felt an itch spreading across her skin. The longer this took, the more likely it was that somebody besides Tarro would get hurt.

They were at the foot of the stairs now, looking up at Tarro where he stood at the edge of the dais. He was flanked by some newly arrived guards, and those Dominas that remained were clustered around him, too, some of them armed. Rhea could not spot Ettore in their number, but then she could barely see anything properly, could barely breathe as the noise around them all continued to mount.

"Please," she said, hoping that wherever he was, he could hear. "What are you waiting for?"

Tarro looked away from them and nodded to the guards. "Those two. Bind their hands and bring them to one of the holding cells while I sort this out."

Rhea's heartbeat stuttered. She fumbled for Falka's hand, ready to flee, but Falka stood firm. "Are you sure those guards will be enough?"

The knot of people around Tarro loosened; the guards started down the stairs, leaving gaps wide enough that Rhea could see Ettore reach into his pocket and pull something metallic out. She frowned, curious despite her fear.

"Almost," Falka whispered.

Something flashed in Ettore's hands, and then, as his fingers moved, every bit of gold—every necklace, every bracelet, every decorative chain, and every circlet—lifted off the Dominas gathered on the dais and twisted into a misshapen braid. It hovered in midair for a moment, as long as Tarro himself, before it wound tightly around his arms and neck, dragging him to his knees and pinning him there before anybody could so much as blink.

A gasp went up in the crowd, muffling the shouts from those pressed against the shut doors. Rhea herself could hardly believe what she was seeing. She knew Ettore's past, had considered privately that his gifts might look different from hers, but this? She could not have imagined it.

"Everyone, please," Ettore said. "There's no need for any panic." His words carried, more commanding than Tarro's, threaded through with more charm. Rhea could spot a number of people in the crowd turning back to listen. "This is nothing more than a bit of family politicking. My son here is just a bit reluctant to give me back my seat." He sighed, his smile broadening. "I have to tell you—it's so good to be home."

The Dominas gathered around Tarro had backed away, fear so clearly written across their faces that Rhea could read it, even from the bottom of the steps. Falka broke away from Rhea, pulling off her half-veil; their gazes swung toward her.

"Dominarazzi," she said, "we've talked about this. It's time. Meet your new Stratagorra, Luco Domina."

Rhea could see the name settle on the shoulders of the other Domina children, could see it push them to the back of the dais with a true awe in their eyes; she could hear it stirring murmurs in the crowd behind her. There were words being spoken, words she didn't understand, but they seemed to please Ettore, who shut his eyes for a moment, all but basking in the whispers. Doubters or not, people would find it hard to argue with the power he'd demonstrated and with the matagios he carried on his tongue.

"Rhea, if you would?"

She startled, the movement sending an ache pulsing through her ribs. He was waving her up the stairs, his eyes intent on her. Was it time? She wasn't ready. But all she could do was what he'd told her to.

She gathered her skirts in one hand and started up the stairs, the little drop on either side enough to make her dizzy. When Ettore took hold of her elbow and ushered her up the last few steps, she was absurdly grateful, even as the sight of Tarro, pinned to the dais on his knees, churned in her stomach.

"I'm sorry," she said. "Can I just— Do you mind if I take a minute?"

Ettore's smile turned grim. "Unfortunately, I do. It's now, Rhea. I need you to do it now."

"Rhea?" came a muffled voice. Tarro, unable to lift his head, but still able to speak. "You've got the Argyros girl?"

This close, Rhea could see the muscles straining in Tarro's shoulders, in his thighs as he tried to stand.

Ettore crouched by Tarro's side. "I've heard you were hoping to do the same, no? What a shame you couldn't get the job done."

Something in the rope of gold loosened, and Tarro tilted his head in Ettore's direction. Bloodshot eyes, spit flecked across his chin—he looked awful. Maybe he wouldn't mind dying.

"Why have you come back?" he said. "If you wanted to punish me for keeping you in that house, you've had ample opportunity before now."

Rhea was not entirely sure what Tarro was referring to, but Ettore clearly was; he nodded and said, "You're right. I have. No, it's not about that. It really isn't even about you, I'm afraid. It's just time. And I can't be who I need to be to these people with you still here." He cupped Tarro's cheek in one hand, surprisingly tender. "It will be a sacrifice. But that's just the sort of thing our gifts require these days."

Sacrifice, Rhea thought. Ettore had said that once before. Maybe it would be what made the prayer the weapon she needed it to be today. For Michali, she had given up spring, had undone the power she held as Thyspira. She had offered up nothing when she'd asked for Nitsos back, and look where it had got her.

So let Ettore's own pain at losing his son bleed through her. Let it sing in the prayer as she spoke it aloud. Payment, for what she was asking the matagios to do.

Ettore straightened, nodding to Rhea as he backed away. Tentatively, she came closer, flinching the moment Tarro's stare slid to her. It had been a long time since they'd met; she couldn't even remember quite when that had been. But she knew him, knew the lines around his eyes and the gregariousness missing from his expression.

"Hello," she said and regretted it immediately. "I . . . I don't think it will hurt."

Over Tarro's shoulder, Ettore moved, but his figure looked blurry, indistinct. Everything was except the lines around Tarro's eyes and the bare stretch of his throat above his jacket collar. If he'd been her consort, that's how she would have done it. A knife, right there where his pulse beat under his jaw. How was this different?

Slowly, she lifted her marked hand and rested it on the crown of Tarro's head. His hair was warm to the touch, as though he'd just been in the sun; it made something convulse in her chest. She took a deep breath, pressing her fingertips against Tarro's scalp. She could feel a tremor run through him. He was trying to speak through the rope of gold that had wound itself across his mouth.

"*Elado,*" Ettore said. "Now."

The sound of Thyzaki washed through her. For a moment she could imagine she was back at the dining table with her father and that he was speaking these words. But it was her mouth that opened, her own voice that she heard.

"*Aftokos ti kriosta. Ta sokomos mou kafotio.*" The prayer came out easily enough, and she could feel it beginning to build, rising in her throat, stinging and sharp. It did not feel the way it had in the mountains, the way it had when she'd spoken the name that had arrived at the back of her mind, but she couldn't stop now, not for anything. "*Aftokos ti kriosta po* Tarro Domina. *Ta sokomos mou kafotio.*"

Tarro's jaw clenched. His eyes fell shut. Rhea waited for him to drop to the dais, for his skin to sap of color or for blood to leak from his ears and nose. Instead, he drew a shuddering breath, and then another, and another, and it was Rhea going cold, her own body turning weak and unsteady.

He was alive. The prayer had not worked. She was Lexos standing in the garden at Stratathoma; she was her own self, kneeling in the rubble at Agiokon, calling Nitsos home and hearing no answer; she was nobody at all.

"Well?" Ettore demanded. "Have you finished?"

She opened her mouth to answer, to explain, but nothing came out. At her feet, Tarro had begun to shake, a strange sound coming from behind the golden rope. Laughter. He was laughing.

"Enough," Ettore said. He came around to stand opposite Rhea, Tarro knelt between them. With one hand, he grabbed a fistful of Tarro's hair and yanked his head back, the gold going loose to allow the movement. With the other hand, he reached under his jacket. "I'll do it myself."

In a heartbeat, he had pulled out a slim little knife, its blade flashing gold. In another, he had drawn it across Tarro's throat. A red line opened—narrow at first, and then wider and wider as blood began to pour out.

Ettore let the knife fall to the dais. Rhea gaped at it, rooted to the spot. She herself had meant to kill Tarro, and still it was more than she could bear to watch his body go limp, with only the strength of the golden rope keeping him upright.

"That's that finished," Ettore said, in Trefza once more. "Falka, do you mind handling the rest? I've had my fill of the public for the day."

"Of course," Falka said. She had come partway up the steps, and though she sounded quite composed, her face had gone a bit ashen. "Consider it done."

"And I'll need a meeting with everyone as soon as possible. Nastia, Milad, Zita, all of them. I don't care if they're busy."

"Of course."

"Very good." Ettore ran one hand through his close-cropped hair and set his shoulders. The tension went out of the golden rope, and with a clatter, it fell to the ground, no longer a rope but back in its disparate pieces. One Domina darted forward and picked her necklace out of the tangle, ignoring Tarro's body where it had collapsed onto its back. As far as they were concerned, this was all over; Rhea could not understand it. Did it matter to none of them that Tarro was dead?

No, she thought it likely mattered more that she had failed. But as Ettore came toward her now, his disappointment sat lightly in the line of his mouth. It was almost worse this way, worse for him to be able to dismiss her and her failure as nothing of consequence.

"I'm sorry," she said as soon as he was near. "I don't know what happened. I thought—"

"You don't need to apologize," Ettore cut in. He laid a hand on her shoulder, reassuring. And he even sounded like he meant it. Maybe everything would be all right. "I didn't have high expectations."

Oh. A cold dread began to spread down the back of Rhea's neck. "What do you mean?"

"You're Irini's child," he said, as if it was obvious. "She might have outlived the others, but she was never good for much. Why should you or your brother be any different?"

"You knew?" She should have been embarrassed by how small her voice was, by how much she sounded like a child caught in a lie, but that's what she was. A daughter again, disappointing yet another father. She was too mortified to even blush.

"I knew Aya Ksiga," Ettore said. "I made Aya Ksiga. Did you really think I wouldn't recognize her in your face?" He shook his head. "It's as I said. Never good for much."

"I—I can try again."

"He's already dead." Ettore pinched her cheek, too hard to be affectionate. "You'll stay, of course, and you'll tell me all about your mother, and where I can find her. But I have to finish taking my city back first, so if you'll excuse me . . ."

He stepped past her, his shoulder knocking against hers; it was enough to send Rhea stumbling to the side. She pressed her marked hand to her chest, her heartbeat quick beneath. She had asked Michali in Ksigori to let her prove her use, and he'd refused, told her there was more to consider than what she could do for him. And she'd believed him. How wrong they'd both been. How naïve. It was only ever about use—Baba had taught her that, and here was the cost of letting herself forget it.

"Falka," Ettore called from behind her, "I'll be going if we're all sorted."

"We are," Falka replied. Rhea turned to see a number of Domina children clustered around her on the stairs as she gestured to various areas in the hall. Some people were still trying to get out, but the guards had managed to subdue most of the chaos. Rhea could already tell—the transition from Tarro to Ettore would be complete by the end of the day. They were used to this kind of bloody change here in Vuomorra, and anyone anywhere would have been hard-pressed to deny the authority of Luco Domina.

But what did that mean for her? Where was she supposed to go now? Down to Falka, to take orders alongside the rest of the Dominas? Or with Ettore? Nothing seemed right. Everybody had somewhere to go, someone to look to, and Rhea was alone. Left on the dais, with Tarro bleeding out at her feet.

She forced herself to move. Step by step, down the stairs, the chatter in the hall too loud one moment and too quiet the next. Rhea focused on the curl of Falka's hair, the curve of her mouth, and let the rest of the room fall away. Falka would take care of her.

The Dominas circling Falka did not move aside as she approached, so Rhea had to content herself with waiting at the edge for her to finish. Her Trefza was too fast for Rhea to make out much, and she didn't think she would've understood much anyway. People's mouths had started looking strange as they spoke, moving slowly or not at all even as their words continued on. Rhea squeezed her eyes shut and held her breath. When she opened them again, the world remained only blackness for a moment too long.

Finally, the Dominas began to disperse. The doors at the back of the hall had been opened at last, and the hall was beginning to empty now that Ettore was gone. Rhea eased forward, sidling up next to Falka as the other woman handed her discarded half-veil to a passing servant.

"What's next?" she asked. "Are we going to your room to settle in?"

"Oh," Falka said apologetically, "I'm not sure that I can. There's just quite a lot to handle at the moment." She caught the eye of someone across the room and nodded toward the back door of the hall. "I'll have someone show you to my room, all right?"

She was gone before Rhea could answer, and Rhea was left alone at the foot of the dais stairs. She watched a servant climb them, carrying a bucket of water and a rag. Someone to clean up Tarro's body—soon the blood would be washed away, and every Domina in Vuomorra would have changed their coat from pale to darker green. And she would still be here. Still alone. At least for Tarro it was over.

She stayed there for a long time, staring at the body, rooted to the spot. It was only when another servant arrived and called her name that she was able to look away.

"Yes?" she said.

The servant was hovering nervously a few yards away. They were holding a note and seemed eager to be elsewhere. "Falka said to apologize again for her exit and to give this to you." They approached, note held out. "She said she can't speak to its accuracy, but that it does seem like something you'd want to know."

Rhea accepted the note. It was thick parchment, and its edges were worn, a smear of dirt along the outside suggesting it had traveled quite a ways.

"Thank you," she said. "I appreciate it."

At last, she broke away from the mess on the dais. She slipped out the back of the hall and into the adjacent garden. The afternoon had begun to deepen; all around her the potted cyprus trees cast long, narrow shadows, and the hedges stretched out, bordering a path that led to an open lawn. She found a small stone bench and sat before opening the parchment.

It was a note from one of Ettore's scouts—like Lexos, he had a network he relied on—specifically regarding the movements of Rhea's brother. According to this scout, Lexos had been seen headed north, across the border into Chuzha. There was quite a lot about the conflict between the Stratagiozi factions that was still forming, but it was already clear that Chuzha would serve as the battlefield for much of it. What was Lexos thinking, walking into danger like that? There was nothing there for him, nothing that would attract an Argyros. No wealth, no power, and no family. But he'd gone anyway, so what did he think he would find?

Her, she thought. Maybe he was looking for her.

She could not say why, really. To take her gifts for his own; to help her; to simply be near her again, because he didn't know what else to do. Whatever the answer, she didn't care. She had lost Nitsos twice, once to the whir of his machines and a second time to the crush of the Agiokon spire. She had pushed Chrysanthi to the edge of their relationship, stretched the bonds between them to breaking so that her sister would never come back. But Lexos was Lexos. He had called her his *kathroula*, and he had been right to; she was part of him. No, it was more than that. They were the same body, the same heart. Why had she ever tried to change that? Why hadn't she understood the gift she'd been given? It was more powerful and more dear than the mark and matagios both. And it meant that Lexos would come when she called. She would never be alone again.

Rhea folded the parchment back up and went inside. She had a letter to write.

CHAPTER FORTY-FOUR

ALEXANDROS

Michali and Piros had told Lexos the general direction they suspected Rhea had gone, so of course Lexos had begun his travel in the exact opposite direction—north, following the gulf coast up toward Chuzha and Prevdjen. He'd managed to find passage on a small skiff that promised to make good time, and it had, leaving him in southern Chuzha only two days after his meeting with Rhea's so-called friends. It of course took longer than it would have on one of Baba's ships, but then, as he was being quite forcibly reminded constantly, he no longer had the access and power that had come with being a Stratagiozi's second.

Even the scout network he'd spent almost a century building had turned away from him. When he had finally managed to meet one near the Chuzhak border, they could only barely be convinced to provide him with a horse and some food. Lexos understood their mistrust, but really, he'd been a bit busy since the fall of Stratathoma. Keeping his scouts informed and—more important—paid had not been possible.

He was not sure why he felt so certain that Rhea had come north. It wasn't at all what he would've done, not when there were centers of power that she had not yet explored. But Rhea had gone to the Sxoriza after that mess at Stratathoma; she had fled the world she was meant for, shirked her duty to her gifts and her family both. It made sense to him that she would have done it again this time and tried to disappear into the northwestern corner of the continent, where Aya Thyspira had never been heard of before. And until he could coax any other information out of what remained of his scout network, he would trust his own instincts and continue on.

At the close of his third day of travel, he found himself nearing a small wood that bordered on one of Chuzha's famous grain fields, which were spread across the country's western half. This particular stretch of land was a good ways away from the road. It had been planted with wheat and mixed grass, which made Lexos nervous that he would be found by some farmhand, but a quick wander around the perimeter proved the field deserted, and what had grown in its furrows was high enough that any strangers coming this way would likely not see Lexos. With the sun beginning to set, he dismounted from his borrowed horse and set up camp right where the trees and the tall grass met.

It was lonely, traveling like this. He'd never had to do it this way before—even his forced touring around Trefazio had put him in the company of some assortment of guards at all times, and before, when he'd ridden alone, it had been with the knowledge that back at Stratathoma, his family was waiting for him. There was nobody waiting now.

He cleared himself a little space just within the woods and lit a fire, huddling close to shield it from the wind that snuck through the trees. The sky had gone purple, stars beginning to emerge. Lexos scowled up at them. Was Falka taking proper care? He thought some of the spring stars looked out of place, but perhaps it was only that he was this far north. Regardless, he reminded himself, it was all her responsibility now. He was on his way to greater power than a needle and thread.

After a simple meal and an unrewarding conversation with his horse, Lexos lay back and shut his eyes. It was getting colder, but the fire was strong, and Rhea could not possibly be far now. Before he knew it, he had drifted off, the exhaustion of days in the saddle taking him so soundly under that he did not wake when the air began to grow warm, nor when the black of the night began to brighten. It was only when a thread of smoke curled around his throat that Lexos sat up, gasping, and found that the trees were on fire.

Flames licking high up their gnarled trunks, the canopy overhead beginning to smolder. Lexos's eyes immediately began to water as he coughed. Frantic, he rolled over toward his campfire, scrabbling in the dirt for something he could use to douse it. But his own fire was still contained properly within the pit he'd dug for it. And beyond, the grass field lay open and waiting, as yet untouched. This blaze was coming from somewhere in the trees; there was no time to wonder what had started it. Lexos had to run, and now, before he lost his way out.

He stumbled to his feet. The heat was painful, somehow sharp, and the roar of it was getting louder with every second as the fire took more of the forest. With one hand shielding his eyes from the smoke, he fought through the undergrowth to where his horse was tied. Already, he could see ash staining her white flanks. Her eyes were rolling, wide with panic, and when he reached for her, she let out a shriek the likes of which he had never heard before. She would throw him as soon as he tried to mount. Better to cut her loose and go on foot.

Once she had gone, galloped out to disappear into the grass, Lexos followed. Even a few steps were enough to feel the difference, a touch of frost in the air, but he couldn't afford to slow down—his lungs had begun to ache, and the fire was quickening as it reached the dry growth of the grass. Swallowing another hacking cough, Lexos began to run.

How had a fire this size started and come so close without him realizing? He'd heard no storms, no lightning that might have given off a stray spark. A house beyond the trees, maybe, or—

An arrow whizzed past his head.

Lexos cursed and threw himself flat against the ground. The earth was warm, the grass sharp against his cheek. Somebody was out here, had perhaps even followed him from Merkher. And though he had a knife in his boot and another in his belt, he knew very well that anybody who could come that close to hitting him in the shadow and flicker of the fire would dispatch him easily. He pushed up to his hands and knees and began to crawl away from the fire at an angle to keep him well away from whoever had fired that shot.

It was as the heat receded that he began to hear shouts. One, and then another, until there were ten, even twenty voices calling, screaming, in a language he couldn't identify right away, and from all sides. Up ahead now he could see the shape of someone crouched in the grass, their figure lit by the glow of the fire. They were armed, and as they surged to their feet and rushed toward the flame, Lexos realized that he'd woken in the middle of a battlefield.

He clambered to his feet. His head low, the grass brushing against his shoulders, he ran. Most of the soldiers seemed to be moving in the opposite direction, but he could hear others at his back, their yells as they fought and died. Each one sent another wave of fear crashing down over him. Hide—there was no other thought.

Sweat poured into his eyes, stinging bitterly. It was easier to breathe out here, but for all he knew he was running right into an enemy camp. For as long as he dared, he stopped running and peered over the rise of the grass. To one side, shadows moving in groups, and to another, torches in the distance. The fire in the trees was still raging, and in its light Lexos could see dark figures struggling, fighting viciously with blades that gleamed red.

There was nowhere to hide, Lexos realized. No abandoned shed, no creature's burrow left empty. There was only the luck that had carried him this far, and the hope that it would carry him a bit farther.

As another soldier in the distance let out a gurgled cry and dropped, Lexos again began to crawl through the grass, this time back toward the fight. It wasn't long before he found himself face-to-face with the half-shut eyes of a dead man. This one had taken a sword to the gut, and blood was still pumping out of him, as hot as the air that shimmered by the forest blaze. Another had collapsed next to him and was facedown, arms lying at an odd angle.

For a moment, Lexos thought of his father. Of sitting at the table every night, listening to Baba speak the names of strangers and doom them to die. Nobody had doomed these soldiers, but some Stratagiozi's child had colored the fire that raged beyond, and someone had set the winds blowing tonight so that the smell of something cooking, of deep burn and ash, would carry so far and so fast. Even a death like this was Stratagiozi work. There was no escaping it, no matter how far from home he went.

But then another battalion of soldiers rushed by with a shout, and the moment passed. Lexos inched his way forward, until he was positioned between the two corpses. All of his caution was gone; he heard something crack and squelch as he shoved himself half under the nearer body and shut his eyes. He could feel the blood seeping in through his jacket, and the gritty smear of earth across his cheek. Good—let anyone who passed think he had died, too.

The fight went on. Lexos listened to the soldiers, picking out bits of Amolovak—or was it Chuzhak?—as they shouted orders. They were well armed, the clash of their weapons so loud his head seemed to rattle with it. Sometimes a stray soldier would rush past, their boots trampling the earth only inches from him, but he did not flinch.

At last, the fighting began to quiet, until finally there was a minute without the yell of an injured man, and he heard a soldier nearby toss their weapon to the ground, breathing heavily. Though he did not know what a battle sounded like when it was done, he thought it might be like this. Low conversations began to drift by on the breeze, punctuated by yells for water, for aid. Chuzhak, he was fairly sure. It was so much easier to understand without all of the screaming.

Still, he did not move. The victors might come looking for their dead.

At last, when the sun had fully risen and he had heard no talk and no movement for what felt like hours, Lexos crawled out from under the corpse and got to his feet. The field was deserted; he was as alone as he'd thought himself when he'd sat down to camp. Flies were hovering above the tall grass, swirling in black clouds as though they were sparrows. It would not be long before they were joined by the carrion.

Averting his eyes, he made his way back toward where he had slept.

The fire had ruined the forest, leaving blackened, bare trunks behind. It still burned in places, but Lexos was surprised at how controlled the damage seemed to be, as though someone had taken precautions to protect certain parts of the forest and funnel the fire forward. And when he got closer to get a better look, he noticed that there were stone blocks, from the look of it, arranged here and there throughout the grass, alongside places where the grass itself had been cut away. Deterrents for the fire, to keep it from spreading too far. One side had driven its enemy here and used the fire to keep any of them from hiding in the trees.

Lexos supposed it was the smart thing to do. But then he wouldn't know, would he? All his strategizing with his father, all his plans—he had never dealt with anything like this.

He approached a nearby corpse and pushed it over onto its back. It was a young woman, wearing colors he did not recognize, but tied around her upper arm was a band of yellow fabric. A Chuzhak soldier, then, fighting for Nastia Rudenko. He didn't have to look to know that others on the battlefield would be marked as Ammar's. They had been fighting over the Vitmar for so long, those two, and Lexos had known somewhere in himself that their fighting was not and would never be only theoretical, but it wasn't—

He had never—

The thing was, Ettore had been right to call him a child. Lexos had argued, but he should have listened instead. A hundred years at his father's side had marked his palm; more and more it seemed that time had done absolutely nothing else.

Lexos bent and picked up the young woman's fallen sword. His hands shook as he cleaned off the blade. If Rhea had come north, had she found herself in some situation like this? Had she pressed herself into the dirt, into the blood and grime, and wanted very much to just go home? They were twins; if he was not built for the world beyond Stratathoma's walls, neither was she.

Before leaving, he took one last look through the remains of his camp, careful not to leave behind any rations or spare clothes. The cold would turn unbearable before he got much farther north.

Most of his supplies had been destroyed, but one bag was still intact, its brown leather stained with smoke. Perched on the buckle was a little hummingbird, its eyes identical to Lexos's own. It cocked its head and Lexos jumped, his breath catching.

"I forgot you can move," he said. "What are you doing here?"

The hummingbird was Rhea's, of course—he'd never seen another like it—but that did not mean it had been her who'd sent it, particularly if Ettore and Falka had got to her first. Although if they had, he couldn't imagine why they wanted to speak to him; they hadn't had anything further to say when they'd left him behind.

"Are you from her?" he asked the hummingbird. "Also, can you understand me?"

The hummingbird hopped in place, drawing attention to the bit of parchment tied to its leg. He supposed that was answer enough.

He had never exchanged messages with his sister this way before, but the bird seemed to know what to do. It darted into the air and hovered near him until he held out one hand. With an odd, hiccuping whir, it alighted there on his index finger. It held perfectly still as he undid the knotted twine keeping the parchment in place. This close, Lexos could see the gears and cogs at work, rust beginning to gnaw at the edges of the bird's wings. That did nothing, though, to make its eyes less unnerving, or to make it feel less like a living creature. When he'd got the message loose, he was relieved to watch the bird lift off again—and grateful that it knew to wait for his reply.

"Does she make a habit of sending you out, then?" he asked as he unrolled the message. "Do you get enough rest?" The hummingbird chirped, blinked at him with its Argyros eyes, and Lexos nodded. "That's right. Machine. I forgot."

He turned then to the letter. Rhea's handwriting was shaky, the strokes thin and hard to read in places. Lexos had to hold the message close to the embers of his trampled fire to get enough light to make it out.

> *Reports tell me you're on your way north. I would caution you against it: If your intent is to find some sort of peace, away from*

all that's happened since we parted, it will only follow you. If your intent is to find me, I am not there.

I know we carry many wounds between us. But what is any of that, really, between kathroulaki? Come to Vuomorra. Come back to me, and I will not let us be parted again.

Vuomorra. So, Ettore had got to her. Lexos reread the message, willing himself to ignore the urge to start heading there right away. He was resolved to find Rhea, but he could do that without responding to this message; in fact, if this wasn't really from her, he might have a better chance at it that way. Think, he told himself. Take care.

Most of it read to him as though anyone could have written it. But one word stood out to him: *kathroulaki*. That was not a word Rhea ever used lightly.

She had used it to close the letter she'd sent him near the end of her time in the Ksigora with Michali, a letter that had made clear to Lexos that she could not be counted on to do her job. It had been an attempt at manipulation then. Was it the same thing this time? Or was she trusting that he would remember? Even hoping he would? Maybe her mind had changed, and she saw now what Lexos always had—that they were mirror images, the pair of them, and that they could never really exist apart from each other. Or maybe it was a signal that she was, in fact, this letter's author. Nobody else would have thought to use that term, and certainly not a Trefzan imitator.

Lexos shut his eyes, breathing deeply for a moment. He could spend days trying to decide what this letter meant, or he could take it for what it was and accept Rhea's invitation. And he wanted very badly to go back to her.

He had nothing in the way of ink, but there was plenty of charcoal to be found. Lexos wrote his reply, hoping that when she read it, Rhea would feel how truly and sincerely he meant it.

It will take me a week. I cannot show my face in the palace. Instead once I arrive I will wait in the northeastern quarter of

*the city. Send your bird to find me; it will show
you the way. Do not worry. I am coming.*

If she wanted him with her, he would be there. She was right—nothing they'd done would matter once they laid eyes on each other. They had never been meant to be apart for this long.

The hummingbird flitted into the air, Lexos's reply fastened securely to it. He traced its path through the air as it started its trip back south, until, between one blink and the next, it had disappeared.

Lexos hoisted his bag onto his back and began to walk after it. He'd told Rhea a week. With any luck, he would be there sooner.

CHAPTER FORTY-FIVE

CHRYSANTHI

This was why they'd stopped burying people a thousand years ago: It was too much work to dig a grave. Chrysanthi's arms were aching. Her back felt as though it might split in two. And she hadn't yet finished scouring even a third of the territory she'd marked off.

She'd been at it for three days, digging through the morning and afternoon before falling asleep early on one of the divans in the sitting room—tucking herself into her parents' bed, which was the only one still intact, was absolutely not an option. The food she'd dug out of the pantry was more than enough to keep her, and though the house was too big and too lonely, there was something peaceful about it. This morning she'd woken to the call of a bird she did not recognize; the grass had been bent with dew, and there had been nobody to watch as she'd pinned her hair up off her neck with an old clip from one of the spare rooms and got to work.

There was still nobody to watch now as she let her shovel fall to the side. With a groan, she climbed out of the hole she'd begun an hour ago. She wasn't sure what she'd expected, except that was a lie, and what she'd expected was that she would lift one shovel's worth of earth and find her mother's face uncovered below. An unerring daughter's intuition, even though Chrysanthi could barely remember what the woman had looked like.

She made her way back to the house, brushing dirt off her clothes as she went. She hadn't bothered to clear the doors when the pantry window served her purpose just fine, but today she was reconsidering it as she hauled herself over the sill, muscles straining in protest. Even camping out with Andrija for weeks on end had not left her this uncomfortable.

She had done her best not to think of him since arriving here, reminding herself that she no longer needed him. She'd got here on her own. Still, she found herself taking note of things she wanted to tell him about later, or wondering, as she lay down to sleep every night, if he would've stretched out on the floor alongside her divan, or kept watch at the nearby window, only sleeping once she had woken again. He'd looked as close as he'd ever come to devastated when she'd left him in the orange grove; had he really deserved that?

Well, yes. He'd known what Ammar was capable of, what Ammar might do, and done nothing to stop it.

But then, hadn't she done much the same thing? She had spent quite a lot of time watching her family, allowing their decisions and their plans to pass by her with little commentary. She knew the guilt of a life like that. She knew, too, though, how impossible it had felt to say anything—to step in front of an arrow that she'd been sure would reach its target anyway.

It took time, she'd told herself in the days since leaving Stratathoma, for someone born at sea to realize there might be a life to be had on land. And if she was going to give herself that time, she supposed she could see how she might owe it to Andrija as well.

But she did not have to like it. Nor did she have to forgive him for the rest—for hiding his true allegiance from her, for reporting on her to Ammar. If she wanted to know what he would've thought about this house, whether he might've been content here or found it too quiet, that was neither here nor there.

After making herself a simple meal in the kitchen, she wandered upstairs, to the hallway where she'd found the family's old bedrooms. It would rain later, judging by the clouds gathering to the west, and she had no wish to get caught in a storm while standing in an empty grave.

She had examined each of the bedrooms upon arriving and found little to draw her back, but the one room, with its bundles of dried herbs—Rhea's room, she was fairly sure—tugged at her now, its door slightly ajar, the light from within cool and inviting. Chrysanthi felt in her pocket for the blackstone stud she'd found there and stepped inside.

Nothing had changed, as expected, but she was still relieved not to find any new sets of footprints or left-behind camp supplies. Even a handful of days in the empty house had not stopped her from expecting to come across another occupant every time she turned a corner.

Just to be careful, Chrysanthi shut the door behind her. This room looked north like Nitsos's did, but it had a better view of the pond. She approached the window, peering down at the water as she ducked under the garland of herb bouquets and leaned her elbows on the sill. The pond was small, perfectly sized for the children they'd been when they lived here. Its banks were fresh with new growth for spring. The winter that Rhea had brought back when she'd raised Michali did not seem so heavy here; there was a bourboula beetle flitting across the water's surface, its green back flashing silver in the pale light.

What would it have been like if they'd stayed here? No Stratathoma, no gifts, some other family leading Thyzakos in their place. She hadn't really considered it before, but faced with the remains of the life she'd had for her first few years, it all felt unfair: both that she had ever had to leave here and that she'd been forced now to come back.

She sighed and turned away from the view, dropping down to sit with her back pressed against the wall. Over her head, the bouquets of herbs rustled in the breeze coming through the open window. Chrysanthi took the blackstone stud out of her pocket, studying it closely as she stretched one leg out. Who had left it here? Out of Irini and her father, Irini seemed more likely—sentiment like this, if it could really be called that, was rare for Baba—but there was so little Chrysanthi knew about her mother that she could turn to now for understanding.

"*Elado*, Mama," she whispered. "Tell me what I'm doing here."

The blackstone caught the fading light, casting a spangled reflection across the ceiling. Chrysanthi laughed; that was probably all the answer she would ever get.

She tipped her head back. From this angle she could see the underside of the windowsill, pale wood marked with odd carvings. She craned her neck to get a better look—it was Rhea's name, etched into the sill by an unsteady hand. Two of the letters had extra lines, and a third was missing its top portion altogether. Rhea would have to have been very young when she wrote it. Chrysanthi was surprised she hadn't written Lexos's name there alongside it.

She twisted around onto her knees, pressing her thumb against the inscription. If Rhea were here with her, maybe everything would have gone differently. Maybe what Rhea had learned about Irini in the Ksigora would have put all this in some new perspective. Maybe—

Chrysanthi narrowed her eyes. Rhea had carved her name into the sill, but there was something else, too: a dot at the end of her name, as though it were the end of a sentence. Chrysanthi couldn't imagine young Rhea bothering to add it. And it was small and neat, nothing like the rest of the lettering. Had Lexos added it?

She couldn't get close enough to be sure, but it looked, too, as though the dot bored somewhat beneath the wood's surface. Not a dot at all, then, but a miniature hole. Just about the size, Chrysanthi thought, of the pin on the back of the blackstone stud.

"All right," she said into the quiet. "Why not?"

She slid the blackstone stud home and heard a click as the end of the pin met something metal. A moment later, a piece of wood no bigger than a coin popped up from the flat of the windowsill, like a little trapdoor. Underneath sat something round, something that cast faint flickers of light across Chrysanthi's finger as she reached for it. Carefully, she tapped it. Not glass, but something equally delicate. Something she recognized very well: a kymitha.

She scooped it out of its hiding place before tipping it into her palm. Irini had taught Rhea to make these. Each little dessert was spun from a story or a memory, and eating one was meant to be like living it over again. Rhea had never been able to achieve that. Her kymithi were just flashes strung together, just fleeting impressions of feeling, but they were still better than anything Chrysanthi or Lexos could do.

Like the kymithi Rhea made, this one was a small sphere, the texture crisp and frail, the color a rich amber with a living wink of something brighter at the center. But as much as it was familiar, it was equally different. This kymitha was clearer, almost fully translucent, and it seemed more compact. From different angles, Chrysanthi could see different layers contained within it. Did that mean it had been spun from multiple stories? How many moments had its maker crystallized?

At least there was no question of who the maker had been. This was Irini's handiwork. Whether or not she had been the one to leave it here, in this secret compartment in Rhea's room, Chrysanthi couldn't say for sure, but it seemed likely. Baba had preferred to pretend that they'd never lived anywhere but Stratathoma; she could not picture him leaving anything behind with such care, as though it was a gift waiting to be opened.

Chrysanthi eased back onto her heels. The kymitha glowed faintly, the lit heart of it harder to make out without any shadow clinging to it. It looked tempting. Sweet. She could practically feel it between her teeth already.

And, well, there was nobody here to tell her not to. So she popped the kymitha into her mouth and bit down.

A crunch, as the first layer gave way. The flavor was fresh, green. Her eyes fell shut, and when she opened them again, the room around her had gone—

She had gone—

Not Chrysanthi, but Irini and a very young Rhea at the edge of the pond. Irini lifted a hand, waving to where Lexos was wading in the shallows on the opposite side.

"You'd better go in, *koros*. Your father was looking for you."

The pond blurred, the sky wheeling overhead, and then Irini was crouched in the water, Rhea's small body tucked against her hip.

"You see?" Irini said. "You let your brother tend to your father. He's the eldest. You let that be his job."

A second layer cracked, and the taste turned rank—sweat and dried blood. Irini stood over a crib. In it lay two infants, side by side, each wrapped in a blanket.

"Rhea," Irini said, "for my mother. And Alexandros, for Vasilis's father."

There came a muffled reply, somewhere from beyond the memory's edges; the room disappeared, leaving Rhea in Irini's arms, a hummed lullaby fading in the distance.

"I'm sorry," Irini said, and Rhea opened her eyes. "Whatever I may have passed to you, whatever you carry now . . . he cannot see a saint working in you. Alexandros will serve him. Alexandros will be his heir. For both of us, you see?" She pressed her forehead to Rhea's pink cheek. "Let this be the only lie I tell you."

The third layer, this time. Salt and a burst of citrus. Irini turned away from the sea, the beach broad behind her, her cloak whipping in the breeze.

"What for?" she asked, and Vasilis held up a hand.

"I haven't told you because I want your opinion," he said. "I've told you because it's what's going to happen."

"You're really marching on Stratathoma?"

Vasilis nodded. His dark coat outlined his silhouette sharply against the city in the distance. "The army will follow me. And the seat is ripe for the taking."

"But you don't need it," Irini said. "We're happy this way. The children are safe and well, and—"

"I will have better than that house," Vasilis cut in, "to give to my son."

Irini opened her mouth as the sea stretched, rose, swallowed her whole, and the fourth layer broke open, the taste of bitter herbs and therolia beneath. She was young, hair long and loose. A scream in the air, a trail of blood left behind her in the snow as she ran, darting into the woods.

"Aya Ksiga," someone called after her. "Irini! You cannot hide for long."

She crumpled to her knees. Her breath coming quick, her blue eyes wide, Irini reached into the air—into the very sky itself. "Please," she whispered. "Help me."

Her outstretched fingers caught a handful of the black between the stars. She pulled it down, wrapped it around her shoulders, and was gone, just as—

The fifth layer, almost painfully sour. A little bed in a comfortable room, with a small child tucked under its covers. Rhea, asleep, and Irini sitting on the bed's edge, stroking her daughter's hair.

"If it were only you and me," she said. "You, and me, and your siblings. If only, *koukla*. But your father has plans for all of us. He will mark your palm before long."

A shadow in the window, and the brush of bare feet against stone. Irini flinched and leaned closer to her daughter. "I watched my friends die for these gifts. I heard the cries of the earth as we first tore them free. Power like that only keeps rotting. I can't imagine how much it demands now."

She sighed, the dark clinging to her body, the walls buckling, then standing firm. "If I could keep you from it, I would. But you may need it, to keep you safe as my gift has kept me." She wrapped a lock of Rhea's hair around her finger and kissed it. "I hope you won't. I hope that even if you do, you will be stronger than I am. Strong enough to put that power back for good."

Finally, the sweet center of the kymitha, hot as an ember pulled from the fire. "Saint's bone and your blood," Irini said to a young Rhea, the two of them in the kitchen as they rolled out dough for a pita. "And a little bit of earth." She grabbed a pinch of flour and spread it on the counter. "Give it a mix, yes? After that it's just as your father will do to you someday soon. That stain will come right back out."

"I don't understand," Rhea said, and Irini laughed.

"I know that you don't." She lifted a sheet of dough. Sun filtering through it, spread thin and soft. "Here, let's— Oh, Vasilis. I didn't know you—"

Chrysanthi gasped, choking on her own spit. She was still there, still sitting on the floor in Rhea's old bedroom. Sweetness lingered on her tongue, the only sign that what she'd seen had been real at all.

That had been a saint's kymitha, she thought. More powerful, more complete. The Irini in each memory had been real, not just a name spoken by Chrysanthi's siblings but flesh and blood. Chrysanthi had felt her mother's fear as she'd run for her life, and again as she'd lied and made Lexos the eldest twin. She'd felt her anger as she'd argued with Baba and her resolve as she'd spoken to Rhea, asleep in this very room. Irini had known what might come from Baba's ascent to Stratagiozi, and she had tried to give her children a way out. A way to undo what she and her fellow saints had done.

Her children—but really, all this had been for Rhea, hadn't it? Irini's firstborn. Her heir, if Lexos had been Baba's. Rhea should have been here, should have found the kymitha and heard what their mother had to say. What she *had* said, in bits and pieces, until Vasilis had heard.

Had it been that night that she'd died?

Chrysanthi shut her eyes tightly, searching for any memory of her own of her mother. But there was only emptiness, and the distant sound of a laugh Chrysanthi recognized as her own. Those images in the kymitha were the most she would ever see of Irini. They were the closest she would ever get.

She sat up. That wasn't true, was it? Yes, if all she ever did was look to the past, she would find nothing. But she could look ahead. She could follow the directions Irini had left, meet the challenge she had offered Rhea: let her gift slip back into the ground. Because Irini was right. For a hundred years, Chrysanthi and all of her siblings had been holding tight to the blade of a sword, all the while wondering why it was making them bleed. It would be strength, now, to let go. To refuse, finally, to let that blade turn against anyone else.

Saint's bone, and her blood, and a little bit of earth. Chrysanthi smiled. That sounded easy enough.

CHAPTER FORTY-SIX

RHEA

A chirp woke Rhea from deep slumber. With a groan, she turned her head toward the sound, Falka's arm jostling her as she did. There was little else in her life at the moment that warmed her as much as the sight of Falka, dark hair against the white bed linens, waiting for her at the end of the day. But if pressed Rhea would have had to admit that lying alongside her did not make for very restful sleep. She often woke pushed near the lip of the bed, with Falka spread out at a diagonal, luxuriating in all of her space.

Tonight was no exception. She was already only inches from the edge, which thankfully meant that Falka did not stir any further as Rhea swung her feet down and stood. The room was dark, the moonlight faint and shifting. They had left the windows open; through them, she could smell the damp gathering in the air, a fresh, earthy scent mixed with the honeysuckle off the vines that climbed past Falka's room. There would be a storm soon, if the clouds scudding across the night sky were anything to go by.

But it was not the weather that had woken her. She squinted into the shadow, searching for the source. When it came again—a mechanical sort of sound, part song and part sequence—she was startled to realize it was her hummingbird, perched only inches away on the top of the headboard.

"Oh," she said. "Hello."

The bird did not answer; no matter how she liked to speak to it, it was not in fact alive.

She lifted it gently from the headboard and carried it toward the window to get a better look at it. She'd been expecting word from Lexos, but crossing borders was not always an easy thing these days, and every day that passed made her less and less certain that she would ever see her brother again.

There was no message tied to the hummingbird's leg. With a sigh, she set it on the windowsill and pressed her palms to her eyes, letting the pressure of it ground her. No message did not mean bad news necessarily. It was still very possible that he was on his way to her.

"Why did you wake me up, then?" she said crossly before dropping her hands to level the bird with a glare. "You know I don't get much rest lately."

The hummingbird looked back at her as it always did. After Nitsos's death, she had worried it would cease to function, and while it had seemed to lose some of its movement—it no longer cocked its head when she spoke—it still gave the distinct impression of listening to her.

"Fine," she said. "Good night."

She turned, meaning to get back into bed, but stopped as a soft whir reached her ears. When she looked over her shoulder, the hummingbird was hovering there, wings moving too quickly to be seen. After a moment, it flitted to the window and through, holding a new position out in the night air.

Rhea's heart jumped. There had been no message because Lexos was here. He had arrived in Vuomorra, and here was the hummingbird, ready to lead her to him.

She rushed for Falka's dressing room, stumbling in her excitement.

A few days prior she'd tucked away a coat and satchel, both filled with everything she could take without anyone noticing: a waterskin and some food for Lexos, in case he'd run out, along with some money, a needle and thread, and other such things. She dug them out of their hiding place now before changing, hurriedly, into a loose shirt, dark trousers, and sturdy boots, all borrowed from Falka. Also borrowed from Falka was the knife that Rhea slid into her belt—with any luck there would be few people out in the city this late, but she hadn't had much luck in quite a while.

Once dressed, she eyed herself in the mirror. Did she have enough supplies for Lexos? Or, for that matter, for both of them? It was her intention to find some way to bring him back to the palace—Ettore and Lexos had met, and surely he would be welcome here—but that wasn't a risk she was prepared to take just yet. And maybe Lexos would have some new plan and usher them both out of Trefazio in the dark of night. It would be very like him, although whether she was ready for that, she didn't know.

She eased back out into the bedroom. Falka had rolled over into the space she'd vacated, and her face was turned toward the dressing room door. Rhea froze—had she woken? No, no, she hadn't. She was still breathing slow and easy.

Though she knew it was a bad idea, Rhea set her satchel down and stepped closer until she could crouch at the edge of the bed, her face level with Falka's. A season ago she had left Michali behind just like this, gone off to search through another city that wasn't hers. But she'd been alone that day, and every day since. Michali, Piros, Chrysanthi, Falka—none of it was real the way Lexos was. And now finally, finally, they would be together again.

She leaned forward and carefully kissed Falka's forehead. She would see her again, if everything went the way she hoped. And maybe then she and Falka could have an honest conversation about Ettore, about what he was doing here. About whether or not Falka ever meant to turn over the power she'd accumulated on the palm of her left hand.

But just in case, before she left the bedroom, Rhea stopped at the threshold and whispered, "Goodbye." Falka had tried to give her everything, tried to fashion a new life for Rhea just like her own, and Rhea was grateful, but she had a chance now to get back some of what she'd lost.

The hummingbird flitted in from the window to hover in front of her. "Off you go," Rhea said to it. "I'm right behind you."

CHAPTER FORTY-SEVEN

RHEA

The northwest quarter of Vuomorra was mostly public land, dominated by a park that Rhea had heard referred to as the jewel of the city. She had never been before, and the path the hummingbird led her on through it was disorienting. The canals here had been built deliberately so as to look natural—like rivers winding through broad lawns of green and wooded thickets that some gardener must have tended to every day. The city was old enough that these trees were fully grown, and standing amongst them, it was easy to forget that only a quarter of a mile away, thousands of homes and shops and markets were shuttered for the night.

There were other people out in the park—sometimes her route led her past one of the lampposts that were scattered sparsely throughout, and she would see shadowed figures gathered there, or stretched out in the shelter of one of the marble gazebos—but nobody so much as looked her way. Even if they had, she didn't think they would have recognized her. Her portrait had become popular in Thyzakos and Merkher, but it did not seem to have reached the same heights here. And while that did smart a little, in the end it suited her well enough.

She had followed the hummingbird along one particular canal for almost an hour before the bird stopped in midair and hovered in place. In the city the canals flowed through tiled trenches, the geometric patterns on the bottom refracted by the water. Here the tiles remained, but they had been carefully chosen to match the grass and soil on the banks, and to replicate the sort of rock riverbed that one might have expected to see out in nature. It was an odd sort of trick to the eye—at once expected and entirely surreal—and it was because of this that Rhea did not immediately recognize her brother, sitting where he was in the grass by the water's edge. Finally, the hummingbird chirped, and he moved, getting to his feet. Rhea startled.

"*Mala,*" she said, "you scared me."

"I wasn't hiding."

Lexos looked older in the moonlight. She studied the added length of his hair, the new sharpness of his cheekbones. More like Baba, she thought, and then wondered if the same could be said for her. After all, they were twins.

And they were used to being parted, to reuniting, but tonight Rhea didn't know whether to move toward Lexos, her arms held wide, or to reach for the knife in her belt. She did not have to decide; he moved first, crossing the space between them in two strides before he took her face in his hands and pressed his forehead against hers.

"I'm sorry," he said, his voice wrenched from somewhere deep within. "Rhea, I'm sorry."

She drew him down, his chin tucked into her shoulder. Together. They were together at last, and she would never be alone again. "It's fine," she whispered. "It doesn't matter."

She held on to him for a moment longer, clutching him as tightly as she could, before pushing herself back. It felt too dangerous to stay out in the open much longer, and besides, she wanted somewhere with a bit more light so they could really look at each other. Her trips away every season had been bearable because she'd known they would end and allow her a bit of respite at home, with Lexos. This time apart had weighed on her more heavily than she'd even realized.

"Come on," she said. "Let's find someplace to sit. I brought food."

She sent the hummingbird on its way, back to keep watch in Falka's room, and once it had gone, she and Lexos followed the canal north, away from the city. It was not long before they encountered one of the bridges that ran from bank to bank. This one was a grand affair, pale stone arcing above the water to form a narrow, colonnaded passage, its roof carved with scrolling embellishments. Rhea led Lexos to the middle and sat between a pair of columns, her feet dangling over the edge. She'd chosen the side facing the city, the distance washing what lamps were still left burning to a soft glow.

Lexos sat down next to her, close enough that his knee knocked against hers, but he propped his back against the column and drew one leg up. She could feel him staring at her, and she wanted more than anything to look back at him—for their eyes to meet, and for everything that had changed about them to equalize, settle the way it always had when they were together. This time, though, she let him look. The circles under her eyes, the bruises she sustained so easily these days. Let him realize what it had done to her to be alone.

"I expected to find you elsewhere," he said finally. "Did the Sxoriza tire of you?"

Ah, so he was angry still. But about what, she wondered. What had stuck with him in the season since that day at Stratathoma? Was it her defection he remembered most? Her accusations regarding Michali's death? Or was it simply the fact that he had not gotten the matagios when he'd expected it? Baba was gone; she was the only target left to him anymore.

"I tired of them," she said. "Things have changed too much since I pledged my loyalty."

"You pledged?"

"It's a figure of speech."

He pulled a face, but she bit her tongue. They could only poke at each other so many times before drawing blood; they carried sharper swords these days. And she didn't want to fight. She just wanted to be near him, to know there was someone who might understand how adrift she had felt since Baba died.

"So Ettore, then," Lexos said.

"Ettore. He said you spent some time with him as well." It had been part of why she'd allowed herself to trust Ettore as far as she had. Not that Lexos ever needed to know that.

"That's one way of putting it." He winced, whether at her own choice of words or some memory he had yet to share. "I think you were right to meet me here. I don't trust him. None of the Dominas."

"Is there anyone you do trust?" she asked dryly.

He laughed. "That's a fair question. You, I guess."

"Don't tease."

"I'm not." His hand brushed her arm; she turned to face him and leaned back against her own column, mirroring his position. "I know that we argued—"

"We did a lot worse than that."

"But that doesn't matter to me tonight." He cleared his throat. "Does it matter to you?"

She could hold the line, embarrass him here. But she had missed him. It seemed that there should have been bigger words for it, but that was the best she could do; he had not been there, and she had wanted him to be, so, so much.

"No," she said. "It doesn't. Where have you been, *koros*?"

He shrugged. "Here and there."

He looked a sight worse than he had the day they'd parted at Stratathoma, which she thought was saying something. Aside from a general air of exhaustion, there was a scrape on his cheek and a new scar on the side of his neck, along with rips in his clothes, which were simple, plain things that did not even have the quality of their construction to recommend them.

"You should have come to me sooner," she said. She plucked at his sleeve before reaching for her satchel, which she'd set to one side. "There's food in here, and water. And some thread to mend your jacket."

"Can you do it for me?" Lexos had bypassed the buckles holding the satchel shut and was already wiggling the waterskin out from under the flap. "You've got steadier hands."

Rhea glanced down at her injured one. The broken fingers had stopped hurting quite so much, but they had not set properly. "Not anymore."

She saw it cross his face—the surprise and the understanding. "From Agiokon?" he asked. She nodded. "Are they taking care of you? Feeding you? Treating you well?"

"I think there is only so much they can do for me, at this point. But they are doing it." Lexos made a noise of disapproval before opening the waterskin and seeming to drain half of it in one sip. "No, really. They are."

"That's not what I mean." He reached into the bag and came up with a little pouch of dried nuts and fruit. "Only so much they can do for you? What are you talking about?"

She wore her bandages during the day, to keep from alarming other people at court, but she had not bothered to rewrap them before going to sleep, or before leaving the palace. So her arm was bare as she uncurled her fingers, extending her marked hand toward Lexos.

He gasped. Quietly but distinctly. It was almost comforting to hear that sort of reaction; Rhea had stopped being surprised when she saw it, or when she woke on a new morning and found herself still unwell. She had stopped expecting to feel any different.

"Ah," he said. "I see." The food and supplies were forgotten. He reached for her instead, meeting her eyes to gauge her response as he took hold of her arm. Carefully, he began to turn it this way and that as he examined the split of her skin, and the garish show of bone beneath.

"It doesn't hurt," she told him, after it had been quiet for a little too long. She wasn't actually sure whether that was true, but if it did hurt, she was so used to it now that she didn't think it counted.

Lexos frowned, pushing his hair out of his eyes. "Maybe not, but, Rhea—"

"I know."

"Ettore mentioned some corrosion, but . . . How long has it been like this?"

"Agiokon." She cleared her throat, unwilling to tell him the truth of what she'd asked her gift to do. He would only laugh at her. "I pushed myself a bit too hard."

"I can see that. Is Chrysanthi's like this, too?"

It seemed a difficult question for him to ask, and she struggled at first to remember why until she caught sight of his own unmarked palm. Right. There was only Chrysanthi to ask about, because Lexos was without power, without a gift to call his own. She'd lived alongside a version like that once, when they were small, but as much as they'd always clung to each other, they had barely known each other then. Nothing like the recognition she felt when she looked at him now after so many years, a feeling as much a part of her as the blood in her veins.

"No," she answered. "I never saw anything like this in her mark. And the Dominas here— No, I don't think it's got that far upstream yet."

Underneath them, the canal meandered along, its current soft but constant. Lexos gave a wry smile. "What an apt metaphor, *koukla*."

"I do try."

He released her hand and sat back, eyeing her. "And what about the other?"

"The other?" Of course she knew what he meant, but there was still a part of her that wanted very much to hear him acknowledge it: She was their father's heir. She always had been.

"The matagios," he said stiffly. "Is it behaving similarly?"

She tried to imagine the face he might make if she reached into her mouth and scraped some of her tongue off with one fingernail. Lexos could barely stand a day's sail without vomiting. She did not think it would go very well for him.

"In a sense," she said. "I'll spare you the details."

"Will you? How kind."

She tipped her head back against the column, the cold of the stone sending a shiver through her. He was looking at her in that way of his: impassive but exacting. He had almost certainly learned it trying to imitate Baba.

"What?" she asked.

Lexos's gaze dropped to her right boot, which she'd drawn up onto the bridge in mirror of him. Its laces had come undone. Without prompting, he set about retying them. "It's just that you don't seem alarmed," he said. "About what it means."

"I'm not, I suppose."

"Yes, but *why* not?" He finished the knot on her right boot and tapped her knee lightly. "This sort of thing . . . it seems to me there's only one way that it ends, and—"

"You don't know that," she interrupted. She was no longer prepared to tolerate his attempts to cast himself as an expert, particularly on things which so intimately concerned her. And besides, this was time with him that she'd longed for. If he kept tugging at this thread, he would unravel it into an argument. "We don't know anything about this. Not really."

"Fine," Lexos said, voice rising, "we don't know specifically that your arm splitting open is bad for you, but I do honestly feel quite comfortable saying that your arm splitting open is bad for you, Rhea!"

"Yes, but—"

"And whatever's causing it—whatever's happening with your mark—is likely to end with the loss of your life." He sat forward, reaching for her hand, and she gave it to him. Of course she did. "You know that, right? You know that matagios doesn't protect you from anything?"

"I know. I promise I do." She could see, she supposed, how it might look to him, how the Rhea he'd known at Stratathoma might not have understood the predicament she found herself in now. That girl had traveled and wed and buried, and still she'd seen so very little of what the world truly was. That was different now.

"But you're still not worried."

"Worried? No."

Lexos's grip tightened. "Why?"

"I wish you would stop asking that."

"I will if you answer me. I mean it, Rhea. Why aren't you afraid?"

"Because it won't kill me." She was tired of this. Of everything. Why couldn't Lexos understand? "Over and over, I have asked these gifts to do something, to be what they were for Baba, and every time they've failed me. Why would they choose now to give me what I want?" She shook her head, pulling her hand free of Lexos's. "This won't kill me. I'm not that lucky."

For a moment the only sound was the rush of the water in the canal below. Rhea stared into it, all too aware of Lexos's eyes on her. She hadn't meant to be quite so honest, but perhaps it was better this way.

He cleared his throat. "Lucky." He sounded very quiet, but she could not bring herself to look up. "You would be lucky to die?"

She lifted one shoulder in a sullen shrug.

"Do you understand," he asked, "why hearing you say that makes me very nervous?"

She sighed, meeting his eyes. She hadn't meant to upset him. "I do."

"And do you understand why I would very much like for it not to happen?"

"Of course I do. Please, I—"

"Don't." He caught himself, jaw clenched, his posture rigid. She would've thought he was angry if not for the wet shine of his eyes. "You can't go."

She shook her head. That wasn't what she wanted, either. What she wanted was to be home again, to be standing at Stratathoma's door for the first time, with the past hundred years ahead of her and Lexos by her side. What she wanted was some peace, just like what she had woken Michali from when she'd called him back. If it was dying that would do it, she couldn't really think of any reason not to.

"It isn't that," she said. "I don't want to go, Lexos. I only—I mean, does a body really disappear when it's burned?"

"Don't you dare say— Rhea—" His voice cracked, and she felt, so clearly it could have been the work of some Stratagiozi gift, her heart inch forward in her chest, just to be that very little bit nearer to him.

"You can't leave me here," he finished. Quiet, resolved. "I won't let you."

She laughed a little; he recoiled, as though the sound of it was offensive. "Good," she said. "I don't *want* to leave you. Not ever again."

"You say that, but you also say that you'll let these marks take you apart."

Their eyes met, his gone stubborn and wild. He was breathing hard, and the stillness he'd held so carefully was beginning to slip.

"All right," she said, lifting her hands in mock surrender. She hated to see him so upset, and there was no point in continuing this way. Lexos had bled their father dry and buried him, but he would not be convinced to stand by and watch as she died.

"All right?"

"I understand you. I do."

He blinked hard, but nevertheless a tear wound down his cheek. "I should hope so."

"And I mean it, *kouklos*. I never want to leave you."

He pushed her hair back from her face, his chin crumpled and trembling as he knotted his fingers at the nape of her neck. His palm was warm cradling her head, the weight borne for her as though they were floating on their backs in the water below.

They had come into this world together. Lived alongside each other, parted and returned again, and everything had always been fine until she decided to join the Sxoriza and abandon her brother. What had they done wrong, the pair of them? How had they ruined things to the point of ending up here, the doors of their home shut to them forever? They had been through so much since they'd parted; if she deserved to rest, so did he. And her peace would only be true, be complete, if he was there with her.

She reached up and clasped Lexos's arm. If she pressed hard enough, she could feel his pulse beating at his wrist.

"What if?" she asked. "What if we went together?"

His face went slack, and though he recovered only a second later, she could tell he was afraid. That was fine. She would be brave for both of them.

"Where?" he asked. "To the palace? Yes, why don't we?"

He moved to get up, but she kept her grip tight on his arm. Rather than struggle, he remained where he was. She pulled herself closer. She could see now: His freckles were coming in with the spring. Hers always took much longer and were so faint you could barely see them even in the height of summer. Such an odd thing, to think they were identical—except, except, except.

"Rhea," Lexos said into the quiet, "I really think we should head for the city. It's late, and you must be tired."

She fought down the urge to laugh, but it lingered as she said, "I am."

"So wouldn't some rest be nice?"

She smiled. Of course he understood. He always knew just what she wanted. They were always the same underneath.

"Yes," she said. "Yes. That's all I want. Let me show you."

She'd thought he'd agree, but instead he pulled away and got to his feet, the arches of the colonnade throwing his face into shadow. "I'm not listening to any more of this," he said. "I'm getting you back to the city if I have to carry you over my shoulder."

"Why? What for?"

"Oh, I don't know—maybe some food and some water and to have Ettore explain what's happened to your arm, because—"

"That isn't what I need."

"Yes," Lexos snapped, "it is." He took hold of her elbows and hauled her to her feet. She let herself go limp; he cursed as he staggered under her weight. "Stand up. Come on."

She leaned back against the marble column, his hands falling away from her. "Say we did go back," she said. "Say we go to the palace, and Ettore welcomes you in. What then? How long until I die and you're left alone?"

"You won't," Lexos said, but she went on.

"It doesn't have to happen that way. It can be you and me forever, just like it is right now."

"No."

"I'll take care of you. I'll take care of both of us." She stepped away from the edge, putting herself between Lexos and the path back to the palace. His figure seemed so slight, as though they were both still children. "Come with me, Lexos. What have we ever done that we have not wished we could do together?"

"I know," he said. "I know. But not this, all right? Let's go back to your room together. Let's share a meal, let's wake up tomorrow. Not this."

She could tell that he meant those things as comfort. He was holding a new day out toward her as though it were a gift and not the thing she dreaded every night, awake and alone in the dark. How could she accept it? Another morning in Vuomorra, eating breakfast across from Falka in a house that wasn't hers, knowing all the while that she could have got it perfect if she'd just had the nerve? She was not strong enough. She didn't think Lexos was, either, if he was being honest with himself.

"I'm sorry," she said and held out her arms. "Will you—"

"Koukla." He had her in an embrace before she could blink, his cheek pressed against hers as they swayed back and forth. He was holding her so tightly that her ribs ached, but she didn't mind.

"I love you," she said, her eyes shut. "I love you so much."

Ettore said the gifts required sacrifice. She could think of none greater than what she meant to do now. It had not worked with Tarro, but she knew why now. His death would have cost her nothing. This was different. This was right.

"I love you, too," Lexos whispered roughly. "I'm here now. We'll sort it."

Yes. She would sort it. She was the eldest. Protecting her brother, even from himself—that was the only thing she'd ever known how to do.

She held him more tightly and said, *"Aftokos ti kriosta. Ta sokomos mou kafotio."* Just like that day in the garden. He'd been right to say her name in that prayer, only this time she would do it properly. This time they would go together.

Lexos went rigid in her grasp. "Rhea," he said, and he tried to pull away, but she had his hair tangled in one hand and his shirt in the other. "Rhea, don't. You can't."

"Aftokos ti kriosta po Alexandros Argyros *ke* Rhea Argyros.*"*

"Stop it!" He broke her hold and pushed her away, sending her stumbling. "What are you doing?"

She caught herself on one of the columns as he looked wildly from one end of the bridge to the other. He knew how the prayer worked; he knew there was nowhere to go, didn't he? The only thing he could do to stop this was to hurt her, and he'd only ever done that at Baba's urging. And Baba was gone now. It was only the two of them. Lexos and Rhea, Rhea and Lexos, as it was meant to be. She had only to finish it now.

She smiled and thought of the woods, of saying that first name. How it had felt when the knot of the prayer had finally come undone. *"Ta sokomos mou kafotio."*

There: the breath leaving her like a sigh, and the coldness already at home in her turning to something different, something that did not belong to the world she knew. Rhea gazed at Lexos as the words of the prayer seemed to echo through her. Let him be the first and last thing she ever saw.

He blinked. One hand reached toward her, faltering, and she reached for him in return, but a lancing pain shot up from her mark, and she heard again the sound of her skin tearing. She looked down in time to see the wound at her wrist rip its way up to above her elbow, its edges blackened and curling as if burned.

"Lexos," she said. "What—"

He dropped to one knee, mouth working. No sound came out. Not a whimper, not a scream. And as he looked up at her, she could have sworn she saw the exact moment that his eyes went empty.

The prayer had worked. It had taken her sacrifice, and now Lexos was gone. But she was still here.

Rhea pressed one hand over her mouth to muffle her own cry as Lexos's body toppled backward off the side of the bridge and into the water below.

CHAPTER FORTY-EIGHT

CHRYSANTHI

On the sixth day, Chrysanthi struck wood. She had been digging for so long now that she had stopped expecting to find anything, but there in a stretch of open lawn near the very edge of what had been her family's land, at the base of an olive tree, the tip of her shovel hit a part of the box that contained Irini Argyros.

She stared down into the hole, her mouth dry, her hair in her eyes. The wood was stained dark with dirt and soft enough that her shovel had left a dent in it. She didn't know much about this sort of thing, but that didn't seem to be a good sign. Still, it had been more than a hundred years since Irini had been buried here. Surely most of the mess had disappeared by now.

Chrysanthi was not, though, in a rush to find out. She tossed her shovel to one side and sat down in the grass a few feet away from the hole she'd created. There were dozens of others like it in this corridor of the grounds, dotted at equal intervals—or as close to it as she'd been able to manage—right up to the base of the house. She'd skipped a bit of land near the middle, where the trees had grown too close together, but otherwise she'd been very thorough, glad to have something to do while she considered what she'd learned from her mother's kymitha.

If she was interpreting it correctly, it had meant that Irini's remains—her bones and teeth ground to powder—could be used in a ritual much like the one her father had performed to give her the mark on her left palm. Only this time, it would take that mark away, and Chrysanthi would be without the gift that had sat at the heart of her for so long.

What would it mean, to let it go? To choose her own way forward? She had been very young when Baba had marked her; she hadn't understood the sort of life he was creating for her then. Would she have let him smear that mix of blood and earth across her palm if she had?

Oh, probably, she thought. She liked nice things. She liked making them nicer. She liked a bit of shine and a fresh coat of paint. Even if all of that had been built into her by an outside hand, that didn't mean she had to resent it. But her paints were lost in Vashnasta, and Stratathoma was someone else's now. What would happen, the longer she did nothing? Would the sun go pale? Would the water in the gulf go silver and glass near the shore?

Irini had returned her gifts to the earth when she'd died. Maybe she'd had the right of it.

Chrysanthi gave herself a little shake. None of that would matter if she opened this box and found nothing inside. So she had better get back to work.

After digging a bit more in every direction, she discovered that she'd unearthed the middle of the box and that it ran parallel to the house, west to east. She was not sure which end was the head, which made her a little nervous, as she hoped to not come face-to-sort-of-face with her mother just yet. But without any markings to guide her, all she could do was clear the dirt off the lid and wedge her shovel underneath it. With a deep breath, she bore down, using all her strength to leverage the lid out of place.

A nail in the corner seemed to think about moving, but that was all. Chrysanthi was not, as it happened, very strong.

The sun had crested and begun its afternoon descent by the time she had all eight nails popped free. She was sweating profusely, and one of the blisters on her right hand had been punctured by a splinter from the shovel's handle, leaving her palm sticky with a substance she had avoided looking at too closely. But the lid moved when she prodded at it with the edge of the shovel's blade. She could see the darkness underneath.

She dropped to her knees in the dirt. The box, when she rested one hand on the lid, was cool to the touch. That surprised her. She'd been sure, somehow, that it would feel as a body might have.

With a grunt of effort, she pushed the lid of the box back. There wasn't much room in the hole she'd dug, but she managed to get it almost halfway off. As she dusted her hands on her trousers, she kept her eyes fixed on the roots of a nearby tree, refusing to take a look just yet. None of this was what she'd expected. She'd felt no lining in the box, nothing to protect the body, and though she'd been braced for a smell—wasn't that the way of rotting things?—there was nothing. Just the stink of her own sweat.

She took a deep breath, a shiver rumbling through her. She had come all this way to unearth her mother's grave. There was nothing left to wait for.

She looked down, and her eyes widened. This end of the box was empty save for some dust and the carcass of a recently deceased rat. Something had gnawed a hole in the bottom plank, and other creatures had clearly made the box a home over the years, leaving behind their own bones, among other things.

As for her mother, all Chrysanthi could see that might have belonged to her was a scattered handful of teeth at the far end of the box. Everything else—her tissue, her clothing, her bones—had turned to dust.

"Hello, Mama," Chrysanthi said. "You're looking well."

She did not have anything beautiful or precious to carry her mother home in, so Chrysanthi scooped up the teeth and poured them into her left-hand pocket. They clicked together as she stood, the noise like a child's rattle. She pressed her palm against them to hold them still; the sound was unnerving, as though her mother were trying to speak.

Back in the kitchen, Chrysanthi stood at the counter examining the array of tools available to her. Ground herbs were fairly common in Thyzak cuisine, but the mortar and pestle by the derelict stove might not be strong enough to wear down Irini's teeth. They'd survived in large fragments, some of them whole.

Best to start with a hammer, the sort her mother or father might have used to crack the walnuts that grew in this part of the country. She thought she'd seen a hammer like that in the pantry.

She had taken to shutting the pantry door when she was not inside it; with the window broken, it could be quite chilly. Opening it now, she was startled to find that the northward view the window usually provided had been blocked by the silhouette of a large horse. Leaning against its shoulder was a tall man with fair hair, dressed in black. Andrija had not listened to her; he had followed, and he was here.

For a moment, she did not move. She couldn't tell whether he had seen her or not. Certainly he knew she was somewhere nearby, but there was a chance still that she could turn away, leave out of the south side of the house and never see him again. Never find out why he'd come back, or where they might have ended up if she hadn't found that letter in the grove.

Chrysanthi stepped up to the window and leaned out into the sun. "Well," she called. "I guess you'd better come in."

CHAPTER FORTY-NINE

CHRYSANTHI

She let Andrija sit at the kitchen table while she gathered her supplies. He had looked so awkward climbing in the pantry window, almost stumbling when she neglected to tell him about a loose floorboard near the base of the wall, and he looked awkward still as he watched her from the other side of the room, his hands folded on the table.

She turned away and began to dig through the dishes left in the cupboard, looking for one without any cracks. If Andrija had something to say, he could break the silence himself.

After a few moments she emerged with a plain wooden bowl. She was not sure of the exact proportions she was meant to use—blood to earth to mother's bone—but she would just have to trust that if there had been anything else important, Irini would have said it.

Andrija cleared his throat. "You found the house," he said, voice lifting at the end in a way she hadn't heard from him before.

She set the bowl down and began fussing with one of the dishrags, scrubbing at a stubborn bit of grime on the counter. "I did."

"I knew you would."

"Really?" she asked and risked a look at him. She expected him to be smiling, making fun, but he was staring back at her solemnly. Chrysanthi felt her mouth go dry and a blush begin at the back of her neck. It was terrifying, to bear the weight of his attention. She looked away before adding, "You can take off your jacket if you want. I won't make you leave just yet."

Andrija did not immediately move, as if he meant to give her time to change her mind. When she said nothing else and only continued her tidying of the kitchen, he rose. Out of the corner of her eye, she watched him take off his black jacket and roll up the sleeves of the white shirt underneath.

He did not seem to know what to do next. Chrysanthi felt a flash of pity, but she would not help him. Carefully, she scooped a handful of teeth from her pocket and poured them into the wooden bowl, making sure not to lose any in the process. It felt like too many teeth to have come from one person, she thought. Then again, she'd never really seen an entire mouthful in this particular setting. Some had already split, their centers gone yellow or brown. Others might take quite a bit of effort to break open, and even more to grind down.

"What are you making?" Andrija asked.

She continued making eye contact with a particularly hefty molar. "A family recipe."

"Can I help?"

She looked up. He had come nearer. In this light she could see the weariness in his eyes, and a braid she'd given him on their journey from Agiokon in his hair. It pleased her that he'd kept it, put a lightness in her limbs that she was unfamiliar with.

"You want to help?" she repeated. He nodded and, well, fine. See what he thought of her project. She tipped the bowl toward him so he could see its contents.

Andrija tilted his head, considering, and then said, "What is it you need?"

"There's a hammer in the pantry. Will you bring it to me? I meant to fetch it earlier." But then she'd seen him out the window and been distracted, which was not at all embarrassing.

He was quick about it, and even set the hammer on the counter rather than force her to take it directly from him, which was kind, if unnecessary. He was being so careful, his silences heavy with anxiety rather than the comfort and sureness she'd got used to. It felt strange, like trying on one of Rhea's old gowns without tailoring it to fit herself. But she wasn't sure how to change it. They'd argued, and though she didn't regret it, she didn't know how to tell him—

Or what to tell him, really. With a suppressed sigh, she fetched the hammer from the counter and slammed it down on the first of the teeth.

Nothing happened, because of course nothing happened. Despite its age, the tooth simply sat there on the counter intact, its dull, almost-white surface doing a poor job of catching the sun. Chrysanthi let the hammer fall from her grasp. Her arms ached from the digging she'd done; the blister on her right hand was starting to beat in time with her pulse.

"Andrija," she said, "you've used a hammer before, right?"

He leaned across the counter from his spot by the end and picked up the tool, its silver filigree at odds with the calluses she could see on his palm. "Such as it is, yes."

"Have at it, then." She pushed the bowl of teeth in his direction and stepped around him, making for the chair he had vacated.

Immediately, he set to work. The kitchen was comfortably warm this time of day, especially with the sun coming in through the south windows. Chrysanthi leaned back in her chair and watched Andrija crack each tooth into smaller chunks. He worked methodically, a frown creasing his brow. She imagined smoothing it out with the pad of her thumb, how he would certainly let her, only for it to return moments later.

She let her eyes shut. When she opened them again, they fell on his jacket where he'd hung it on the door into the hallway beyond. It didn't look the worse for wear since she'd seen it last—no rips from travel or slices from someone else's blade.

"Where did you go?" she asked.

"Hm?" Andrija brought the hammer down on one stubborn incisor and examined the results, nodding to himself.

"I mean, you haven't been following me since I left, have you?"

He looked up, alarm flashing in his eyes. "No. No, you asked me not to."

"Yes, all right," she said, smiling. "So where did you go, then?"

He swept the incisor bits into his palm and dumped them into the mortar she'd set on the end of the counter. She knew very well his hesitation might mean he was about to lie to her, but she could practically hear him considering every word, could see him testing the heft of each one as though it were a sword to be wielded in her defense. Perhaps that was more charitable than he deserved; certainly it was more charitable than she was inclined to be for anyone else.

"Essentially," he said, "nowhere."

Chrysanthi raised an eyebrow. What about that answer had required so much thought?

"I stayed much where you left me for the first few days," he went on. "I never meant to follow you. I just wanted to be where you could find me, if you needed me."

"But you're here."

"Yes." He set another tooth in place. It split neatly in two under a swing of the hammer. "I saw a carriage traveling not far off from where I was camped. It seemed a bit rich for this area, and I worried . . . I thought perhaps Zita had sent someone after you."

"Zita? What would she—"

"It wasn't her." Another tooth; another sure stroke of the hammer. "I followed it. South, for the most part, and a bit west."

"Yes, all right," Chrysanthi said, growing impatient, "but who was inside it?"

"Falka Domina. The girl collecting gifts for herself." Andrija looked grim—Chrysanthi wasn't sure why until he went on: "And then she picked up your sister."

Chrysanthi pressed her hands to her stomach, just the way Rhea had done to settle herself before a choosing. She felt ill, as though the ground under her had suddenly tilted. What was her sister doing in Thyzakos? And furthermore, what would this Falka Domina want with her? Did she have plans to take Rhea's gifts?

"Where did they go?" she asked. Maybe they could follow after and pull Rhea out of whatever mess she'd got tangled up in. It would be difficult to convince her to come along after their argument, but Chrysanthi would do it if she had to.

"The two of them backtracked north," Andrija said, "and then I followed them to a port on the western coast." He set aside the hammer, turning to look Chrysanthi in the eye. "Your sister's sailed for Vuomorra. By this time she'll have been there at least a week. I tried to find out more, but short of sailing for the city myself, there wasn't much I could do. What I know is that she's there; what I know is that she's in the company of two Dominas, Falka being one."

A second Domina was all they needed. "Who is the other?"

"A man. Tall, relatively. Dark hair." Andrija shrugged. "I did not recognize him."

Chrysanthi decided to set aside the question of whether she could trust that he was telling her the truth. The identity of the second Domina changed nothing about the message her mother had left behind and the duty it had placed in her hands. Although really, Falka probably had a better shot at taking Rhea's gifts than Chrysanthi did at the moment.

She leaned back in her chair, breathing deeply. Some of the anxiousness had gone out of her, but still, it helped to focus on the moss that had begun growing in the corner of the ceiling. "Why did you follow them so closely?" she asked. Out of the corner of her eye, she saw Andrija return to his work. "You could have come to find me the second you saw Rhea climb into Falka's carriage."

"I wanted to bring you as much information as I could. I . . ."

If he'd been uncomfortable before, he seemed truly nervous now. She smiled. "Go on."

She saw his knuckles go white as he gripped the hammer, holding it down by his side. "I thought," he said, "that given what Zita told us, it might be good for you to know where Falka is. In case you need that mark gone from your hand."

Chrysanthi blinked. Nervous over that? But then, she reminded herself, he had no knowledge of what she'd discovered in Rhea's old bedroom. He probably thought suggesting the removal of her mark was an insult she wouldn't stand for.

"I agree," she said. Andrija's eyes widened very slightly. "I think getting rid of my gifts and of Rhea's will be important."

She stood and went to his side, nudging him out of the way. The recipe her mother had left her rang in her head. Had Irini called them hers, those people who worshipped her? What would she have made of all of this?

Tucking her hair behind her ears, Chrysanthi peered into the mortar. That looked like enough bone chips; time to start grinding to powder. "It's a good thing," she said, "that I have no need of Falka Domina, then."

There was a heartbeat of quiet, Andrija so near that her shoulder knocked against his chest as she straightened. "Is that so?" he said.

She tapped the edge of the mortar. "Family recipe, remember?"

"I hate to think of what the other ingredients might be."

"Speaking of."

She led him to the pantry and told him where to find Irini's grave. The ritual instructions had no specifications regarding where the earth was meant to come from, but Chrysanthi figured that she could do no better than the dirt the woman herself had been buried in. Andrija did not balk when she told him what she needed, and returned promptly with a bowl full of fresh soil.

"That was quite a project out there," he said as he climbed back in through the window, coming to stand only inches from her.

"Yes, it was." She accepted the bowl from him. Near the rim, a worm thin as a bit of thread raised its head, and then ducked back into the dirt.

Behind her, the door to the kitchen was open, and more teeth were waiting to be powdered, but Chrysanthi did not move. There was so much she wanted to ask Andrija, so much she wanted to hear from him, only it seemed the most difficult thing to start. All she could do was look up at him and then—

"You've got dirt on you," she said.

"Have I?" He scrubbed at a spot near his temple. "Is that it?"

"No, it's just there, by your nose." She reached up, and when he did not shy away, thumbed at the smudge across his cheek. "Sorry. I think I made it worse."

Something shifted in his expression—that alarm surfacing again, perhaps—and he swayed toward her for a moment. "Chrysanthi," he said. "About before."

A gust of wind came billowing in through the open window, but she did not feel it. "Yes?"

"I never apologized."

She waited for him to go on, but that seemed to be the end of it. It was a very Argyros sort of apology, she thought, if that was the only thing he meant to say on the matter, and she had learned long ago not to accept any of those.

"All right," she said. "I have more work to do, so if you wouldn't mind—"

"I wanted to. I still do." He winced. "I don't think I deserve to yet."

"You could let me decide that."

"Maybe," he agreed, "but yours isn't the only apology I owe."

The image of the Agiokon square hovered before her eyes for a moment, rubble and dust and Nitsos buried somewhere beneath it all. Chrysanthi blinked it away. It was much easier to be angry about the rest of it, about Andrija's presence among the Sxoriza and alongside her—no matter what he had tried to tell her before she'd left the orange grove.

She turned and went back into the kitchen, confident he would follow. "How did you come to work for Ammar?" she asked over her shoulder. "To send you to find my sister—that seems like an important task, no? He must have trusted you."

"He did." Andrija lingered at the threshold, arms folded across his chest. "The Korabret . . . he keeps his own army. Young people, mostly.

Most of Amolova is like the Ksigora. Outside of the army, we do not have many chances at something like this." He gestured to the room around them, and Chrysanthi was reminded of how Baba had come to own the house in the first place. Another young boy, starving for something better than what he had.

"You joined, then?" she asked, busying herself with the mortar and pestle.

He nodded. "I was left alone very young. A bit of money, a bed in the barracks. It was all I needed. And I did well."

"I'm sure you did."

"I am not good with people," he said, looking somewhat sheepish. "Not like you are. But I listen. They started sending me places. Giving me questions to ask. The Korabret likes someone without anything to lose."

"So, he sent you to follow Rhea." She leaned against the counter and mirrored his posture, her chin lifted, lips pursed. "And then in spite of your loyalty to him, of everything you owed him, you left your assignment to come looking for my brother with me."

"Yes," Andrija replied. "Yes, that's what I chose."

"Why?"

"You—" His jaw worked, a muscle jumping on one side. "You *did* have something to lose."

"So did lots of other people."

She would have preferred that he argue with her, to give her something she could use to shore up the wall between them. Instead, watching him stand there, her words landing like a hail of arrows, it felt unfair. She sighed, rubbed at her eyes.

"What it is, I think," she said, "is that I recognized it. The position you were in."

Andrija tilted his head. "Which position was that?"

"With your Korabret. The letter you didn't send." She frowned, the nausea rising again in her gut as if summoned by the memory. "He wouldn't have listened to you if you had, would he?"

"I don't know," Andrija said quietly. "I can say I don't think so, but I don't know."

"So you kept it to yourself. You let it pass." Chrysanthi heard her voice tremble but kept going. She had to say this bit out loud. She had to say it to someone who might understand. "You never met my father."

Andrija took a small step toward her. "Are you—"

"He was hard to live with," she said. "He yelled, and when he didn't yell it was worse, and . . ." She scrubbed one hand across her face. "That's not what I'm talking about."

"What is it, then?"

She felt a rush of gratitude—there was no judgment in Andrija's voice, no confusion. He only wanted to know.

"I was his favorite," she said. "Things were difficult, but I could always tell that he loved me, in his way. And I would see how he was with the others, how he could be, but as long as he wasn't like that with me . . . well, that was what was important." She let out a long breath, studiously avoiding Andrija's eyes. She had never said any of this before, and if he looked even a little bit skeptical, she wasn't sure she'd be able to handle it. "I don't mean that it's the same. Just that I recognized it when you told me about the Korabret. And it suited me to be angry with you, rather than with both of us."

She chanced a look in his direction. He was still in the threshold, but he looked as though it was costing him to stay there. "I would take that for you," he said. "Every time."

Chrysanthi felt the knot of her nerves release. He wasn't leaving. He had heard it and understood, and there was so much left for them both to do, but they might do it together. "First things first," she said, beginning to smile. "I think you should say it."

"What?"

"What you owe me. I think you should say it now."

Recognition washed over him; she saw him swallow hard, a cautious smile already starting at one corner of his mouth. "Chrysanthi," he said, "I am so sorry."

She felt a settling somewhere behind her ribs, warm and familiar. For a moment she was in the orange grove again, looking down at Andrija in the blue before dawn, only she wasn't there anymore at all. She was here, in her mother's old house.

"He didn't send you to me," she said.

"No."

"You followed me on your own."

Andrija's cheeks began to redden, but he did not look away. "Yes."

"Why?" She would wait as long as it took, until he said it himself, until he called her name, because it was her that he wanted. Year after year at Stratathoma, watching her siblings come and go, watching their lives take shapes she had never seen before—she was patient. She could wait a bit longer.

He opened his mouth, closed it again and then took a deep breath.

Actually, she wasn't that patient at all.

She had crossed the room before Andrija could get a single word out. His eyes widened, and he took hold of her waist to keep her balanced as she rose onto tiptoe, her body pressing into his, but Chrysanthi did not care if they toppled over, if they ended up flat on their backs with dust eddying around them. She drew him down to her, hands skimming along the line of his jaw as she felt him shiver.

"I'll ask you again later," she said and kissed him.

That night, when Chrysanthi stood under the apple trees and looked up at the black sky, there was a new shape stitched into the stars. Rudimentary and vague, but so large and so perfectly centered overhead that it could not be missed—a hummingbird clutching an arrow that pointed to some spot farther south in the sky. Next to the point of the arrow sat another shape, one that looked almost like the letter *F*.

"What is it?" Andrija asked, his shoulder brushing hers.

"I'm not sure," she said, "but it could be from Falka Domina."

"Is it a message for you, then?"

She shook her head. "I think it's a message for anyone who knows to read it. I think it means that Rhea's going home."

"Rhea's coming here?"

Chrysanthi imagined the arrow being loosed, imagined it falling from the sky to land in the grass at her father's house. No—that was not the path it would take. "Not here," she said. "Stratathoma."

CHAPTER FIFTY

RHEA

There was no going back to the palace. Rhea bound her wounds and fled the city, the image of Lexos's corpse stamped onto the world everywhere she looked. In the harbor, as she bargained for passage on a ship across the gulf. On Thyzak soil, as she stumbled up to a farmer's front door and traded her jewelry for a horse. And on the path along the cliffside, as she rode ever closer to Stratathoma.

She was going home. She was not sure when she'd made that decision, or really if she'd ever made it at all. Perhaps it had been built into her as it had been for Nitsos's creatures: that sense, always, of where she belonged. And with the tie between her and Lexos cut, where else was left for her? Every door she'd ever tried was closed to her. The Sxoriza, the Dominas . . . even death itself had refused her, had taken Lexos and left her here. All she could think to do now was turn back. Return to Stratathoma, and hope against hope that somehow it would fix everything.

It wasn't far now. She knew this approach as well as anything, knew the view of the sea off to the left and the roll of the countryside to her right. Soon she would have reached the perimeter wall of the house.

She'd heard it had been left empty, but even if it was guarded by the Sperosi, or overrun with Dominas, none of that would matter. She was an Argyros, and she had the matagios on her tongue. Stratathoma would let her in.

One of her legs was beginning to go numb from the long ride; Rhea drew her horse to a halt before dismounting stiffly. The horse was exhausted, sweat foaming down its neck, its breath labored. They'd been riding without stopping for at least a day; it wouldn't last much longer. Without a second thought, she undid the cinch holding the saddle in place.

"There," she told her horse and pushed the saddle off. It hit the ground with a dull thud, followed soon after by the bridle.

The horse looked at her warily as she turned and continued up the path on foot. There was nothing else she needed that poor creature for. It had worked as hard as it was able.

She knew she should have been worn-out, too, but instead she felt almost painfully awake. How could she sleep knowing that she would have to wake again, and to a world without Lexos in it? And while her body ached, and the injuries she'd sustained during the spire collapse still hurt, all of that pain had faded, become as regular as her heartbeat. She hadn't bothered looking at the mark on her palm since leaving Vuomorra, or at the wound that branched from it, now reaching above her elbow. What was the point, when she knew what she would see?

She kept on another hour. Something was slippery in the foot of her boot; when she bent to check, she found the sole of her left foot had begun to bleed, but she did not stop. None of it mattered. Bodies lived and died and lived again, and her own had taken so much hurt, held on to it, and survived even when she hadn't wanted to. She should be so lucky, she thought, to die, but going home would have to do.

At the close of her second hour on foot, a shape began to form where the path disappeared into the horizon. The house, its familiar stone-tiled roof cresting above the curve of the cliff. Rhea stopped short for a moment. It was still standing. A shudder ran through her, as though her bones were settling back into place. Why had she ever left?

Every time she'd left Stratathoma, all she'd ever wanted was to come home again—yes, even knowing Baba was waiting for her. There was a certain ease to being his daughter. A freedom to knowing that despite his demands of perfection, he'd never truly thought she was capable of it.

How right he had been. About her, and about all of her siblings. They'd never been free of him, of their drive to earn a spot at his side. Not even after his death.

Rhea continued her trudge up the trail, a gust of wind catching her hair, tugging at the hem of her heavy black coat. Always in mourning black to come back to Stratathoma. And though she had no consort's blood on her hands this time, there was Lexos's to keep them red.

Back in Vuomorra, somebody would have discovered his body by now. Would he burn, like so many had, in the great hall of the palace? No, it was more likely that whoever found him would not know who he was. Lexos would go to rest stripped of everything he'd held dear—his name, his gift, his family. Maybe coming back to Stratathoma was as much for him as it was for her.

She was expecting to encounter some sort of guard before arriving at the perimeter walls, but the trail stayed clear, the countryside around it just the same as it had always been—low, gentle foothills, browned wildflowers and dried grass that stretched south, toward the mountains. No sentries posted, no flags flying from behind the wall.

"Hello?" she called. She'd rather be found now; at least she would know what waited for her. Instead her voice was alone as it drifted out over the ocean.

The path followed the line of the wall, around to where Rhea knew the doors into the grounds would be waiting. She kept on, listening hard as she went, trying to pick out any sort of conversation or movement; the only sound, other than the wind and the heave of her own breath, was the cry of a lone bird overhead. Carrion, she thought at first, come to pick some corpse clean, but it was a gull, riding the breeze here before making for a busier port. A familiar sight, just like the shape of the house where it rose above the wall.

In fact, everything was just as it might have been on any given day at Stratathoma, as if the Dominas and their fleet had never come. A strange, unmoored sort of joy caught her in the ribs, so unexpected that it nearly staggered her. Imagine: Lexos waiting at the innermost doors, that scent to him like old stone and wine. Chrysanthi in the kitchen, rolling out dough for a pita. Nitsos up in his workshop, too deep in his work to notice she was home. She had called Michali back to life. Why not call her old life back, too?

She rounded the curve of the wall, her heart rising as she caught sight of the deep blue doors which led through into the grounds. They stood wide open, one half off its hinges, and ahead, a cobblestone path continued toward the first of the two courtyards. It was too far away to be sure, but Rhea thought those interior doors might be open, too.

So, this was how the Dominas had left it. Stratathoma laid bare, unguarded as though there were nothing of value inside, not even a steward worth protecting.

A spasm shot through her left leg, lancing from hip to ankle. Her muscles would begin cramping soon, she knew, for want of rest. With a swallowed groan of pain, she cradled her marked hand against her chest and started forward again. She could rest in her own bed, in her own house.

The outer courtyard was in disarray, the flagstone cracked in places, the grass overgrown and dying. The roses were still growing across the courtyard walls, but they'd throttled themselves, scattering the stone beneath with rotten petals. In Chrysanthi's wild inner courtyard, it was even worse. Already predisposed to a precarious sort of chaos, it had tumbled into ruin in its keeper's absence. The olive tree Chrysanthi had cherished had been cut down by some Domina weapon, and the fountain spat only a trickle of brown sludge from its lion's mouth.

Rhea looked away. Still, it did nothing to keep her from thinking of the square at Agiokon, of Chrysanthi weeping as she reached for her. Chrysanthi had left behind everything she had ever loved to join Rhea in the Ksigora. And then Rhea had made sure she could never get it back.

It was only fair, wasn't it? It was an Argyros's lot in life to suffer that way, to find themselves adrift in a world they were not built for. Chrysanthi had escaped so much by virtue of being the youngest. Rhea had refused to let her escape this.

She cleared her throat and swallowed a mouthful of something that tasted too much like blood before passing through the interior court-yard and into the house itself. The great room was dark, the air damp and cold, broken only by the sound of her footsteps as she continued past the threshold. There was something scattered across the floor: little bits of color, about as big as a fingernail. She scraped one up. It was paint, which meant—

She looked up. Baba had had the ceiling painted when they'd been new to their titles. Under Chrysanthi's direction, a cadre of artists had covered the surface with a depiction of the Argyros line: Baba, his forefathers, and their forefathers beyond, all depicted in the style of a traditional icon. For years, Rhea had lived under the watchful, accus-ing eyes of prior Argyrosi, none of whom would ever have dreamed that their son Vasilis would carry them all the way to Stratathoma. Now, there was almost nothing of them left. Across the ceiling, great gouges wound through the colorful design. Most of the portraits had had their eyes scratched out, and some had even been painted over in black.

Rhea studied Baba's portrait, which held the center of the ceiling. The shape of him had been destroyed; all that remained were the fin-gers of one hand and a sliver of what might have been his right eye. She could imagine it, some Domina soldier climbing up hastily erected scaffolding before lifting a blade to Stratathoma's ceiling and gouging deep into the paint.

She let the fleck of paint she'd been cupping in her palm fall. What else had the Dominas done to this place? She thought of her room, of her wardrobe full of carefully sewn gowns and the tin of kymithi she'd stowed away, a treat to give Chrysanthi on some special occasion. It would all be ransacked—she knew that. Her things destroyed like the portraits overhead, or simply stolen by the Dominas or by whoever might have come to Stratathoma since. There would be no rest there for her.

Instead of taking the stairs up toward the bedrooms, or following the hallway that led from the great room through the rest of the house toward the kitchen, Rhea turned to the right, sidling through a narrow little door set out of the way and taking one of the servants' passages. With every step, she could feel her weariness weighing on her more heavily, as though passing through Stratathoma's doors had given her body permission to acknowledge how much she had asked it to endure.

The grounds had seemed, on her walk through them, to be mostly untouched, the mechanical creatures that lived out amongst the trees keeping to themselves just as they had under Nitsos's care, so when she arrived at the door that opened out onto the north side of the house, she shouldered it open and stepped through, back into the sunlight. The grass here was in better shape, with even a few wildflowers on their way to blooming scattered here and there. Rhea breathed deeply, ignoring the protest from her ribs. With the house at her back, she could almost pretend it had not lost any of its dignity. Waiting for her in the distance were the walls of Nitsos's clockwork garden.

For a moment she was there again, and Lexos was kneeling over Baba's body; Lexos was looking at her with a terrible, terrible fire, speaking their father's prayer and adding in her name. And then she blinked, and there was only empty air.

She reached behind her, steadying herself against the doorframe. Had they been hurtling toward this end since that day? Had Lexos speaking the prayer doomed her to do the same? They were twins, mirrors in so many things. Even in this.

At least that day in the garden had not been their last moment together. At least they'd gotten another chance to say goodbye.

She followed her own footsteps forward, to where the garden door could be found. It was shut, the wood warped and so crusted with salt that Rhea thought she might not be able to get it open. But when she tried the handle, the door swung easily, only juddering slightly as it caught on something she could not see.

It had been barely morning when she'd been here last, and Nitsos's garden had been a place of soft light and blood, dawn only just catching the top of the copper cherry tree. Today it was past noon, the shadows angled and growing. The sun fell through Nitsos's fabric leaves and glass flowers, sending shafts of colored light scattering across the ground. Rhea ducked through the door.

The garden had not been touched by Tarro and his soldiers. Whether that was the result of some negotiation by Nitsos or pure luck, she didn't know, but the garden was unassuming from the outside, enough so that she and Lexos had barely paid it any attention until it had been too late. And that meant that everything was as it had been when Lexos had left her there: the broken flowers, the lantern Nitsos had set aside. The body of her father, half buried in a shallow grave at the foot of the cherry tree.

He was there. Only a few yards away, his torso tipped at an awkward angle from where the rest of his body had begun to sink into the earth. The birds had got at him, torn the skin from his cheek and punctured one of his eyes, and Rhea could feel her stomach clenching, sick working its way up her throat, but it was nothing—a gnat buzzing by her ear only to be carried away by the wind.

"Baba," she said. "I'm home."

With slow steps, she approached him. Her argument with Lexos here had kept her, then, from looking too closely at what he'd done to their father, and in the months since it had been enough for her to know that he was dead and who had killed him. Now, though, she felt new wounds opening under her skin as she took in the lie of Baba's body and the decay that had begun to pick it apart.

With the unfinished way Lexos had buried him, Baba's head lolled back; now that she was closer, Rhea could see places where his scalp had separated from his skull and where worms had burrowed through.

The rest of Baba had not fared any better. The skin that remained on his arms was mottled green and black, and the nightgown he'd been buried in was riddled with holes, enough to show a glimpse of white beneath. Rhea had never seen anyone this far past death, anyone caught halfway between body and bone.

What an indignity for this man. It was enough to make her want to weep, to reach out and shut his remaining eye. Instead, she dropped to her knees in the dirt beside him.

"I'm sorry," she said. "You deserved to burn, at least."

He did not answer, and she let out a grating laugh as she realized that she had, in fact, expected him to. She could almost hear it anyway, his voice spooling out from somewhere over her shoulder, saying, "I still could."

She supposed that was true. The Dominas and the Sperosi had probably left some flint behind somewhere. She wouldn't even have to worry about the fire catching and spreading. There was nothing left in Stratathoma that could be saved. But a fire alone wouldn't be equal to what he'd deserved.

"It would only be me to witness it," she said. "Chrysanthi is gone. Nitsos is dead." And then, because she knew very well what her father did and did not care about: "Lexos is dead, too."

On the body, a fly crawled out of Baba's nostril. "Dead?" said the voice behind her. "Is that all?"

Rhea felt a tremor run through her, settling at the base of her neck. She could hear something coming from under her skin. A hum, perhaps, or the whir of a set of gears. "I don't know what you mean."

"How did he die, *koukla*?"

She tipped her head back, working for breath. There was a word for what she'd done, a word she had yet to speak aloud. It hadn't been meant to turn out that way. If she'd gone with him . . . But she hadn't. She had stood on that bridge and watched him tumble into the water, and she'd had the chance—a prayer was not the only way people died—but she hadn't taken it.

"I killed him," she said. That was the truth. She was too exhausted to keep hiding from it.

"I know you did."

Rhea could've sworn a shadow fell across her, almost like a hand on her shoulder. Baba's body was there in front of her, lifeless and rotting, but the longer she looked at it, the harder it was to understand. One moment it looked as though it had been made of paper; the next its edges seemed to turn liquid and spill onto the ground.

"Baba?" she said. "Where are you?"

"I'm here," the voice said. It was so close now. "I'm proud of you, Rhea."

Her cheeks went hot, a smile beginning at the corner of her mouth. Had Baba ever said that to her before? "Really?"

"You and your brother spent all your lives pretending not to see it. You told yourselves it could always be the two of you, side by side." The voice was low, threaded right into her ear. "But one of you was always born first."

"Me," she said.

"You." The Baba behind her sounded as though he was smiling. "At last, it can be only you."

Her at Baba's side. His second, his heir. She'd never cared about any of that, but then, was that right? Maybe she had. Maybe she'd gone out into the world, been married and widowed, and wanted all the while to be in Lexos's place. If Baba said so, he couldn't be wrong.

But what did any of that matter? He was dead, like Lexos. She could see the gleam of his skull in the setting sun. She could feel the earth squelching under her knees, softened to muck by the melt of his body.

Tears welled up in her eyes; one fell, landing in the folds of Baba's nightgown. "I wish you were here," she whispered. "I can't do this on my own. I never could."

The garden around her went still, the silence heavy. A minute passed without answer, and every heartbeat brought Baba's body closer and closer, until it was all Rhea could see, no matter where she turned. He looked so frail, so shattered. How could Lexos have done it? Didn't he see that they needed Baba? They'd tried to be without him, and look what had happened.

"It doesn't have to be a wish," the voice said finally. "I can be something more. Something real."

She let out a juddering breath and sank into herself, digging her scarred hand into the dirt. "Real?" she asked. "You mean—"

"I do."

She shook her head. She had tried to raise Nitsos, and it hadn't worked. She didn't think she could bear another failure like that. "What if I call you and you don't come?"

"I will." She felt something brush against her forehead, as though someone had pressed a kiss to her temple. "You've sacrificed enough. There's nothing more you need to do." The voice began to recede. "*Elado*, Rhea. Call me home."

"Wait." No answer again, but this time she could feel a looseness in the air, an emptiness. "Wait!" She twisted around, looking frantically over her shoulder, but there was nobody there. No figure ducking through the garden door. Just her and Baba's body.

She turned back toward it. With her scarred hand, she cradled her marked one to her chest, breathing slowly as her pulse echoed in her ears. Baba was halfway to disappearing. Some living grass had taken root on the beds of his fingernails; she could see a bubble lifting the skin on his one intact cheek. Surely it was too much to fix. Surely he had been gone too long.

No, she told herself. He told you it would work. He wants to come home. He wouldn't lie.

Rhea leaned forward, digging her palms into the earth. She could feel the wound in her marked arm begin to tear, the pain so bright it pulled her through to some new place, where it wasn't pain at all. A worm inched down from Baba's fingerbone and began to climb the back of her hand.

There was no prayer to speak. When she'd called to Michali, it had been with only the strength of her own will and the want that she kept burning at the core of her. She wasn't sure she had her will anymore. But she wanted—she wanted—she wanted so much.

"Come back," she said to Baba's body. "Please, come back."

Something stirred in the air as a familiar heat poured down her throat from the matagios on her tongue. There, that was it. It was starting to work. She reached more deeply into the earth, as though she might take hold of Stratathoma's very foundations.

"I am asking you as the Thyzak Stratagiozi," she said, shutting her eyes. "As the head of this family. As your daughter."

The heat grew stronger. It spread down into her chest, pressed out through her veins to gather at the tips of her fingers. The gift of the matagios, bending to her. She was almost there.

"Come home, Baba. I need you."

Her heart thundered, her vision swimming. Just a bit longer, she thought, even as she felt herself fall, collapsing into the dirt alongside Baba. All that pain had been too big to live in her body, but it was back now, crashing through her, holding so tightly to the bones of her that they began to crack. Rhea screamed as the wound on her arm split wider, the line of it reaching now up to her shoulder, to her chest, to her neck. She could not see anymore. There was too much blood in her eyes.

At last, she twitched and went still. And all the while, the body of Vasilis Argyros did not move.

CHAPTER FIFTY-ONE

CHRYSANTHI

She had thought before about showing Stratathoma to Andrija, but in those images she'd dreamed up, it had never looked quite like this.

When they'd arrived at the outermost doors, everything had seemed to be in order, and Chrysanthi had gotten ahead of herself, telling Andrija about all her favorite spots in the house and what sort of compliments she would require him to give each one. Now, standing at the edge of her courtyard, the house ahead, that all seemed so foolish as to be absolutely mortifying. Everything she'd planted here, all the flowers she'd painted and repainted each season—they had been destroyed, and what she could see of the house through its open doors did not seem any better.

"I'm sorry," she said to Andrija. "It looked different before. It was beautiful."

"It still is." His hand came to rest on her shoulder. "Do you want me to go in with you?"

She had thought about that before, too. Every day on the short trip here, wondering if Rhea would be alone or not, and if Chrysanthi might need Andrija's protection from her own sister.

"No," she said. "I'll go." There was nothing Rhea could do anymore to hurt her, but especially not now that they were both home, both children again in their father's house.

Andrija nodded, although she could tell he was not pleased. "Here," he said and pulled a knife from his belt, holding it out to her. "Take this, at least."

"I'm not going to stab my sister."

"Of course not."

She eyed the blade, remembering her sister's screams in Agiokon. Maybe he had a point. "Fine."

Once the knife was safely slotted into her boot, he caught her hand in his and kissed the back of it. "Be safe," he said. "I'll wait by the door."

She could feel her cheeks going red. She'd expected him to be shy, to let her lead him in whatever it was they were doing now. But now that he knew how she felt, he was as quietly confident with her as he was with speaking perfect Thyzaki, or with finding the right trail through rough terrain. It was welcome, she thought, looking up at him for a moment longer. There was so much uncertainty in everything else; there was none in the way Andrija said her name.

"I won't be too long," she said and gripped his hand more tightly before letting go and heading for the door.

Inside the great room, there were clear signs of more destruction, but Chrysanthi refused to let herself be distracted. She was here to find Rhea, and that would be hard enough—she didn't need anything else to upset her.

"Hello?" she called. "Rhea?"

No answer came, which was not all that surprising. Rhea was probably holed up in some far corner of the house, if she really was here at all. Chrysanthi sighed, steeled herself, and began her search.

It took the better part of the afternoon to make her way through the entirety of the building. And all of it, from Lexos's observatory to the bottommost storeroom, was empty. Her sister was not inside. With a growing suspicion nagging at her, Chrysanthi slipped out through a servants' passage into the grounds along the northern side. Andrija would be annoyed that she had not come to find him, but now that she was sure the house was a dead end, she had some idea of where Rhea might have gone: the wind-up garden.

Like the rest of the house, the garden's door had been damaged, but luckily it was already open as she approached. She had never seen it in the aftermath of what Rhea had described—the confrontation between the other three siblings, from which Chrysanthi had been excluded (or protected, as Rhea might have countered)—and so it had been difficult to imagine all of Nitsos's beautiful things destroyed. But there they were: the glass flowers crushed to bits, the earth disturbed, the artificial snow she'd helped design now torn and dirtied underfoot. And at the far end, collapsed near the foot of the copper cherry tree, a body.

No. Two. Baba's corpse, half in and half out of his grave. And another, sprawled at his side, dark hair covering her face.

"Rhea," Chrysanthi breathed. "Rhea, can you hear me?"

Her sister shifted very slightly, and Chrysanthi heard a noise like the low moan of a wounded animal. What had happened to Rhea? And what was she doing here in the first place?

Chrysanthi started across the garden, panic simmering under her skin. Rhea was fine. She was only resting, and if she was ill or injured, it would be nothing they couldn't sort out together. She would get Rhea out of here, use the ritual their mother had left to them, and everything would be all right.

Nitsos's glass flowers crunched underfoot as she stopped at Rhea's side. Baba's body had disintegrated into the earth and the smell coming off him was enough to make her eyes water, but she only held her breath and knelt next to her sister, keeping her eyes fixed on the fall of Rhea's hair. She wasn't here for Baba. And besides, she'd seen quite enough of her parents' bones lately.

"Rhea," she said. "Are you awake? Are you hurt?"

Carefully, she pushed her sister's hair back to get a good look at her face. Rhea was breathing, but her eyes were shut, and dark stains trailed down from her mouth to the base of her neck. Blood, Chrysanthi thought, and something else, too, something gray and cloudy. Whatever had happened, it had left Rhea in far worse condition than the last time she had seen her. And being out here, so near Baba, wasn't helping. Chrysanthi needed Andrija to help carry her inside.

She moved to get up, but before she could, Rhea drew a guttering breath. "Chrysanthi?"

Her voice was barely more than a whisper and so rough Chrysanthi thought it must have hurt her to use it. But it was there, real and dear. She shuffled around to cradle Rhea's head in her lap.

"It's me." She rested one hand on Rhea's shoulder and tried not to flinch—Rhea was too warm, and enough blood had seeped through her coat to leave Chrysanthi's palm wet and red. "We have to stop finding each other like this, eh?"

Rhea did not laugh. She stared up at Chrysanthi, her pupils blown wide, her breathing so labored that she shook with it. "How are you here?"

"Me? What about you, *kora*?" Chrysanthi smoothed her palm across Rhea's forehead. Why hadn't she brought any water? "Why did you come back here?"

Rhea reached weakly for Baba's body. Chrysanthi caught her hand, holding it tight. Dirt was crusted under her nails, and her fingers, which had been broken at Agiokon, were set at unnatural angles.

"Is he there?" she asked. "Did it work?"

"He's there, but . . ." Chrysanthi risked a look at Baba, suddenly afraid that she knew exactly what Rhea had come here for. "What do you mean, 'work'?"

Rhea coughed, struggling to lift her head. "I tried," she said. "I tried to bring him back for us, but . . ." A whimper escaped her. "It hurts."

"I know it does," Chrysanthi said. The thought of Baba alive again sent a swell of nausea washing over her. She'd never wanted that, not even right when she'd left Stratathoma. So why was Rhea so willing to suffer for it? Couldn't she see how much better off they were without him? His life was not worth hers; it never had been.

But now was no time for an argument, not with Rhea in such a state. "Look, I'm here now, all right? I can help."

Rhea did not seem to hear her. Her gaze had drifted to something in the distance; a moment later, her body went rigid, and she clutched at Chrysanthi, her expression desperate. "You believe that I tried, don't you?"

"Of course I do. You always try."

"I can try again."

"No," Chrysanthi said, voice tight with alarm. "You need to rest."

"I can do it."

She watched, at a loss, as Rhea tried to twist onto her side. Her movement was enough that Chrysanthi could see now how the wound that ran up from her mark had radiated across her chest. A heavy tear curled around the base of Rhea's neck; another's outline was clear through her shirt, the fabric clinging to the fresh blood that welled up as Rhea continued to strain.

"Don't," Chrysanthi said. This was too much: too much hurt, too much blood, too much for Rhea to bear. How much longer could she survive like this? Or was it already over, even as she drew another breath?

"No," Rhea said, "you don't understand. I have to. Otherwise he's gone for nothing."

"Baba?"

Rhea grabbed a fistful of Chrysanthi's shirt. Chrysanthi could see every tendon in her wrist standing out, almost pushing through the skin.

"No," she said, "Lexos." Her voice cracked, tears fresh in her eyes. "I meant for it to be both of us, but it was only him, and if—I want Baba to be proud, and I—how can he be proud I killed Lexos if he isn't here?"

Shock hit Chrysanthi like a punch to the gut. For a moment she could only open her mouth and close it again. Rhea's grip on her went weak and she slumped back into Chrysanthi's lap. Absently, Chrysanthi patted her on the shoulder, even as her mind reeled.

Lexos, gone. That meant she and Rhea were the only two left, and it was that way because Rhea had . . . What? Killed him? Yes, Rhea had wanted Nitsos dead, but that had been different—justified by the bonds between them all that Nitsos had been too willing to break. Lexos was Lexos. Leaving aside what Rhea had wanted for herself, Chrysanthi had never thought Rhea could be capable of hurting her twin. But then, she hadn't thought Rhea would ever leave her behind.

And now here she was. Back in their father's house, begging at his grave.

Chrysanthi eased out from under her. She had to do what she'd come here to do. She owed her family that much.

"Listen to me," she said. "All right? I can help you."

Rhea's eyes fluttered, her skin horribly pale where it was not sticky with blood. "Help?"

"Your gifts. They're eating away at you. Let me take them." Rhea gasped, spittle gurgling. Chrysanthi pressed on. "It won't hurt. I promise. It'll be like what Falka does."

"You want them?"

"No, I want us to give them up. It's what our mother wanted us to do one day." There wasn't time to explain more—Rhea didn't have long. Chrysanthi took Rhea's face in her hands, trying to keep her attention. A minute ago she had been too warm; now she was far too cold. "I'll show you after, all right? I'll take you to the old house. We'll talk about it, if you just let me do this now."

"You can't." Her chest heaved, but her gaze was intent on Chrysanthi. "You can't do that. I need them."

"You don't need them at all. I can take them away now. Andrija is waiting. He has everything I need. I just—"

"No," Rhea spat. "Don't touch me."

She tried to push herself up onto one arm, to heave herself away from Chrysanthi. Her arm crumpled before she'd moved an inch; Chrysanthi thought she heard the wet crunch of bone as Rhea dropped flat on her back, her head in the crook of what was left of Baba's neck.

"I'll try again," Rhea said faintly. "Baba. I only . . . I'll rest and then I'll . . ."

As her sister trailed off, Chrysanthi looked up to where the sun was disappearing behind the garden wall. She had been here before, in the streets of Agiokon. She knew what it was to watch Rhea hold tight to what was hurting her and turn the point of its blade toward someone else.

And she understood it. Of course she did—she'd done the same herself. Baba had built all of his children for that very purpose. Like Nitsos with his machines, Vasilis had sculpted muscle and flesh. He'd taken a hammer to the shape of them, set a rod of iron running through the core. He'd painted weapons onto their palms and told them where to strike, and they had. For better and for so much worse, they had.

There was only one way to escape from under all of it: ripping that rod of iron right out. Picking up a hammer of one's own, and crafting a new shape.

Chrysanthi could admit it was terrifying. It would not stitch up the wounds Rhea had suffered. It would keep them from getting worse, though, and it would give her time to heal. Rhea just had to be willing.

But she wasn't, and now she would never have another chance to be. Chrysanthi swallowed hard as the light in Rhea's eyes began to fade. Even if she ran to fetch Andrija, she wouldn't make it back in time. There was no fight left to have.

"All right," she heard herself say. "All right, *koukla*." Rhea had deserved better than the father rotting behind her, better than a lonely little garden and an empty house. Chrysanthi couldn't give her those things. But for at least a moment more, she could offer her a bit of company.

It wasn't long before Rhea's breathing slowed. Chrysanthi sat next to her, her tears landing on their clasped hands. The sky was burning orange and gold, and the evening birds had started to stir, their calls plaintive and soft. Chrysanthi hummed along to the ones she recognized. Anything to keep from hearing the moment when her sister fell silent.

She was still humming some time later when a figure appeared at the garden door. Andrija ducked through, a lantern in his hands.

"Chrysanthi?" he said. "Do you need anything?"

She shook her head.

"Is she . . . is she gone?"

She nodded.

"Would you like more time alone?"

Chrysanthi took a deep breath and wiped a stray tear. "No," she said. "I think I've had long enough."

She released Rhea's hand, laying it gently on her chest. She didn't know how people were meant to say goodbye, but she knew what their mother had done and so she gathered the heft of Rhea's hair, heavy and loose, and wound it around her palm before lifting it to kiss the band of it. Gloss and curl, and the smell of sea air.

"*Apoxara,*" she whispered. "I'm sorry."

Rhea would never have accepted that apology. Still, Chrysanthi felt lighter for giving it.

Wearily, she got to her feet and turned away from the copper cherry tree. Andrija would carry Rhea out, and they would bury her on the grounds, under an olive tree just like Mama. Rhea would be home always, part of the place she'd loved so much.

But as deeply as Chrysanthi would mourn her, she knew already she would never come back to stand by her grave. She had spent enough time here behind these walls, in the shadow of Baba's house; there was the world ahead of her now. Let her mourn Rhea there. Let her stand instead on the banks of the Dovikos, or at the corner of a crowded street in a city she'd never visited before.

I will find you there, she thought as she stepped through the garden door. I will find you there wherever I go.

CHAPTER FIFTY-TWO

CHRYSANTHI

Chrysanthi sat in the kitchen, a wet cloth pressed to the palm of her marked hand and a letter sitting open on the table. It had come that morning, attached to the leg of a messenger bird she had not recognized, which itself was now waiting for a reply, hopping around in the pantry and making quite a lot of noise.

The letter was not from Stavra, which had been a surprise. Chrysanthi was still waiting for a reply from her upon her return here, to her mother's house. Of anyone, she supposed Stavra would want to hear the news about Rhea and Lexos. She'd meant to tell her about Irini's ritual for getting rid of the mark, too, and to offer to perform it for her, but as she'd written and rewritten her message, she'd thought better of it. Word spread in Stratagiozi circles, and Chrysanthi didn't want to wake up one morning and find herself caught between warring forces, particularly now that Ammar and Nastia were fighting openly in the north. Better to discuss that in person when they met again.

The letter was not from Piros, either, but that was less of a surprise. He had already written. His messenger bird had alighted at Stratathoma just as Chrysanthi and Andrija had been preparing to leave, Rhea's body only a day buried. He'd seen the hummingbird Falka had stitched into the sky, he'd said, and Michali had been dead, again, by the following night. He hadn't needed anyone to tell him what that meant.

Chrysanthi knew she would not likely see him again as long as he stayed with the Sxoriza. All the same, she held out hope. As wide and strange as the world seemed, it was also smaller than she'd ever understood before leaving Stratathoma.

But that, too, came with its dangers, because this letter, sitting in front of her on the kitchen table, was from Falka Domina. Chrysanthi still had yet to make the woman's acquaintance, which, frankly, she thought might be the reason she was still alive. She had read it so many times she nearly had it memorized, but that didn't stop her from leaning over it once more.

> Chrysanthi,
>
> We haven't met yet, but I feel as if I know you already. My name is Falka Domina, and I serve as the second to Luco Domina, who recently reclaimed his seat as the Saint and Stratagorra of Trefazio. I knew all your family, but your sister best of all, which is why I wanted to write to you to extend my condolences. I was so sorry to hear she had passed. When I observed her leaving Vuomorra, I had hoped that my message might allow someone — particularly you — to reach her. What a shame to learn that was not possible.
>
> I confess I do have another reason to write to you. Please consider this an open invitation from Luco and myself to come join us in Vuomorra. We are, at present, hosting a number of other federation members as we discuss our best options regarding the conflict that has arisen between our Chuzhak friends and Ammar Basha. It would be my honor to have you join us as a representative of Thyzakos. Luco has no interest in maintaining the hostilities between our two families started by his son.
>
> I await your reply at your earliest convenience. And let me

say again how deeply your sister will be missed. She had many
friends in Vuomorra, and we will always think of her fondly.

Yours,

Falka

I should also apologize for not sending Rhea's hummingbird back
to you. I find it brings me a bit of comfort. Do forgive me.

"Are you worrying about that still?" came Andrija's voice.

Chrysanthi looked over her shoulder as he ducked in from the hall-way carrying a fresh bowl of earth. They'd been home from Stra-tathoma for a week or so, and every day she expected that he would tell her he was heading back to his country. Instead, every day he woke up by her side and asked her what she wanted to do that day. Her answer was usually, "Sleep in," but today she had said, "It's time," and so here they were. Here he was.

"Not worrying," she said, pulling the letter closer again. "In fact, nobody seems to be worrying. She sounds so calm. I don't know what I'm supposed to say—isn't it war that she's talking about? With Nastia and Ammar?"

"To her, maybe not," Andrija said. "To the people dying, certainly."

Chrysanthi watched him for a moment as he set the bowl of earth down next to an empty one. "I won't go to Vuomorra," she said. "If Falka and her lot want to get hold of me, they can come here them-selves. But you know I would go back with you to Amolova. Maybe there are people you want to find? To see that they're safe?" She peered at him, trying to read his expression. "Or maybe you want to get to Ammar yourself?"

"I do," he said darkly, "but I know an impossibility when I see it. Besides, a death like that would only make his people love him more. The coalition . . . who can say what will happen after they win? But I do believe they'll win." He took the pouch of bone dust off his belt and began pouring it into the empty bowl. "Those people need food; they need relief I cannot offer. If you want to tell Falka something, tell her that."

She reached for the letter. "All right."

"I meant after this is finished."

"But you're taking ages."

He began to mix the bone and earth together, the white disappearing into the dark soil. "We need to have a discussion about your concept of time."

Another age later, he had still not finished preparing and instead was kneeling in front of her, dabbing at a popped blister on her palm with a wet cloth.

"We need blood to finish it," she reminded him. "I think we can dispense with cleaning my wounds."

"Blood, yes." Andrija's nose wrinkled. "Not whatever's coming out of this. And are we sure it has to be yours?"

"We are." At this angle, she could see the blackstone stud in his tongue when he spoke—a reminder that for the past week, she'd borne the real thing on her body. Already it was taking its toll, but for every time she shivered, too cold despite the late spring sun, she'd just told herself that it had never been meant for her. And her blood mixed into that bowl meant that it would never be anyone else's.

"Let's hurry," she said. "I'm ready." Death had belonged to the Thyzak Stratagiozi for too long.

Reluctantly, Andrija allowed her to stand and took hold of the knife she offered him. She held her unmarked hand out over the bowl of earth and bone. Adding the blood would turn the whole thing into a paste, which he had agreed to help apply to her mark and to the matagios. She could only imagine how this process seemed to him, but to her it felt inevitable, as though this moment had been waiting at the end of the road for her since the day her father had marked her. The youngest of the Argyrosi, and now the last left alive, relinquishing the gifts her father had killed for.

She could admit that she was a little bit scared. Not of losing her gift, but of what would be left of her once she did. Everything outside this house was changing. The Stratagiozis and their gifts, the structures they'd built to keep themselves strong—it might all come crashing down in a day. In a week. There was no telling what time anyone had left, or whether, afterward, the world might find itself become something new. If it did, would there be any room for her in it?

She didn't know. But she had Andrija, and this house, and the road beyond waiting to be traveled, and if all that seemed like more than she was owed, she knew how to pay for it.

She held out her palm to Andrija and flinched as he cut deeply into her flesh. Blood dripped down, pooling oddly on top of the mixture. After a few moments, she stepped back. Andrija began to stir.

In a minute he would apply it to the lines across her skin, to her tongue. In a minute they would wash themselves clean, and no Argyros would ever again call to the dead.

But Chrysanthi wasn't thinking about that. The matagios, the pain and power it commanded—it had ruled her family for too long. It had taken her siblings, one by one. She refused to give it anything more.

No, she was imagining a summer evening. Shadows turning purple, stretching out in long, bold strokes. Dots of gold in the air as fireflies winked in and out. The shifting black stippled across the surface of the little pond and the watercolor shine of Andrija's eyes as she reached for his hand. None of it dreamed up in Stratathoma's gardens. Just light and color, gone home to the earth.

Chrysanthi smiled as the painting took shape. She would spend years at her easel if that's what it took to capture it all. She couldn't wait to see.

ACKNOWLEDGMENTS

I've been so grateful to work with such an incredible team on this duology. I owe so much to Sarah Peed, and to Daniel Carpenter at Titan—thank you for the care and thoughtfulness with which you've shepherded this series to its close. Thank you, too, to my agents, Kim Witherspoon, Jessica Mileo, and Daisy Parente. Your support and guidance are more valuable than I can say.

Massive thanks to Del Rey—Keith Clayton, Alex Larned, Tricia Narwani, Scott Shannon—and to everyone in publicity and marketing, particularly David Moench, Jordan Pace, Ada Maduka, Ashleigh Heaton, Sabrina Shen, Tori Henson, and Matt Schwartz. I am, as ever, honored to be on your team.

To Catherine Bucaria, Rob Guzman, Ellen Folan, Molly Lo Re, Jesse Vilinsky, and Abby Oladipo, thank you so much for the time and detail you put into these audiobooks.

Thank you to David G. Stevenson, Tim Green, and Faceout Studio, for the gorgeous hardcover (and for your patience as I rambled on about shades of green), and to Regina Flath and Elena Masci for the incredible paperback refresh. Thank you, too, to everybody who helped make the inside as beautiful as the outside, particularly Sara Bereta for the interior design, and Cara DuBois, Sam Wetzler, and Pam Alders in production.

Heartfelt thanks to my friends—JD, CH, RB, MH, ET, RT, and more—and family for their support and good humor, to my early readers for their assistance and feedback, and to all those who helped me direct my research. I also want to thank everybody who has supported this series: booksellers, reviewers, bloggers, and creators on TikTok and Instagram, among others. I appreciate the work you do for this community so much.

Perhaps most important, thank you to you for picking up this book. And to my cat, Scallion, who cannot read it (we hope) but who will delight in biting the corner of a hardcover copy for the rest of her days.

ABOUT THE AUTHOR

RORY POWER lives in Rhode Island. She has an MA in prose fiction from the University of East Anglia and is the *New York Times* bestselling author of *In a Garden Burning Gold, Wilder Girls,* and *Burn Our Bodies Down.*

itsrorypower.com
Instagram: @itsrorypower

ABOUT THE TYPE

This book was set in Baskerville, a typeface designed by John Baskerville (1706–75), an amateur printer and typefounder, and cut for him by John Handy in 1750. The type became popular again when the Lanston Monotype Corporation of London revived the classic roman face in 1923. The Mergenthaler Linotype Company in England and the United States cut a version of Baskerville in 1931, making it one of the most widely used typefaces today.

21982320739661